D1355249

The
LAKE HOUSE

KATE MORTON grew up in the mountains of south-east Queensland and lives now with her husband and young sons in London. She has degrees in dramatic art and English literature, specializing in nineteenth-century tragedy and contemporary gothic novels.

Kate has sold over ten million copies of her novels in 33 languages, across 38 countries. *The Shifting Fog*, published internationally as *The House at Riverton*, *The Forgotten Garden*, *The Distant Hours* and *The Secret Keeper* have all been number one bestsellers around the world. Each novel won the Australian Book Industry award for General Fiction Book of the Year.

You can find more information about
Kate Morton and her books at katemorton.com
or facebook.com/KateMortonAuthor

Also by Kate Morton

THE HOUSE AT RIVERTON

THE FORGOTTEN GARDEN

THE DISTANT HOURS

THE SECRET KEEPER

The
LAKE HOUSE
KATE
MORTON

PAN BOOKS

First published 2015 by Mantle

This paperback edition published 2016 by Pan Books
an imprint of Pan Macmillan
20 New Wharf Road, London N1 9RR
Associated companies throughout the world
www.panmacmillan.com

ISBN 978-1-5098-1646-0

1 3 5 7 9 8 6 4 2

A CIP catalogue record for this book is available from the British Library.

Typeset by Ellipsis Digital Limited, Glasgow
Printed and bound by CPI Group (UK) Ltd, Croydon, CR0 4YY

For Henry, my littlest pearl

One

The rain was heavy now and the hem of her dress was splattered with mud. She'd have to hide it afterwards; no one could know that she'd been out.

Clouds covered the moon, a stroke of luck she didn't deserve, and she made her way through the thick, black night as quickly as she could. She'd come earlier to dig the hole, but only now, under veil of darkness, would she finish the job. Rain stippled the surface of the trout stream, drummed relentlessly on the earth beside it. Something bolted through the bracken nearby, but she didn't flinch, didn't stop. She'd been in and out of the woods all her life and knew the way by heart.

Back when it first happened she'd considered confessing, and perhaps, in the beginning, she might have. She'd missed her chance though and now it was too late. Too much had happened: the search parties, the policemen, the articles in the newspapers pleading for information. There was no one she could tell, no way to fix it, no way they would ever forgive her. The only thing left was to bury the evidence.

She reached the place she'd chosen. The bag, with its box inside, was surprisingly heavy and it was a relief to put it down. On hands and knees, she pulled away the camouflage

of ferns and branches. The smell of sodden soil was overwhelming, of wood mouse and mushrooms, of other
mouldering things. Her father had told her once that generations had walked these woods and been buried deep
beneath the heavy earth. It made him glad, she knew, to
think of it that way. He found comfort in the continuity of
nature, believing that the stability of the long past had the
power to alleviate present troubles. And maybe in some
cases it had, but not this time, not these troubles.

She lowered the bag into the hole and for a split second
the moon seemed to peer from behind a cloud. Tears threatened as she scooped the dirt back, but she fought them. To
cry, here and now, was an indulgence she refused to grant
herself. She patted the ground flat, slapped her hands against
it, and stomped down hard with her boots until she was out
of breath.

There. It was done.

It crossed her mind that she should say something before
she left this lonely place. Something about the death of innocence, the deep remorse that would follow her always; but
she didn't. The inclination made her feel ashamed.

She made her way back quickly through the woods,
careful to avoid the boathouse and its memories. Dawn
was breaking as she reached the house; the rain was light.
The lake's water lapped at its banks and the last of the
nightingales called farewell. The blackcaps and warblers
were waking, and far in the distance a horse whinnied. She
didn't know it then, but she would never be rid of them,
those sounds; they would follow her from this place, this
time, invading her dreams and nightmares, reminding her
always of what she had done.

Two

The best view of the lake was from the Mulberry Room but Alice decided to make do with the bathroom window. Mr Llewellyn was still down by the stream with his easel, but he always retired early for a rest and she didn't want to risk an encounter. The old man was harmless enough, but he was eccentric and needy, especially of late, and she feared her unexpected presence in his room would send the wrong sort of signal. Alice wrinkled her nose. She'd been enormously fond of him once, when she was younger, and he of her. Odd to think of it now, at sixteen, the stories he'd told, the little sketches he'd drawn that she'd treasured, the air of wonder he'd trailed behind him like a song. At any rate, the bathroom was closer than the Mulberry Room, and with only a matter of minutes before Mother realised the first-floor rooms lacked flowers, Alice had no time to waste in climbing stairs. As a skein of housemaids waving polishing cloths flew eagerly down the hall, she slipped through the doorway and hurried to the window.

But where was he? Alice felt her stomach swoop, thrill to despair in an instant. Her hands pressed warm against the glass as her gaze swept the scene below: cream and pink roses, petals shining as if they'd been buffed; precious peaches clinging to the sheltered garden wall; the long silver lake gleaming in the mid-morning light. The whole estate had already been preened and primped to a state of impossible perfection, and yet there was still bustle everywhere.

Hired musicians slid gilt chairs across the temporary bandstand, and as the caterers' vans took turns stirring dust on the driveway, the half-assembled marquee ballooned in the summer breeze. The single static note amidst the swirl of activity was Grandmother deShiel, who sat small and hunched on the cast-iron garden seat outside the library, lost in her cobwebbed memories and completely oblivious to the round glass lanterns being strung up in the trees around her—

Alice drew a sudden breath.

Him.

The smile spread across her face before she could stop it. Joy, delicious star-spangled joy as she spotted him on the small island in the middle of the lake, a great log balanced on one shoulder. She lifted a hand to wave, an impulse, and a foolish one because he wasn't looking towards the house. Even if he had been, he wouldn't have waved back. Both of them knew they had to be more careful than that.

Her fingers found the ribbon of hair that always fell loose by her ear and she wound it between her fingers, back and forth, over and over. She liked watching him like this, in secret. It made her feel powerful, not like when they were together, when she brought him lemonade in the garden, or managed to sneak away to surprise him when he was working in the far-off reaches of the estate; when he asked after her novel, her family, her life, and she told him stories and made him laugh and had to struggle not to lose herself within the pools of his deep green eyes with their golden specks.

Beneath her gaze he bent, pausing to steady the log's weight before easing it into place atop the others. He was strong and that was good. Alice wasn't sure why, only that it mattered to her in a deep and unexplored place. Her cheeks were hot; she was blushing.

Alice Edevane wasn't shy. She'd known boys before. Not many, it was true – with the exception of their traditional Midsummer party her parents were famously reserved, preferring one another's company – but she'd managed, on occasion, to exchange surreptitious words with the village boys, or the tenant farmers' sons who tugged their caps and lowered their eyes and followed their fathers about the estate. This, though – this was . . . Well, it was just *different*, and she knew how breathless that sounded, how awfully like the sort of thing her big sister Deborah might say, but it happened to be true.

Benjamin Munro was his name. She mouthed the syllables silently, Benjamin James Munro, twenty-six years old, late of London. He had no dependents, was a hard worker, a man not given to baseless talk. He'd been born in Sussex and grown up in the Far East, the son of archaeologists. He liked green tea, the scent of jasmine and hot days that built towards rain.

He hadn't told her all of that. He wasn't one of those pompous men who bassooned on about himself and his achievements as if a girl were just a pretty-enough face between a pair of willing ears. Instead, she'd listened and observed and gleaned, and, when the opportunity presented, crept inside the storehouse to check the head gardener's employment book. Alice had always fancied herself a sleuth, and sure enough, pinned behind a page of Mr Harris's careful planting notes, she'd found Benjamin Munro's application. The letter itself had been brief, written in a hand Mother would have deplored, and Alice had scanned the whole, memorising the important bits, thrilling at the way the words gave depth and colour to the image she'd created and been keeping for herself, like a flower pressed between pages. Like the flower he'd given her just last month. 'Look, Alice – ' the stem had been green and fragile in his broad, strong hand – 'the first gardenia of the season.'

She smiled at the memory and reached inside her pocket to stroke the smooth surface of her leather-bound notebook. It was a habit she'd brought with her from childhood, with which she'd been driving her mother mad since receiving her very first notebook on her eighth birthday. How she'd loved that little nut-brown book! How clever Daddy had been to choose it for her. He was a journal-keeper, too, he'd said, with a seriousness Alice had admired and appreciated. She'd written her full name – Alice Cecilia Edevane – slowly, under Mother's watchful eye, on the pale sepia line in the frontispiece, and felt immediately that she was now a more real person than she had been before.

Mother objected to Alice's habit of caressing her pocketed book because it made her look 'shifty, like you're up to no good', a description Alice had decided she didn't mind one bit. Her mother's disapproval was merely a bonus; Alice would have continued to reach for her book even if it didn't make that faint frown appear on Eleanor Edevane's lovely face; she did it because her notebook was a touchstone, a reminder of who she was. It was also her closest confidante and, as such, quite an authority on Ben Munro.

It had been almost a whole year since she'd first laid eyes on him. He'd arrived at Loeanneth late in the summer of 1932, during that glorious dry stretch when, with all the excitement of Midsummer behind them, there'd been nothing left to do but surrender themselves to the soporific heat. A divine spirit of indolent tranquillity had descended on the estate so that even Mother, eight months pregnant and glowing pink, had taken to unbuttoning her pearl cuffs and rolling her silk sleeves to the elbow.

Alice had been sitting that day on the swing beneath the willow, swaying idly and pondering her Significant Problem. Sounds of family life, had she been listening, were all around – Mother and Mr Llewellyn laughing distantly as the boat oars splashed a lazy rhythm; Clemmie muttering beneath her breath while she turned circles in the meadow, arms outstretched like wings; Deborah relaying to Nanny Rose all the scandals of the recent London Season – but Alice was intent only on herself and heard nothing more than the mild burr of summer insects.

She'd been in the same spot for almost an hour, and hadn't even noticed the creeping black ink stain her new fountain pen was bleeding on her white cotton dress, when he materialised from the dark wooded grove onto the sunlit reach of the drive. He was carrying a canvas kitbag over one shoulder and what appeared to be a coat in his hand, and walked with a steady, muscular gait, the rhythm of which made her slow her swinging. She watched his progress, the rope rough against her cheek as she strained to see around the willow's weeping bough.

By quirk of geography, people did not come unexpect-edly to Loeanneth. The estate sat deep in a dell, surrounded by thick, briar-tangled woods, just like houses must in fairy tales. (And nightmares, as it turned out, though Alice had no cause to think that then.) It was their own sunny patch, home to generations of deShiels, her mother's ances-tral home. And yet here he was, a stranger in their midst, and just like that the afternoon's spell was broken.

Alice had a natural bent towards nosiness – people had been telling her so all her life and she took it as a compli-ment; it was a trait she intended to put to good use – but her interest that day was fuelled more by frustration and a sudden willingness to be distracted than it was by curiosity. All summer long she'd been working feverishly on a novel of passion and mystery, but three days earlier her progress had stalled. It was all the fault of her heroine, Laura, who, after chapters devoted to illustrating her rich inner life, now refused to cooperate. Faced with the introduction of a tall, dark, handsome gentleman, the dashingly named Lord Hallington, she'd suddenly lost all her wit and pith and become decidedly dull.

Well, Alice decided as she watched the young man walk-ing up the driveway, Laura would just have to wait. There were other matters come to hand.

A narrow stream chattered its way across the estate, delighting in the brief sunny respite before being reeled in-exorably back towards the woods, and a stone bridge, the legacy of some long-ago great-uncle, straddled the banks allowing access to Loeanneth. As the stranger reached the bridge, he stopped. He turned slowly back to face the dir-ection from which he'd come and seemed to glance at something in his hand. A scrap of paper? A trick of the light? Something in the tilt of his head, his lingering focus on the dense woods, spoke of deliberation and Alice narrowed her eyes. She was a writer; she understood people; she knew vulnerability when she saw it. What was he so uncertain about, and why? He turned again, coming full circle, lifting a hand to his brow as he cast his gaze all the way up the thistle-lined drive to where the house stood behind its loyal guard of yew trees. He didn't move, didn't appear to do so much as breathe, and then, as she watched, he set down his bag and coat, straightened his braces to the top of his shoulders, and released a sigh.

Alice experienced one of her swift certainties then. She wasn't sure where they came from, these insights into other people's states of mind, only that they arrived unexpectedly and fully formed. She just *knew* things sometimes. To wit: this was not the sort of place he was used to. But he was a man on a date with destiny, and although there was a part of him that wanted to turn around and leave the estate before he'd even properly arrived, one did not – *could* not – turn one's back on fate. It was an intoxicating proposition and Alice found herself gripping the swing's rope more tightly, ideas beginning to jostle, as she watched for the stranger's next move.

Sure enough, picking up his coat and hoisting his bag over his shoulder, he continued up the drive towards the hidden house. A new determination had entered his bearing and he now gave every appearance, to those who knew no better, of being resolute, his mission uncomplicated. Alice allowed herself a smile, slight and self-satisfied, before being hit by a burst of blinding clarity that almost knocked her from the swing seat. In the same instant that she noticed the ink stain on her skirt, Alice realised the solution to her Significant Problem. Why, it was all so clear! Laura, grappling with the arrival of her own intriguing stranger, also gifted with greater perception than most, would surely glimpse beneath the man's façade, discover his terrible secret, his guilty past, and whisper, in a quiet moment when she had him to herself—

'Alice?'

Back in the Loeanneth bathroom, Alice jumped, hitting her cheek on the wooden window frame.

'Alice Edevane! Where are you?'

She shot a glance at the closed door behind her. Pleasant memories of the previous summer, the heady thrill of falling in love, the early days of her relationship with Ben and its intoxicating link to her writing, scattered around her. The bronze doorknob vibrated slightly in response to rapid footsteps in the hallway and Alice held her breath.

Mother had been a nervous wreck all week. That was typical. She wasn't a natural hostess, but the Midsummer party was the deShiel family's great tradition and Mother had been enormously fond of her father, Henri, so the event was held annually in his memory. She always got herself into a spin – it was constitutional – but this year she was worse than usual.

'I know you're here, Alice. Deborah saw you only moments ago.'

Deborah: big sister, chief exemplar, prime menace. Alice gritted her teeth. As if it weren't enough having the famed and feted Eleanor Edevane for a mother, wasn't it just her luck to follow an older sister who was almost as perfect?

Beautiful, clever, engaged to be married to the catch of the Season . . . Thank God for Clementine, who came after, and was such a curious scrap of a girl that even Alice couldn't help but seem vaguely normal by comparison.

As Mother stormed down the hall, Edwina padding behind her, Alice cracked the window ajar and let the warm breeze, fragrant with fresh-cut grass and salt from the sea, bathe her face. Edwina was the only person (and she was a golden retriever, after all, not *really* a person) who could stand Mother when she was like this. Even poor Daddy had escaped to the attic hours before, no doubt enjoying the quiet good company of his great work of natural history. The problem was that Eleanor Edevane was a perfectionist and every detail of the Midsummer party had to meet her exacting standards. Although she'd kept the fact hidden beneath a veneer of stubborn indifference, it had bothered Alice for a long time that she fell so far short of her mother's expectations. She'd looked in the mirror and despaired of her too-tall body, her unobliging mouse-brown hair, her preference for the company of made-up people over real ones.

But not anymore. Alice smiled as Ben hoisted another log onto what was fast becoming a towering pyre. She might not be charming like Deborah, and she'd certainly never been immortalised, like Mother had, as the subject of a much-loved children's book, but it didn't matter. She was something else entirely. 'You're a storyteller, Alice Edevane,' Ben had told her late one afternoon, as the river tripped coolly by and the pigeons came home to roost. 'I've never met a person with such a clever imagination, such good ideas.' His voice had been gentle and his gaze intense; Alice had seen herself then through his eyes and she'd liked what she saw.

Mother's voice flew past the bathroom door, something further about flowers, before disappearing around a corner. 'Yes, Mother dearest,' Alice muttered, with delicious condescension. 'No need to get your knickers all in a tangle.' There was a glorious sacrilege in acknowledging the fact of Eleanor Edevane's underwear and Alice had to clamp her lips to keep from laughing.

With a final glance towards the lake she left the bathroom, tiptoeing quickly along the hall to her bedroom to liberate the precious folder from beneath her mattress. Managing not to trip in her haste on a tatty patch of the red Baluch carpet runner Great-grandfather Horace had sent back from his adventures in the Middle East, Alice took the stairs two by two, seized a basket from the middle of the hall table, and leapt outside into the brand-new day.

And it had to be said the weather was perfect. Alice couldn't help humming to herself as she made her way along the flagstone path. The basket was almost half filled and she hadn't even been near the wildflower meadows yet; the prettiest blooms grew there, the unexpected ones as opposed to the usual tame, showy suspects, but Alice had been biding her time. She'd spent the morning avoiding her mother, waiting until Mr Harris took his lunch break so she could catch Ben alone.

The last time she saw him he'd said he had something for her and Alice had laughed. He'd offered her that half-smile of his then, the one that made her weak at the knees, and asked, 'What's so funny?' And Alice had drawn herself up to her full height and told him it just so happened she had something to give him, too.

She stopped behind the largest yew tree at the end of the stone path. It had been neatly hedged for the party, its leaves tight and freshly cut, and Alice peered around it. Ben was still out on the island, and Mr Harris was all the way down at the far end of the lake helping his son Adam ready logs to be boated across. Poor Adam. Alice watched as he scratched behind his ear. He'd been the pride of his family once, according to Mrs Stevenson, strong and strapping and bright, until a flying piece of shrapnel at Passchendaele lodged in the side of his head and left him simple. War was a dreadful thing, the cook liked to opine, pounding her rolling pin into a blameless lump of dough on the kitchen table, 'taking a boy like that, so full o' promise, chewing 'im up and spitting 'im out a dull broken version of his old self'.

The one blessing, according to Mrs Stevenson, was that Adam himself seemed not to notice the change, seemed almost lightened by it. 'That's not the norm,' she always added, lest she betray the deep Scottish pessimism at her core. 'There's plenty more come back with all the laughter hollowed out of 'em.'

It was Daddy who'd insisted on employing Adam on the estate. 'He's got a job here for life,' she'd overheard him saying to Mr Harris, his voice reedy with the strength of his feeling. 'I've told you that before. As long as he needs it, there's a place here for young Adam.'

Alice became aware of a soft whirring near her left ear, the faintest breath of wind against her cheek. She glanced sideways at the dragonfly hovering in her peripheral vision. It was a rare one, a yellow-winged darter, and she felt a surge of old excitement. She pictured Daddy in his study, hiding from Mother in her Midsummer state. If Alice were quick she could catch the darter and run it upstairs for his collection, bask in the pleasure she knew the gift would bring, and feel herself elevated in her father's esteem, the way she had as a little girl, when the privilege of being the chosen one, permitted inside the dusty room of science books and white gloves and glass display cabinets, was enough to make her overlook the horror of the shining silver pins.

But of course there wasn't time to go now. Why, even in considering it she was falling victim to distraction. Alice frowned. Time had a funny way of losing shape when her mind got busy on a matter. She checked her watch. Almost ten past twelve. Twenty more minutes and the head gardener would retreat to his shed as he did each day for his cheese-and-piccalilli sandwich, and then contemplation of the racing pages. He was a man of habits and Alice, for one, respected that.

Forgetting the dragonfly, she crossed the path at a clip and made her furtive way around the lake, avoiding the lawn and the band of groundsmen sweeping near the elaborate fireworks contraption, keeping to the shadows until she reached the Sunken Garden. She sat on the sun-warmed steps of the old fountain and set the basket beside her. It was the perfect vantage point, she decided; the nearby hawthorn hedge provided ample cover, while small gaps in its foliage permitted a fine view of the new jetty.

While she waited to catch Ben alone, Alice watched a pair of rooks tumbling together in the sea-blue sky above. Her gaze fell to the house where men on ladders were weaving huge wreaths of greenery along the brick façade and a couple of housemaids were busy attaching delicate paper lanterns to fine strings beneath the eaves. The sun had lit up the top row of leadlight windows and the family home, polished to within an inch of its life, was sparkling like a bejewelled old dame, dressed for her annual opera outing.

A great swelling wave of affection came suddenly upon Alice. For as long as she could remember, she'd been aware that the house and the gardens of Loeanneth lived and breathed for her in a way they didn't for her sisters. While London was a lure to Deborah, Alice was never happier, never quite as much herself, as she was here; sitting on the edge of the stream, toes dangling in the slow current; lying in bed before the dawn, listening to the busy family of swifts who'd built their nest above her window; winding her way around the lake, notebook always tucked beneath her arm.

She had been seven years old when she realised that one day she would grow up and that grown-ups didn't, in the usual order of things, continue to live in their parents' home. She'd felt a great chasm of existential dread open up inside her then, and had taken to engraving her name whenever and wherever she could: in the hard English oak of the morning-room window frames, the filmy grouting between the gunroom tiles, the Strawberry Thief wallpaper in the entrance hall, as if by such small acts she might somehow tie herself to the place in a tangible and enduring way. Alice had gone without pudding for the entire summer when Mother discovered this particular expression of affection, a punishment she could have borne but for the injustice of being cast as a wanton vandal. 'I thought you of all people would have more respect for the house,' her mother had hissed, white with fury. 'That a child of mine could behave with such careless disregard, be the author of such a cruel and thoughtless prank!' The shame Alice had felt, the heartbreak, at hearing herself described in such a way, at having the results of her passionate need for possession reduced to a general mischief, had been profound.

But never mind that now. She stretched her legs out in front of her, lining up her toes, and sighed with deep contentment. It was in the past, water under the bridge, a childish fixation. Sunlight was everywhere, glittering gold off the bright green leaves of the garden. A blackcap, concealed within the foliage of a nearby willow, sang a sweet fanfare and a pair of mallards fought over a particularly juicy snail. The orchestra was rehearsing a dance number and music skimmed across the surface of the lake. How lucky they were to get a day like this one! After weeks of agonising, of studying the dawn, of consulting Those Who Ought to Know, the sun had risen, burning off any lingering cloud, just as it should on Midsummer's Eve. The evening would be warm, the breeze light, the party as bewitching as ever.

Alice had been aware of Midsummer Eve's magic long before she was old enough to stay up for the party, back when Nanny Bruen would bring them downstairs, Alice and her two sisters in their finest dresses, and prod them into line for presentation to the guests. The party was still in its opening throes then, well-dressed adults behaving with stilted decorum as they waited for night's fall; but later, when she was supposed to be asleep, Alice would listen for Nanny's breaths to grow deep and slumbersome, and then she'd creep to the nursery window and kneel on a chair to watch the lanterns glowing like night-ripe fruit, the raging bonfire that appeared to float on the moon-silvered water, the enchanted world in which places and people were *almost* as she remembered them, but not quite.

And tonight she'd be among them; a night that was going to be extra special. Alice smiled, shivering lightly with anticipation. She checked her watch and then took out the folder she'd tucked inside the basket, opening it to reveal the precious cargo inside. The manuscript was one of two copies she'd painstakingly typed on the Remington portable, her latest effort and the culmination of a year's work. There was a small error in the title where she'd accidentally hit a 'u' rather than a 'y', but other than that it was perfect. Ben wouldn't mind; he'd be the first to tell her it was far more important to send the pristine copy to Victor Gollancz. When it was published he could have his very own first edition, she'd even sign it for him, right beneath the dedication.

Bye Baby Bunting: Alice read the title under her breath, enjoying the little shiver it still sent down her spine. She was very proud of the story; it was her best so far and she had high hopes for its publication. It was a murder mystery, a proper one. After studying the preface to *Best Detective Stories*, she'd sat down with her notebook and made a list of the rules according to Mr Ronald Knox. She'd realised her mistake in trying to marry two disparate genres, killed off Laura, and then started again from scratch, dreaming up, instead, a country house, a detective and a household full of worthy suspects. The puzzle had been the tricky bit, figuring out how to keep whodunit from her readers. That's when she'd decided she needed a sounding board, a Watson to her Holmes, so to speak. Happily, she'd found him. She'd found more than that.

For B.M., partner in crime, accomplice in life

She ran her thumb over the dedication. Once the novel was published everyone would know about them, but Alice didn't care. There was a part of her that couldn't wait. So many times she'd almost blurted it out to Deborah, or even to Clemmie, so desperate was she to hear the words said aloud, and she'd been dodging conversations with Mother, who harboured suspicions, Alice knew. But it was right, somehow, that they should find out when they read her first published book.

Bye Baby Bunting had been born out of conversations with Ben; she couldn't have done it without him, and now, having plucked their thoughts from the air and put them down as words on paper, she'd taken something intangible, a mere possibility, and made it real. Alice couldn't help but feel that by giving him his copy she was making the promise that stretched unspoken between them more real, too. Promises were important in the Edevane family. It was something they'd learned from Mother, the adage drummed into them from as soon as they could talk: a promise should never be made that one wasn't prepared to keep.

Voices sounded on the other side of the hawthorn hedge and instinctively Alice snatched up the manuscript, hugging it to her. She listened, alert, and then hurried to the hedge, peering through a small diamond-shaped gap in the leaves. Ben was no longer out on the island and the boat was back at the jetty, but Alice found the three men together near the remaining pile of logs. She watched as Ben drank from his tin canteen, the knot in his throat that moved as he swallowed, the shadow of stubble along his jawline, the curl of dark hair that reached his collar. Perspiration had left a damp patch on his shirt and Alice's throat caught; she loved his smell, it was so earthy and real.

Mr Harris gathered up his tool bag and issued some parting instructions, to which Ben gave a nod, the hint of a smile. Alice smiled with him, taking in the dimple in his left cheek, his strong shoulders, his exposed forearm glistening beneath the fierce sun. As she watched he straightened, a noise in the distance having caught his attention. She followed his gaze as it left Mr Harris and settled on something in the wild gardens beyond.

Visible, just, in the tangle of foxtail lilies and verbena, Alice spotted a small figure making his way, jouncy and intrepid, towards the house. Theo. The glimpse of her baby brother broadened Alice's smile; the large black shadow hovering behind, however, doused it. She understood now why Ben was frowning; she felt the same way about Nanny Bruen. She didn't like her one bit, but then one tended not to develop fond feelings for people with despotic dispositions. Why the sweet, pretty Nanny Rose had been fired was anyone's guess. She'd obviously adored Theo, doted on him in fact, and there wasn't anyone who didn't like her. Even Daddy had been seen chatting with her in the garden while Theo tripped after the ducks, and Daddy was a very discerning judge of character.

Something had got up Mother's nose, though. Two weeks ago, Alice had seen her arguing with Nanny Rose, an exchange of heated whispers outside the nursery. The disagreement had been to do with Theo, but vexingly Alice had been too far away to hear precisely what was said. The next thing anyone knew, Nanny Rose was gone and Nanny Bruen had been dusted off for duty. Alice had thought they'd seen the last of the ancient battleaxe with her whiskery chin and bottle of castor oil. Indeed, she'd always felt a certain jot of personal pride, having overheard Grandmother deShiel commenting that it was unruly Alice who had broken the last of the old nanny's spirit. But now, here she was, back again, more crotchety than ever.

Alice was still lamenting the loss of Nanny Rose when she realised she was no longer alone on her side of the hedge. A twig snapped behind her and she straightened abruptly, swinging around.

'Mr Llewellyn!' Alice exclaimed, when she saw the hunched figure standing there, an easel under one arm, a large sketch block clutched awkwardly to his other side. 'You frightened me.'

'Sorry, Alice, dear. It would appear I don't know my own stealth. I was hoping we might have a little chat.'

'Now, Mr Llewellyn?' Despite her affection for the old man, she fought a wave of frustration. He didn't seem to understand that the days of Alice sitting with him while he sketched, of bobbing downstream together in the rowing boat, of her confessing all her childish secrets as they hunted fairies were gone. He'd been important to her once, there was no denying that; a treasured friend when she was small and a mentor when she was first getting started with her writing. Many times she'd run to present him with the small childish stories she'd scribbled in a fit of inspiration and he'd made a great show of providing earnest critique. But now, at sixteen, she had other interests, things she couldn't share with him. 'I'm rather busy, you see.'

His gaze drifted towards the hole in the hedge and Alice felt her cheeks glow with sudden warmth.

'I'm keeping an eye on party preparations,' she said quickly, and when Mr Llewellyn smiled in a way that suggested he knew precisely whom she'd been watching and why, she added, 'I've been gathering flowers for Mother.'

He glanced at her discarded basket, the blooms wilting now in the midday heat.

'A task I really should be getting on with.'

'Of course,' he said with a nod, 'and I wouldn't normally dream of interrupting while you're so busy helping. But there's something rather important I need to talk to you about.'

'I'm afraid I really can't spare the time.'

Mr Llewellyn seemed unusually disappointed and it occurred to Alice that he'd been quite flat lately. Not moping exactly, but distracted and sad. The buttons of his satin vest were done up crookedly, she noticed, and the scarf around his neck was tatty. She felt a sudden wave of sympathy and nodded towards his sketch block, an attempt to make amends. 'It's very good.' It was, too. She hadn't known him to draw Theo before and the likeness was exceptional, the lingering hint of babyhood in his round cheeks and full lips, the wide trusting eyes. Dear Mr Llewellyn had always been able to see the best in all of them. 'Shall we meet after tea, perhaps?' she suggested with an encouraging smile. 'Sometime before the party?'

Mr Llewellyn gathered his sketch block closer, considering Alice's proposal before frowning slightly, 'What about at the bonfire tonight?'

'You're coming?' This *was* a surprise. Mr Llewellyn was not a social gentleman and ordinarily went out of his way to avoid crowds – especially those crowds comprising people intent on meeting *him*. He adored Mother, but even she had never managed to entice him to attend Midsummer before. Her mother's precious first edition of *Eleanor's Magic Doorway* would be on display, as it always was, and people would be vying to meet its creator. They never tired of kneeling down by the hedge and hunting for the buried top of the old stone pillar. 'Look, Simeon, I can see it! The brass ring from the map, just as it says in the book!' Little did they know that the tunnel had been sealed for years against the explorations of curious guests like them.

Ordinarily Alice might have probed further, but a burst of male laughter from the other side of the hedge, followed by a comradely shout of, 'It'll keep, Adam – go with your dad and have some lunch, no need to lift them all at once!' jolted her back to her purpose. 'Well, then,' she said, 'tonight, yes. At the party.'

'Shall we say half past eleven, beneath the arbour?'

'Yes, yes.'

'It's important, Alice.'

'Half past eleven,' she repeated, a touch impatiently. 'I'll be there.'

Still he didn't leave but remained, seemingly glued to the spot, wearing that serious, melancholy expression and staring straight at her, almost as if he were trying to memorise her features.

'Mr Llewellyn?'

'Do you remember the time we took the boat out on Clemmie's birthday?'

'Yes,' she said. 'Yes, it was a lovely day. A rare treat.' Alice made a point of gathering her basket from the fountain steps, and Mr Llewellyn must have taken the hint, because when she finished he was gone.

Alice felt the nag of an unspecified regret and sighed

deeply. She supposed it was being in love that made her feel this way, a sort of general pity for everyone who wasn't her. Poor old Mr Llewellyn. She'd thought him a magician once; now she saw only a stooped and rather sad man, old before his time, constrained by the Victorian dress and habits with which he refused to part. He'd had a breakdown in his youth – it was supposed to be a secret, but Alice knew a lot of things she shouldn't. It had happened back when Mother was just a girl and Mr Llewellyn a firm friend of Henri deShiel. He'd given up his professional life in London and that was when he'd come up with *Eleanor's Magic Doorway*.

As to what had prompted his breakdown, Alice didn't know. It occurred to her now, vaguely, that she ought to make a better job of finding out, but not today; it wasn't a task for today. There simply wasn't time for the past when the future was right there waiting for her on the other side of the hedge. Another glance confirmed that Ben was by himself, gathering his things, about to go back through the garden to his accommodations for lunch. Alice promptly forgot about Mr Llewellyn. She lifted her face towards the sun and relished the blaze that graced her cheeks. What a joy it was to be her, right now, in this precise moment. She couldn't imagine that anyone, anywhere, could be more content. And then she stepped towards the jetty, manuscript in hand, intoxicated by an enticing sense of herself as a girl on the precipice of a glimmering future.

Three

Sun cut between the leaves, and Sadie ran so that her lungs begged her to stop. She didn't, though; she ran harder, savouring the reassurance of her footfalls. The rhythmic thud, the faint echo caused by damp, mossy earth and dense trampled undergrowth.

The dogs had disappeared off the narrow track some time ago, noses to the ground, slipping like streaks of molasses through the glistening brambles on either side. It was possible they were more relieved than she that the rain had finally stopped and they were free. It surprised Sadie how much she enjoyed having the pair of them alongside her. She'd been resistant when her grandfather first suggested it, but Bertie – already suspicious of her sudden arrival on his doorstep ('Since when do you take holidays?') – had proven characteristically stubborn: 'Those woods are deep in places and you're not familiar with them. It wouldn't take much to get lost.' When he'd started making noises about asking one of the local lads to meet up with her 'for company', regarding her with a look that said he was on the brink of asking questions she didn't want to answer, Sadie had swiftly agreed the dogs could do with the run.

Sadie always ran alone. She'd been doing so since long

before the Bailey case blew up and her life in London imploded. It was best. There were people who ran for exercise, those who ran for pleasure, and then there was Sadie, who ran like someone trying to escape her own death. A long-ago boyfriend had told her that. He'd said it accusingly, bent over double trying to catch his breath in the middle of Hampstead Heath. Sadie had shrugged, puzzling over why that might be considered a bad thing, and she'd known then, with surprisingly little regret, that it wasn't going to work out between them.

A gust of wind slipped through the branches, spraying last night's raindrops against her face. Sadie shook her head but didn't slow down. Wild rambling roses had started to appear on the sides of the path; creatures of habit making their yearly bids between the bracken and the fallen logs. It was good such things existed. It was proof there really was beauty and goodness in the world, just like the poems and platitudes said. It was easy to lose sight of that fact in her line of work.

There'd been more in the London papers over the weekend. Sadie had caught a glimpse over the shoulder of a man in the Harbour Cafe while she and Bertie were having breakfast. That is, while she was having breakfast and he was having some sort of green smoothie that smelled like grass. It was only a small piece, a single column on page five, but the name Maggie Bailey was a magnet to Sadie's eye and she'd stopped speaking mid-sentence, scanning the small print hungrily. She'd learned nothing new from the article, which meant there'd been no change. And why would there be? The case was closed. Derek Maitland had the byline. No surprise he was still clinging to the story like a dog with his neighbour's bone; that was his nature. Maybe on some level it was why she'd chosen him in the first place?

Sadie started as Ash leapt from behind a bank of trees and cut in front of her, ears flapping, mouth open in a wide, wet grin. She pushed herself not to fall too far behind, clenched her fists so her fingers drove into her palms and ran harder. She wasn't supposed to be reading the newspapers. She was supposed to be 'taking a break from it all' while she sorted herself out and waited for things in London to cool down. Donald's advice. He was trying to protect her from having her nose rubbed in her own stupidity, she knew, which was kind of him, but really it was a bit too late for that.

It had been all over the papers at the time, and the TV news, and it hadn't slowed down in the weeks since, only broadened in scope from articles reporting Sadie's specific comments to gleeful claims of internal division within the Met, implications of cover-ups. No wonder Ashford was angry. The Super never missed a chance to trumpet his views on loyalty, hoicking up his lunch-stained trousers and giving the assembled detectives a spittle-laden blast: 'Nothing worse than a canary, you hear? You got a gripe, you keep it in-house. Nothing more damaging to the department than coppers who start whistling to outsiders.' Special mention was always made then of that most heinous of outsiders, the journalist, Ashford's chin shaking with the force of his loathing: 'Bloodsuckers, the lot of them.'

Thank God he didn't know it was Sadie who'd done this particular spot of whistling. Donald had covered for her, the same way he had when she first started making mistakes at work. 'That's what partners do,' he'd said back then, brushing away her clumsy gratitude with customary gruffness. It had been a bit of a joke between them, the minor lapses in her usual fastidious conduct, but this latest infraction was different. As Senior Investigating Officer, Donald was responsible for the actions of his DC, and while forgetting to bring a notepad to an interview merited a good-natured ribbing, letting slip claims the department had botched an investigation was something else entirely.

Donald had known she was the leak as soon as the story broke. He'd taken her out for a pint at the Fox and Hounds and advised her, in terms that left very little room for disagreement, that she needed to get out of London. Take the leave she was owed and stay away until she got whatever was bothering her out of her system. 'I'm not kidding, Sparrow,' he'd said, wiping lager froth off his steel-bristle moustache. 'I don't know what's got into you lately, but Ashford isn't stupid, he's going to be watching like a hawk. Your grandfather's in Cornwall now, isn't he? For your own sake – for both our sakes – get yourself down there and don't come back until you've got yourself sorted.'

A fallen log came at her from nowhere and Sadie leapt over it, catching the tip of her running shoe. Adrenalin spread beneath her skin like hot syrup and she harnessed it, ran harder. *Don't come back until you've got yourself sorted.* That was a whole lot easier said than done. Donald might not know the cause of her distraction and blundering, but Sadie did. She pictured the envelope and its contents, tucked away in the bedside cabinet of the spare room at Bertie's place: the pretty paper, the flowery handwriting, the iced-water shock of the message inside. She could mark the start of her troubles from the evening, six weeks ago, when she'd trodden on that bloody letter lying on the doormat of her London flat. At first it had just been occasional lapses in concentration, little mistakes that were easy enough to cover, but then the Bailey case had come along, that little motherless girl, and *kapow!* The perfect storm.

With a final burst of energy, Sadie forced herself to sprint to the black stump, her turn-around point. She didn't ease up until she reached it, lurching forwards to strike one hand against the damp, jagged top, then collapsing, palms on knees, as she caught her breath. Her diaphragm swung in and out, her vision starred. She hurt and she was glad. Ash was nosing around nearby, sniffing at the end of a moss-covered log that jutted from the steep, muddy rise. Sadie drank greedily from her water bottle and then squeezed some into the dog's ready mouth. She stroked the smooth glossy darkness between his ears. 'Where's your brother?' she said, to which Ash cocked his head and just stared at her with his clever eyes. 'Where's Ramsay?'

Sadie scanned the wild tangle of greenery surrounding them. Ferns were striving towards the light, spiralled stems uncoiling into fronds. The sweet scent of honeysuckle mingled with the earthiness of recent rain. Summer rain. She'd always loved that smell, even more so when Bertie told her it was caused by a type of bacteria. It proved that good things could come from bad if the right conditions were applied. Sadie had a vested interest in believing that was true.

They were thick woods, and it struck her as she looked for Ramsay that Bertie was right. It would be possible to become lost forever in a place like this. Not Sadie, not with the dogs by her side, keen noses trained on the way back home, but someone else, an innocent, the girl from a fairy

story. That girl, her head filled with romance, might easily
venture too deep inside woods like these and be lost.

Sadie didn't know many fairy stories, not beyond the
obvious ones. It was one of the gaping holes she'd come to
recognise in her experience compared with that of her peers
(fairy tales, A levels, parental warmth). Even the little Bailey
girl's bedroom, though sparsely furnished, had contained a
shelf of books and a well-thumbed volume of Grimm's tales.
But there'd been no whispered stories of 'Once upon a time'
in Sadie's childhood: her mother hadn't been the whispering
type, her father less so, the two of them equal in their adamant distaste for the fanciful.

Regardless, Sadie had absorbed enough as a citizen of the
world to know that people went missing in fairy tales, and
that there were usually deep dark woods involved. People
went missing often enough in real life, too. Sadie knew that
from experience. Some were lost by misadventure, others by
choice: the disappeared as opposed to the missing, the ones
who didn't want to be found. People like Maggie Bailey.

'Run off.' Donald had called it early, the same day they
found little Caitlyn alone in the apartment, weeks before
they found the note that proved him right. 'Responsibility
got too much. Kids, making ends meet, life. If I had a quid
for every time I'd seen it . . .'

But Sadie had refused to believe that theory. She'd gone
off on a tangent of her own, floated fantastic suppositions
about foul play, the sort that belonged only in mystery
novels, insisting that a mother wouldn't walk out on her kid
like that, bleating on and on about combing through the
evidence again, searching for the vital clue they'd missed.

'You're looking for something you'll never find,' Donald

had told her. 'Sometimes, Sparrow – not bloody often, but sometimes – things really are as simple as they seem.'

'Like you, you mean.'

He'd laughed. 'Cheeky mare.' And then his tone had softened, turning almost fatherly, which, as far as Sadie could see, was a whole lot worse than if he'd started yelling. 'Happens to the best of us. Work this job long enough and eventually a case gets under your skin. Means you're human, but it doesn't mean you're right.'

Sadie's breaths had steadied but there was still no sign of Ramsay. She called out to him and her voice echoed back from damp, dark places, *Ramsay . . . Ramsay . . . Ramsay . . .* the last frail repeat fading into nothing. He was the more reserved of the two dogs and it had taken longer to gain his trust. Fair or not, he was her favourite because of it. Sadie had always been wary of easy affection. It was a trait she'd also recognised in Nancy Bailey, Maggie's mother; one she suspected had brought them closer together. A *folie à deux* it was called, a shared madness, two otherwise sane people encouraging each other in the same delusion. Sadie could see now that's what she and Nancy Bailey had done, each feeding the other's fantasy, convincing themselves there was more to Maggie's disappearance than met the eye.

And it *had* been madness. Ten years on the police force, five as a detective, and everything she'd learned had gone out the window the moment she saw that little girl alone in the stale flat; fine and dainty, backlit so her messed-up blonde hair formed a halo, eyes wide and watchful as she took in the two adult strangers who'd just burst through the front door. Sadie had been the one to go to her, taking her hands and saying, in a bright, clear voice she didn't recognise,

'Hello there, lovely. Who's that on the front of your nightie? What's her name?' The child's vulnerability, her smallness and uncertainty, had hit hard right in the place Sadie usually kept steeled against emotion. During the days that followed, she'd felt the ghostly imprint of the child's small hands in hers, and at night when she tried to sleep she'd heard that quiet, querulous voice saying, *Mama? Where's my mama?* She'd been consumed by a fierce need to make things right, to return the little girl's mother to her, and Nancy Bailey had proved to be the perfect partner. But while Nancy could be forgiven for clutching at straws, was understandably desperate to excuse her daughter's callous behaviour, ameliorate the shock of her little granddaughter having been left alone like that and assuage her own guilt ('if only I hadn't gone away with girlfriends that week I'd have found her myself'), Sadie ought to have known better. Her entire career, her entire adult *life*, had been built on knowing better.

'Ramsay,' she called again.

Again, only silence in return, the sort marked by leaves rustling and distant water running down a rain-sodden ditch. Natural noises that had a way of making a person feel more alone. Sadie stretched her arms above her head. The urge to contact Nancy was physical, a great big weight inside her chest, a pair of sweaty fists closed tight around her lungs. Her own ignominy she could bear, but the shame when she thought of Nancy was crushing. She still felt the pressing need to apologise, to explain that it had all been a terrible lapse in judgement, that she'd never meant to peddle in false hope. Donald knew her well: 'And Sparrow – ' his parting words before he packed her off to Cornwall – 'don't even think about making contact with the grandmother.'

Louder this time: 'Ramsay! Where are you, boy?'

Sadie strained, listening. A startled bird, the beat of heavy wings high in the canopy. Her gaze was drawn up through the lattice of branches to the white speck of a plane unpeeling the pale-blue sky behind it. The plane was heading east towards London and she watched its progress with an odd sense of dislocation. Unfathomable to think that the swirl of life, *her* life, continued there without her.

She hadn't heard from Donald since she'd left. She hadn't expected to, not really, not yet, it had only been a week and he'd insisted she take a full month's leave. 'I can come back earlier if I want to, right?' Sadie had said to the young man in HR, his confusion making it evident this was the first time he'd been asked. 'You'd better not,' Donald had growled afterwards. 'I see you back here before you're ready and I kid you not, Sparrow, I'll go straight to Ashford.' He would, too, she knew. He was heading for retirement and not about to let his unhinged deputy ruin it for him. With no other choice, Sadie had packed a bag, tucked her tail between her legs, and driven down to Cornwall. She'd left Donald with Bertie's phone number, told him mobile reception was a bit hit and miss, and held out hope he'd summon her back.

A low rumbling came from beside her and she glanced down. Ash was standing as rigid as a statue, staring into the woods beyond. 'What's the matter, boy? Don't like the smell of self-pity?' The fur of his neck bristled, his ears swivelled, but his focus didn't shift. And then Sadie heard it too, far off in the distance. Ramsay, a bark – not of alarm, perhaps, but unusual all the same.

An uncharacteristic maternal streak, vaguely disturbing, had come over Sadie since the dogs had adopted her, and when Ash gave another deep growl she capped her water bottle. 'Come on then,' she said, tapping her thigh. 'Let's go find that brother of yours.'

Her grandparents hadn't had dogs when they'd lived in London; Ruth had been allergic. But after Ruth died and Bertie retired to Cornwall, he'd floundered. 'I'm doing all right,' he'd told Sadie down the whistling phone line. 'I like it here. I keep busy during the day. The nights are quiet, though; I find myself arguing with the telly. Worse, I have a strong suspicion I'm losing.'

It had been an attempt to make light of things but Sadie had heard the crack in his voice. Her grandparents had fallen in love as teenagers. Ruth's father had made deliveries to Bertie's parents' shop in Hackney, and they'd been inseparable ever since. Her grandfather's grief was palpable and Sadie had wanted to say the perfect thing, to make it all better. Words had never been her strong suit, though, and so, instead, she'd suggested he might stand a better chance arguing with a Labrador. He'd laughed and told her he'd think about it, and next day he'd gone down to the animal shelter. In typical Bertie fashion, he'd come home with not one but two dogs and a cranky cat in tow. From what she'd observed in the week since she arrived in Cornwall, they'd formed quite the contented family, the four of them, even if the cat spent most of his time hiding behind the sofa; her grandfather seemed happier than he had since before Ruth got sick. All the more reason Sadie wasn't about to return home without his dogs.

Ash's pace picked up and Sadie had to hustle not to lose sight of him. The vegetation was changing, she noticed. The air was getting lighter. Beneath the thinning trees, the brambles had taken advantage of the brighter sun, multiplying and thickening gleefully. Branches grabbed and clutched at the hems of Sadie's shorts as she pushed through their knots. If she'd been given to fancy she might have imagined they were trying to stop her.

She scrambled up the steep sloping ground, avoiding large scattered rocks, until she reached the top and found herself at the edge of the woods. Sadie paused, surveying the landscape before her. She'd never come this far before. A field of long grass stretched ahead and in the distance she could just make out a fence and what appeared to be a lopsided gate. Beyond it was more of the same, another wide grassy space interrupted in places by huge trees with rich leafy foliage. Sadie drew breath. There was a child, a small girl, standing alone in the centre of the field, a silhouette, backlit, Sadie couldn't see her face. She opened her mouth to call out but when she blinked the child disintegrated into little more than a patch of yellow-white glare.

She shook her head. Her brain was tired. Her eyes were tired. She ought to get them checked for floaters.

Ash, who'd bounded ahead, looked over his shoulder to check her progress, barking impatiently when he judged it insufficient. Sadie started across the field after him, pushing aside the vague unwelcome notion she was doing something she shouldn't. The sensation was not a familiar one. As a rule, Sadie didn't worry about that sort of thing, but the recent trouble at work had her spooked. She didn't like being spooked. Spooked was a bit too close to vulnerable for Sadie's liking and she'd decided years ago it was better to march straight up to trouble than have it sneak up behind her.

The gate, she saw when she reached it, was made of timber: sun-bleached, splintered and hanging from its hinges with a deep sagging ennui that suggested it had been doing so for a very long time. A leafy climber with trumpeting purple flowers had tied itself in comprehensive knots around the posts, and Sadie had to climb through a gap between the pieces of bowing wood. Ash, reassured by this sign his mistress was following, let out a rousing bark and picked up speed, disappearing towards the horizon.

Grass brushed Sadie's bare knees, making them itch where her sweat had dried. Something niggled about this place. An odd feeling had come over her since she'd climbed through the gate, an inexplicable sense of things being not quite right. Sadie didn't go in for presentiments – there was no need for a sixth sense when the other five were being properly employed – and sure enough, there was a rational explanation for the oddness. Sadie had been walking for ten minutes or so when she realised what it was. The field was empty. Not of trees and grass and birds, they were everywhere; it was all the rest that was missing. There were no tractors puttering over the fields, no farmers out mending fences, no animals grazing. In this part of the world that was unusual.

Sadie glanced around, searching for something to prove her wrong. She could hear running water not too far away, and a bird that might have been a raven was watching her from the branch of a nearby willow. She noted great stretches of long rustling grass and the occasional gnarled tree, but nothing human as far as the eye could see.

A black gleam moved on the edge of her vision and Sadie flinched. The bird had launched itself from its perch and was cutting through the air in her direction. Sadie shifted sideways to avoid being hit and as she did her foot caught on something. She fell onto her hands and knees in a stretch of boggy mud beneath the massive willow. She glanced back accusingly and saw a mildewed piece of rope hooked over her left foot.

Rope.

Instinct, experience perhaps – a grisly melange of crime scenes from old investigations – made her look up. There, tied around the tree's thickest bough, visible only as a nobbled ridge beneath the bark, was the rope's frayed other end. There was another matching one beside it, dangling towards the ground where it trailed a damp plank of disintegrating wood. Not a noose then, but a swing.

Sadie stood up, brushed off her muddied knees, and paced a slow circumference around the dangling rope. There was something mildly unsettling about the tattered remnant of childish activity in this lonely place, but before she could give it further thought, Ash was off again, his brief concern for Sadie replaced by the urgent need to find his brother.

With a last glance at the ropes, Sadie followed. This time, however, she began to notice things she'd missed before. A strip of unruly yew trees ahead now re-presented itself as a hedge, neglected and wild but a hedge nonetheless; on the northern horizon between two dense clumps of wildflowers, she could make out what appeared to be the span of a bridge; the broken gate she'd climbed through no longer seemed a rudimentary division between two natural spaces but an overrun border between civilisation and the wilderness. Which meant this plot of land she traversed wasn't an uncultivated field, but a garden. At least, it had been once.

A howl came from the other side of the yew hedge and Ash answered loudly before disappearing through a gap in the greenery. Sadie did the same, but stopped abruptly when she reached the other side. An ink-like mass of stagnant water lay before her, glassy in the still of the dense clearing. Willows made a ring around the water's edge, and from its centre there rose a great muddy mound, an island of sorts. There were ducks everywhere, coots and moorhens, too, and the smell was rich and grubbily fertile. The feeling was uncanny, of avian eyes watching, dark and shiny.

Ramsay howled again, and Sadie followed his call around the lake's wet bank, decades of duck mess making it slimy underfoot. It was slippery and she went carefully beneath the trees. Ash was barking now too, standing on the far side of the lake on a wooden jetty, his nose raised skywards as he sounded the alarm.

Sadie brushed aside the weeping fingers of a willow, leaning to avoid a peculiar glass dome hanging from a rusted length of chain. She passed another four orbs along the way, all similarly clouded with dirt, their insides layered with generations of spidery web. She ran her hand lightly around the base of one, admiring its strange allure, wondering at its purpose. These were odd fruit hanging there amongst the leaves.

When she reached the jetty, Sadie saw that one of Ramsay's hind legs had broken through a hole in the rotting timber. He was panicking, and she picked her way quickly but carefully across the planks. She knelt, stroking his ears to calm him as she established there was no serious injury and considered the best way to get him out. In the end she could think of nothing better than to hold him in a clinch and heave. Ramsay was less than grateful, scrabbling his claws against the decking, barking with pained indignation. 'I know, I know,' muttered Sadie. 'Some of us just aren't very good at being helped.'

Finally she managed to extricate him, collapsing on her back to catch her breath as the dog, ruffled but evidently unhurt, leapt clear of the jetty. Sadie closed her eyes and laughed when Ash gave her neck an appreciative lick. A small voice warned that the boards might collapse at any moment but she was too exhausted to pay it any heed.

The sun had risen now, high in the sky, and its warmth on her face was godly. Sadie had never been the meditating type, but in this moment she understood what people were on about. A sigh of contentment escaped her lips, even though contented was the last word she'd have chosen to describe herself of late. She could hear her own breaths, her pulse pumping beneath the thin skin of her temple, as loudly as if she held a conch shell to her ear to eavesdrop on the ocean.

Without sight to get in the way of things, the whole world was suddenly alive with sound: the lapping of water as it washed around the posts below her, the splashing and skimming of ducks as they landed on the lake's surface, the wooden planks stretching beneath the sun's glare. As she listened, Sadie became aware of a thick blanketing hum behind it all, like hundreds of tiny motors whirring at once. It was a sound synonymous with summer, difficult to place at first, but then she realised. Insects, a hell of a lot of insects.

Sadie sat up, blinking into the brightness. The world was briefly white before everything righted itself. Lily pads glistened, heart-shaped tiles on the water's surface, flowers reaching for the sky like pretty, grasping hands. The air surrounding them was filled with hundreds of small winged creatures. She scrambled to her feet and was about to call for the dogs when something on the other side of the lake caught her attention.

In the middle of a sunlit clearing stood a house. A brick house with twin gables and a front door tucked beneath a portico. Multiple chimneys rose from the tiled roof and three levels of leadlight windows winked conspiratorially in the sun. A climber, green-leafed and voracious, clung to the brick face of the building and small birds flew busily in and out of the fretwork of tendrils, creating an effect of constant movement. Sadie whistled under her breath. 'What's a grand old lady like you doing in a place like this?' She'd only spoken quietly but her voice was foreign and unwelcome, her humour forced, an intrusion on the profound natural exuberance of the garden.

Sadie started around the lake towards the house; its pull was magnetic. The ducks and wild birds ignored her, their obliviousness combining somehow with the warmth of the day, the moist humidity of the lake, to feed the atmosphere of cloying enclosure.

There was a path, she noted as she reached the other side, mostly grown over due to encroaching hawthorn, but leading all the way to the front door. She scuffed the toe of her running shoe against the surface. Stone. Probably pale pinkish-brown once, like the rest of the local stone in the village buildings, but time and neglect had tarred it black.

The house, she saw as she drew nearer, had been as thoroughly forgotten as the garden. Tiles were missing from the roof, some of them lying shattered where they'd fallen, and one of the windowpanes on the top floor was broken. The remaining glass wore a thick render of bird droppings and white stalactites drooped from the sill, spilling onto the glossy leaves below.

As if to lay claim to the impressive clumps, a small bird launched itself from behind the broken glass, diving in a direct line before correcting to swoop fast and close by Sadie's ear. She flinched but stood her ground. They were everywhere, those little birds she'd glimpsed from the lake, darting in and out of the creeper's dark spaces and calling to one another in urgent chirrups. Not just birds, either; the foliage teemed with insects of all descriptions – butterflies, bees and others she couldn't name – giving the building an appearance of constant animation at odds with its dilapidated state.

It was tempting to assume the house was empty, but Sadie had been sent on call to enough homes of the elderly to know that the appearance of abandonment often presaged a sorry story inside. A dull brass knocker shaped like a fox's head hung lopsided from the chipped wooden door and she lifted a hand towards it before lowering it again. What would she say if someone answered? Sadie flexed her fingers one by one, considering. There was no reason she should be here today. No excuse she could give. A trespassing charge was the last thing she needed. But even as she thought it, Sadie knew she was speculating unnecessarily. The house before her was deserted. It was hard to put into words, but there was a look about it, an aura it gave off. She just knew.

A panel of decorative glass had been set above the door: four figures in long robes, each depicted against a background representing a different season. It wasn't a religious picture, as far as Sadie could tell, but the effect was similar. There was an earnestness to the design – a reverence, she supposed – that made her think of the stained-glass windows in churches. Sadie manoeuvred a large dirty planter closer to the door and climbed gingerly onto the rim.

Through a largish piece of clear glass, she glimpsed an entrance hall with an oval table at its centre. A vase stood on the tabletop, a bulb-shaped china jug with flowers painted on its side and – she squinted – a faint gold pattern snaking up the handle. A few thin branches of something brittle, willow perhaps, were arranged haphazardly within and there were dry leaves scattered beneath. A chandelier – crystal, glass, something fancy – was suspended from a plaster rose on the ceiling and a wide flight of stairs with worn red carpet curled upwards and away at the back of the hall. There was a round mirror on the wall to the left, hanging by a closed door.

Sadie jumped off the planter. A knotted garden ran along the front of the house beside the portico and she clambered through it, prickles catching her T-shirt as she picked a path through the brambles. There was a strong but not unpleasant smell – moist earth, decomposing leaf matter, new flowers beginning to catch the day's sun – and great fat bumblebees were busy already collecting pollen from a profusion of small pink and white blooms. Blackberries: Sadie surprised herself by dredging up the knowledge. They were blackberry flowers, and in a few months' time the bushes would be heavy with fruit.

When she reached the window, Sadie noticed that something had been etched into the wooden frame, some letters, an A, maybe an E, crudely carved and dark green with mould. She traced her fingers along the deep grooves, wondering idly who had made them. A curled piece of iron jutted out from amid the thick overgrowth beneath the sill and Sadie pulled the branches aside to discover the rusted remnants of a garden seat. She glanced over her shoulder at the jungle she'd just traversed. Difficult to imagine that a person had once been able to sit here comfortably, looking out over what must then have been a well-kept garden.

That strange, almost ominous, feeling was there again but Sadie shook it off. She dealt in facts, not feelings, and after recent events it was as well to remind herself of that. She steepled her hands against a glass pane and pressed her face to them, peering through the window.

The room was dim, but as her eyes adjusted certain objects began to stand out from the gloom: a grand piano in the corner by the door, a sofa in the centre with a pair of armchairs turned to face it, a fireplace in the far wall. Sadie experienced the familiar, agreeable sensation of opening the lid on someone else's life. She considered such moments a perk of her job, even if she often saw ugly things; she'd always been fascinated by the way other people lived. And although this wasn't a crime scene and she wasn't a detective on duty, Sadie automatically started making mental notes.

The walls were papered in a faded floral design, greyish-mauve, and covered with shelves that sagged beneath the weight of a thousand books. A large painted portrait stood sentinel above the fireplace, a woman with a fine nose and a secretive smile. A pair of French doors bordered by thick damask curtains were set in the adjacent wall. Presumably the doors had led once to a side garden, and sun had spilled through the glass on mornings like this to cast warm, bright squares on the carpet floor. But not anymore. A tenacious weave of ivy made sure of that, clinging to the glass and letting in only the merest specks of light. Beside the doors stood a narrow wooden table on which a photograph was displayed in a fancy frame. It was too dark to see the subject, and even if the light had been better an old-fashioned teacup and saucer blocked Sadie's view.

She sucked in her lips, considering. In some ways – the open piano lid, the sofa cushions askew, the teacup on the table – the room gave the impression that whoever had been there last had only just left and would be back any minute; yet at the same time there was an eerie, somehow permanent, stillness about the world on the other side of the glass. The room seemed frozen, its contents suspended, as if even the air, that most relentless of all elements, had been shut outside, as if it would be difficult to breathe inside. There was something else, too. Something that suggested the room had been that way for a long time. Sadie had thought at first it was her straining eyes, before she realised that the room's dull glaze was actually caused by a thick layer of dust.

She could see it clearly now on the desk beneath the window, where a shaft of light revealed a coating over every object: the inkwell, the lampshade and the collection of open books spread haphazardly between them. A sheet of paper on top of the pile caught Sadie's eye, the sketch of a child's face, a beautiful face with large serious eyes and soft lips and hair that fell either side of small ears so that he (or she; it was hard to tell) looked more like a garden pixie than a real child. The drawing was smudged in places, she noticed, the black ink smeared, the strong lines blurred, and something had been written in the bottom corner, a signature and a date: *June 23rd, 1933*.

Loud noise and a barrelling movement behind her made Sadie start, bumping her forehead on the glass. Two black, panting dogs burst through the brambles to sniff at her feet. 'You want your breakfast,' she said as a cold wet nose prodded her palm. Sadie's own stomach took up the suggestion, letting out a low grumble. 'Come on then,' she said, stepping back from the window. 'Let's get you home.'

Sadie took one last look at the house before following the dogs back through the overgrown yew hedge. The climbing sun had slipped behind a cloud and the windows no longer glinted at the lake. The building had taken on a sullen cast, like a spoiled child who enjoyed being the centre of attention and now wasn't happy being ignored. Even the birds were more brazen than before, criss-crossing the hazy clearing with calls that sounded eerily like laughter, and the insect choir was growing louder with the day's expanding heat.

The lake's flat surface glistened in a secretive, slatey way and Sadie suddenly felt every bit the intruder she was. It was hard to say what made her so certain, but as she turned to leave, ducked through the hole in the yew and started chasing the dogs home, she knew, in that twist-of-the-gut way a police detective had better hope she developed, that something terrible had happened in that house.

Four

The girls were laughing, and of course they all whooped with glee when it nearly took the top off Mother's head! Alice brought her hands together in excitement as Clementine thudded after the little glider.

'Just don't throw that thing too near the baby,' warned Mother, patting the top of her hair to make sure every pin was still in place.

If Clemmie heard the warning she gave no sign. She was running like her life depended on it, hands in the air, skirt flying, ready to catch the plane if it even looked like crash landing.

A clatter of curious ducks had waddled up from the lake to observe the commotion and they scattered now in a flurry of feathers and indignant quacks as the glider, with Clemmie close behind it, came skidding to a halt among their party.

Daddy smiled over the book of poetry he'd been reading. 'Beautiful landing!' he called from his seat by the old planter. 'Just beautiful.'

The glider had been his idea. He'd seen an advertisement in a magazine and sent away to America especially. It was supposed to be a secret but Alice had known about it for months – she always knew who was giving what to whom well ahead of time; she'd seen him point to the advertisement one evening back in spring and say, 'Look at this. Perfect for Clemmie's birthday, don't you think?'

Mother had been less keen, asking him whether he really thought a wooden glider was the most appropriate gift for a twelve-year-old girl, but Daddy had only smiled and said that Clementine wasn't an ordinary twelve-year-old girl. He'd been right about that: Clemmie was decidedly different – 'The son we never had,' Daddy had been fond of saying before Theo came along. He'd been right about the glider, too; Clemmie had torn off the wrapping at the table after lunch, her eyes widening as the gift was revealed, and then she'd actually squealed with delight. She'd leapt from her seat, dragging the tablecloth behind her in her rush to reach the door.

'Clemmie, no,' Mother had implored, reaching out to catch a tumbling vase. 'We're not finished yet.' And then, glancing beseechingly at the others, 'Oh, let's not go outside. I thought perhaps charades in the library . . .'

But it was rather difficult to celebrate a birthday party when the guest of honour had fled the scene, and thus, to Mother's obvious chagrin, there'd been nothing for it but to abandon the carefully arranged table and move the afternoon's festivities to the garden.

And so here they were, the whole family, Mr Llewellyn, Grandmother and Nanny Rose too, spread out over the lawn of Loeanneth, as the long shadows of afternoon began to spill across the deep green grass. The day was glorious, autumn but not yet cold. The clematis was still blooming on the wall of the house, little birds twittering as they whipped across the clearing, and even baby Theo had been brought out in his Moses basket.

A farmer was burning heather in one of the neighbouring fields and the smell was wonderful. It always made Alice happy, that smell, something to do with the change of seasons, and standing there watching Clemmie tend the wooden glider, the sun warm on her neck, the ground cool beneath her bare feet, she experienced a delicious moment of profound well-being.

Alice dug into her pocket and pulled out her notebook, hurrying to make a note of the sensation and the day and the people in it, chewing on the end of her fountain pen as her gaze tripped over the sunlit house, the willow trees, the shimmering lake and the yellow roses climbing on the iron gate. It was like the garden from a storybook – it *was* the garden from a storybook – and Alice loved it. She was never going to leave Loeanneth. Never. She could picture herself growing old here. A happy old woman, with long white hair and cats – yes, certainly a few cats to keep her company. (And Clemmie would visit, but probably not Deborah, who would be far happier in London, with a grand house and a wealthy husband and a team of housemaids to arrange her clothes . . .)

It was one of those days, Alice thought, as she scribbled happily, when everyone seemed to feel the same way. Daddy had taken a break from his study, Mr Llewellyn had removed his formal jacket and was getting about in his shirt and waistcoat, Grandmother deShiel looked almost cheerful as she dozed beneath the willow. Mother was the notable exception, but then she never liked having her careful plans flouted, so a certain amount of curt displeasure was only to be expected.

Even Deborah, who wasn't usually one for toys, considering herself far too grown-up and ladylike, had found Clemmie's enthusiasm contagious. The fact had made her understandably cross, so she'd insisted on sitting alone on the garden seat beneath the library window and speaking, when she deigned, at a brusque clip, as if she really did have far better things to do and they were just lucky she'd decided to bless them with her presence. 'See if you can make it turn a circle,' she called now, holding up the box in which the glider had arrived. 'It says here that if you get the rubber bands just right you can make it turn a loop.'

'Tea is ready,' said Mother, her tone of censure sharpening as the afternoon's progress spiralled further away from that which she'd envisaged. 'The pot's fresh but it will only get colder.'

They'd had a large lunch and nobody much felt like tea, but Mr Llewellyn was a faithful friend, fronting up as requested and accepting the cup and saucer Mother thrust upon him.

Deborah, by contrast, ignored the entreaty entirely. 'Hurry up, Clemmie,' she said. 'Give it another toss.'

Clemmie, who was fastening the glider inside the satin sash of her dress, didn't answer. She tucked the hem of her skirt into her knickers and craned her neck to take in the top of the sycamore tree.

'Clemmie!' Deborah called, imperious now.

'Give me a boost?' came their youngest sister's reply.

Mother, though busy foisting cake on Mr Llewellyn, was always alert for signs of impending trouble, and didn't drop a crumb as she said, 'No, Clemmie! Absolutely not!' She glanced towards Daddy, seeking agreement, but he was back behind his book, happily ensconced in the world of Keats.

'Let her go,' soothed Mr Llewellyn. 'Everything's all right.'

Deborah could resist the call of the afternoon no longer, tossing the box onto the seat beside her and hurrying down to the base of the tree. Nanny Rose was cajoled into linking arms to form a step, and Clemmie hoisted herself up. After a moment of scrabbling and a few false starts, she disappeared into the lower boughs.

'Be careful, Clementine,' Mother admonished, gravitating towards the site of the action. 'Do be careful.' She hovered beneath the tree, sighing with exasperation as she tried to follow Clemmie's progress through the thick foliage.

At last, there came a triumphant whoop, and an arm appeared, waving from the top of the tree. Alice squinted into the afternoon sun, grinning as her younger sister positioned herself in the highest fork and inched the glider free from where she'd strapped it. Clemmie wound the elastic bands tight, lifted her arm, making sure to keep the whole thing at the optimum launch angle, and then, then, there came – release!

The glider flew like a bird, soaring across the pale-blue sky, dipping slightly and then straightening, until the air speed slowed and the pressure on the tail lessened, and the rear part angled up.

'Watch!' shouted Clemmie. 'Watch it now!'

Sure enough, the glider started to turn a great loop, right out over the lake, a sight so spectacular that even Mr Harris and the new gardener stopped what they were doing down at the jetty and gazed up towards the sky. Spontaneous applause broke out as the glider completed its stunt and continued its cruise, clearing the water and landing with a gentle slide on the flat grassed area by the fountain on the other side of the lake.

The whole world seemed to have stalled as the little plane described its circle, so it was with some surprise that Alice realised the baby was crying. Poor little mite! With all the excitement, he was being quite ignored in his basket. Alice, accustomed to thinking herself an observer, glanced around, waiting for someone to step in, before realising she was the only person free to help. She was on the verge of starting for Theo's basket when she saw Daddy was going to beat her to it.

There were some fathers, or so Alice was led to believe, who would've thought it outside their remit to comfort a little baby, but Daddy wasn't like that. He was the best father in the world, kind and gentle and really, really clever. He loved nature and science, and was even writing a book about the earth. He'd been working on his tome for over a decade and (although she wouldn't have admitted the fact out loud) it was the only thing Alice would've changed about him if she could. She was glad he was clever, and proud of him of course, but he spent far too much time in the company of that book. She'd much rather they had him all for themselves.

'Alice!'

Deborah was calling, and whatever she wanted to say must've been important because she'd forgotten to sound disdainful. 'Alice, hurry up! Mr Llewellyn is going to take us in the boat!'

The boat! Ripping! Such a rare treat – it had been

Mother's as a girl and was thus considered an antique and Not For Use. Alice beamed and her heart danced and the afternoon sunlight was suddenly brighter than it had been before. This really was turning into the best day ever!

Five

'We're back!' Sadie kicked off her muddy running shoes in the small entrance hall of her grandfather's place, herding them into line against the skirting board with her toes. The cliff-top cottage was thick with the smell of something warm and savoury and her stomach, starved of breakfast, pleaded loudly.

'Hey, Bertie, you're not going to believe what we found.' She rattled out a serving of dog biscuits from the tub beneath the coat rack. 'Granddad?'

'In the kitchen,' came his reply.

Sadie gave the ravenous dogs a final pat and went inside.

Her grandfather was at the round wooden dining table, but he wasn't alone. A small energetic-looking woman with short grey hair and spectacles sat across from him, a mug in her hands and a joyous smile of greeting on her face.

'Oh,' Sadie said. 'Sorry. I didn't realise—'

Her grandfather waved the apology aside. 'Kettle's still hot, Sadie, love. Pour yourself a cup and join us? This is Louise Clarke from the hospital, here to collect toys for the Solstice Festival.' As Sadie smiled hello, he added, 'She's kindly brought a stew for our supper.'

'It was the least I could do,' said Louise, half standing to shake Sadie's hand. She was wearing faded jeans and her T-shirt, which was the same vibrant green as the frame of her spectacles, read: *Magic Happens!* She had one of those faces that seemed lit from within, as if she were getting better sleep than the rest of the population; Sadie felt dusty, creased and scowling by comparison. 'Beautiful work your grandfather does, such fine carving. The hospital stall's going to be brilliant this year. We're incredibly lucky to have him.'

Sadie couldn't have agreed more, but, knowing her grandfather's distaste for public praise, she didn't say so. Instead, she planted a kiss on top of his bald head as she squeezed behind his chair. 'I can see I'm going to have to crack the whip and keep him working,' she said as she reached the bench. 'That stew smells amazing.'

Louise beamed. 'It's my very own recipe – lentils and love.'

There were any number of rejoinders to choose from, but before Sadie could settle on one Bertie had interjected. 'Sadie's stopping with me for a while, down from London.'

'A holiday, how lovely. Will you still be with us in a fortnight when the festival rolls around?'

'Maybe,' said Sadie, avoiding her grandfather's gaze. She'd been less than specific when he asked about her plans; 'I'm playing it by ear.'

'Letting the universe decide,' Louise said approvingly.

'Something like that.'

Bertie raised his brows, but evidently thought better of pressing. He nodded at her muddy clothing. 'You've been in the wars.'

'You should see the other guy.'

Louise's eyes widened.

'My granddaughter's a runner,' Bertie explained. 'One of those curious people who seem to enjoy discomfort. The weather this past week has given her cabin fever and it seems she's been taking it out on the local tracks.'

Louise laughed. 'It's often like that for newcomers. The fogs can be oppressive for those that haven't grown up with them.'

'No fog today, I'm pleased to report,' Sadie said, carving a thick slice of Bertie's daily sourdough. 'It's crystal clear out there.'

'Just as well.' Louise drained the last of her tea. 'I've got thirty-two dangerously excited children back at the hospital waiting for their seaside picnic. Another postponement and I fear I'd have had a mutiny on my hands.'

'Here, I'll help you with these,' said Bertie. 'Don't want to give the little inmates cause for insurrection.'

While he and Louise wrapped tissue paper around the carved toys, packing them carefully into a cardboard box, Sadie spread butter and marmalade on her bread. She was impatient to tell Bertie about the house she'd found in the woods. Its strange, lonely atmosphere had followed her home and she listened only vaguely as they picked up the tail end of a conversation about a man on their committee named Jack. 'I'll go and visit him,' Bertie was saying, 'and take one of those pear cakes he likes, see if I can talk him round.'

Sadie glanced through the kitchen window, beyond her grandfather's garden and down over the harbour to where scores of fishing boats were bobbing on the velvet sea. It was remarkable how quickly Bertie had managed to find a place for himself in this new community. Only a little over twelve months since he'd arrived and already it seemed he'd formed connections that ran as deep as if he'd been here all his life. Sadie wasn't even sure she could name all her neighbours in the block of flats she'd lived in for seven years.

She sat down at the table, trying to remember whether the man in the upstairs flat was Bob or Todd or Rod, but let it slip away unresolved when Bertie said, 'Go on then, Sadie, love – tell us what you found. You look as if you fell down an old copper mine.' He paused in his wrapping. 'You didn't, did you?'

She rolled her eyes with affectionate impatience. Bertie was a worrier, at least he was when it came to Sadie. He had been since Ruth died.

'Buried treasure? Are we rich?'

'Sadly not.'

'Never know your luck around here,' Louise said, 'what with all the smugglers' tunnels pitted along the coast. Did you run around the headland?'

'The woods,' Sadie replied. She explained briefly about Ramsay, how he'd gone missing and she and Ash had been forced to leave the path to find him.

'Sadie—'

'I know, Granddad, the woods are thick and I'm a city-slicker, but Ash was with me, and it was just as well we went looking because when we finally caught up with Ramsay he'd got himself stuck down a hole in an old jetty.'

'A jetty? In the woods?'

'Not right in the woods, it was in a clearing, an estate. The jetty was by a lake in the middle of the most incredible overgrown garden. You'd have loved it. There were willows and massive hedges and I think it might once have been rather spectacular. There was a house, too. Abandoned.'

'The Edevane place,' Louise said quietly. 'Loeanneth.'

The name when spoken had that magical, whispering quality of so many Cornish words and Sadie couldn't help but remember the odd feeling the insects had given her, as if the house itself was alive. 'Loeanneth,' she repeated.

'It means "Lake House".'

'Yes . . .' Sadie pictured the muddy lake and its eerie avian population. 'Yes, that's it. What happened there?'

'A terrible business,' Louise said, with a sad shake of the head. 'Back in the thirties, before I was born. My mother used to talk about it, though – usually when she wanted to stop us kids from wandering too far. A child went missing on the night of a grand party. It was a big story at the time; the family was wealthy and the national press paid a lot of attention. There was a huge police investigation, and they even brought down the top brass from London. Not that any of it helped.' She slipped the last toy into place and folded the box shut. 'Poor lad, he was little more than a babe.'

'I've never heard of the case.'

'Sadie's in the police,' Bertie explained. 'A detective,' he added with a lick of pride that made her wince.

'Well, it was a long time ago, I suppose,' said Louise. 'Every decade or so the whole thing rears its head again. Someone calls the police with a lead that goes nowhere; a fellow comes out of God knows where to claim he's the missing boy. Never makes it further than the local papers, though.'

Sadie pictured the dusty library, the open books on the

desk, the sketch, the portrait on the wall. Personal effects that must once have meant something to someone. 'How did the house come to be abandoned?'

'The family just left. Locked the doors and went back to London. Over time people forgot that it was there. It's become our very own Sleeping Beauty house. Deep in the woods like that, it's not the sort of place you go near unless you've got good reason. They say it was lovely once, a beautiful garden, a great big lake. A sort of paradise. But it was all lost when the little lad disappeared into thin air.'

Bertie sighed with deep satisfaction and brought his hands together in a soft clap. 'Yes,' he said. 'Yes, that's just the sort of thing I was led to believe I'd find in Cornwall.'

Sadie frowned, surprised by her usually pragmatic grandfather. It was a romantic story, to be sure, but her police instincts quivered. No one just disappeared, thin air or otherwise. Leaving Bertie's reaction for another time, she turned to Louise. 'The police investigation . . .' she said. 'I take it there were suspects?'

'I suppose there must've been, but no one was convicted. It was a real mystery from what I can remember. No clear leads. There was a huge search for the boy, an initial theory that he might merely have wandered off, but no trace of him was ever found.'

'And the family never came back?'

'Never.'

'They didn't sell the house?'

'Not as far as I'm aware.'

'Strange,' Bertie said, 'just to let it sit there, locked and lonely, all this time.'

'I expect it was too sad for them,' Louise said. 'Too many

memories. One can only imagine what it's like to lose a child. All that grief, the sense of impotence. I can understand why they'd have fled the scene, decided to make a fresh start somewhere else. A clean break.'

Sadie murmured agreement. She didn't add that in her experience, no matter how hard a person ran, no matter how fresh the start they gave themselves, the past had a way of reaching across the years to catch them.

That evening, in the room Bertie had made up for her on the first floor, Sadie took out the envelope, just as she had the night before and the one before that. She didn't slip the letter from inside, though. There was no need; she'd memorised its contents weeks ago. She ran a thumb over the front, the message written in capital letters above the address: DO NOT BEND, PHOTOGRAPH INSIDE. She'd memorised the picture, too. Proof. Tangible evidence of what she'd done.

The dogs shifted at the foot of her bed and Ramsay whimpered in his sleep. Sadie laid a hand on his warm flank to calm him. 'There now, old fellow, everything's going to be all right.' It crossed her mind she was saying it as much for herself as for him. Fifteen years the past had taken to find her. Fifteen years in which she'd focused on moving forwards, determined never to look back. Incredible, really, that after all her efforts to build a barrier between then and now, it only took one letter to bring it down. If she closed her eyes, she could see herself so clearly, sixteen years old and waiting on the brick wall out the front of her parents' neat semi-detached. She saw the cheap cotton dress she'd been wearing, the extra coat of lip gloss, her kohl-rimmed eyes. She could still remember applying it, the smudgy stub of eye pencil, her reflection in the mirror, her desire to draw circles thick enough to hide behind.

A man and woman Sadie didn't know – acquaintances of her grandparents, was all she'd been told – had come to collect her. He'd stayed in the driver's seat, polishing the black steering wheel with a cloth, while she, all pearlescent coral lipstick and bustling efficiency, had climbed out of the passenger seat and trotted around to the kerb. 'Morning,' she'd called, with the strident cheer of someone who knew she was being helpful and rather liked herself for it. 'You must be Sadie.'

Sadie had been sitting there all morning, having decided there was no point staying inside the empty house and being unable to think of anywhere else she'd rather go. When the henna-haired social worker first gave her the details of when and where to wait she'd considered not turning up, but only for a minute; Sadie knew this was the best option she had. She might have been foolish – her parents never tired of telling her she was – but she wasn't stupid.

'Sadie Sparrow?' the woman persisted, a thin lace of perspiration on the blonde hairs above her top lip.

Sadie didn't answer; her compliance had limits. She tightened her mouth instead and pretended great interest in a flock of starlings soaring through the sky.

The woman, for her part, remained splendidly undeterred. 'I'm Mrs Gardiner, and that's Mr Gardiner up front. Your Grandma Ruth asked us to collect you seeing as neither she nor your granddad drive, and we were only too happy to help. We're neighbours, and as it happens we spend quite a bit of time out this way.' When Sadie said nothing, she nodded her lacquered hairdo in the direction of the British

Airways bag Sadie's father had brought back from his business trip to Frankfurt the year before. 'That's everything then?'

Sadie tightened her grip on the bag's handles and dragged it across the concrete until it touched her thigh.

'A light traveller. Mr Gardiner will be impressed.' The woman swatted at a fly by the end of her nose and Sadie thought of Peter Rabbit. Of all the things to enter her head as she left home for good, a nursery-book character. It would have been funny except that right then Sadie couldn't imagine anything being funny ever again.

She hadn't wanted to do something as wet as turning back to look at the house she'd lived in all her life, but as Mr Gardiner steered the great vehicle away from the kerb, her faithless gaze flickered sideways. There was no one home and there was nothing to see that hadn't been seen a thousand times before. At the window next door, a sheer curtain twitched and then fell, an official signal that the brief rupture of Sadie's exit had ended and the sameness of suburban life was free to continue its flow. Mr Gardiner's car turned at the end of the street and they started west towards London, and Sadie's own fresh start at the home of the grandparents she hardly knew, who'd agreed to take her in when she had nowhere else to go.

A number of soft thuds came from overhead and Sadie let go of the memory, blinking herself back into the dimly lit, whitewashed bedroom with its sloping ceiling and the dormer window overlooking the vast, dark ocean. A single picture was hanging on the wall, the same framed print Ruth had put above Sadie's bed in London, of a storm-whipped sea and an enormous wave threatening to engulf three tiny fishing boats. 'We bought it on our honeymoon,' she'd told Sadie one night. 'I loved it at once, the tension of that great wave caught on the verge of its inevitable collapse. The brave, experienced fishermen, heads bowed, holding on for dear life.' Sadie had glimpsed the thread of advice; Ruth hadn't needed to spell it out.

Another thud. Bertie was in the attic again.

Sadie had discerned a pattern in the week she'd been staying at Seaview Cottage. While her grandfather's days were busy, filled with his new life and friends, his garden and endless preparations for the upcoming festival, nights were a different story. Sometime after dinner each evening, Bertie would take himself up the rickety ladder under the guise of searching for a particular saucepan/whisk/cookbook he suddenly needed. There'd be an initial series of bumps as he rummaged about in the moving boxes, and then the spaces between would lengthen and the sweet, cloying smell of pipe smoke would drift down through the gaps in the floor-boards.

She knew what he was really doing. Some of Ruth's clothing he'd already given to Oxfam, but there was still a large number of boxes full of things he couldn't bear to part with. They were the collections of a lifetime and he their curator. 'They'll keep for another day,' he'd said quickly when Sadie offered to help him sort through them. And then, as if regretting the sharpish tone, 'They're doing no harm. I like to think there's so much of her here, under this roof.'

It had been a surprise when her grandfather told her he'd sold up and was moving to Cornwall. He and Ruth had lived in the one home all their married life, a home Sadie had loved, that had been a haven for her. She had presumed he'd stay forever, loath to leave the place where happy memories moved like old projector images in the dusty corners. Then again, Sadie had never loved another person with the sort of devotion shared by Bertie and Ruth, so what would she know. It turned out the move was something they'd talked about doing together for years. A customer had put the idea in Bertie's head when he was still a boy, telling him stories about the fine weather in the west, the glorious gardens, the salt and the sea and the rich folklore. 'The time just never came,' he'd told Sadie sadly some weeks after the funeral. 'You always presume there's time ahead, until one day you realise there isn't.' When Sadie had asked him whether he'd miss London, he'd shrugged and said that of course he would, it was his home, the place he'd been born and grown up, where he'd met his wife and raised his family. 'But it's the past, Sadie, love; I'll carry that with me wherever I go. Doing something new, though, something that Ruth and I talked about – in some way it feels like I'm giving her a future, too.'

Sadie was aware, suddenly, of footfalls on the landing, a knock at the door. Quickly, she hid the envelope behind her pillow. 'Come in.'

The door opened and Bertie was there, cake tin in hand.

She smiled too broadly, her heart racing as if she were guilty of an indiscretion. 'Found what you were looking for?'

'The very thing. I'm going to bake tomorrow, one of my signature pear cakes.' He frowned lightly. 'Though it occurs to me I haven't any pears.'

'I'm no expert, but I'm guessing that could be a problem.'

'I don't suppose you'd pick some up for me in the village tomorrow morning?'

'Well, I'll have to check my diary . . .'

Bertie laughed. 'Thanks, Sadie, love.'

He lingered in such a way that Sadie knew he had more to say. Sure enough: 'I found something else while I was up there.' He reached inside the tin and took out a dog-eared book, holding it up so she could see the cover. 'Good as new, eh?'

Sadie recognised it at once. It was like opening the door unexpectedly to an old friend, the sort who'd been along for the ride during an especially difficult and bruising period. She couldn't believe Bertie and Ruth had kept it. Hard to imagine now, the prominence the book of brainteasers had had in her life back then, when she'd first come to live with them. She'd cloistered herself away in the spare bedroom at her grandparents' house, the little room above the shop that Ruth had done up specially for her, and she'd worked through the whole thing, page by page, front to back, her commitment verging on the religious.

'Got them all out, didn't you?' Bertie said. 'Every puzzle.'

Sadie was touched by the pride in his voice. 'I did.'

'Didn't even need to look at the answers.'

'Certainly not.' She eyed the rough edges at the back where she'd torn out the solutions so she wouldn't, couldn't, be tempted. It had been very important to her, that. Her answers must be her own, her achievements clean and absolute, above suspicion. She'd been trying to prove something, of course. That she wasn't stupid or hopeless or 'a bad egg', no matter what her parents might think. That problems, no matter how big, could be solved; that a great wave could crash and the fishermen survive. 'Ruth bought it for me.'

'That she did.'

It had been the perfect gift at the perfect time, though Sadie suspected she'd been less than grateful. She couldn't remember what she'd said when her grandmother gave it to her. Probably nothing; she hadn't been particularly communicative back then. A sixteen-year-old knot of insolence and monosyllabic disdain for everyone and everything, including (especially) these unknown relatives who'd swept in to rescue her. 'I wonder how she knew?'

'She was good like that, kind and clever. She saw people, even when they did their best to hide.' Bertie smiled and they both pretended talk of Ruth hadn't made his eyes glisten. He put the puzzle book on the bedside table. 'Might have to get yourself another one while you're down here. Maybe even a novel to read. That's the sort of thing people do when they're on holiday.'

'Is it?'

'So I hear.'

'Perhaps I will then.'

He lifted a single brow. He was curious about her visit, but he knew her well enough not to force the matter. 'Well,' he said instead, 'time for me to turn in. Nothing like the sea air, eh?'

Sadie agreed and wished him a good night's sleep, but when the door closed behind him she noticed his footsteps went back up towards the attic rather than across the hall to bed.

As pipe smoke drifted through the floorboards and the dogs dreamed fitfully beside her and her grandfather confronted his own past upstairs, Sadie glanced through the book. Just a humble collection of brainteasers, nothing fancy, and yet it had saved her life. She hadn't known she was smart until her grandmother gave her that book. She hadn't known she was good at puzzles, or that their solution would deliver her the kind of high other kids got from skipping school. But it turned out she was, and it did, and so a door was opened and her life was set upon a path she'd never imagined. She grew up and away from her teenage troubles and found herself a job with real puzzles to solve and consequences if she failed that went far beyond her own intellectual frustration.

Was it a coincidence, she wondered, that Bertie had given it to her tonight, this book that so strongly signified that other time? Or had he guessed somehow that her current visit was linked to the events fifteen years before that had first brought her to stay with him and Ruth?

Sadie retrieved the envelope, studying again the censorious handwriting, her own name and address spelled out like a criticism across its front. The letter inside was her own personal time bomb, tick-tick-ticking while she worked out how to defuse it. She needed to defuse it. It had made a mess of everything and would continue to do so until she fixed it. She wished she'd never received the damn thing. That the postman had dropped it from his bag, and the wind had whipped it away, and a dog somewhere had chased and chewed it until all that remained was a soggy pulp. Sadie sighed unhappily and tucked the envelope inside the book of puzzles. She wasn't naive; she knew there was no such thing as 'fair'. Nonetheless, she felt sorry for herself as she closed the book and tucked it away. It didn't seem right, somehow, that a person's life should be derailed twice by the one mistake.

*

The solution came to her on the edge of sleep. She'd been slipping, as was normal now, into the dream about the little backlit girl in the doorway, holding out her hands and calling for her mother, when she opened her eyes, instantly awake. The answer (to all her problems, it seemed to Sadie in the clarity of night) was so simple she couldn't believe it had taken her six weeks to find it. She, who prided herself on her ability to unravel puzzles. She'd wished the letter hadn't reached her, and who was there to say it had? Sadie threw back her duvet and retrieved the envelope from inside the book of brainteasers, rummaged about on her bedside table for a pen. *No Longer at this Address*, she scribbled hastily on the front, eagerness making her writing more jagged than usual. *Return to Sender*. A great sigh of relief escaped her as she studied her handiwork. Her shoulders lightened. Resisting the urge to look again at the photograph, she resealed the envelope carefully so that no one would be any the wiser.

Early next morning, while Bertie and the dogs slept, Sadie pulled on her running gear and jogged along the dark silent streets, letter in hand. She dropped it into the village's only postbox to be spirited back to London.

Sadie couldn't stop smiling as she continued around the headland. Her feet pounded with renewed energy, and as the sun rose golden in the pink sky, she basked in the knowledge that the whole unpleasant business was over and done with. To all intents and purposes, it was as if the letter had never found her. Bertie would never need to know the truth behind her sudden visit to Cornwall, and Sadie could get back to work. Without the letter's contents clouding her judgement, she'd be able to let the Bailey case go once and for all, and creep out from under whatever madness it was that had cloaked her. The only thing left to do was to tell Donald.

When she went out again later for Bertie's pears, Sadie walked the long way into the village, over the cliff towards the lookout and then down the steep western path into the playground. There was no denying this was a beautiful part of the world. Sadie could see why Bertie had fallen in love with it. 'I knew immediately,' he'd told her, with unexpected, born-again zeal. 'There's just something about the place that called me.' He'd been so keen to believe there were mysterious external forces at work, that the move was somehow 'meant to be', that Sadie had merely smiled and nodded, and refrained from telling him there were very few people who *wouldn't* have felt that life here was calling to them.

She took the coins from her pocket and jiggled them in anticipation. Mobile reception was unreliable in the village, but there was a public phone box in the park and she was going to take advantage of being out of Bertie's earshot. She dropped her coins into the slot and waited, drumming her thumb against her lip as she stood there.

'Raynes,' his grunt came down the line.

'Donald, it's Sadie.'

'Sparrow? I can hardly hear you. How's the leave?'

'Yeah, great.' She hesitated and then added, 'Restful,' because it seemed the sort of thing a person ought to say about a holiday.

'Good, good.'

The phone line hissed. Neither of them went in much for small talk so she decided to come straight to the point.

'Listen, I've done a lot of thinking and I'm ready to come back.'

Silence.

'To work,' she added.

'It's only been a week.'

'And it's been very clarifying. Sea air and all that.'

'I thought I made it clear, Sparrow. Four weeks, no buts.'

'I know, Don, but look . . .' Sadie glanced over her shoulder and saw a woman pushing a child on a swing. She lowered her voice. 'I know I was out of line. I got it completely wrong, I overreacted and I handled it badly. You were right, there was some other stuff going on, personal stuff, but it's over now, dealt with, and—'

'Hang on a tick.'

Sadie heard someone muttering in the background at the other end.

Donald murmured a reply before coming back to her. 'Listen, Sparrow,' he said, 'something's happening here.'

'Really? A new case?'

'I've got to go.'

'Yeah, right, of course. I was just saying, I'm ready—'

'It's a bad line. Give us a call in a few days, eh? Next week sometime. We'll discuss it properly.'

'But, I—'

Sadie cursed into the receiver as the phone line went dead and dug around in her pockets for more change. She redialled but the call went straight to Donald's voicemail. She waited a few seconds before trying again. Same thing. Sadie left no message.

She sat for a while on the bench near the playground. A couple of seagulls were fighting over a pile of spilled chips in a newspaper shroud. The child on the swing was crying, the chains of the swing creaking in sympathy. Sadie wondered if it was possible Donald had ignored her subsequent calls on purpose. She decided it was. She wondered if there was anyone else she should contact while she was sitting by the phone with coins in her pocket. She realised there wasn't. Sadie bounced her knees up and down, restless. The need to get back to London, where she was useful and there was more to do in a day than buy pears, was almost painful. Frustration, impotence and the sudden quelling of excitement jostled about inside her. The child on the swing was having a full-blown tantrum now, arching his little body and refusing his mother's attempts to wipe his smeary face. Sadie would have rather liked to join in.

'Going cheap,' the woman said to Sadie as she walked by, the same eye-rolling tone all parents adopted when they joked about giving away their children.

Sadie smiled thinly and continued to the village, where she made a greater job than was necessary of choosing the pears, scrutinising each one like a suspect in a line-up before making her selection, paying at the till and starting for home.

She'd passed the library before – the stone building was on the High Street and an unavoidable landmark between her grandfather's house and the village proper – but she'd never thought to go inside. She wasn't a library person. Too many books, too much quiet. Now, though, the display in the window made her stop abruptly. It was a pyramid of mystery novels, lots of them, with black covers and the name A. C. Edevane spelled out across the front in bold silver. Sadie was familiar with the author, of course. A. C. Edevane was one of the few crime writers actually read by police officers, and a national institution besides. When Louise had spoken about the Edevane family and their house by the lake, Sadie hadn't made the connection. Now, though, glancing at the poster strung above the display – LOCAL AUTHOR TO PUBLISH FIFTIETH BOOK – she felt the singular thrill of two seemingly unconnected elements coming together.

Without another thought, Sadie entered the building. A helpful-looking man of gnome-like proportions and with a nametag pinned to his shirt assured her that yes, of course they had a local history section; was there anything in particular he could help her with? 'Actually,' said Sadie, setting down her string bag of pears, 'there is. I need to find out everything I can about a house. And an old police case. And, while I'm at it, I'll take a recommendation for your favourite A. C. Edevane novel.'

Six

London, 2003

Peter almost dropped the parcel as he ran for the bus. Thankfully a lifetime of clumsiness had given him practice at catching things and he managed to pinion it to his body with an elbow without breaking his stride. He took his bus pass from his pocket, pushed a curtain of hair from his eyes, and spotted a single vacant seat. 'Excuse me,' he said, to nobody in particular, making his way down the aisle as the bus lurched forwards. 'Excuse me, please. Sorry. So sorry.'

The pursed-lipped woman occupying the window seat frowned over her open copy of *The Times* as the bus turned a corner and Peter fell into the space beside her. Her sideways shuffle and small-but-pointed sigh of indignation suggested he'd brought an unwelcome whirlwind of fluster and bother with him. It was something Peter had always suspected about himself and so the insinuation didn't offend him in the least. 'Thought I was going to be walking for a minute there,' he said affably, letting his satchel and the parcel slide to the floor between his feet. 'Long way to Hampstead from here, especially in this heat.'

The woman returned his smile, in a withering sort of way that might have been classed a grimace by someone less generous than Peter, before glancing back at her paper and giving the broadsheet a lavish shake to straighten its pages. It was a reading style that necessarily ignored her seatmate's presence entirely, but Peter wasn't a large man and found that if he leaned back hard against his seat the pages barely skimmed him. What was more, by this arrangement he was able to glean the day's headlines, saving him a stop at the newsagent's when he got to Hampstead.

Alice expected him to keep up with the news. She could be a hungry conversationalist when the mood struck her, and she didn't suffer fools gladly. The latter he'd learned from Alice herself; she'd announced the fact during their first day of working together, her eyes narrowing perceptibly as if she possessed the superhuman ability to scan a person and detect foolishness at a glance.

Peter let his own gaze wander over page two, laid out helpfully by his seat mate across his lap: the latest MORI poll put Labour and the Conservatives on even terms, six members of the Royal Military Police had been killed in Iraq, and Margaret Hodge was being tipped as the first Minister for Children. At least the Bailey case had fallen off the front pages. It had been a terrible thing, a child left alone like that for days, abandoned by the very person you'd think might be counted on to care for her. Peter had said as much during tea one afternoon when the case was at its hottest and Alice had surprised him, staring fixedly over her cup before replying that they'd no business passing judgement when they didn't know the full story. 'You're young,' she'd continued briskly. 'Life will cure you of naive assumptions. The only thing one can count on is that no one else can truly be counted on.'

Alice's constitutional acerbity had been challenging at

first. Peter had spent the first month of his employment convinced he was on the brink of being let go, before coming to understand it was just part of her nature, a sort of humour, scathing at times but never really nasty. Peter's problem was that he was too earnest. It was a character flaw, he knew, and one he tried hard to correct, or at least disguise. It wasn't always easy; he'd been that way for as long as he could remember. His mum and dad, his big brothers, too, were a joyous lot, all fond of having a laugh, and throughout Peter's childhood they'd shaken their heads and chuckled and tousled his hair whenever he puzzled too long over jokes and teases, saying what a cuckoo he was, what a serious little cuckoo, arrived in their nest from nowhere, bless him.

The description had bothered Peter, but only a little. The fact was he *had* always been different, and not just in matters of sincerity. His two older brothers had been broad, sturdy boys who'd grown into broad, sturdy men, the sort who looked right with a pint of bitter in one hand and a football in the other. And then there was Peter: skinny, pale and tall, with a tendency to 'mark easily'. His mother hadn't said it as a criticism, more with a note of wonder that she and his father could have created this odd little changeling with bruisable skin and a quaint, unfathomable passion for his library card. 'He likes reading,' his parents had told their friends in the same awed tones they might have used to announce he'd been awarded the Victoria Cross.

Peter *did* like reading. He'd read his way through the entire children's section of the Kilburn Library by the time he was eight, a feat that might have been a source of pride and celebration but for the problem posed by his still being years off acquiring the coveted adult borrowing card. Thank

God for Miss Talbot, who'd bitten her lip and straightened the library name badge on her lemon cardigan, and told him – a faint quiver of purpose enlivening her usually soft, smooth voice – that she would personally ensure he *never* ran out of things to read. She was a magician, as far as Peter was concerned. Decipherer of secret codes, master of index cards and Dewey decimal, opener of doors to wonderful places.

Those afternoons in the library, breathing the stale sun-warmed dust of a thousand stories (accented by the collective mildew of a hundred years of rising damp), had been enchanted. Two decades ago now, and yet here, on the No. 168 bus towards Hampstead Heath, Peter was beset with an almost bodily sense of being back there. His limbs twitched with the memory of being nine years old and lanky as a foal. His mood lifted as he remembered how large, how filled with possibilities, and yet, at once, how safe and navigable the world had seemed when he was shut within those four brick walls.

Peter risked his seat mate's put-upon sigh, reaching past the newspaper to rummage through his satchel for the programme. He'd tucked it inside the front cover of the dog-eared copy of *Great Expectations* he was rereading in honour of Miss Talbot, and now studied the smiling portrait on the front.

When Peter had told Alice he needed Tuesday morning off to attend a funeral she'd been typically curious. She was, as a rule, rapaciously interested in the details of his life. She quizzed him whenever the mood took her, asking questions of the type one might more reasonably have expected from an alien student of the human race than from an eighty-six-year-old member of its ranks. Peter, who might, if he'd given it any thought, have described his life to that point as so ordinary as to be beneath notice, had found the older woman's interest unnerving at first. He was far more comfortable reading about the lives and ideas of others than describing his own. But Alice wasn't the sort to brook opposition and he had got better, with time and practice, at answering her questions straightforwardly. It wasn't that he'd gained any greater sense of his own importance as much as he'd realised Alice's interest in him wasn't exclusive. She was equally inquisitive about the habits of the rangy foxes eking out a living behind her garden shed.

'A funeral?' she'd said, glancing up sharply from the books she was signing for her Spanish publisher.

'First I've ever been to.'

'Won't be the last,' she'd said matter-of-factly, scratching a flourish across the page before her. 'One collects them over a lifetime. When you get to my age you find you've put more people in the ground than you could gather for morning tea. Necessary, of course; nothing good comes from a death without a funeral.' Peter might have wondered at that remark but before he could give it further thought Alice continued, 'Family member, is it? Friend? Always worse when a young person dies.'

Peter told her then about Miss Talbot, surprising himself with the things he remembered, the odd little details that had lodged within his nine-year-old brain. The delicate rose-gold watch she'd worn, her habit of rubbing the tip of her index finger against her thumb when she was thinking, the way her skin had smelled like musk and petals.

'A guide,' Alice had said, silvery brows raised. 'A mentor.

How fortunate you were. And you kept in contact all this time?'

'Not exactly. We lost touch when I left for university.'

'You visited, though.' A statement, not a question.

'Not enough.'

Not ever, but he'd been too ashamed to admit that to Alice. He'd thought about visiting the library, meant to, but life was busy and he'd just never got around to it. He'd only learned of Miss Talbot's death by chance. He'd been running an errand for Alice at the British Library, flicking idly through a copy of the *SCONUL Newsletter* while waiting for a German book on poisons to be delivered from the archives, when her name leapt out at him. Miss Talbot – *Lucy* Talbot, because of course she'd had a first name – had lost her battle with cancer, the funeral would be held on Tuesday, June the tenth. Peter had experienced an electric flash of shock. He hadn't even known that she was ill. No reason he should, really. He told himself it was the way of things, children grew, and grew away, and in any case he was overthinking it, memory had embroidered his friendship with Miss Talbot. He'd imagined a special connection between them when in reality she'd just been doing her job, he'd only ever been one of many.

'Doubtful,' Alice said to this. 'Far more probable that the number of children she saw and didn't connect with specially made the one with whom she did particularly important to her.'

Peter hadn't flattered himself that Alice was trying to bolster his esteem. The pronouncement was her considered opinion, expressed with characteristic candour, and if it made him feel a right heel, well, what concern was that of hers?

He'd thought it the end of the matter, until hours later, when he was engrossed in his daily task of transferring Alice's morning scenes onto the new computer she refused to use, she'd said, 'Did she ever give you one of mine?'

Peter had looked up from the heavily edited typewritten sentence he was transposing. He had no idea what Alice was talking about. He hadn't even realised she was still in the room with him. It was highly unusual for Alice to stick around while he did his work; she went out like clockwork most afternoons, to run mysterious errands the purpose of which she didn't disclose.

'Your librarian. Did she ever give you one of my books?'

He'd considered lying but only for a second. Alice had a nose for dishonesty. When he said that she had not, Alice surprised him by laughing. 'A good thing, too. Not meant for children, not the things I write.'

Which was true enough. Alice's books were English mysteries, but there was nothing cosy about them. They were the sort of crime novels reviewers liked to describe as 'psychologically taut' and 'morally ambiguous', whydunits as much as they were whos or hows. As she herself had famously said in an interview with the BBC, murder in and of itself was not engaging; it was the drive to kill, the human factor, the fervours and furies motivating the dreadful act that rendered it compelling. Alice had a formidable grasp on those fervours and furies. She'd nodded when the interviewer said as much, listened politely as he implied she was, in fact, just a little *too* perceptive on the matter for his comfort, and then she'd replied: 'But of course one does not need to have committed murder to write about it, any more than one needs a time machine to write about the Battle of Agincourt. One simply requires an acquaintance with man's dark depths, and the inclination to explore them to their very end.' She'd smiled then, almost sweetly. 'Besides, haven't we all experienced the desire to kill, if only for a moment?'

Sales of her books had gone through the roof in the days following the interview, not that she'd needed them to. She was hugely successful and had been for decades. The name A. C. Edevane was shorthand for the entire procedural crime genre and her fictional detective, Diggory Brent, the curmudgeonly ex-soldier with a penchant for patchwork, was more beloved by a great swathe of readers than their own fathers. That wasn't just Peter's hyperbole; a recent poll in the *Sunday Times* had posed the question and the responses from readers had proved it. 'Remarkable,' Alice had said after her publicist telephoned with the news. And then, lest Peter think for a moment she cared one jot for pleasing others, 'And certainly not what I intended.'

Peter had never told Alice, but he hadn't read any of her books when he started work as her assistant. He hadn't read much contemporary fiction at all, for that matter. Miss Talbot, who'd taken her responsibility as a dealer of illicit adult books to a minor very seriously, had vacillated briefly over whether non-fiction might be the best place to start (what harm, she'd reasoned aloud, could possibly come to a child's mind from the pages of history?), before deciding a grounding in the classics was capital and plucking the library's copy of *Great Expectations* from the shelves. Peter had fallen hard for gaslight, frock coats and horse-drawn

coaches, and never looked back. (Or forwards, as the case
may be.)

Funnily enough, it was his obsessive consumption of
nineteenth-century fiction that had brought him together
with Alice. Peter had been at a crossroads after he graduated
from university – there didn't seem to be many jobs for
people with postgraduate degrees in Constellations of Fig-
uration: Enlightenment, Self, and Sensibility in Victorian
Novels, 1875–1893 – and had given himself the summer to
come up with a firm plan. The rent still needed to be paid so
he was making some extra money by helping his brother
David in his pest-extermination business; Alice's call had
come through first thing on a Monday morning. There was
an ominous ticking noise in her wall that had kept her awake
all weekend and she needed someone to see to it at once.

'Thorny old girl,' David had told Peter as they hopped
out of the van on Heath Street and headed towards Alice's
place. 'But harmless enough. Strange habit of calling me out
and then telling me what she thinks I'm going to find. Even
stranger habit of being right.'

'I suspect the deathwatch beetle,' she'd said as David
unpacked his kit at the base of her bedroom wall and
pressed his listening glass to the plaster. '*Xestobium*—'

'—*rufovillosum*,' Peter had murmured simultaneously.
And then, because David was staring at him as if he'd started
talking in tongues, 'Like in "The Tell-Tale Heart".'

There'd been a brief, cool silence and then, 'Who is this?'
Alice had spoken in just the sort of voice the Queen might
have used had she dropped by to inspect the pest-eradication
progress. 'I don't recall your having had an assistant, Mr
Obel?'

David had explained that he didn't have an assistant; that Peter was his little brother, helping out for a few weeks while he worked out what to do next. 'Needed a break from all those books,' he'd added. 'Getting too smart for his own good.'

Alice had given an almost imperceptible nod before retreating, her footsteps echoing as she climbed the stairs to the room in the roof Peter knew now as her writing bower.

David had clipped him on the shoulder later, when they were sitting in the smoky back booth at the Dog and Whistle. 'So you woke the dragon and lived to tell the tale,' he'd said, draining the last of his beer and gathering up the darts. 'What was it you said to her, anyway – that thing about the heart?'

Peter had explained about Poe and his unnamed narrator, the careful precision of the murder he committed, his claims to sanity and his eventual undoing by guilt, while David, not of a gothic temperament, continued to hit one bullseye after another. Darts spent, he'd suggested cheerily it was lucky Alice hadn't put Peter in the wall. 'That's what she does, you know: murder. Not real ones – at least, not that I know of. Commits all her crimes on paper.'

Alice's letter had arrived a week later, tucked inside the same envelope as the cheque to settle her account. It had been typewritten on a machine with a faulty 'e' and signed in navy-blue ink. The message was simply expressed. She was interviewing for a temporary assistant, someone to fill in while her permanent person was away. She would see him at midday on Friday.

Why had he fronted up obediently as ordered? Hard to remember now, other than to say that observation had since taught him people tended to follow Alice Edevane's instructions. He'd rung the doorbell at midday sharp and been admitted to the jade-green sitting room on the ground floor. Alice had been dressed handsomely in a pair of twill trousers and a silk blouse, a combination he now thought of as her uniform, and she'd worn a large gold locket on a chain around her neck. Her white hair had been neat and unfussy, set back from her face in waves that terminated with an obedient curl behind each ear. She'd seated herself at a mahogany desk, indicated that he should take the upholstered chair on the other side, and then made a bridge of her hands over which she proceeded to fire off a series of questions that didn't seem remotely relevant to the position she meant to fill. He'd been mid-sentence when she glanced sharply at a ship's clock on the mantelpiece, stood abruptly and reached to shake his hand. He could still remember how unexpectedly cool and birdlike it had felt. The interview was over, she'd said curtly. She had things to see to now; he should start the following week.

The 168 bus slowed to pull in against the kerb at the top of Fitzjohn's Avenue and Peter gathered his things. That meeting with Alice had been three years ago. The permanent person had mysteriously never returned and Peter had never left.

Alice was working on a particularly knotty scene, a transition. They were always the hardest to write. It was their very insignificance that rendered them problematic, the seemingly simple task of getting one's character from important moment A to important moment B without losing the reader's interest in the process. She'd never admit it to anyone, certainly not the press, but the wretched things continued to bring her unstuck even after forty-nine novels.

She pushed her reading glasses further up the bridge of her nose, flicked the typewriter's paper guide out of the way, and reread her most recent line: *Diggory Brent left the morgue and started back towards his office.*

Perfunctory, clear, directional, and the following lines should be just as straightforward. She knew the drill. Give him some thoughts pertinent to the novel's theme, an occasional update on his physical progress to remind the reader he's making some, then a final sentence bringing him through his office door to where – *voila!* – the next surprise is waiting to propel him further through the narrative.

The trouble was she'd already written just about every scenario she could think of and Alice was bored. It was not a feeling with which she was familiar, nor one she intended to indulge. Boredom, as her mother had always told them, was a state to be pitied, the province of the witless. Fingers poised above the keys, Alice considered weaving in some thoughts as to the quilt piece he was working on; an allegory, perhaps, for the unexpected turn the case had taken.

They were useful, those little fabric squares. They'd rescued her more than once. Terrific to think they'd been a happy accident. She'd been seeking to give Diggory a hobby that would highlight his instinct for patterns at precisely the time her sister Deborah had fallen pregnant and, in a wildly uncharacteristic turn, taken up needle and thread. 'It relaxes me,' she'd said. 'Keeps my mind from worrying about all the things that might go wrong.' It had seemed just the sort of remedial activity a man like Diggory Brent might adopt in order to occupy the long night-time hours his young family had once filled. Critics continued to claim the hobby was an attempt by Alice to soften her detective's rough edges, but it wasn't true. Alice liked rough edges; and she was deeply suspicious of people determined not to have any.

Diggory Brent left the morgue and started back towards his office. And . . . ? Alice's fingers hovered above the typewriter keys. What then? *As he walked, he considered . . .* What?

Her mind drew a blank.

Frustrated, Alice flipped the paper guide back into place, laid down her glasses and surrendered her attention to the view from her window. It was a warm day in early June and the sky was a brilliant blue. As a girl she'd have found it impossible to resist the call of the outside world on a day like this, with its smell of sunlit leaves and honeysuckle, the ticking sound of concrete baking and crickets hunkering down in the cool undergrowth. But Alice hadn't been that girl in a long time and there were few places she preferred to be now, even when her creative powers had deserted her, than here in her writing room.

The room was at the very top of the house, in a red-brick Victorian terrace high on Holly Hill. It was small with an angled ceiling and bore the distinction, according to the estate agent who'd shown Alice through the property, of having been used by a previous owner to keep his mother locked away. She'd become an inconvenience, one presumed. Alice was glad she'd never had children. The room was the reason she'd bought the house, though not because of its unhappy past. She had enough of that in her own family, thank you very much, and was quite immune to the folly of mistaking history for romance. It was the room's position that had driven Alice to possess it. It was like a nest, an eyrie, a watchtower.

From where she sat to write, she could look out over Hampstead towards the heath, as far as the ladies' pool and beyond to the spires of Highgate. Behind her, a small round ship's window offered a view of the back garden, all the way to the mossy brick wall and small wooden shed marking the rear limit of her property. The garden was dense, the legacy of another past owner, this one a horticulturalist who'd worked at Kew and devoted herself to creating a 'Garden of Earthly Delights' in her own backyard. It had been allowed to grow unruly under Alice's care, but not through accident or neglect. She was most fond of woods, preferred spaces that defied manicure.

Downstairs, the latch on the front door shook and the entry floorboards creaked. There was a thump as something dropped. Peter. It wasn't that he was clumsy so much as his long limbs had a habit of getting in his way. Alice glanced at her wristwatch and noted, with surprise, that it had just gone two. No wonder she was hungry. She laced her fingers and stretched her arms forwards. She stood up. Frustrating to lose an entire morning to the rigours of pushing Diggory Brent from A to B, but there was nothing to be done about it now. Half a century as a professional writer had taught her there were some days when the best thing to do was to walk away. Diggory Brent would just have to pass the night in the no-man's-land betwixt morgue and office. Alice washed her hands at the little basin by the back window, dried them on the towel, and then started down the narrow stairs.

She knew why she was having trouble, of course, and it wasn't as simple as boredom. It was the damned anniversary and the fuss her publishers intended to make when she reached it. An honour, well-meant, and ordinarily Alice would have enjoyed a bit of ceremony in her name, but the book was going badly. At least, she suspected it was going badly – and that was half the problem: how was she to know, really? Her editor, Jane, was clever and enthusiastic, but she was also young and awed. Criticism, *real* criticism, was too much to hope for.

In her darkest moments, Alice feared there was no one left to tell her when the standard dropped. That it must eventually drop she didn't doubt; Alice had kept up with the works by other writers of her generation and genre and knew there was always a book in which it happened: the author's grasp on the mores and minds of the modern world began to loosen. It wasn't always glaring – the slight over-explanation of a technology readers took for granted; the use of a formal term when its abbreviation was the norm; a cultural reference that belonged to the year before – but it was enough to render the whole thing false. For Alice, who prided herself on the verisimilitude of her books, who'd been showered throughout her career with compliments, the idea of being allowed to publish beyond her best was chilling.

Which was why she rode the Tube, every afternoon, sometimes to places she didn't need to go. All her life, Alice had been interested in people. She didn't always like them, she rarely sought their company for reasons of social fulfilment, but she did find them fascinating. And there was nowhere better for seeing people than in the rabbit warrens of the Underground. All of London passed through those tunnels, a steady flow of humanity in its many weird and wonderful forms, and among them Alice slipped like a ghost.

To age was contemptible, but the single silver lining was the cloak of invisibility gifted by the years. Nobody noticed the little old lady sitting primly in a corner of the carriage, handbag on her knee.

'Hiya, Alice,' Peter called up from the kitchen. 'Lunch in a jiffy.'

Alice hesitated on the first-floor landing but couldn't bring herself to shout back. Echoes of her mother's long-ago lectures on decorum still rang too loudly in her ears. That was Eleanor, Alice thought as she started down the last flight of stairs; almost seventy years since they'd lived beneath the same roof and still she was setting the house rules, even here, in this house she'd never laid eyes on. Alice wondered sometimes, had her mother lived longer, what she might have made of her daughter's life, whether she'd have approved of Alice's career, her clothes, her lack of a husband. Eleanor had had very firm ideas about monogamy and its bonds of loyalty, but then she'd married her childhood sweetheart, so it wasn't entirely a fair comparison. Mother loomed so large in the memories Alice kept of childhood, was so much a figure of the distant past, that it was almost impossible to imagine she might have moved with the changing times. She remained, for Alice, a beautiful, untouchable lady, beloved but distant, made brittle in the end by loss, the only person for whom Alice yearned, at times, with the fierce, bitter longing of a wounded child.

She was not otherwise of a needy disposition. Alice had lived alone most of her adult life, a fact of which she was neither proud nor ashamed. She'd had lovers, each of whom had brought their clothes and toothbrushes across the threshold, some of whom had stayed for stretches, but it wasn't the same thing. She had never extended an official invitation or made the mental transition to considering 'my' house 'ours'. It might have been different – Alice had been engaged once – but the Second World War had put paid to the affair as it had so many things. Life was like that, doors of possibility constantly opening and closing as one blindly made one's way through.

She reached the kitchen to find a saucepan steaming on the stovetop and Peter standing at the far end of the table, a small parcel of correspondence open in front of him. He looked up when she came through the door and said, 'Hello there,' right as the timer started ringing on the benchtop. 'Perfect timing, as always.'

He had a lovely smile, did Peter, quite curly, always genuine. It was one of the reasons she'd hired him. That, and he'd been the only applicant to arrive on the dot of the specified time. He'd since proven himself highly capable, which was no surprise; Alice considered herself to be an excellent judge of character. At least, she did now. There had been mistakes in the past, some more regrettable than others.

'Anything urgent among them?' she asked, seating herself in front of the newspaper she'd left open at the crossword puzzle that morning.

'Angus Wilson from the *Guardian*, hoping to set something up in time for the anniversary. Jane would like you to do it.'

'I bet she would.' Alice poured herself a cup of freshly brewed Darjeeling.

'The Natural History Museum asking you to speak at the opening of an exhibition they're planning, an invitation to attend the celebration evening for *Death Will Have His*

Day's ten-year run, and a card from Deborah confirming the appointment this Friday for your mother's anniversary. The rest, as far as I can tell, are from readers – I'll get started on those after lunch.'

Alice nodded as Peter set a plate in front of her, a boiled egg on toast. Alice had eaten the same lunch every day for the past two decades – though not, of course, on occasions when she dined out. She appreciated the efficiency of routine but she wasn't a slave to it, not like Diggory Brent, who'd been known to instruct waitresses on the precise method of his preferred egg preparation. She spooned the almost-hard yolk onto her piece of toast and cut it into quarters, watching as Peter continued to sort the mail.

He was not an overly conversational fellow, a fact that was greatly to his credit. Exasperating when she sought to draw him out on a subject, but preferable to the more loquacious assistants she'd had in the past. She decided she liked his hair that little bit longer. With his lanky limbs and dark-brown eyes, it made him look like one of those Britpop musicians, though perhaps it was only the unusually formal clothing he was wearing today, the dark velvet suit, that made her think so. And then Alice remembered. He'd been at his old friend's funeral, the librarian's, that's why he was late for work. She felt somewhat cheered, eager to have his report. Alice had been struck when he told her about the woman, his mentor. Her mind had been cast back to Mr Llewellyn. She didn't think of the old man often – her feelings for him were so bound up with that awful summer she made a point not to – but when Peter told her about his Miss Talbot, the lasting impression she had made on him, the interest she'd taken in his younger self, Alice had been beset with unusually visceral memories: the smell of damp river mud, and the plink of water bugs all around them as they drifted downstream in the old rowing boat, discussing their favourite stories. Alice was quite sure she'd not felt such perfect contentment since.

She took another sip of tea, blotting out unwelcome thoughts of the past. 'You saw off your friend then?' It was his first funeral, he'd said, and Alice had told him there'd be plenty more to come. 'Was it as you expected?'

'I suppose so. Sad, but interesting in a way, too.'

'In what way?'

Peter considered. 'I only ever knew her as Miss Talbot. Hearing other people speak, though – her husband, her son . . . it was moving.' He shifted his fringe from his eyes. 'That sounds stupid, doesn't it? A cliché . . .' He tried again: 'There was more to her than I knew and I enjoyed hearing it. People are fascinating, aren't they, the closer you get to knowing what makes them tick?'

Alice gave a slight, satisfied smile of agreement. She had found there were very few genuinely dull people; the trick was to ask them the right questions. It was a technique she employed when she was creating characters. Everybody knew the best guilty characters were those the reader didn't suspect, but motive was key. It was all very well to surprise people with a murderous granny, but the rationale must be watertight. Love, hate, envy, each was as plausible as the other; it was all a matter of passion. Discover what excited a person's passions and the rest would follow.

'Here's something a bit different.' Peter had returned to his work, opening reader letters, and his dark brows drew together in a frown as he scanned the one in hand.

Alice's tea was suddenly bitter. One was never entirely inured to criticism. 'One of those, is it?'

'It's from a police officer, Detective Constable Sparrow.'

'Ah, one of *those*.' In Alice's experience there were two types of police officer: those who could be relied upon to help with matters of procedure during the creative process, and the other blighters who liked to read the books and point out problems *after* publication. 'And what pearl of procedural wisdom does DC Sparrow have to share with us?'

'No, it's nothing like that, she's not a reader. She's writing to you about a real-life case, a disappearance.'

'Let me guess. She's stumbled upon a Great Idea and thought if I wrote it we might go halves on the profits?'

'A missing child,' he continued, 'back in the 1930s. An estate in Cornwall, a case that was never solved.'

And to her dying day Alice would never be able to say for sure whether the room grew cold right then, a sudden breeze off the heath, or whether it was her own internal thermostat, the wash of real life, the past hitting her like a wave that had drawn back a long time ago and been waiting for the tide to turn. For of course she knew exactly what the letter was about, and that it had nothing at all to do with the neat made-up mysteries she put inside her books.

Such an ordinary piece of paper, Alice noticed, flimsy and cheap, not at all the sort readers usually chose when they wrote to her, certainly not the type with which she'd have furnished a character in one of her novels, charged with delivering such a potent detonation from the past.

Peter was reading aloud now, and although Alice would have liked him not to, the words to say so had dried up. She listened as he delivered an efficient summary of the known circumstances surrounding the long-ago case. Sourced from the newspaper files, Alice supposed, or that deplorable book by that Pickering fellow. And there was nothing to stop people from accessing public records, from sending letters out of the blue to those they'd never met, from bringing the pernicious past to the lunch table of a person who'd done everything she could to avoid ever going back to that place, that time.

'She seems to think you'll know what she's talking about?'

Images fell inside her mind, one after the other, like cards being dealt from a pack: searchers knee-deep in the glistening lake; that fat policeman sweating in the fetid heat of the library, his green young deputy taking notes; her father and mother, ashen-faced, as they fronted the local news photographer. She could almost feel herself pressed against the French doors watching them, sick with the secret she hadn't been able to make herself tell, the guilt she'd nursed deep inside ever since.

Alice noticed that her hand was shaking very slightly and urged herself to remember the fact for when she next needed to depict the bodily effects of shock, its ice wash hitting a person who had, over a lifetime, schooled herself in the appearance of composure. She moved her treacherous hands into her lap, pressing one firmly over the other, and said with an imperious jut of the chin, 'Put it in the bin.' Her tone was surprisingly even; there were very few people left alive who'd have marked the faint note of underlying tension.

'You don't want me to do anything? Not even to write back?'

'No point, is there?' Alice kept her gaze direct. 'I'm afraid this DC Sparrow's made a mistake. She has me confused with someone else.'

Seven

The man was talking. His mouth was moving, words were swarming, but Eleanor couldn't catch them, not in a way that made sense. Just one here and another there: missing . . . wandered . . . lost . . . Her mind was a fog, a blessed fog; Dr Gibbons had seen to that.

A trickle of perspiration slipped beneath her collar, finding its way between her shoulder blades. The cool of it made her shiver, and Anthony, sitting beside her, strengthened his gentle hold. His hand rested on hers, large upon small, eminently familiar and yet today rendered foreign by the nightmarish turn of events. There were features she'd never noticed before, hairs and lines and pale-blue veins, like roads on a map beneath his skin.

The heat had held. The storm that threatened had never come. The thunder had rumbled all night before rolling out to sea. Just as well, the policeman had said, for rain would have washed away the clues. The same policeman, the younger one, had told them speaking to the newspaper would help. 'We'll have a thousand pairs of eyes that way, all on the lookout for your boy.'

Eleanor was sick with worry, immobilised by fear; it was a relief that Anthony was answering the reporter's questions.

She could hear his voice, as if from a great distance. Yes, the boy was young, not quite eleven months, but he'd walked early – all the Edevane children had walked early. He was a bonny child, strong and healthy . . . his hair was blond and his eyes were blue . . . of course they'd be able to supply a photograph.

Through the window, Eleanor could see all the way across the sunny garden to the lake. There were men there, policemen in their uniforms, and others, too, men she didn't know. Most were standing together on the grassy bank but some were out on the water. The lake was as smooth as glass today, a great silver mirror with a dull impression of the sky rippling on it. The ducks had fled the water, but a man in a black diving suit and mask had been searching from a small rowing boat all morning. They did that before they used the hooks, Eleanor had heard someone say.

When she was a girl, she'd had a little boat all of her own. Her father had bought it for her and painted her name on the side. It had a set of wooden oars and a hand-fashioned white sail and she'd taken it out most mornings. Mr Llewellyn had called her Eleanor the Adventuress, waving from behind his sketchpad on the overgrown bank as she sailed past him, inventing stories about her travels that he told them over lunch, making Eleanor clap and her father laugh and her mother smile with grim impatience.

Mother despised Mr Llewellyn and his stories. She hated any sort of softness in a person, 'weakness of character' she called it, and he was certainly a far gentler soul than she. He'd had a breakdown when they were younger and still suffered bouts of melancholy; Constance greeted such occasions with contempt. She also loathed what she saw as the 'unhealthy attention' her husband lavished on their daughter. Such focus, she insisted, couldn't help but spoil a child, particularly one already in possession of 'a worrying spirit of mutiny'. Besides, there were better things, surely, that he could have spent his money on? This was a common refrain between them, money or the lack thereof, the disparity between the life they led and that which Eleanor's mother wished them to lead. Many nights Eleanor heard them arguing in the library, her mother's sharp tone and her father's soft, placatory replies. She wondered sometimes how he stood the constant criticism. 'Love,' Mr Llewellyn had said when she ventured as much to him. 'We do not always have a choice in where and how and whom, and love gives us the courage to withstand that which we never thought we could.'

'Mrs Edevane?'

Eleanor opened her eyes and found herself inside the library. She was on the sofa, Anthony beside her, his large hand still protectively over hers. She was briefly surprised to see a man sitting across from them with a small spiral-ringed notepad in hand and a pencil behind his ear. Reality came funnelling back.

He was a reporter. Here to talk about Theo.

Her arms were suddenly heavy with her baby's absence. She remembered that first night when it had been just the two of them. He'd been the only one of her four children to arrive early, and she could feel his heels moving against her hand as she cradled him, the same little marble joints she'd felt only days before through the skin of her belly. She'd whispered to him in the dark, promised she would always keep him safe—

'Mrs Edevane?'

With Theo it was different from the start. Eleanor had loved all her babies – not perhaps, if she were honest, at first sight, but certainly by the time they took their first steps – but with Theo it was more than love. She *cherished* him. After his birth she'd taken him into her bed, swaddled in his blanket, and she'd looked into his eyes and seen there all the wisdom babies are born with before it slips away. He stared back, trying to tell her the secrets of the cosmos, his little mouth opening and closing around words he didn't yet know, or perhaps no longer remembered. It reminded her of when her father died. He'd done the same thing, staring at her with bottomless eyes, filled with all the things he'd never now have the chance to say.

'Mrs Edevane, the photographer is going to take your picture.' Eleanor blinked. The reporter. His notepad made her think of Alice. Where was she? And where were Deborah and Clemmie, for that matter? Someone, presumably, was taking care of the girls. Not her mother, but Mr Llewellyn, perhaps? That would explain why she hadn't seen him yet this morning: he must've stepped in to help with the girls, keeping them out of trouble's way just as she'd asked him to do in the past.

'Right then, Mr and Mrs Edevane.' A second man, portly, red with heat, waved a hand from behind his tripod. 'Look this way, if you wouldn't mind.'

Eleanor was used to having her picture taken – she was the little girl from the fairy tale and had been painted, sketched and photographed all her life – but now she flinched. She wanted to lie down in the dark and close her eyes, to stay that way and talk to no one until things were right again. She was tired, unthinkably tired.

'Come, my love.' Anthony's voice, kind and quiet by her ear. 'Let's get this over with. I have your hand.'

'It's so hot,' she whispered in reply. The silk of her blouse was sticking to her back; her skirt worried at her waist where the seams gathered.

'Look this way, Mrs Edevane.'

'I can't breathe, Anthony. I need—'

'I'm here, I'm with you. I'll always be here with you.'

'Ready, and . . .' The photographer's flash burst with white light, and as Eleanor's sight starred, she thought she saw a figure by the French doors. Alice, she was sure of it, standing very still, watching.

'Alice,' she said, blinking her dazzled vision clear. 'Alice?'

But then a cry came from the lake, a man's voice, loud and sharp, and the reporter leapt from his chair and hurried to the window. Anthony stood and Eleanor did the same, stumbling on legs that were suddenly weak, waiting as time seemed to stand still, until finally the young reporter turned and shook his head.

'False alarm,' he said, excitement giving way to disappointment as he took out a handkerchief to wipe his brow. 'Just an old boot, not a body at all.'

Eleanor's knees threatened to give way. She turned back towards the French doors, but Alice was no longer there. She caught, instead, the eyes of her own reflection in the mirror by the mantelpiece. She almost didn't recognise herself. The careful poise of 'Mother' was gone and instead she found herself face to face with a girl who used to live in this house a long time ago, unmannered, wild, exposed; a girl she'd almost forgotten.

'That's enough.' Anthony's voice came sharply, suddenly. Her love, her saviour. 'Have some pity, man, my wife is in shock, her child is gone. This interview is over.'

Eleanor was floating.

'I assure you, Mr Edevane, they're very powerful barbiturates. Just one will be enough to keep her sleeping all afternoon.'

'Thank you, Doctor. She's been beside herself.'

She knew that voice; it was Anthony's.

And now the other one again, the doctor: 'I'm not surprised. Terrible business, just terrible.'

'The police are doing everything they can.'

'They're confident they'll find him?'

'We must stay positive and trust they will do their best.'

Her husband's hand was on her forehead now, warm, firm, smoothing her hair. Eleanor tried to speak, but her mouth was lazy and the words wouldn't come.

He hushed her. 'There, my love. Sleep now.'

His voice was everywhere, all around her like the voice of God. Her body was heavy but slow, as if she were sinking through clouds. Falling, falling, backwards through the layers of her life. Before she became Mother, before she came home to Loeanneth, through the summer she met Anthony, back beyond the loss of her father, and into the long, boundless stretch of her childhood. She had a vague sense that something was lost and she ought to be looking for it, but her brain was sluggish and she couldn't grasp the thing. It was eluding her, like a tiger, a yellow-and-black tiger, slinking away from her through the long strands of the meadow. It was the Loeanneth meadow, the woods dark and glistening in the distance, and Eleanor reached out her hands to brush the tips of the grass.

There was a tiger in Eleanor's bedroom when she was small. His name was Zephyr and he lived beneath her bed. He'd come with them from the big house, smuggled out in the move, a little the worse for wear, his proud coat reeking of smoke. Her father's father, Horace, had captured him in India, in the great time of before. Eleanor had heard about the time of before, stories that her father told her from when the estate was large and the deShiels lived in a grand house with twenty-eight bedrooms and a coach house filled not with pumpkins but with real coaches, some of them decorated with gold. Not much was left now, only the burned shell of the house, too far away from Loeanneth to be seen. But it was Mr Llewellyn who'd told her the story of the tiger and the pearl.

When she was a girl, Eleanor had completely believed the tale. That Zephyr brought her back from India with him, a pearl that he'd swallowed, that had remained hidden deep within his jaw when he was shot, skinned, sold and shipped, during the decades his pelt was put on proud display at the big house and through his subsequent repair to reduced circumstances at the Lake House. It was there, one day, when the tiger's head was tilted just so, that the pearl rolled out of his lifeless mouth and became lost in the long weave of the library carpet. It was trodden on, bypassed and all but forgotten, until one dark night, while the household slept, it was found by fairies on a mission of theft. They took the pearl deep into the woods, where it was laid on a bed of leaves, studied and pondered and tentatively stroked, before being stolen by a bird, who mistook it for an egg.

High in the treetops, the pearl began to grow and grow and grow, until the bird became frightened her own eggs would be crushed and she rolled the argent orb back down the side of the tree, where it landed with a soft thud on a bed of leaf-fall. There, in the light of the full moon, surrounded by curious fairy folk, the egg began to hatch and a baby emerged. The fairies gathered nectar to feed her and took turns rocking the babe to sleep, but soon no amount of nectar was enough, and even fairy magic could not keep the child content. A meeting was held and it was decided the woods were no place for a human child and she must be returned to the house, laid on the doorstep in a wrap of woven leaves.

As far as Eleanor was concerned, it explained everything: why she felt such an affinity with the woods, why she'd always been able to glimpse the fairies in the meadows where other people saw only grass, why birds had gathered on the ledge outside the nursery window when she was an infant. It also explained the fierce tiger rage that welled up inside her at times, that made her spit and scream and stomp, so that Nanny Bruen hissed and told her she'd come to no good if she didn't learn to control herself. Mr Llewellyn, on the other hand, said there were worse things in life than a temper, that it only proved one had an opinion. And a pulse, he added, the alternative to which was dire! He said a girl like Eleanor would do well to keep the coals of her impudence warm, for society would seek to cool them soon enough. Eleanor put a lot of stock in the things Mr Llewellyn said. He wasn't like the other grown-ups.

Eleanor did not make a habit of telling people the story of her birth – unlike *Eleanor's Magic Doorway*, which had been turned into a book for children everywhere, 'The Tiger and the Pearl' was hers and hers alone – but when she was eight years old her cousin Beatrice came with her parents on a visit to Loeanneth. This was not usual. Eleanor's mother, Constance, did not, as a rule, get on with her sister, Vera. With eleven months between them, the two had always been competitive, their entire lives comprising a tournament of minor sibling battles, the culmination of one leading necessarily to the commencement of another. Constance's marriage to Henri deShiel, a seeming triumph at its start, had been tarnished irreparably when her sister (younger!) made a vastly superior match with a newly minted Scottish earl who'd dug a fortune out of the ground in Africa. The sisters had not spoken for five years afterwards, but now, it seemed, a shaky truce had been achieved.

One rainy day, the girls had been sent to the nursery, where Eleanor was trying to read Edmund Spenser's *The Faerie Queene* (it was Mr Llewellyn's favourite and she wanted to impress him) and Beatrice was finishing her latest tapestry. Eleanor had been away with her thoughts when a terrified squeal made her lose her rhythm altogether. Beatrice was standing bolt upright, pointing beneath the bed with tears lacquering her blotched face. 'A monster . . . my needle . . . I dropped . . . and there's . . . I saw . . . a *monster*!' Eleanor realised at once what had happened and pulled Zephyr from beneath her bed, explaining that he was her

treasure, kept concealed only so he might be saved from
Mother's wrath. Beatrice, still gulping and sniffing, was so
pink-eyed and snotty that Eleanor felt sorry for her. The rain
was drumming against the window, the world outside was
cold and grey: the perfect conditions for storytelling. And so
she encouraged her cousin to sit beside her on the bed and
explained all about the pearl and the woods and her unusual
arrival at Loeanneth. Beatrice had laughed when she finished
and said that it was a fun tale and well told, but surely she
must know she came from inside her mother's stomach. It
had been Eleanor's turn then to laugh, in delight, but more
than that surprise. Beatrice was a doughy, ordinary sort of
girl with a penchant for lace and ribbons, resolutely simple,
not given to fancy or storytelling. To think that she could
concoct such a wild and wonderful tale! Her mother's
stomach indeed! Eleanor's mother was tall and lean, winched
and cinched each morning into dresses that never wrinkled
and certainly didn't stretch. It was unthinkable that anything
could possibly have grown inside her. Not a pearl, and certainly not Eleanor.

The story made Eleanor warm to Beatrice and despite
their differences the two girls started to become friends.
Eleanor didn't have many friends, only her father and Mr
Llewellyn, and the novelty of a girl of her own age to play
with was enormous. She showed her cousin all her special
places. The trout stream in the woods, the bend in it where
the water suddenly deepened, the tallest tree from which, if
one climbed all the way to the top, the burned shell of the
big house could be glimpsed in the distance. She even gave
Beatrice a tour of the old boathouse, beloved setting of all
her most important pastimes. She had thought they were

having a grand visit, until one night, lying in their twin beds, her cousin said, 'But you must get so *lonely* here, just you, by yourself, in the middle of nowhere with nothing to do.' Eleanor had been struck by the wrong-headedness of the description. How could Beatrice say such a thing when there was so *much* to do at Loeanneth? Clearly, it was time to introduce her cousin to her favourite and most secret game.

Before daybreak the next morning, she shook Beatrice awake, signalled to her to be quiet, and then led her down to the lake where the trees grew wild and the eels slithered in the shadowy depths. There, she initiated her cousin into the ongoing Adventures of Grandfather Horace. The great man's diaries were upstairs in the study, tied together with a yellow ribbon. She wasn't supposed to know they were there, but Eleanor was always in trouble for going places that were out of bounds, for listening to things she ought not to hear, and she knew them all by heart. She re-enacted the ones he'd described, his trips through Peru and Africa and over the ice in northern Canada, and others she made up. Now, with the help of Zephyr, she performed for Beatrice's edification and entertainment her pièce de résistance, the old man's grisly death, as detailed in the letter addressed to 'whom it may concern' and tucked inside the back cover of the final, unfinished diary. Beatrice looked on wide-eyed, and then clapped and laughed, and said with cheerful admiration, 'No wonder your mother says you're a little savage.'

'Does she?' Eleanor blinked, surprised and rather pleased by the unexpectedness of the description.

'She told my mother she despaired of ever having you fit for London.'

'London?' Eleanor wrinkled her nose. 'But I'm not going to London.' She'd heard the word before – London, rhymes with 'undone'. Whenever her parents argued, the word was parried like a sword. 'I'm fading away in this godforsaken place,' Eleanor's mother would say. 'I want to go to London. I know that frightens you, Henri, but it's where I belong. I should be mixing with the right sort of people. Don't forget I was invited to the palace once when I was young!'

Eleanor had heard *that* particular story a thousand times and so paid it no heed. She had been curious, though: she'd never known her father to be frightened of anything, and imagined London the home of lawlessness and mayhem. 'It's a big city,' he'd said when she asked him, 'full of motorcars and omnibuses and people.'

Eleanor had sensed the unspoken shadow behind his answer. 'And temptations?'

He'd looked up swiftly, his eyes searching hers. 'Now where did you hear a thing like that?'

Eleanor had shrugged artlessly. The word had come from her father's own lips, when he and Mr Llewellyn were talking by the boathouse and she was stealing wild strawberries from the bushes beside the stream.

He'd sighed. 'For some. Yes. A place of temptations.'

And he'd looked so sad that Eleanor put her small hand in his and said vehemently, 'I'm never going there. I'm never leaving Loeanneth.'

She said the same thing now to cousin Beatrice, who smiled at her in much the same fond, pitying way her father had. 'Well, of course you will, silly. How are you ever going to find a husband living in a place like this?'

*

Eleanor didn't want to go to London and she didn't want to find a husband, but in 1911, when she was sixteen years old, she did both. She hadn't meant to. Her father was dead, Loeanneth had been placed in the hands of an estate agent, and her mother had taken her to London in order to marry her off to the highest bidder. In her fury and impotence, Eleanor had steadfastly promised herself *not* to fall in love. They were staying with Aunt Vera in a large house on the fringe of Mayfair. It had been decided Beatrice and Eleanor should take part in the Season together and, predictably enough for Constance and Vera, the sibling battlelines had been drawn around the marriage prospects of their respective daughters.

So it was, on a fine afternoon in late June, in a second-storey London bedroom, with a summer's day turning to haze outside the window, a lady's maid with perspiration beading on her brow pulled at her recalcitrant subject's bodice and said, 'Stand still, Miss Eleanor. I'll never give you a bosom if you don't jolly well stand still.'

None of the maids enjoyed dressing Eleanor; she knew this for a fact. There was a nook in the library with a vent behind it connecting to the cupboard where the housemaids went to avoid the butler. Eleanor had overheard them when she was doing her own bit of hiding from her mother. Accompanied by a faint waft of cigarette smoke, she'd caught the following: 'Never stands still . . .'; 'Stains on her clothes!'; 'With a bit of effort . . .'; 'If she'd only try . . .'; 'But dearie me, that hair!'

Eleanor stared now at her reflection. Her hair *was* wild, it always had been, a mess of dark brown ripples that resisted all attempts to tame it. The effect, in combination with stubbornly lean limbs and a habit of studious wide-eyed focus, was resolutely uncoquettish. Her nature, she'd been given to understand, was similarly defective. Nanny Bruen had been fond of clicking her tongue and lamenting aloud 'the sparing of rod' and 'unfettered feeding of a wicked passion' that had allowed the child to develop into 'a disappointment to Mother' and, worse, 'to God!' God's feelings remained a mystery, but Eleanor's mother's disappointment was written all over her face.

Speak of the devil: Constance deShiel arrived at the bedroom door dressed in her finest, her hair (neat, blonde, smooth) piled on top of her head in elaborate curls, jewels dripping from her neck. Eleanor bared her teeth. The sale of jewels like that would have saved Loeanneth. Her mother waved the maid aside and took over lacing Eleanor's stays. She pulled with enough vigour to make Eleanor gasp, and launched directly into a recitation of the eligible young men who'd be at the Rothschild dance that night. It was difficult to believe this was the same person who'd resolutely refused to answer Father's questions about extravagant purchases, claiming airily, 'You know I haven't a head for details.' The summary was exhaustive, no feature of any prospective suitor deemed too petty for inclusion.

No doubt there were some mothers and daughters for whom this routine would have proved enjoyable; Eleanor and Constance deShiel, however, were not among them. Her mother was a stranger to Eleanor, a cold, distant figure who'd never liked her. Eleanor wasn't sure why *exactly* (there'd been whispers between the servants at Loeanneth that the mistress had always wanted a son) and she didn't particularly care. The feeling was mutual. There was a manic edge to

Constance's enthusiasm today. Cousin Beatrice (who, in the intervening years, had developed a buxom figure and an unhealthy addiction to Elinor Glyn novels) had been mentioned in the most recent Court Circular and suddenly the contest had become a great deal more urgent.

'. . . the eldest son of a viscount,' Constance was saying. 'His grandfather made a fortune in some sort of deal with the East India Trading Company . . . fabulously wealthy . . . stocks and bonds . . . American interests . . .'

Eleanor frowned at her own reflection, hating the way these conversations implied collusion. These words, these clothes, these expectations were constraints from which she longed to escape. She didn't belong here in this London of stucco and paving stones; of morning dress fittings at Madame Lucille's in Hanover Square and afternoon carriages delivering white appointment cards arranging yet another round of tea and chatter. She cared not a jot for the fervent advice doled out by *The Lady* magazine on servant management, home decoration and what to do with superfluous nasal hair.

Her hand went to the chain she wore around her neck, the pendant she kept concealed beneath her clothing – not a locket, but a tiger's tooth set in silver, a gift from her father. Caressing its familiar smooth edges, she let her vision glaze so she no longer saw herself, only a vaguely human shape. As her outline wavered, so did her concentration. Her mother's voice became a faint background drone, until suddenly she was no longer in this room in London, but at home, her real home, Loeanneth, sitting by the stream with her father and Mr Llewellyn, everything right with the world.

*

That night, Eleanor stood on the edge of the dance floor watching her mother twirl by. It was grotesque the way Constance gambolled around the ballroom, lips large and red, bosom heaving, jewels twinkling as she waltzed and laughed with one pink-faced partner after another. Why couldn't she be like all the other dutiful dowagers? Take her place on a seat against the wall and admire the garlands of lilies, while secretly nursing a desire to be home in a warm bath, her bed turned down and her hot-water bottle waiting for her. Her current dance partner spoke close to her ear and when Constance laughed and her hand leapt to her décolletage, things came back to Eleanor: whispers that had passed between the servants when she was a girl, footsteps in the hallway at dawn, strange men in their stockinged feet slinking back to their own rooms. Every tiny muscle in Eleanor's own face tightened and a tiger's rage flared hot inside her. As far as she was concerned, there was no sin greater than disloyalty. The worst thing a person could do was to break a promise.

'Eleanor! Look!' Beatrice was breathing quickly beside her, excitement expressing itself, as always, in the form of mild respiratory distress. Eleanor followed her cousin's gaze and saw a boisterous young man with a spotty chin approaching in the flickering candlelight. She felt an emotion similar to despair. Was this love? This transaction? The dressing in one's best clothing, the painting of a mask on one's face, the dance of learned steps, of scripted questions and replies? 'Of course it is!' Beatrice exclaimed, when Eleanor said as much.

'But shouldn't there be more to it? Shouldn't there be an element of recognition?'

'Oh, Eleanor, you're such an ingénue! Life isn't a fairy

tale, you know. That's all very well in books, but there's no such thing as magic.'

Not for the first time since her swift removal to London, Eleanor ached for Mr Llewellyn's company. Ordinarily she was a devotee of written correspondence, treasuring every letter she received and keeping copies of those she wrote in special books of triplicate, but there were some occasions where only the immediacy of a real, proper conversation with an understanding soul would do. What she'd have given for the fundamental comfort of knowing herself understood! She wasn't talking about magic. She was talking about an essential truth. Love as a fait accompli, a matter of fact, rather than a mutually beneficial arrangement between two suitable parties. She was debating whether to say so when Beatrice sang through the teeth of her most charming smile, 'Now come along, dear one, do put on a happy face and let's see how many glances we can win.'

Eleanor deflated. It was hopeless. She had no interest in procuring glances from men for whom she cared nothing; pampered men leading bland lives of selfish pleasure. Her father had once said that the poor might suffer poverty, but the rich had to contend with uselessness, and there was nothing like idleness to eat away at a person's soul. When Beatrice was otherwise engaged, Eleanor slipped through the crowd towards the exit.

She went up the stairs, flight by flight, with no destination in mind, content so long as the music was fading behind her. It had become her routine, to leave the ballroom at the earliest moment and then to explore the house in which the dance was being held. She was good at it; she'd had practice, sneaking through the woods of Loeanneth with the ghost of grandfather Horace, making herself invisible. She reached a landing where one door stood ajar and decided it was as good a place as any to start.

It was dark inside the room, but moonlight spilled through the window like mercury and Eleanor could see that it was a study of some kind. The far wall was lined with bookshelves and a large desk stood on a carpet in the middle. She went to sit behind the desk. Perhaps it was the leathery smell, perhaps it was simply that he was never far from her thoughts, but Eleanor pictured her father, the study at Loeanneth in which she'd often found him towards the end, head bent over a list of figures as he grappled with the family's debts. He'd weakened in his final months and was no longer able to roam with her as he once had across the meadows and through the woods. Eleanor had set herself the task of bringing his beloved natural world to him, collecting objects in the early morning and then carrying them back to show him, recounting all the things she'd seen and heard and smelled. One day she'd been rabbiting on about the changing weather when he'd held up his hand to stop her. He told her that he'd spoken to his solicitor. 'I'm no longer a wealthy man, my lovely girl, but this house is safe. I've made a provision so that Loeanneth can't be sold and you will never be without your home.' When the time came, though, the documents had disappeared and Eleanor's mother denied all knowledge of them. 'He spoke a lot of nonsense at the end,' she said.

With a glance at the shut door, Eleanor turned on the desk lamp and a broad rectangle of yellow light appeared on the table's surface. She tapped her fingertips on the wood as she considered the accoutrements. A carved ivory pen-holder, an ink blotter, a cotton-bound journal. A newspaper was open and she began idly to flick through its pages. Later, the whole sequence of events would be folded into the story of How They Met and acquire an air of reverence and inevitability. At the time, though, Eleanor was simply escaping the predictability and boredom of the dance below. She had no idea when she read the headline PAIR OF TIGERS FROM FAR EAST ARRIVE AT LONDON ZOO that a door had opened. She knew only that Zephyr's tooth was suddenly warm against her skin and that she had to see those tigers for herself.

Eight

Eleanor's chance came two days later. A trip to the Festival of Empire had been planned and everyone in Vera's household was suitably excited. 'To think,' Beatrice had exclaimed over sherry the night before, 'real live tribesmen, all the way from Africa!'

'A flying machine,' cried Vera, 'a pageant!'

'A triumph for Mr Lascelles,' agreed Constance, before adding somewhat hopefully, 'I wonder if the man himself will be there? I hear that he's a great friend of the King's.'

The Crystal Palace shone in the sunlight as the Daimler pulled up at its entrance. Eleanor's mother, aunt and cousin were helped from the car and Eleanor followed, lifting her gaze to take in the spectacular glass building. It was beautiful and impressive, just as everyone said, and Eleanor felt her cheeks flush with anticipation. Not, though, because she was looking forward to a day spent ogling the treasures of the Empire; Eleanor had something else entirely planned. Their party made its way inside the All British section and a good half-hour was spent agreeing on the superiority of everything within, before moving on to the exotic delights of the colonies. There were blooms to be admired in the floricultural section, athletic figures to be appreciated in the Overseas

Dominions Cadets Camp, the pageant site itself to be thoroughly critiqued. Eleanor, trailing behind, forced herself to nod attentively when required. Finally, when they reached the Medieval Maze she glimpsed her chance. The maze was busy and it wasn't difficult for Eleanor to separate from her group. She simply turned left when the others turned right, and then doubled back and escaped the way they'd come.

She walked quickly, her head bowed against the terrible possibility of seeing someone her mother knew, past the Empire Sports Arena, towards the Small Holdings, not stopping until she reached the railway entrance on Sydenham Avenue. There, her spirit performed a gleeful flip. Eleanor took out the map she'd borrowed from Uncle Vernon's study and checked again the route she'd plotted in the bathroom the night before. According to her research, all she had to do was wave down the number 78 tram on nearby Norwood Road and it would take her all the way to Victoria station. She could walk the rest of the way from there, through Hyde Park, across Marylebone and into Regent's Park. It was preferable to stick to the parks. The streets of London were like rivers of molten noise rushing through the city, and it was all so fast and furious that sometimes Eleanor could *feel* what it would be like to be hit and knocked down.

Today, though, she was too excited to be fearful. She hurried along the pavement to the tram stop, her heart galloping at the prospect of seeing the tigers and, more than that, with the immense joy of being alone for the first time in weeks. The number 78 tram came trundling towards her. She flagged it down, paid her fare with the coins she'd borrowed from Uncle Vernon's study, and just like that she was on her way. When she took her seat, she could barely keep from

grinning. She felt grown-up and intrepid, an adventurer setting out to conquer all obstacles in her path. Ties she'd
thought broken were strengthened now, to her childhood, to
her life before, to her old self, and she experienced a thrill
similar to that she'd relished when playing The Adventures
of Grandfather Horace. As the tram finally crossed Vauxhall
Bridge and slid on its rails through Belgravia, Eleanor
caressed the tiger's-tooth pendant on its chain beneath her
blouse.

Victoria station was chaos, with people moving every
which way, a sea of top hats and walking canes and long
swishing skirts. Eleanor alighted from the tram and slipped
through the crowd as quickly as she could, emerging onto
the street where horse-drawn carriages and coaches jostled
this way and that on their way to teatime appointments. She
could have jumped for joy not to be on board one of them.

She took a moment to gather her bearings and then set
off along Grosvenor Place. She was moving quickly and her
breaths were short. London had a distinctive smell, the
unpleasant mingling of manure with exhaust fumes, of old
and new, and she was glad when she turned into Hyde Park
and caught the scent of roses. Nannies in starched uniforms
paraded large prams along the red dirt of Rotten Row, and
the expanse of lawn was covered with green sixpenny deck-
chairs. Rowing boats speckled the Serpentine like enormous
ducks.

'Get your mementoes here!' shouted a street vendor, his
stall stocked with coronation flags and pictures of the enormous new peace statue that stood before Buckingham Palace.
('Peace?' her uncle was fond of snorting each time their
carriage passed by the enormous statue, its white marble glis-

tening against the dirty black stonework of the palace. 'We'll
be lucky to see out the decade without another war!' A smug
look would settle on his dour face after the pronouncement
– he liked nothing more than the anticipation of bad news –
and, 'Don't be such a killjoy, Daddy,' Beatrice would scold,
before her attention was diverted by a passing coach. 'Oh,
look! Is that the Manners' carriage? Did you hear the latest
about Lady Diana? She dressed as a black swan to attend the
all-white charity ball! Can you imagine Lady Sheffield's
fury!')

Eleanor was hurrying now. Towards Bayswater Road,
under Marble Arch, through the edge of Mayfair and into
Marylebone. The sign for Baker Street made her think again
of Uncle Vernon, who rated himself something of a sleuth
and enjoyed pitting his wits against Sherlock Holmes. Eleanor had borrowed some of the mystery books from her
uncle's study but wasn't a convert. The arrogance of rationalism was at odds with her beloved fairy tales. Even now,
Holmes's cocksure assumption that there was nothing that
couldn't be explained by process of human deduction made
her hot under the collar. So hot that as she approached
Regent's Park she forgot all about the mechanised river she
had to cross. She stepped right out onto the road without
looking and didn't notice the omnibus until it was almost
upon her. In that instant, as the enormous advertisement for
LIPTON'S TEA bore down on her, Eleanor knew she was going
to die. Her thoughts came swiftly – she would be with her
father again, she would no longer have to worry about
losing Loeanneth, but, oh, what a shame not to have seen the
tigers! She screwed her eyes shut, waiting for the pain and
oblivion to hit.

The shock when it came took her breath away, a force around her waist as she was thrown sideways, the wind knocked out of her as she fell hard to the ground. Death was not at all as she'd expected. Sound was swirling, her ears rang and her head swooned. When she opened her eyes, her vision filled with an image of the most beautiful face she'd ever seen. Eleanor would never confess the fact to anyone, but for years after she would smile to remember that in that moment she'd thought herself face to face with God.

It wasn't God. It was a boy, a man, young, not much older than she was, with sandy-brown hair and skin she had a sudden urge to touch. He was on the ground beside her, one arm beneath her shoulders. His lips were moving, he was saying something that Eleanor couldn't make out, and he was looking at her intensely, first into one eye and then into the other. Finally, as noise and movement whirled around them – they'd gathered quite a crowd – a smile came to his face, and she thought what a glorious mouth he had, and then she promptly fainted.

His name was Anthony Edevane and he was studying at Cambridge to become a doctor, a surgeon to be precise. Eleanor learned this at the refreshments counter of Baker Street station, where he took her after the altercation with the bus and bought her a lemonade. He was meeting a friend there, a boy with dark, curly hair and spectacles, the sort of boy whose clothing, Eleanor could tell just by looking at him, would always appear hastily arranged, whose hair would never sit quite as it was meant to. Eleanor could relate to that. She took a liking to him at once. 'Howard Mann – '

Anthony gestured towards the dishevelled boy – 'this is Eleanor deShiel.'

'It's a pleasure to meet you, Eleanor,' said Howard, taking her hand. 'What a charming surprise. How do you know this old boy?'

Eleanor heard herself say, 'He just saved my life,' and thought what an unlikely scenario it presented.

Howard, however, didn't skip a beat. 'Did he now? Not surprising. That's the sort of thing he does. If he weren't my best friend I think I'd have to hate him.'

It might have been awkward, this bantering conversation in an Underground station cafe with two male strangers, but, as Eleanor discovered, being saved from certain death had a way of freeing a person from the usual strictures of what to say and how. They talked easily and freely, and the more she heard the more she liked them both. Anthony and Howard joked around with one another a lot, but their manner was affable and therefore somehow inclusive. She found herself voicing opinions in a way she hadn't done in a very long time, laughing and nodding and disagreeing at times with a vehemence that would have horrified her mother.

The three of them spoke fiercely about science and nature, politics and honour, family and friendship. Eleanor gleaned that Anthony wanted to be a surgeon more than anything in the world, and had done since he was a little boy and his favourite housemaid died of appendicitis for lack of a qualified doctor. That Howard was the only son of an extremely wealthy earl who spent his days on the French Riviera with his fourth wife, and sent money for his son's care to a trust administered by a bank manager at Lloyds of London. That the two boys had met on the first day of school when Anthony lent Howard his spare uniform hat so he wouldn't be given a caning by the housemaster and that they'd been inseparable ever since. 'More like brothers,' Anthony said, giving Howard a warm smile.

Time flew and when, during a rare pause in conversation, Howard frowned lightly and said to Eleanor, 'Not to break up the party, but it occurs to me someone must be missing you,' she was shocked to glance at her father's watch (she'd worn it since he died, much to her mother's annoyance) and realise that three hours had passed since she'd lost her family in the maze. She experienced a sudden vision of her mother in a state of emotional apoplexy.

'Yes,' she agreed grimly. 'It's a distinct possibility.'

'Well then,' said Howard, 'we should get you home. Shouldn't we, Anthony?'

'Yes,' said Anthony, frowning at his own watch, tapping the glass as if the time it told were surely wrong. 'Yes, of course.' Eleanor wondered whether she imagined the note of reluctance in his voice. 'Terribly selfish of us to keep you here talking when you really ought to be resting your head.'

Suddenly, Eleanor was filled with a desperate desire not to part company from them. From him. She started to demur. The day had turned out to be a glorious one; she felt absolutely fine; home was the last place she planned on going. She'd come all this way, she was so near the zoo, she hadn't even seen the tigers yet! Anthony was saying something about her head and the impact of her fall, which was kind of him, but really, she insisted, she felt fine. A little dizzy, now that she tried to stand up, but that was only to be expected; it was very warm inside the cafe, and she hadn't eaten lunch, and – oh! Perhaps if she just sat for a moment longer, caught her breath, waited for her vision to clear.

He was insistent; she was stubborn; Howard was the decider. With a small smile of apology he took her other arm as Anthony went to pay the bill.

Eleanor watched him go. He was clever, and kind, and possessed an obvious fascination with the world and all it had to offer. He was also very handsome. That thick dark-blond hair and sun-browned skin, a gaze that was electric with curiosity and a passion for learning. She couldn't be absolutely certain that it wasn't her near-death experience playing tricks with her eyes, but he seemed to shine. He was so filled with enthusiasm and energy and confidence that he was somehow more alive than everybody else in the room.

'He's something, isn't he?' said Howard.

Eleanor's skin flared. She hadn't meant to be so obvious.

'He's the smartest boy in class, he won most of the academic prizes at our school graduation. Not that he'd ever tell you himself, he's modest to a fault.'

'Is he?' She pretended only a mild, polite interest.

'When he qualifies, he plans to establish a surgery for those who can least afford it. The number of children who go without vital operations for want of the money to pay a surgeon is shameful.'

They drove her back to Mayfair in Howard's Rolls-Royce Silver Ghost. Vera's butler opened the door, but Beatrice, who'd been watching from her bedroom window, came flying down the stairs, hot on his heels. 'Oh my goodness, Eleanor,' she breathed, 'your mother is *livid*!' Then, noticing Anthony and Howard, she regathered herself and fluttered her eyelashes. 'How do you do?'

'Beatrice,' said Eleanor with a smile, 'allow me to introduce Howard Mann and Anthony Edevane. Mr Edevane just saved my life.'

'Well then,' said Beatrice, without skipping a beat, 'I expect you'd better come in for tea.'

The story was told again over tea and lemon cake. Constance, her brows arched and her lips tight, was simmering with unasked questions as to why Eleanor had been in Marylebone in the first place, but she held firmly to her composure as she thanked Anthony. 'Edevane?' she asked hopefully. 'Not *Lord* Edevane's son?'

'That's right,' said Anthony cheerfully, taking a second piece of cake. 'The youngest of his three.'

Constance's smile evaporated. ('Third son?' she was later heard barking at Vera. '*Third* son?! A third son has no business walking the streets rescuing impressionable young girls. He's supposed to join the ministry, for goodness' sake!')

To Eleanor, though, it explained everything. His easy, unassuming nature, the inexplicable, almost regal air he carried with him, the way they'd met. He was the third son. 'You were born to be the hero of a story,' she said.

Anthony laughed. 'I don't know about that, but I do count myself lucky to be the third.'

'Oh?' Constance's chill tone lowered the room's temperature by degrees. 'And why, pray tell, is that?'

'My father already has an heir and a spare, which leaves me free to do as I please.'

'And what exactly is that, Mr Edevane?'

'I'm going to be a doctor.'

Eleanor started to explain that Anthony was, in fact, studying to be a surgeon, that he'd committed his life to helping people less fortunate, that he'd won all sorts of important academic prizes, but such details were lost on Constance, who curtly interrupted. 'Surely a man of your class needn't work for a living. I wouldn't have thought your father approved of that.'

Anthony looked at her and the strength of his gaze was such that all remaining warmth was sucked from the room. The air was charged. Eleanor had never seen anyone stand up to her mother and she held her breath, waiting to see what he would say.

'My father, Mrs deShiel, has seen, as have I, what becomes of bored, privileged men who've been spared the effort of wage-earning. I don't plan to spend my days sitting around looking for ways to fill the stretch of time. I want to help people. I intend to be useful.' And then he turned to Eleanor, as if they were the only people in the room, and said, 'What about you, Miss deShiel? What do you want from life?'

Something changed in that moment. It was a small shift but a decisive one. He was dazzling, and it became clear to Eleanor that their meeting that morning had been fated. The tie between them was so strong she could almost see it. There was so much to tell him, and yet at the same time, she knew with a strange but clarifying certainty that she didn't have to tell him anything at all. She could see it in his eyes, the way he looked at her. He already *knew* what she wanted from life. That she had no intention of becoming one of those women who sat around playing bridge and gossiping and waiting for their drivers to take them out in carriages; that she wanted so much else and more, far too much to put into words now. And so she said only, 'I want to see those tigers.'

He laughed and a beatific smile spread across his face as he held his palms outstretched. 'Well, that's not difficult to arrange. Rest your head this afternoon and I'll take you tomorrow.' He turned to Eleanor's mother and added, 'If you have no objections, Mrs deShiel.'

It was clear to all who knew her that Constance was brimming with objections, itching to say no, to forbid this overconfident youth – this third son! – from taking her daughter anywhere. Eleanor wasn't sure she'd ever seen her mother dislike anyone so much, but there was very little Constance could do. He came from a good family, he had saved her daughter's life, he was offering to take her to the very place she'd just professed a deep desire to visit. It would have been bad form to say no. Constance planted a sour smile on her face and managed a small noise of assent. It was merely a formality. Everyone in the room could feel that the power balance had tilted, and from that moment on Constance was to play very little part in her daughter's courtship.

Eleanor walked the two boys to the door after tea. Howard said warmly, 'I hope to see you again soon, Miss deShiel,' before glancing at Anthony with a knowing smile. 'I might just go and get the Ghost warmed up.'

Anthony and Eleanor, left alone, were both all at once lost for words.

'So,' he said.

'So.'

'The zoo. Tomorrow.'

'Yes.'

'Promise me you won't step in front of a bus before then?'

She laughed. 'I promise.'

A light frown settled on his brow.

'What is it?' she said, suddenly self-conscious.

'Nothing. It's nothing. Only, I like your hair.'

'This?' Her hand went to touch the mop, at its wildest after the day's unexpected excitement.

He smiled, and deep inside her something quivered. 'That. I like it. A lot.'

And then he said goodbye and she watched him go, and when she went inside and closed the door behind her, Eleanor knew, quite simply and clearly, that *everything* had changed.

It would be wrong to say they fell in love over the next couple of weeks, for they were already in love that first day. And throughout the following fortnight, with cousin Beatrice proving a benevolently lax chaperone, they were hardly apart. They went to the zoo, where Eleanor finally saw the tigers, they lost entire days in Hampstead, discovering hidden green pockets of the heath and learning each other's secrets, they explored the Victoria and Albert Museum, and the Natural History Museum, and saw the visiting Imperial Ballet perform eight times. Eleanor attended no more balls unless Anthony was going to be there, too. Instead, they walked along the Thames, talking and laughing as if they'd known one another forever.

At the end of his holidays, on the morning he was due to return to Cambridge, he made a detour to see her. He didn't wait until they went inside but said to her, there on the doorstep, 'I came with the idea of asking you to wait for me.'

Eleanor's heart had begun to pound beneath her dress

but her breath caught when he added, 'And then I realised it wasn't right.'

'You did? It isn't?'

'No, I could hardly think of asking you to do something I wouldn't do myself.'

'I *can* wait—'

'Well, I *can't*, not for another day. I can't live without you, Eleanor. I have to ask – do you think – will you marry me?'

Eleanor grinned. She didn't need to think twice. 'Yes,' she said. 'Yes, a thousand times! Of course I will!'

Anthony swept her off her feet and spun her around, kissing her as he set her back down. 'I will never love anyone but you,' he said, smoothing strands of hair away from her face. He said it with a certainty that made her shiver. The sky was blue, north opposed south, and he, Anthony Edevane, would love only her.

She promised him the same and he smiled, pleased, but not surprised, as if he'd already known it was true.

'You know, I'm not a wealthy man,' he said. 'I'll never be rich.'

'I don't care.'

'I can't give you a home like this one.' He gestured at Aunt Vera's grand house.

Indignant. 'You *know* I don't care about those things.'

'Or a home like the one you grew up in, Loeanneth.'

'I don't need that,' she said, and for the first time she believed it. 'You're my home now.'

They were happy in Cambridge. Anthony's digs were small but clean, and Eleanor made them homely. Anthony was in the final years of his degree and sat hunched over his texts most nights after dinner; Eleanor drew and wrote. His intelligence, his goodness, were apparent even in the way he frowned at the books, his hands moving sometimes as he read about the best way to perform a certain operation. They were clever hands, gentle and deft. 'He was always able to build and make and fix things,' his mother had told Eleanor the first time they met. 'As a little boy, he liked nothing better than to take apart my husband's heirloom clock. Lucky for us – and him! – he was always able to put it back to rights.'

Their life together was not elaborate; they didn't attend big society parties, but entertained their nearest and dearest in small, intimate gatherings. Howard came often to share a meal, staying long into the night to talk and laugh and argue over a bottle of wine; Anthony's parents paid occasional visits, perplexed but too polite to comment on the straitened circumstances in which their youngest and his new wife chose to live; and Mr Llewellyn was a regular guest. With his wisdom and good humour, and his evident fatherly love for Eleanor, he soon became a treasured friend to Anthony, too; the bond was further strengthened when Anthony learned that long before his gift for storytelling made him an accidental literary star, the older man had also trained in medicine (though as a physician and not a surgeon). 'Did you never long to go back and practise?' Anthony asked more than once, unable to fathom what could possibly keep a man from his calling. But Mr Llewellyn always smiled and shook his head. 'I found something to which I was more suited. Better that I leave such matters to able men like you whose blood burns with the need to help and heal.' When

Anthony graduated from his pre-clinical training with first-class honours and a university medal, it was Mr Llewellyn he invited to sit beside Eleanor and his parents to watch him receive his degree. As the vice chancellor delivered his rousing speech about manhood and duty – 'If a man cannot be useful to his country, he is better dead' – Mr Llewellyn leaned to whisper wryly in Eleanor's ear, 'What a jolly fellow – he reminds me rather of your mother,' and she had to stifle a laugh. But the older man's eyes glistened with pride as he watched his young friend graduate.

Anthony meant it when he said money held no interest for him, as did Eleanor, but life could be devious and it turned out they were soon to be very rich indeed. They'd been married for nine months when they stood together on the Southampton docks and bade farewell to his parents and older brothers, who were leaving together for New York.

'Do you wish we were going?' Anthony said over the noise of the cheering crowd.

There'd been talk of travelling with the family, but Anthony's budget wouldn't stretch to cover the tickets and he'd baulked at letting his parents foot the bill. He felt badly, she knew, embarrassed that he couldn't afford such luxuries. Eleanor couldn't have cared less. She shrugged. 'I get seasick.'

'New York's an incredible city.'

She squeezed his hand. 'I don't mind where I am, so long as it's with you.'

He shot her a smile so filled with love that her breath caught. As they both turned back to wave, Eleanor wondered whether it was possible to be too happy. Seagulls dipped and dived and boys in cloth hats ran along beside the departing ship, leaping over each and every obstacle. 'Unsinkable,' said Anthony, shaking his head as the great ship pulled away. 'Just think of that.'

On their second wedding anniversary, Anthony suggested they go away for the weekend to a little seaside place he knew. After months spent mourning the loss of his parents and brothers to the icy cold Atlantic Ocean, at last they had something momentous to celebrate. 'A *baby*,' he'd said when she told him, a look of profound amazement on his face. 'Imagine! A tiny mix of you and me.'

They caught an early train from Cambridge to London and then changed at Paddington. The journey was long but Eleanor had packed a picnic and they ate lunch along the way, filling the hours with chatting and reading, the latest spirited game of cards in an ongoing contest, and periods of sitting contentedly, side by side, holding hands and watching through the window as the fields fled by.

When at last they reached their station a driver was waiting and Anthony helped Eleanor into the motorcar. They set off along a narrow, winding road and in the warm enclosure of the vehicle the day's travel finally caught up with her. She yawned and leaned her head back against the car seat. 'Are you all right?' Anthony asked gently, and when Eleanor said that she was she meant it. She hadn't been sure, when he first mentioned the trip, how it would feel to skirt so close to the place of her childhood; whether she'd endure the loss of her father and her home anew. Now, though, she realised that of course she would, but while there was no escaping the fact that there'd been sadness in the past, the future was still hers – theirs – to seize. 'I'm glad we've come here,' she said, resting her palm on her gently rounded belly as the road tapered to follow the line of the ocean. 'It's been such a long time since I saw the sea.'

Anthony smiled and reached across to her. She looked at his hand over hers, large over small, and wondered how she could possibly be so happy.

It was in the company of such memories that she fell asleep. It happened easily now that she was pregnant; she'd never been so tired. The motorcar's engine continued to thrum, Anthony's hand remained warm on hers, and the smell of salt infused the air. Eleanor wasn't sure how much time passed before he nudged her and said, 'Wake up, Sleeping Beauty.'

She sat and stretched, blinking into the blue light of the warm day and letting the world take shape again before her eyes.

Eleanor drew breath.

For there was Loeanneth, her dear, beloved, lost home. The gardens were becoming overgrown, the house was more run-down than she remembered, and yet it was perfection.

'Welcome home,' Anthony said, lifting her hand to kiss it. 'Happy birthday, happy anniversary, happy start of everything.'

Sound came before sight. An insect was buzzing against a glass windowpane, short, fierce bursts of static anxiety followed by momentary quiet, and another noise sat behind it, softer but more insistent, a ceaseless scratching Eleanor recognised but could not name. She opened her eyes to find herself in a place that was dark except for a dazzling slice of light between drawn curtains. The smells were familiar, of a room closed against the heat of summer, of thick brocade drapes and shadowy cool skirting boards, of stale sunlight. It was her bedroom, she realised, the one she shared with Anthony. Loeanneth.

Eleanor closed her eyes again. Her head was swimming. She was groggy, and it was awfully hot. It had been hot like this the summer they arrived together, in 1913. The pair of them, little more than children, had lived for a glorious time without the wider world and its rhythms. The house had been in dire need of repairs so they'd set up camp in the boathouse, the cherished play site of her childhood. The accommodation was primitive – a bed, a table, basic kitchen facilities and a little washroom – but they were young and in love and used to living on next to nothing. For years afterwards, when Anthony was away at war and she missed him, whenever she felt sad or alone or overwhelmed, she would take herself down to the boathouse, bringing with her the love letters he'd written home to her, and there, more than anywhere else, she'd be able to touch the happiness and truth she'd felt that summer before the war came along to spoil their paradise.

They'd eaten every meal outdoors, hard-boiled eggs and cheese from a picnic basket, and drunk wine under the lilac tree in the walled garden. They'd disappeared inside the woods, and stolen apples from the farm next door, and floated down the stream in her little boat as one silken hour spun itself into the next. On a clear, still night, they'd dug the old bicycles out of the shed and cycled together along the dusty lane, racing, laughing, breathing in salt from the warm air as moonlight made the stones, still hot from the day, shine lustrous white.

It had been the perfect summer. She'd known that at the time. The long sunny spell, their youth, this new and all-consuming love they'd found; but there'd been larger forces at work, too. That summer was a beginning for the two of them – their new family, their life together – but it was also the end of something. They, along with the rest of human-kind, had stood at a precipice; the rhythms of their lifetime, unchanged for generations, were about to be given a seismic jolt. There were people who'd glimpsed what was coming, but not Eleanor. The future had seemed unimaginable. She'd been happily cocooned in the sublime and heady present where all that mattered was today. But war clouds had been gathering, the future waiting in the wings . . .

The insect was still thrashing against the leadlight win-dows and Eleanor endured another wave of grief as the present seeped back in. Theo. The reporter's questions, the photographer, Alice in the doorway to the library. The look on Alice's face had been one that Eleanor recognised. It was the same expression she'd worn when Eleanor caught her scratching her name into the architraves of the house, the same as when Cook sent her upstairs as a tot for stealing sugar mice from the larder, as when she ruined her new dress with great splotches of black ink.

Alice had looked guilty, certainly, but there was more to it than that. She'd appeared to be on the cusp of speak-ing. But what could Alice have wanted to say? And to whom? Did she know something? She'd had her interview with the policeman, as had everyone in the house. Was it possible she had information about Theo's whereabouts that she hadn't yet mentioned?

'How could she?' came a voice in the dark. 'She's still but a child herself.'

Eleanor hadn't intended to speak aloud and the realisation that she had was disquieting. She peered through the dim of the room. Her mouth was dry – an effect, presumably, of the medication Dr Gibbons had given her. She reached for the glass of water on the bedside table and the person beyond it clarified in the gloom: her mother, sitting in the brown velvet chair by the bureau. Eleanor said quickly, 'Is there news?'

'Not yet.' Her mother was writing letters, her pen scratching across the vellum. 'But the nice policeman, the older one with the poorly eye, told me they've received information that might be of assistance.'

'Information?'

Scritchety-scratch. 'Now, now, Eleanor, you know I haven't a head for details.'

Eleanor took a sip of water. Her hand shook and her throat burned. It had to be Alice. She could just picture her second daughter fronting up to the policeman in charge, confidence animating her eager features as she pulled out that journal of hers and proceeded to deliver crisp notes. Observations and theories she was 'just positive' were relevant.

And maybe Alice really *could* help; perhaps she had seen something that would lead the police to Theo. The girl had developed an uncanny habit for being where she shouldn't.

'I need to speak to Alice.'

'You need to rest. Those sleeping tablets of Dr Gibbons' pack quite a punch, or so I'm told.'

'Mother, please.'

A sigh. 'I don't know where she is. You know what that girl's like. You ought to know; you were just the same at that age, each of you as stubborn as the other.'

Eleanor didn't deny the comparison. Neither, if she were honest, could she contradict the description, though 'stubborn' was perhaps a lazy choice. There were plenty that were more suitable. Eleanor preferred to think of her younger self as tenacious. Devoted, even. 'Mr Llewellyn then. Please, Mother. He'll know where to find Alice.'

'I haven't seen *him* either. As a matter of fact, the police were looking for the man. I heard they couldn't find him anywhere – there was talk he'd taken off. Very peculiar, but then he never was especially reliable and he's been jumpier than a cat lately.'

Eleanor tried to sit up. She didn't have the capacity today to admit her mother's ancient contempt for Mr Llewellyn. She was going to have to find Alice herself. Oh, but her head was thumping. She cradled it in her hands and Edwina whimpered at the end of the bed.

Just another minute or two to steady herself, that was all she needed. To stop her thoughts from jumbling, to make her head stop spinning. Constance was simply stirring up mischief; Eleanor knew there was no way Mr Llewellyn would desert her at a time like this. He *had* been anxious over the past few weeks, that much was true, but he was her dearest friend. He was bound to be in the garden somewhere, taking care of the girls; it was the only thing that explained his absence from her side. And when she found him, she'd find Alice.

For no matter how muddy her mind, no matter how desperately she wanted to sink back into her bed and hide beneath the covers, to deny the horror of the day, Eleanor was determined to speak with Alice. Her daughter knew something about Theo's disappearance, Eleanor was certain of it.

Nine

It had been almost a week since she first stumbled upon Loeanneth and Sadie had been back every day. No matter which way she headed out on her morning run, she always ended up in the overgrown garden. Her favourite place to sit was on the wide rim of a stone fountain overlooking the lake, and this morning as she sat down, she spotted a crude carving in the shadowy contour of the fountain base. A-L-I-C-E. Sadie ran her finger along the cool indentations of the letters. 'Hello there, Alice,' she said. 'It seems we meet again.'

They were all over the place, these engravings. On the trunks of trees, the soft wood of the windowsills, the slippery moss-green platform of the boathouse she'd discovered and explored the other day. Sadie had started to feel as if she and Alice Edevane were playing an elaborate game of cat-and-mouse across the decades, a connection accentuated by the fact that she'd been dipping in and out of *A Dish Served Cold* all week while she played at holidays (for Bertie's benefit) and tried to sort things out with Donald (she'd left six messages since Monday, made countless other calls, and still heard nothing back). Despite some initial doubts, reading had proved a surprisingly agreeable pastime. Sadie liked the crabby detective, Diggory Brent, and was taking an inordinate amount of pleasure in spotting the clues before he did. It was hard to imagine that the stern-faced woman pictured inside the back covers of the crime novels had once been a junior delinquent, defacing the family home, but it had made Sadie warm to Alice in some inexplicable way. It intrigued her, too, that a writer famous for inventing complex mysteries had been involved, however peripherally, in a real-life crime investigation, particularly one that had never been solved. She wondered which had come first, the choice of genre or the disappearance of a baby brother.

All week, faced with Donald's silence, while she battled a deep sense of impotence, Sadie had caught herself brooding on the neglected house and the missing child, intrigued by its puzzle. She would rather have been back in London at her real job, but anything was better than watching the clock count time away, and her interest had not gone unnoticed. 'Solved it yet?' Bertie had taken to calling whenever she and the dogs clattered through the front door to his cottage. There was a smile in his voice when he said it, as if he were pleased to see her occupied but guardedly so. Apparently she had not altogether convinced him with her holidaymaker act. She caught him watching her sometimes, a thoughtful frown on his face, and she knew questions about her sudden visit to Cornwall, the highly unusual absence from her job, were damming up behind his lips. Sadie had got good at escaping the house, backpack slung over her shoulders and dogs at her heel, whenever it looked like that dam might be on the brink of bursting.

The dogs, for their part, were thrilled with the new arrangement. They raced ahead of Sadie, swapping places as they wove through the woods, before veering off the track together, chasing one another into the long grass and sliding beneath the yew hedge to take up yesterday's quarrel with the ducks. Sadie lagged behind, but then books weren't light and her backpack was full of them these days, care of her new friend Alastair Hawker, village librarian.

From the first time she'd met him, he'd been as helpful as his limited collection allowed. Unfortunately, that wasn't saying much. It was Hitler's fault. A bomb during the Second World War had destroyed the newspaper records for the years prior to January 1941. 'I'm really very sorry,' Alastair had said. 'They're not online but I can order them from the British Library, find you something else to get you started?'

Sadie had told him that suited her very well and he'd got down to business, tapping keenly on a computer keyboard and flicking through old file cards in a set of wooden drawers, before excusing himself to disappear at a brisk pace behind a door marked *Archives*.

'Success,' he said on his return, brushing dust from the top of a small stack of books. '*Notable Cornish Families*,' he read, turning to the table of contents and running a long finger down the list, stopping at a spot midway. 'Chapter eight: The deShiels of Havelyn.'

Sadie looked at him, unconvinced. 'The house I'm interested in is called Loeanneth.'

'The Lake House, yes, but it used to be part of a much larger estate. I believe Loeanneth was originally the head gardener's residence.'

'And the deShiels?'

'They were local gentry, hugely powerful in their day. Same old story: strength and influence waned along with the family's bank balance. Some unwise business decisions, a few bad eggs, the obligatory series of aristocratic scandals.' He waved the book. 'You'll find it all in here.'

Sadie had left with a shiny new library card, her first; a photocopy of 'Chapter eight: The deShiels of Havelyn'; and Arnold Pickering's *The Edevane Boy*, a rapturously written account of the disappearance she had the dubious honour of being the first to borrow since August 1972. She'd also borrowed a well-thumbed copy of *A Dish Served Cold*.

That afternoon, while Bertie was busy baking pear cake, Sadie had set up in the courtyard of the cottage, listening to the sigh and heave of the sea and reading about the deShiel family. It was, as the librarian said, a tale of greatness and decline. Sadie skimmed through the first few hundred years – the knighting by Elizabeth I of some seafaring deShiel who'd managed to pilfer great masses of gold from the Spanish, the awarding of lands and titles, the various deaths, marriages and inheritances that followed – becoming interested again around 1850, when the family's fortunes took a sharp turn for the worse. There was the suggestion of a fleecing, something to do with a sugar plantation in the West Indies, and a great gambling debt, and then a fire on Christmas Day, 1878, that started in the servants' hall and went on to destroy much of the manor house. Over the next thirty years, the estate was carved into pieces and sold off bit by bit until all that remained to the deShiel family was the Lake House and its surrounding acres.

The Edevanes, it turned out, were just a footnote in the house's history. Three paragraphs from the end of the chapter the author noted that Eleanor deShiel, the last in the family line, had married Anthony Edevane in 1911, after which Loeanneth was restored and retained for use as their

country residence. There was no mention of Theodore
Edevane's disappearance, a fact that had surprised Sadie
until she established that *Notable Cornish Families* had been
published in 1925, almost a decade before the little boy went
missing; indeed, a good eight years before he'd been born.

In the absence of this intrigue, the author had focused on
Eleanor deShiel's status as the inspiration for Daffyd Llewellyn's *Eleanor's Magic Doorway*, a children's storybook that
had enjoyed great success in the first decade of the twentieth
century. 'If not for the unlikely rapport between Llewellyn
and the perspicacious daughter of his friend, he might have
remained a physician, never discovering his gift for storytelling, and generations of children would have been deprived
of a treasured tale.' Llewellyn had continued to write and
illustrate and in the 1934 Honours was awarded a posthumous OBE for services to literature. According to Alastair
Hawker the book was still around but hadn't stood the test
of time as well as some of its contemporaries. Sadie had had
to take his word for it. She hadn't read the book as a child;
there'd been a copy, she thought, a gift from her grandparents, but her mum and dad had declared it 'nonsense',
taking predictable exception to the magical elements of the
story and filing it distastefully wherever the Enid Blytons
went to die.

The edition she had now on her lap had been published
in 1936. The paper was soft and powdery, interspersed with
shiny picture pages that were starting to spot around the
edge. Plates, Alastair had called them, when she borrowed it
from him on Monday. The story was about a little girl who
lived in a big, lonely house with her kind but ineffective
father and an ice-cold, social-climbing stepmother. One day,

when her parents were away in London, the girl was rattling around the draughty house and found herself before a door she'd never noticed. On the other side she found a wizened, white-haired man, 'like Old Father Time himself', the walls around his bed covered from floor to ceiling in hand-drawn maps and carefully sketched landscapes. 'What are you doing here?' she asked, as well one might; 'I've been waiting for you,' he said in response, before beginning the tale of a far-off magic land in which once upon a time a terrible wrong was done that ruptured the peace and allowed war and strife to flourish. 'There is only one person who can make things right, and that is you,' he said.

By following his maps, the girl discovered a tunnel in the overgrown garden that took her to the magic land. There she joined with a trusty band of oppressed locals and undertook a number of adventures and battles to trounce the wicked usurper and restore peace and happiness to the land. When at last she made her way back through the tunnel, it was to discover that no time had passed at all and yet her home had changed entirely. Her father was happy, her mother still alive, and the house and garden had lost their gloom. She ran to tell the old man of her success, only to find the room was empty. Her parents told her she must have dreamed the whole thing, and the girl almost believed them until she found, hidden beneath the wallpaper in the spare bedroom, a single map of the magic land.

Sitting on the rim of the fountain, Sadie took a bite of the cheese sandwich she'd brought in her backpack and held the book up in front of her, comparing an illustration of the storybook house to the real one behind. She'd asked Alastair to find her some additional information on the author,

Daffyd Llewellyn. According to the preface at the beginning of the book, he was a close family friend to the Edevanes, and there was no doubting he'd taken his inspiration from Loeanneth. The house in Llewellyn's illustration was a dead ringer for the real thing; he'd even captured the leaning angle of the window on the far left-hand side. It had taken Sadie days of close inspection to notice that the window wasn't square. She turned to the plate marked *fig. ii*, an illustration of a wild-haired little girl in old-fashioned clothing, standing beside a stone pillar with a brass ring at its base. The sun's glare was impossibly bright and Sadie had to squint to read the line of text beneath the picture: *There, under the deepest, darkest, most whispering willow, Eleanor found what the old man's map had promised. 'Pull the ring,' the air around her seemed to breathe, 'pull the ring and see what happens.'*

Sadie threw the crust of her sandwich to an insistent cluster of cygnets and wiped her hand on her tracksuit bottoms. From what she could gather, these kids' books were all alike. Isolated child finds doorway into magical world; adventures and heroism ensue. Evil is vanquished, old-man storytellers are freed from the curses that detain them, and everything is made right with the world. It seemed a lot of kids dreamed about escaping childhood, of having power over their own destiny. Sadie could relate to that. Some went through the back of a wardrobe, others to the top of an enchanted tree, Eleanor had found an escape hatch in the garden. Unlike some doorways, Eleanor's had been real. Sadie had been chuffed when she found it on Tuesday morning, the brass ring and the pillar, just like the story said, hidden beneath a particularly virulent willow on the far side of the lake. Naturally, she'd tried to open it, but despite summoning all her strength, the trapdoor hadn't budged.

Their childhoods might have been decidedly different, but Sadie felt a kinship with Eleanor Edevane all the same. She *liked* the little girl in the fairy story, with her spirit of honour and bravery and mischief; she was just the kind of girl Sadie would have loved to be when she was small. But it was more than that, too. Sadie felt bonded to Eleanor because of something she'd found in the old boathouse the other day, down by the stream. She'd climbed through a broken window into a room that had been set up with a bed, a table and a few other basic furnishings. Everything was covered in dust and dirt and a moist blanket of age, and after a thorough search Sadie had turned up nothing useful and only one item that could rightly be termed interesting. The envelope had slipped behind the head of the bed and been lost for the better part of a century. Inside was a single sheet of paper with an elaborate design of deep green ivy leaves around the edges, the second page of a letter with Eleanor's name at the end.

It was a love letter, written while she was pregnant, in which, amid intimate declarations that his love had saved her life, she tried to convey to her husband the miraculous changes taking place as their baby grew – *a tiny mix of you and me*. Sadie had presumed at first that the baby was Theo Edevane, until she noted Eleanor's poignant lament that her love was too far away, that she wished he could be near, that she missed him desperately. She'd realised then that the letter must have been written when Anthony was in France during the First World War. According to 'The deShiels of Havelyn', the Edevanes had had three daughters: Deborah born before the war, Clementine afterwards, and Alice smack bang in the middle. Thus, the baby whose birth Eleanor anticipated with such longing must be Alice. Passionate and honest, the letter provided such a strong insight into Eleanor's character that Sadie could almost hear the other woman's voice, clear and true, across the passage of ninety years.

Now, she closed the library book with a clap, sending a colony of dust spores hurtling. The sun was high and moisture was evaporating from the lake's surface. Reflected light danced on the underside of leaning branches and leaves glistened, impossibly green. Despite the day's warmth, Sadie shivered as she looked up towards the house. Even without its link to *Eleanor's Magic Doorway*, this place still gave her the uncanny sense of having stumbled into the pages of a fairy story. The more time she spent in the Loeanneth garden, the more she learned about the house and the people who'd lived inside it, with each new imprint of A-L-I-C-E she discovered, the less she felt like an intruder. And yet she couldn't shake the feeling that the house was watching her.

Ridiculous, fanciful nonsense. It was the sort of thing Bertie's new friend Louise might think; Donald was guffawing in her mind. It was the stillness she was responding to, the lack of human habitation and its legacy. Houses weren't meant to stand empty. A house without occupants, especially one like this, still filled with a family's possessions, was the saddest, most pointless thing on earth.

Sadie followed a flock of mirrored clouds as they drifted across the leadlight windows on the top floor, her gaze stopping at the window on the far left. The nursery, the last place Theo Edevane had been seen before he went missing. She took up a pebble, rolling it thoughtfully between her thumb and index finger, judging its weight idly in her palm. That, there, was the crux of it. This house might easily have been forgotten but for the story attached to it, the infamy of that little boy's disappearance. Over time the infamy had gained an echo and eventually it had ripened into folklore. The fairy story of a little boy lost and a house cast into an eternal sleep, holding its breath as the garden continued to tumble and grow around it.

Sadie cast the pebble in a lazy arc towards the lake, where it landed with a rich *plink*. No doubt about it, the fairy-tale element was one of the trickiest aspects of the case. Cold cases were always a challenge, but this one had the added folklore factor. The story had been told and retold so many times that people had come to accept its mystery. If they were honest, most people didn't want an answer – outsiders, that is, people who weren't involved; that the mystery was unsolvable was part of its appeal. But it hadn't been witchcraft or magic, and children did not spontaneously dematerialise. They were lost, or stolen, or trafficked. Killed, sometimes, too, but mostly given or taken away. Sadie frowned. There were so many shadow children out there, separated from their parents, tugging at their mothers' skirts. Where had this one gone?

Alastair had been as good as his word, putting in an order for copies of the original newspaper articles, and Bertie's friend Louise, who seemed to be 'just popping in' whenever Sadie entered the kitchen, had promised to ask around the old people's wing of the hospital for anyone who might know something. Sadie had confirmed with the Land Registry Office that the house was currently owned by Alice Edevane, but despite proud claims to the contrary, it transpired the 'local' author lived in London and hadn't been spotted in the village for decades. Sadie had found a street address but no email; she hadn't had an answer to either of her letters yet. In the meantime, she was making do with the library copy of *The Edevane Boy* by Arnold Pickering.

The book had been published in 1955 as part of a series called *Cornish Mysteries* that also included a volume of collated fairy sightings and the story of a notorious ghost ship that appeared in the bay. These stablemates had not filled Sadie with confidence, and sure enough, Pickering's account suggested a far greater love for intrigue than for truth. The book didn't venture a sensible theory, preferring to remain in thrall to 'the mysterious disappearance that Midsummer's Eve'. It did, however, contain what appeared to be a decent summary of events, and beggars couldn't be choosers.

Sadie took out her notes, newly encased in a folder she'd labelled *Edevane*. It was becoming something of a daily ritual to read them through, here on the edge of the old fountain. It was how Sadie always worked, inputting every detail of a case, over and over, until she could recite the contents of a file by memory. Donald called it obsessive (he was more a ponder-by-pint man), but Sadie figured one man's obsession was another girl's devotion, and if there was a better way to discover flaws, holes and discrepancies in the evidence, she was yet to find it.

According to Pickering, Theodore Edevane was last seen at eleven on the night of the party, when his mother went to the nursery to check on him. It was the same time she looked in each evening before retiring to bed, and the boy's habit was then to sleep until morning. He was a good sleeper,

Eleanor Edevane had told police, and he rarely woke during the night.

Her visit to the nursery on the evening of the party was verified by one of the maids, who saw Mrs Edevane leave the room and stop to speak briefly with another servant on the stairs. The maid confirmed the time as just after eleven and said she knew this because she was carrying a tray of used champagne flutes back to the kitchen in order that they might be cleaned so the guests would have them for the fireworks display at midnight. The footman on duty by the front door reported seeing Mrs Edevane leave the house just after eleven, after which time none of the guests or family members re-entered, except to visit the bathroom on the ground floor, until the end of the party.

Mrs Edevane spent the rest of the evening at the boat-house, where gondolas were taking partygoers for joyrides down the lantern-lit stream, and retired to bed just after sunrise, when the last guests had left, presuming her children were all where they should be. She fell asleep quickly and stayed that way until she was woken at eight by a maid who informed her that Theo wasn't in his cot.

The family carried out a preliminary search, but without any great sense of urgency, and without alerting those guests who'd stayed overnight. One of the Edevane daughters – the youngest, Clementine – had a habit of slipping out of the house early and had been known, on occasion, to take her little brother with her if he were awake when she passed the nursery. It was presumed to be the case in this instance.

Breakfast was still being served in the dining room when Clementine Edevane returned to the house, alone, just after ten. When she professed no knowledge of her brother's whereabouts, reporting that the door to his nursery had been closed when she passed at six, police were called to the house. The boy was officially declared missing and a massive search was launched.

Although Pickering seemed happy to believe that the boy had simply vanished into the night, he did include a small summary of the police investigations, outlining two official explanations for Theodore Edevane's disappearance: the boy had wandered or he had been abducted. The wandering theory was lent credence when it was discovered his favourite toy puppy was also gone, but as the search widened and no trace of the child was found, and in light of the family's wealth, police became convinced the latter was more likely. At some point between eleven o'clock on Midsummer's Eve and eight the following morning, someone had crept into the nursery and removed the boy.

It seemed a reasonable assumption and one with which Sadie was inclined to agree. She looked across the lake towards the house and tried to imagine herself into the night-time party as described by Pickering: people everywhere, lanterns and flares, gondolas with laughing passengers drifting down the lamp-lit stream, a bonfire in the middle of the lake. Music and laughter and the noise of three hundred people chatting.

If the boy had wandered – and Pickering quoted a newspaper report in which Anthony Edevane said his son had recently started climbing from his cot and had once or twice made his way down the stairs – then what chance was there that no one at the party had seen him? Pickering alluded to a few uncertain reports from guests who 'might have' noticed a child, but evidently there was nothing concrete. And if the eleven-month-old had somehow managed to avoid detection as he crossed the garden, how far was it reasonable to presume he might have travelled? Sadie didn't know much about children and their milestones, but presumably even an advanced walker would have run out of steam pretty quickly? Police had searched for miles in all directions and uncovered nothing. Besides, it was incredibly unlikely that seventy years had passed without anything turning up: no body, no bones, not even a shred of clothing.

There were problems with the abduction theory, too. Namely, how someone could have got inside, taken the child and then left again without arousing suspicion. There'd been hundreds of people cluttering up the house and garden, and as far as Sadie could tell there were no solid reports of anyone seeing or hearing anything. She'd spent all of Wednesday morning scouting about the house looking for exits and found two, other than the front door, that seemed viable: the French doors leading from the library and another door at the back of the house. The library was out, surely, because the party had spilled around to the garden there, but Sadie had wondered about that back door.

She'd tried to look through the keyhole and had given the door a hearty shake in the hopes it might swing open; there was a difference, after all, between breaking and entering and just plain entering. Ordinarily, Sadie wasn't one for splitting hairs, and it wasn't as though there was anyone around to mind if she broke the latch to get inside, but with things as sticky as they were with Donald, and the looming shadow of Ashford, who had the power and possibly the inclination to kick her off the force, she figured it was wise to be on her best behaviour. Climbing through the window into a virtually empty boathouse was one thing, breaking into a fully furnished manor house was quite another. The room beyond the door would remain a mystery until Alastair was enlisted to find her a floorplan in the county collection. 'I'm a nut for maps and plans,' he'd said, barely able to conceal his glee at having been asked to obtain one. It had taken him no time at all and thus by Thursday Sadie had learned that the door was the servants' entrance into the kitchen.

Which didn't exactly help matters. The kitchen would have been buzzing on the night of the party. Surely there was no way anyone could have sneaked out undetected with Theo Edevane under one arm?

Sadie glanced again at Alice's name engraved in its secret spot at the base of the fountain. 'Come on, Alice,' she said. 'You were there. Throw a girl a bone.'

The silence was deafening.

Well, no, not silence, for it was never silent here. Each day, as the sun rose higher into the sky, the choir of insects hovering amongst the reeds warmed to a feverish static; it was the lack of clues that was deafening.

Frustrated, Sadie cast her notes aside. Trying to find gaps in the evidence was all well and good, but the method relied, funnily enough, on having evidence to sift through. Real evidence: witness statements, police theories, reliable information. Right now, Sadie was working with only the flimsiest of outlines.

She gathered her things, slipping the books and file inside her backpack, and called to the dogs. They came reluctantly, but soon fell into step as Sadie made her way through the back garden, away from the house. Her explorations earlier in the week had revealed a stream at the rear of the estate that could be followed all the way to the village.

In a matter of days, God willing, she'd have some concrete material. One of the most useful things she'd gleaned from Pickering's book was the name of the investigating officers, the youngest of whom, it turned out, was still alive and living in the area. According to Pickering, it had been Clive Robinson's first case after joining up with the local police force. He'd been seventeen at the time and assistant to the local police inspector, DI Hargreaves.

It hadn't been difficult to track down Clive Robinson's address; not for Sadie, who still had friends in Traffic. *A* friend, at any rate. An amiable-enough fellow with whom she'd shared a drunken fumble after a police night out a few years back. Neither of them had mentioned it since, but he was always happy to expedite her requests for information. She'd jotted down the address and driven into nearby Polperro on Wednesday afternoon. There'd been no answer when she knocked, however the next-door neighbour had been most forthcoming. Clive was on holiday in Cyprus with his daughter and son-in-law, but would be back the following day. The neighbour knew this, she volunteered, because she was busy being neighbourly, collecting mail and keeping Clive's pot plants alive until he returned. Sadie had written out a note requesting a meeting and then slipped it through the letterbox. She'd thanked the woman and commented that the plants appeared to be thriving. Sadie held a special affection for neighbours like Doris, so willing to share.

The dogs raced ahead, crossing the stream at its narrowest bend, but Sadie paused. There was something in the shallows and she fetched it up from the mud, turning it over in her fingers. A smooth oval stone, flat as a coin, the perfect skimmer. Bertie had taught her how to find them, back when she first went to live with her grandparents in London and they'd gone for walks, the three of them, around the bathing pond in Victoria Park. She tossed it underarm, pleased when it bounced obligingly across the water's surface.

She searched between the reeds and had just found another lovely skimmer when a flash of light and movement on the other side of the stream caught her eye. Sadie knew what it was at once. She tightened her lips and blinked long and hard. Sure enough, when she looked again the backlit child with her hands raised for help was gone. Sadie launched the stone, watching grimly as it chased its mate across the water. When finally it sank without a trace, she crossed the rocks to the other side and didn't let herself look back.

Ten

'You need to find a really flat one,' Anthony said, digging in the shallow water at the edge of the stream. 'Just like this beauty here.' He held the small oval-shaped stone between his fingertips, admiring it as he turned it this way and that. Sunlight glinted behind him as he placed it in little Deborah's waiting hand.

She gazed at it in wonder, her downy hair falling forwards to graze the top of her wide blue eyes. She blinked and then heaved a great happy sigh, so emphatically pleased with the situation that she couldn't help but stamp her little feet in a burst of explosive glee. Somewhat foreseeably, the stone slipped from her palm and fell with a splash back into the water.

Deborah's mouth formed an 'O' of surprise and after a brief inspection of her empty hand a plump finger shot out indignantly to point at the place where it had disappeared.

Anthony laughed and brushed her soft hair back and forth. 'Never mind, poppet. There are plenty more where that one came from.'

From where she sat on the fallen log beneath the willow, Eleanor smiled. This, here, was everything. This late summer's day, the smell of the distant sea, the people she loved most in the world all in the same place. On days like today it felt as if the sun had cast its spell and it would never be winter again, and she could almost convince herself she'd imagined the whole awful thing . . . But then she would telescope out of the perfect moment and the panic would return, a rabid gnawing in her stomach, because each day was going faster than the one before it and no matter how determinedly she tried to slow time down, it was slipping through her fingers like water, like those flat little river stones through Deborah's fingers.

She must have sighed or frowned or otherwise expressed her inner turmoil because Howard, sitting beside her, leaned to bump her shoulder lightly with his own. 'It won't go on for long,' he said. 'He'll be back before you know it.'

'By Christmas, they say.'

'Not even four months.'

'Barely three.'

He took her hand and squeezed it and Eleanor felt a chill of presentiment. She told herself she was being silly, and focused instead on the dragonfly hovering in the sunlit reeds. Dragonflies didn't imagine they could sense the future; they just flew about, enjoying the sun on their wings. 'Have you heard from your Catherine?' she said brightly.

'Only to tell me she'd become engaged to some red-haired cousin from the north.'

'No!'

'I'd thought going into uniform might impress her, but alas . . .'

'More fool her. She doesn't deserve you.'

'No . . . only I'd rather hoped I might deserve her.'

He said it lightly, but Eleanor knew beneath his humour

he was smarting. He'd fallen deeply for Catherine; according to Anthony he'd been on the brink of proposing marriage.

'There are plenty more fish in the sea,' she said, wincing because it sounded so glib.

'Yes. Only Catherine was a very lovely fish. Maybe if I come back from the war with a small but impressive injury . . .'

'A limp, perhaps?'

'I was thinking more along the lines of an eyepatch. Just enough to lend me a certain roguish charm.'

'You're far too nice to be a rogue.'

'I was afraid you'd say that. War will toughen me up, surely?'

'Not too much, I hope.'

Over by the stream, little Deborah laughed with delight as Anthony dunked her toes in the cooler, deeper stretch of water. The sun had slipped a little in the sky and the pair of them were bathed in light. The baby chuckle was infectious and Eleanor and Howard smiled at one another.

'He's a lucky man,' Howard said, his tone unusually serious. 'I've never envied Anthony before – though God knows I've had more than enough reason – but I do envy him that. Being a father.'

'Your turn next.'

'You think so?'

'I know so.'

'Yes, I suppose you're right. Who could resist me?' He puffed out his chest and then frowned. 'Other than sweet Catherine, of course.'

Little Deborah toddled over to where they were sitting, the short journey made treacherous by her small stature and newness to walking. She held out her hand, presenting a little stone with all the solemnity of a royal bestowal.

'It's beautiful, darling.' Eleanor took the pebble in her fingers. It was warm and smooth and she rubbed her thumb over its surface.

'Da,' said Deborah importantly. 'Da-da.'

Eleanor smiled. 'Yes, Da-da.'

'Come on, little D,' said Howard, swinging her up onto his shoulders. 'Let's go and see what those greedy ducks are doing on the lake.'

Eleanor watched them go, her daughter squealing with laughter, enjoying the ride as Uncle Howard bobbed and weaved his way through the trees.

He was such a good, kind man, yet for as long as she'd known him there'd been something profoundly solitary about Howard. Even his sense of humour, his habit of making people laugh, seemed somehow only to isolate him further. 'That's because he is alone,' Anthony had said when Eleanor mentioned it. 'Except for us. He has been all his life. No brothers or sisters, his mother long dead and a father who couldn't be bothered.' Eleanor had a feeling that was why she liked him so much; because they were the same, the two of them, only she'd been fortunate enough to find her soulmate on a busy London street, while Howard was still searching.

'I'll make a champion skimmer of her yet,' said Anthony, coming towards her from the stream.

Eleanor shook away sad thoughts and smiled. His shirt-sleeves were rolled to his elbows and she thought for the thousandth time what wonderful arms he had, what splendid hands. No more or less than what she'd been born with, and yet his were capable of fixing broken people. At least they would be when he completed his clinical training, once the war was over. 'I expect you will,' she said. 'Only I'm concerned you waited so long to start her instruction. She's almost eleven months old.'

'She's a fast learner.'

'And clearly gifted.'

'She takes after her mother in that respect.' Anthony leaned down to kiss her, cupping her chin in his hands, and Eleanor drank in the smell of him, his presence and warmth, trying to fix this moment in her memory.

He sat beside her on the log and sighed with deep satisfaction. How she wished she could be like him: certain, confident, at peace. Instead she worried constantly. How would she manage when he left? How would she make it right for little D? Already their daughter adored her father especially, seeking him out each morning, her face widening in a smile of sheer delight when she saw that, yes, joy of joys, he was still here. Eleanor couldn't bear to imagine the first time that little face sought her father in vain, remaining poised on the anticipation of delight. Worse – the first day she forgot to seek him altogether.

'I have something for you.'

Eleanor blinked. Her fears were like flies at a picnic: as fast as she swatted them away, there were more to replace them. 'You do?'

He rummaged in the basket they'd brought down from the house and handed her a small flat package.

'What is it?'

'Open it and see.'

'It's a book,' she said.

'It's not. And you really shouldn't guess like that.'

'Why not?'

'One day you'll be right and you'll spoil the surprise.'

'I'm never right.'

'That's a good point.'

'Thank you.'

'Though there's a first time for everything.'

'I'm going to open this now.'

'I wish you would.'

She tore off the paper and drew breath. Inside was the most beautiful ream of writing paper she'd ever seen. Eleanor ran her fingertips over the soft cotton sheets, following the elegant green vine of ivy leaves that twined its way around the borders.

'It's so you can write to me,' he said.

'I know what it's for.'

'I don't want to miss anything while I'm gone.'

The word 'gone' brought home the reality of what was about to happen. She'd been trying so hard to contain her worries. He was so strong and sure and she wanted to be equal to him, didn't want to disappoint him, but at times her fear threatened to consume her.

'You don't like it?' he said.

'I love it.'

'Then . . . ?'

'Oh, Anthony.' Her words came in a rush. 'I know it's not very brave of me, and we're all supposed to be very brave at times like these, but—'

He pressed a finger lightly to her lips.

'I don't think I can bear—'

'I know. But you can and you will. You're as strong as anyone I've ever met.'

He kissed her, and she sank into his embrace. Anthony thought she was strong. Maybe she could be? Maybe for the sake of Deborah she could manage to overcome her own emotions? She pushed aside her fears and allowed herself to disappear into the perfect satisfaction and fulfilment of this moment. The stream burbled on its way towards the sea, just as it always had, and she rested her head on his warm chest, listening to the steady thud of his heart. 'Come home to me.'

'Nothing will stop me.'

'Promise you won't let it?'

'I promise.'

Eleven

Sadie went home by way of the library. The dogs knew the drill by now, kicking about a bit before settling at the corner of the building near the stainless-steel water bowl Alastair had started leaving for them.

It was dim inside, but after some scouting Sadie spotted the librarian crouched behind a stack of books in the large-print section.

He smiled when he saw her. 'I've got something for you.'

He fetched an A4-sized envelope from beneath the desk.

'Is it what I think it is?'

'*Polperro Post*,' he said. 'The day after the disappearance.'

Sadie let out a small, satisfied breath.

'That's not all.' He handed her a thick stack of bound pages with her name attached to the front with a rubber band. 'Fictional Escap(e)ades: Mothers, Monsters and Metaphysics in Children's Fiction, a doctoral dissertation featuring a chapter on Daffyd Llewellyn and *Eleanor's Magic Doorway*.'

Sadie's eyebrows arched.

'And last but not least . . .'

'There's more?'

'We aim to please. Another map of the property, including plans for the house. Rather special, this one. Quite a stroke of luck. It came from a set of documents that were only discovered a few years ago. They were stored in an old trunk – God only knows who put them there – and found when renovations were being undertaken for the millennium. The originals were badly water-damaged but were sent off for restoration. They only came back to the County Archives last month.'

Sadie was nodding keenly in the hope it would hurry him along. It took every ounce of patience she had not to tear open the newspaper archive envelope and devour its contents in a single gulp, but listening to Alastair's enthusiastic research-related narrations was part of the deal. Never mind that she already had a perfectly adequate plan of the house and property. Alastair chattered, Sadie nodded, until finally he drew breath and she was able to squeeze in a thank you and something about the dogs needing to get home.

Her mood was strangely light as she emerged back into the brilliance of the sunlit day, packages in hand. Sadie would never have guessed in a million years that a person could gain this sort of satisfaction from a visit to the library, certainly not a person like her.

There was a small white-rendered hotel just down the road, with giddy sprays of flowers in hanging baskets, views to the harbour and a convenient wooden bench seat out front. Sadie sat against a neat sign reading HOTEL GUESTS ONLY!, tore open the envelope and scoured the article inside.

Her heart sank as she realised the information wasn't new. Clearly this was where Pickering had done his research. There were, at least, two photographs she hadn't seen before: one of an elegant, smiling woman sitting beneath a tree with three little girls in summer white dresses gathered around her and a copy of *Eleanor's Magic Doorway* on her lap; and another featuring the same woman, only this time her face was serious and drawn and a tall, handsome man had his arm around her, his hand resting on her waist by way of support. Sadie could identify the room as the Loeanneth library. It was unchanged, right down to the framed picture on the table by the French doors. DISTRAUGHT PARENTS! the headline clamoured, before continuing: *Mr and Mrs Anthony Edevane urge anyone with information on the whereabouts of their young son, Theodore, to come forward.*

There was a depth of sorrow in the woman's face that Sadie recognised. This was a woman who'd lost a part of herself. Although the letter on the ivy-rimmed paper had been written during an earlier pregnancy, the longing and love expressed for her unborn child made it clear that Eleanor was the sort of woman for whom motherhood was a blessing, her children a joy. The intervening decades had given the photograph an additional layer of resonance. It had been captured when the horror of the disappearance was hot and new, when Eleanor Edevane still believed her son would be returned and that the raw, empty hole torn by his absence was temporary. Sadie, observing the frozen moment from the future, knew better. The loss was one Eleanor would always carry, and beyond the loss itself, the agony of uncertainty. Not knowing whether her baby was dead or alive, loved or suffering, whether he cried for her through the long nights.

She set the paper aside and looked down the cobbled

lane towards the shimmer of water. Maggie Bailey's daughter
had cried for her. When Sadie and Donald discovered
Caitlyn alone in the flat in Holborn, the little girl's face had
been stained with old tears. The two of them had pushed
their way through the stack of junk mail piled behind the
door and been met with a smell so foul even steel-gutted
Donald had retched; the kitchen bin, in full sun by the
counter, had been buzzing with flies.

Sadie would never forget her first glimpse of the Bailey
child – she'd been halfway down the corridor when the
small, wide-eyed girl materialised like a ghost in her Dora
the Explorer nightie – but then they hadn't been expecting
a child. The neighbour who'd reported the smell, when ques-
tioned about the occupant of the apartment, had described a
woman who kept to herself, occasional loud music, a mother
who came to visit sometimes. She hadn't mentioned a child.
Afterwards, when Sadie asked her why not, she'd shrugged
and said, 'It didn't seem important.'

All hell had broken loose when they found her. Jesus
Christ, a child, alone for a week in a locked apartment?
Donald had called it in while Sadie sat on the floor with the
girl, with Caitlyn – they'd learned her name by then – playing with a toy bus, struggling to remember the lyrics to a
single nursery rhyme, and trying to get her head around how
this turn of events changed things. It changed them a lot.
Little girls left all alone tended to bring the services out in
force, and more police, forensics and child protection all
seemed to come at once, milling about in the tiny apartment,
measuring and searching and dusting. At some point, as the
day turned into night, the little girl had been taken away.

Sadie didn't cry over her work, not ever, despite the sad and awful things she saw, but she'd run hard that night, thudding along the pavements of Islington, through Highgate, across the darkened heath, shuffling pieces of the puzzle until they blurred into a furious fug. Sadie had trained herself not to get hung up on the emotive, human parts of crime-solving. Her job was to unravel puzzles; the people involved were important only insofar as their characters could be usefully applied to that end, determining matters of motive and confirming or collapsing alibis. But that little girl with her rumpled nightie, her bird's-nest hair, and those frightened eyes as she called for her mother, kept getting in the way.

Hell, she was still getting in the way. Sadie blinked the image out of her mind, angry with herself for having let her thoughts drift again to that bloody flat. The case was closed. She focused on the harbour instead, the fishing boats coming back to roost, the gulls circling above them, swooping and soaring.

It was the parallels between the cases, of course: mothers and their children, the removal of one from the other. The photograph of Eleanor Edevane, her face hollowed by loss, by fear when faced with separation from her son, poked at Sadie's soft spot. It exposed the same weakness that had allowed the Bailey case to weasel its way beneath her skin, that had kept her awake at night, convinced that Maggie Bailey couldn't have done it, walked out like that, left a child of two alone in a locked flat with no guarantee she'd be found in time.

'Don't mean to disappoint you, Sparrow,' Donald had

said, 'but it happens more than you'd like to think. Not everyone's cut out to be a mother.'

Sadie hadn't disagreed. She knew he was right; she knew it better than anyone. It was the manner in which Maggie appeared to have left her daughter, the carelessness, that didn't compute. 'Not like that,' she'd insisted. 'Maggie might not have been able to stick it out as the child's mother, but she wouldn't have risked her daughter suffering. She'd have called someone, made some sort of arrangement.'

And Sadie had been right, in a way. It turned out Maggie *had* made arrangements. She'd walked out of Caitlyn's life on a Thursday, the same day the little girl's father always called to collect her for his weekend custody visit. Only that week he'd been out of town on a fishing trip in Lyme Regis. 'I told her,' he'd said, cradling his cheap takeaway cup in the interview room at the Met. 'I made her write it down on a piece of paper so she wouldn't forget. I hardly ever go away, but my brother gave me a charter trip for my birthday. I wrote it down for her.' The man had been beside himself, worrying away small pieces of polystyrene as he spoke. 'If I'd only known, if she'd only said. When I think what might have happened . . .'

He'd given them information that painted a very different picture of Maggie to the one her mother, Nancy Bailey, had supplied. Not a surprise. It was maternal instinct, Sadie supposed, to paint the best possible portrait of one's child. Still, in this case it had been particularly unhelpful. It was a pity Sadie hadn't met the father, Steve, first, before she bought Nancy's story, lock, stock and barrel. 'You know the problem?' Donald had said helpfully when all was done and dusted. 'You and the grandmother, the pair of you got too chummy. Rookie mistake.' Of all the comments he'd made, that one had stung the most. Loss of objectivity, the intrusion of emotion into the realm of the rational – they were among the worst criticisms you could level at a detective.

Especially a detective for whom the accusation rang true. *Don't even think about making contact with the grandmother.* Donald was right. Sadie *had* liked Nancy, all the more because she'd said the things Sadie wanted to hear. That Maggie was a responsible, caring mother who'd have sooner died than left her child unattended, that the police were wrong, that they ought to be looking for evidence of foul play. 'Why would she lie?' Sadie had demanded of Donald. 'What's in it for her?' He'd only shaken his head and smiled with fond sympathy. 'It's her daughter, you goose. What else is she going to say?'

Sadie had been cautioned against making any further attempts to visit Caitlyn after Steve filed his complaint, but she'd seen the little girl once again, just after the case was officially closed. Caitlyn had been walking between her father and his wife, Gemma, holding their hands as they left the Met, a kind-looking couple with neat haircuts and nice clothes. Someone had brushed out the tangles and put plaits in Caitlyn's hair, and as Sadie watched, Gemma stopped to listen to something the little girl said before swinging her up onto her hip, making her laugh in the process.

It was only a brief glimpse, from a distance, but it was enough to know that things had turned out all right. The other woman in her silk wrap dress, with her kind face and tender gestures, was just what Caitlyn needed. Sadie could tell just by looking at her that Gemma was the sort of person who'd always know just what to say and do, who'd know exactly who Dora the Explorer was, and have the lyrics to any number of soothing lullabies at the ready. Evidently Donald had thought so too. 'Best thing the mother could've done for her,' he'd said later in the Fox and Hounds. 'Blind Freddy can see the kid's better off with her dad and that wife of his.' And children deserved that, didn't they, the best possible chance to thrive? God knew there were enough pitfalls out there waiting to trip them up.

Sadie's thoughts went to the letter she'd dropped in the postbox. It would have reached the girl by now. Good thing she'd printed her return address nice and clearly on the back of the envelope. No doubt they taught that sort of thing in the fancy school she went to. Charlotte Sutherland. It was a good name, Sadie had decided; not the name Sadie had given her, but a lovely name all the same. It was rich-sounding, educated and successful. The name of someone who enjoyed hockey and horses and never bit her tongue for fear of sounding stupid. All the things Sadie had wanted and wished for when she handed the tiny girl over to the nurse and watched through glazed eyes as she was carried away to a better future.

A jolting noise behind her and Sadie jumped. A stiff sash window was being jiggled and lifted in spurts. The lace curtain was drawn aside and a woman with a green plastic watering can appeared in its place, a distinctly proprietorial tilt to her nose as she glared down at the seat (HOTEL GUESTS ONLY!), and more specifically at Sadie on it.

The dogs had finished their exploring and were sitting, ears cocked, watching Sadie earnestly for a sign that it was time to go. As the hotelier began pouring water into the hanging basket directly above her, Sadie gave them a nod.

Ash and Ramsay paced ahead towards Bertie's place, while Sadie followed, trying to ignore the backlit shadow child who'd fallen into step behind her.

'Solved it yet?' Bertie called as Sadie and the dogs clattered through the front door.

She found him in the courtyard beyond the kitchen, pruning shears in hand, a small pile of weeds and trimmings on the bricks beside him. 'Almost,' she said, dropping her backpack onto the slatted garden table. 'Just the small matters of who, how and why.'

'Small matters indeed.'

Sadie leaned against the rock border wall that stopped the garden from sliding down the steep hill into the sea. She took in a deep breath and released it steadily; it was the sort of thing you had to do when confronted with a view like that. The spill of wind-silvered grass, white sand tucked into a cove between two headlands, the vast silken sea unfurling from azure to ink. Picture perfect. Just the kind of view sunburned holidaymakers posted back home to make their friends and family jealous. She wondered if she ought to buy a postcard for Donald.

'You can smell the tide rising, can't you?' Bertie said.

'And here I was blaming the dogs.'

Bertie laughed and made a judicious snip to the stem of a small flowering tree.

Sadie sat on the seat beside him, propping her feet on the steel rim of a watering can. Her grandfather had green fingers, no doubt about that. Aside from the small paved square in the centre of the garden, the rest was given over to flowers and foliage that tumbled together like sea foam.

Amid the ordered disorder, a cluster of small blue flowers with yellow starlike centres caught her eye. 'Chatham Island forget-me-nots,' she said, remembering suddenly the garden he and Ruth had created in the courtyard behind their place in London. 'I always liked them.' He'd kept them in terracotta pots back then, hung on the brick walls; amazing what he'd been able to do with nine square metres and an hour of full sun each day. She'd used to sit with him and Ruth in the evenings after the shop was closed; not at first, but later, when she'd been there a few months and the due date was drawing near. Ruth with her steaming cup of Earl Grey and her kind eyes, her infinite goodness: *Whatever you decide, Sadie, love, we'll support you.*

Sadie was surprised by a fresh surge of grief. Shocking the way it could creep up on her even now, a year later. How deeply she missed her grandmother; what she'd have given to have her here today, warm and familiar, seemingly eternal. No, not here. To have Ruth back and for Bertie never to have left their London home. It seemed like all the important decisions had been made in that tiny, walled garden with its pots and hanging baskets, so different from this open, sunlit place. She felt a deep, sudden resistance to change well up inside her, a childish swirl of petulant rage she swallowed like a bitter pill. 'Must be nice to have more garden room,' she said with brittle brightness.

Bertie smiled at her in agreement, and then gestured towards a tatty folder of papers beneath two used teacups with what looked like sludgy grass clippings in the bottom. 'You just missed Louise. Those are for you. Not much help with the case, but she thought you might like to see them anyway.'

Louise. Sadie bristled before reminding herself that the other woman was a perfectly genial human being who had just done her a favour. She glanced through the pile. They were newspapers of a sort, amateurish, each a single sheet with a masthead reading *The Loeanneth Gazette*, written in Old English font and embellished with a pen-and-ink sketch of the house and its lake. The pages were blotched and discoloured, and a couple of silverfish made bids for freedom as she turned them. The paper smelled of mildew and neglect; the headlines, however, still sparked with life, trumpeting such events as: NEW ARRIVAL: BABY BOY AT LAST!; INTERVIEW WITH MR LLEWELLYN, AUTHOR EXTRAORDINAIRE!; RARE SIGHTING: SHORT-TAILED BLUE SPOTTED IN LOEANNETH GARDEN! Each article was accompanied by an illustration credited to Clementine, Deborah or Alice Edevane, but the bylines belonged without exception to Alice.

Sadie's gaze lingered on the name and she experienced the same tightening knot of connection she felt each time one of the A-L-I-C-E engravings revealed itself at Loeanneth. 'Where did they come from?' she asked.

'One of Louise's patients at the hospital had an aunt who was a housemaid at the Lake House. She stopped working for the Edevanes back in the thirties when the family left Cornwall but these must've got mixed up with her other possessions. There was a printing press in the schoolroom, apparently, up in the attic near the maids' accommodation. The children of the house used to play with it.'

'Listen to this . . .' Sadie held the paper out of the glare and read aloud: 'INTERVIEW WITH A GROSS DEPORTER: THE ACCUSED SPEAKS! *Today we publish an exclusive interview with Clementine Edevane, who stands accused by*

The Mother of "gross deportment" after a recent incident in which she offended Nanny Rose. "But she did look fat," the accused was heard to shout from behind the gaol of her closed bedroom door. "I was only being truthful!" Truth or travesty? You, dear reader, be the judge. Story by Alice Edevane, investigative reporter.'

'Alice Edevane,' Bertie said. 'She's the one who owns the house.'

Sadie nodded. 'Also known as A. C. Edevane, crime writer extraordinaire. I wish she'd write back to my letters.'

'It hasn't been a week yet.'

'So?' said Sadie, who didn't count patience among her virtues. 'Four perfectly good days of postal service.'

'Your faith in the Royal Mail is touching.'

To be honest, Sadie had presumed Alice Edevane would be thrilled to hear from her. A bona fide police detective willing to reopen, if only unofficially, the case of her brother's disappearance? She'd expected to hear back by return post. Even if, as Bertie said, the postal service was less than perfect, she should have heard by now.

'People can be funny about the past,' said Bertie, running his fingers lightly along a fine stem. 'Especially after something painful.'

His tone remained even, his focus on the tree didn't falter, yet within his words Sadie felt the heat of an unasked question. He couldn't possibly know about Charlotte Sutherland and the letter that had brought the whole awful business back into the present. A gull cawed, slicing through the sky above them, and for a split second Sadie considered telling him about the girl with the clear, confident handwriting and clever turn of phrase.

But it would be a stupid thing to do, especially when she'd just got rid of the letter. He'd want to talk things over and there'd be no forgetting the whole thing then, and so, instead, she said, 'The newspaper report finally arrived,' pulling her research from the backpack, making a small stack on her lap of library books, archive folders and the writing pad she'd picked up at WHSmith. 'There were some photos I hadn't seen, but nothing particularly useful.'

She thought she heard him sigh, sensing perhaps the unspoken confidence, and was beset by a sudden sliver of awareness that he was the only person in the world she loved, that if she lost him she'd be all alone. 'So,' he said, knowing better than to push, 'we're pretty sure he was taken, but we're no closer to knowing how or by whom.'

'Right.'

'Any theories as to why?'

'Well, I think we can rule out opportunistic predators. There was a party going on, and the house is well off the beaten track. Not the sort of place a person just happens upon.'

'Unless they're chasing a dog, of course.'

Sadie returned his smile. 'Which leaves two possibilities. He was taken because someone wanted money, or because they wanted a child for themselves.'

'But there was no ransom note?'

'Not according to Pickering, but police don't always make these things public. It's on the list for Clive Robinson.'

'You've heard from him?'

'No, but he was due back yesterday, so fingers crossed.'

Bertie pruned another stem from his tree. 'Let's say it wasn't about money.'

'Then it was about the boy. And this boy in particular. It doesn't make sense that someone who simply wanted a child would choose the son of a wealthy, upper-class family with all possible resources at their fingertips to find him.'

'It would seem a foolish choice,' Bertie agreed. 'There must've been easier pickings.'

'Which means whoever took Theo Edevane wanted him because of who he was. But why?' Sadie jittered her pen on the writing pad. It was cheap paper, thin to the point of near-translucence, and sunlight picked out the imprints from the last letter she'd written. She sighed. 'It's no use. Until I get more information – hear back from Alice Edevane, speak to Clive Robinson, get a better feel for the people involved and find out who had means, motive and opportunity – it's all just guesswork.'

There was a new sense of frustration in her voice and Bertie noticed. 'You're really intent on solving it, aren't you?'

'I don't like loose ends.'

'It's been a long time. Most of the people who might have missed that little boy are long gone.'

'That's not the point. He was taken; it isn't right; his family deserve to know what happened to him. Here . . .' She held out the newspaper. 'Look at his mother, look at her face. She created him, named him, loved him. He was her child and she lived the whole rest of her life without him, never knowing what happened, what he grew up to be, whether he was happy. Never being certain if he was alive or dead.'

Bertie hardly glanced at the paper, fixing Sadie instead with a look of kind perplexity. 'Sadie, love—'

'It's a puzzle,' she went on quickly, aware that she was sounding strident but unable to rein it in. 'You know me, you know I can't let them go unsolved. How on earth was a child removed from a house filled with people? There's something I'm not seeing. Doors, windows, a ladder like in the Lindbergh kidnapping?'

'Sadie, this holiday of yours—'

Ash barked suddenly and both dogs scrambled to their feet, racing to the rock wall on the side of the garden that bordered the lane.

Sadie heard it too, then, a small motorbike approaching the cottage and stopping. There was a squeak and a soft thud as the letterbox on the front door opened and a clutch of letters dropped through onto the mat. 'Post,' she said.

'I'll go.' Bertie set down his pruning shears and dusted his hands on his gardening apron. He gave Sadie a light, thoughtful frown before ducking his head and disappearing through the door into the kitchen.

Sadie waited until he was gone before letting her smile collapse. Her face ached. It was getting harder to hold off Bertie's questions. She hated lying to him, it made fools of both of them, but she couldn't bear for him to know she'd messed up so prodigiously at work. What she'd done, going to the press, was embarrassing, shameful even. Worse, he'd be bound to ask *why* she'd behaved so wildly out of character. Which brought them back to Charlotte Sutherland and her letter. She couldn't tell him about that. She didn't think she'd be able to stand seeing his kind face contorting in sympathy as he listened. She had a terrible fear that to speak about it would make it real somehow and she'd be back there, trapped inside the body of her panicked, powerless younger self, cowering before the giant wave that was coming for her. She wasn't that girl anymore. She refused to be.

So why was she acting like it? Sadie frowned. That's exactly what she was doing, wasn't it? Letting Donald call all the shots while she languished indefinitely in limbo, waiting to be invited back to a job at which she excelled. At which she'd worked damn hard to succeed. She'd faced down countless adversities to rise in the ranks; why was she behaving so meekly now, hiding out beside the flat summery sea behind a case with a trail that had gone cold seventy years before?

On a whim, Sadie took her mobile from her pocket. She jostled it lightly back and forth between her hands for a few seconds, and then, with a decisive sigh, went over to the furthermost point of the garden. She climbed up onto the rock wall and leaned as far as she could away from the house until a single bar of connectivity showed up on her screen. She dialled Donald's number and waited, muttering beneath her breath, 'Come on, come on . . .'

The phone went straight to voicemail and Sadie cursed into the breeze. Rather than hang up and try again, she listened to Donald's curt message and then left her own. 'Yeah, Donald, look, it's Sadie. Just to let you know, I'm coming up to London. I've sorted things my end and I'm ready to get back to work, Monday week. It'd be great to catch up beforehand. You know, show you my holiday snaps . . .' The small joke fell flat even to her own ears, and she pressed on. 'Anyway, let me know when and where suits. Sometime next week?' She left it at that, statement as question, and then she ended the call.

There. Sadie heaved a purposeful sigh. It was done. Now, when Bertie asked her about her plans she'd be able to give him some proper answers: after a short, pleasant trip to Cornwall, she'd be going home to London next week.

She tucked the phone back into her pocket and returned to her seat near Bertie's tree, waiting for the onset of welcome peace of mind. But her mind was far from peaceful. Now that she'd done it, her thoughts comprised a list of things she should have done differently. She should have been more specific as to place and time. She should have been gentler, more apologetic, made it seem like it was his idea.

Sadie remembered now his threat to go to Ashford if she didn't follow his instructions to the letter. Donald was her partner, though; he was a reasonable man. He'd had her best interests at heart when he forced her to take leave and she'd learned her lesson, she wouldn't be leaking to journalists in the future; but the Bailey case was closed now, it had all but disappeared from the papers, no real harm had been done. (So long as she didn't take Nancy Bailey into account. Sadie winced as she pictured the look on the woman's face when they'd informed her the investigation was over. 'But I thought you believed me, that my girl never would've left like that. I thought you were going to find her?')

Pushing Nancy Bailey from her mind (*Don't even think about making contact with the grandmother*), Sadie told herself she'd done the right thing and concentrated on believing it.

The new map of the Loeanneth estate was still on her lap and she forced her attention back to it, a resolute attempt at diversion. It was much older than the one Alastair had given her earlier – 1664, according to the title at the top – drawn back when the Lake House had still been a smaller adjunct to the large manor on the property. Despite some antiquated spelling and a font that rendered certain words illegible, the layout was nonetheless instantly recognisable to Sadie, who'd spent the past week studying the floorplan in the hope she could somehow intuit the path taken by Theo's abductor that night. The rooms and spaces were all where they should be.

Except . . . Sadie looked more closely.

She took the original map out of her folder and laid the two side by side to compare.

There *was* a variation in this floorplan after all. A little room or cavity, right near the nursery, that wasn't marked on the more recent map.

But what was it? A cupboard? Did they have built-in cupboards in the seventeenth century? Sadie suspected not. And even if they did, why include this one in the floorplan and not others?

Sadie tapped her lips thoughtfully. She looked from Bertie's tree, to the dogs settled now at the base of the rock wall, and finally out to sea. Her gaze settled on the dark blip of a ship balanced on the horizon.

And then, the vague flicker of a light bulb.

Sadie riffled through her papers until she found the notes she'd made from 'Chapter eight: The deShiels of Havelyn'.

There it was: the house was built during the reign of Henry VIII by a long-ago seafaring deShiel who'd purloined gold from Spain. There was another name for people like that.

Connections were flaring in Sadie's mind like ancient warning beacons, each causing the next to catch alight: a possible deShiel pirate . . . Louise's talk of smugglers . . . of tunnels dug into the Cornish coastline . . . the tunnel in

Eleanor's Magic Doorway with its real-world counterpart . . . the pillar and ring Sadie had seen with her own eyes . . .

'Something for you,' said Bertie, back from collecting the post and holding out a small envelope.

She took it wordlessly, so distracted by the theory forming in her mind that she hardly registered the name printed neatly on the top left-hand corner.

'It's from the police officer,' Bertie urged. 'Clive Robinson from Polperro. Aren't you going to . . . ?' He faltered. 'What is it, what did I miss? You look as if you've seen a ghost.'

Sadie might not have seen a ghost, but she had a feeling she'd just glimpsed a shadow. 'This room,' she said, as Bertie came to peer over her shoulder. 'This tiny alcove – I think I might have found the escape route.'

Twelve

London, 2003

This particular corner of South Kensington was thick with ghosts, which was why the Edevane sisters had chosen it in the first place. They took tea at the V&A every year on the anniversary of Eleanor's death, but they met at the Natural History Museum first. Their father had donated his entire collection to the museum in his will, and it seemed to Alice there was more of his spirit in this building than lingered anywhere else.

It made sense to remember their parents formally on the same day. Theirs had been the sort of romance that writers trumpeted and real people envied, two beautiful young strangers who'd met by chance, loved at first sight, before being separated, tested and strengthened by the First World War. Alice and her sisters had accepted the relationship unquestioningly as children, growing to adulthood in the embrace of Eleanor and Anthony's devotion. But it was the sort of love that rendered all other people outsiders. Except for a small, stable circle of friends, they socialised rarely and reluctantly, and in retrospect it was their very isolation that added an extra layer of magic and wonder to the annual Midsummer party. When Eleanor had died suddenly like that, unexpectedly, and so soon after her husband, people had shaken their heads at the tragedy before assuring the sisters that, 'Of course, they belonged together, the two of them.' Those same smarmy people had gone on behind the sisters' backs, in whispers laced with implication: 'It's like she couldn't *bear* to be parted from him.'

Alice got to the museum first, just as she always did. It was part of their habit; a tacit agreement allowing Alice to feel punctual and Deborah bustling. She settled herself on a bench in the Central Hall and reached into her bag, stroking the smooth, worn leather of her notebook before taking it out and laying it on her lap. This was not unusual; ordinarily Alice enjoyed nothing more than watching people and she'd learned over time that what was considered nosy under usual circumstances passed for distracted, even charming, when done with pen and paper in hand. Today, though, she had no intention of taking notes. She was far too preoccupied with her own plight to bother with strangers.

She opened the notebook and eyeballed the letter she'd filed inside. She didn't reread it, there was no need. It was the second she'd received, similar in content to the first. The detective had pressed again for an interview but been deliberately vague as to her current knowledge of the Edevane case (as she called it). A wise move and precisely what Alice would have written for Diggory Brent had he developed a fierce interest in an unsolved crime while holidaying in Cornwall. Any detective worth her salt knew that providing only the barest scaffolding left the biggest hole into which an unsuspecting witness might fall. Unfortunately for Sadie Sparrow, Alice wasn't unsuspecting and had no intention of being tricked into revealing anything she didn't want to. Deborah, on the other hand . . .

Alice closed the book and used it to fan her cheeks. She'd been lying in bed the night before, wondering how best to handle the situation, weighing up the odds this Sparrow person would discover anything important, reassuring herself that it had all taken place so long ago that there could be nothing left to find, when it struck her that Deborah might also have received a letter. An invisible blade of panic had sliced cold through her at the realisation.

She'd considered the possibility from all angles before deciding that Deborah, innocent of all wrongdoing, would have got in touch immediately had she been contacted. With Tom's political legacy to safeguard, she'd have been horrified to think of some eager young stranger raking through the family's coals and keen to enlist Alice's help. It wasn't until this morning, as the taxi wended its way through St John's Wood, that it occurred to Alice that Deborah might be waiting to discuss the matter in person. That with Eleanor's anniversary meeting so conveniently near, she might simply have tucked the letter in her handbag and was preparing herself even now to broach the subject.

Alice exhaled bracingly and looked again towards the entrance. There was no sign of Deborah yet, but a hapless man in black jeans was creating something of a fuss by the doors. Alice had noticed him when she arrived. He'd been holding the hand of a small girl in a bright pink singlet and denim dungarees. The girl had been pointing and jumping, the man – her father, Alice supposed – trying to temper her enthusiasm while he reached to retrieve something (a water bottle, perhaps? Children these days always seemed in need of rehydration) from the small backpack he was carrying.

The man was in quite a state now, hands flapping at a

security guard, and the little girl was no longer with him. The searing panic of a parent who'd lost a child; Alice could spot it from a mile away. Her gaze drifted beyond the enormous diplodocus skeleton to the grand stone stairwell at the end of the cavernous room. The little girl had been pointing that way when Alice saw her, she'd had a ball clasped in her other hand, the sort that fired when shaken, as if made from electricity, and there'd been an unmistakable glint of determination in her eyes. Sure enough, the child was standing now at the top of the stairs, cheek resting on the cool, flat stone of the balustrade, lining the ball up in front of her face, readying to let it roll.

Elementary, my dear Watson. Alice tried to enjoy the familiar comfort of being correct. She'd always had a good memory – more than that, an ability to draw conclusions based on available evidence. It was a skill she credited her father with honing. He'd played games with them when they were young, possessing an insatiable appetite for the sort of play other adults found tiresome. He'd taken them with him on his nature rambles, letting them carry this tool or that, the coveted butterfly net if they were lucky, stopping every so often to crouch at their eye level and point out a scene. 'Paint a picture in your mind,' he would say, 'but don't just see the tree. Notice the lichen on its trunk, the holes made by the woodpecker, the thinner leaves where the sun doesn't reach.' Later, sometimes days later, when it was least expected, he'd say, 'Alice! The tree in the wood, ten things.' And then he'd close his eyes and count on his fingers as she conjured the scene for him, memory by memory.

Even now, echoes of the thrill of being the one to make him smile stirred her. He'd been a terrific smiler, one of those people whose whole face was captive to his mood; so different from Eleanor, whose fine breeding had made her strait-laced and wary. One of the great mysteries of Alice's childhood was how Eleanor of the fairy tales, that adventurous sprite of a girl, could possibly have grown into such a stern, predictable adult. The hovering presence of Mother was an enduring childhood memory, watching and waiting for one of them to step out of line so she could seize the opportunity, send them away and have Anthony for herself. It had taken Alice years to understand that her mother was envious of them, of the close relationship they shared with their father, of how much he loved them.

'Yes, but it's rather more complex than that,' Deborah had said when they'd spoken of it. Alice had pushed her as to how, and after choosing her words carefully, Deborah had said, 'I think she was envious of him, too, in a way. Do you remember during the war, when we were little, how different she was, how fun and playful? How it used to feel as if she were one of us, rather than a proper grown-up like Grandmother or Nanny Bruen?' Alice had nodded uncertainly as Deborah's words stirred faraway memories of hide-and-seek and enchanted stories. 'But then Daddy came home and we adored him, and she sort of lost us. Everything changed. *She* changed after that, became a different, stricter person. She couldn't – ' Deborah had stopped abruptly then, as if thinking better of whatever it was she'd been about to say. 'Well,' she'd continued with a wave of the hand. 'There wasn't room for both of them to be the favourite, was there?'

A familiar figure by the door caught Alice's eye. Deborah, her arm linked through James's for support. As they reached the hall, Deborah laughed at something her young driver said. She patted his hand fondly and bade him farewell. Alice exhaled. Her sister didn't look like someone who'd received a grenade in the post.

Deborah remained where she was for a moment after James left, the general fluster of other people's meetings and greetings swirling around her. She was practised, as were all politician's wives, at maintaining a pleasant visage, but Alice had always been able to see beneath the mask: a slight tightening about the mouth, the habit brought with her from childhood of pressing her fingertips together in agitation. Neither was in evidence this morning. Alice felt her tension recede, but didn't glance away. One rarely took the time to look closely at those one knew well. Deborah was still tall and poised, even as she approached ninety, still elegant, wearing the same satin dresses she'd worn throughout the 1930s, cinched at the waist and with dainty pearl buttons climbing from belt to lace collar. She was like one of Daddy's butterflies, caught at the peak of her beauty and frozen in time, eternally feminine. Quite the opposite of Alice in her trousers and brogues.

Alice stood and waved, catching her sister's attention. Deborah was walking with a cane today so Alice knew her leg was troubling her. She knew, too, that when she enquired after her health, Deborah would smile and claim she'd never felt better. It was inconceivable that any of the Edevane girls might admit to frailty, pain or regret. Emotional fortitude was part of Eleanor's legacy, along with prompt letter-writing and a contempt for sloppy grammar.

'Sorry I'm late,' said Deborah, arriving at the bench. 'My morning's been quite mad. I haven't kept you long?'

'Not at all, I had my notebook with me.'

'Have you been in to see the collection?'

Alice said that she had not, and they went in mutual silence to deposit Deborah's summer coat at the cloakroom. An outside observer might have described their greeting as cool, but there was nothing of Deborah's current emotional condition to be read there. They never kissed hello when they met, neither did they hug. Alice deplored the modern trend for crying and sharing, and she and Deborah were united in their disdain for giddy emotional displays.

'Well, you two must be sisters,' the young cloakroom attendant sang with a broad smile.

'Yes,' Deborah said, before Alice could respond from habit, too wryly, 'Must we?'

It was true they looked more alike in old age than they had at any other time in their lives, but then all old people looked alike to the young. The fading of hair, eyes, skin and lips, the loss of individual details as a person's real face retreated behind the mask of lines. They weren't alike really. Deborah was still beautiful – that is, she still wore the remnants of beauty – just as she'd always been. The summer she became engaged to Tom, the last summer at Loeanneth, there'd been an article in *The Times* naming her the prettiest young lady of the Season. Alice and Clemmie had been merciless in their teasing, but only for sport. The article told them nothing they hadn't already known. *In every group of sisters there was one who outshone the others.* Alice had written that line in a book, her eighth, *Death Shall Call*. She'd given the observation to Diggory Brent, who had an uncanny knack for seeing the world very much as Alice did. He was a man, though, and therefore able to think such thoughts without seeming bitter or unkind.

No, Alice decided, as Deborah laughed gaily at something the attendant had said, her sister hadn't received a
letter from Sadie Sparrow. Alice's relief was tempered by her
awareness that it was only a matter of time. That unless she
found a way to satisfy the detective's curiosity, Deborah
would almost certainly be brought in. Happily, Alice knew a
thing or two about redirection. She just needed to be calm
and methodical, more so than she had been to this point.
Alice wasn't sure what she'd been thinking when she'd told
Peter the first letter had come to the wrong address, that she
knew nothing about the missing child. She hadn't been
thinking, she'd been panicking. She intended to do less of
that.

'You're well? You look it,' Deborah said appraisingly as
she turned from the cloakroom counter.

'Very well. You?'

'Never better.' Deborah nodded in the direction of the
hall, the merest hint of distaste twisting her lips. She had
never liked Daddy's insects and their silver pins, however
much she'd fought to take her turn assisting him when they
were girls. 'Well then,' she said, leaning gingerly on her cane.
'Let's get it over with, shall we, so we can go and have tea.'

Alice and Deborah said very little as they did the rounds,
other than to note that the butterflies were all in place. The
museum curator had taken the creatures from Anthony's
display cases, redistributing them to augment the existing
collection, but Alice had no difficulty picking out those she'd
helped to gather. Each one told a story; she could almost
hear her father's gentle words as she took in the familiar
wings, the shapes and colours.

Deborah didn't complain, but it was evident her leg was troubling her, so Alice called an early end to the pilgrimage and they went across the road to the V&A. The cafe was bustling but they found a corner by the unlit fireplace in the smaller room. Alice suggested her sister mind the table while she fetched their tea, and by the time she returned, tray in hand, Deborah had a pair of reading glasses perched on the end of her nose and was peering over them at her mobile phone. 'Damn thing,' she said, stabbing at the keypad with a crimson fingernail. 'I never seem to hear it ring and do you think I can get the messages to play?'

Alice offered a small sympathetic shrug and poured the milk.

She sat back, watching the steam rise from her cup. It had occurred to her that before she spoke to the detective it would be wise to ascertain just how much her sister knew. The question was, how to begin.

While Deborah continued to fiddle with her phone, shifting it further away and then close again, muttering as she tried to read the display, Alice took a sip of tea.

Deborah frowned and pressed a key. 'Maybe if I . . . ?'

Alice set down her cup. 'I've been thinking lately of Loeanneth.'

Deborah expressed only the faintest flicker of surprise. 'Oh?'

Carefully, Alice reminded herself, *go carefully*. 'When Daddy came back from the war, do you remember how excited Mother was? The room upstairs she filled with all his favourite things: the microscope and specimen boxes, the rows of books, his old gramophone and dance records. We used to sneak upstairs to spy through the keyhole at the tall, handsome stranger in our midst.'

Deborah put down her phone and regarded Alice through slightly narrowed eyes. 'Goodness,' she said at length. 'We are nostalgic today.'

Alice ignored the implied question as to why that might be. 'Not nostalgic,' she said. 'I don't long romantically for the past. I'm simply raising the topic for discussion.'

'You and your semantics.' Deborah shook her head, amused. 'Well, if you say so. God forbid anyone accuse you of sentimentality! And yes, for the record, I do remember. They used to dance up there and you and I tried to do the same. Of course you had two left feet . . .' Deborah smiled.

'She was saving him.'

'Whatever do you mean by that?'

'Only that he must have been exhausted – the war, all those years away – and she cherished him back to his old self.'

'I suppose she did.'

'He did the same for her, later, didn't he? After Theo.' Alice strove for nonchalance. 'They were lucky to have one another. The loss of a child, the not knowing. Not many marriages would survive it.'

'That's true.' Deborah spoke cautiously, no doubt wondering why Alice was dragging the conversation in a direction they'd tacitly agreed never to go. But Alice couldn't afford to stop now. She was preparing her next question when Deborah said, 'The night before my wedding she came to my bedroom and delivered a little pep talk. She quoted 1 Corinthians.'

"Love is patient, love is kind?"

"Love keeps no record of wrongs."

'That's rather grim. Whatever did she mean?'

'I can't imagine.'

'You didn't ask her?'

'I did not.' An old acerbity had crept into Deborah's voice, though she tried valiantly to mask it, and Alice remembered something she'd forgotten. Her mother and sister had been at odds in the lead-up to Deborah's wedding, snapping at each other and inflicting long periods of silence on the rest of the household. The Edevane family had returned to London by then. Deborah's wedding to Tom had taken place only five months after Theo's disappearance and family life at Loeanneth was over. It would never resume, though none of them knew that at the time; the police case had been wound down but they still clung to hope. There'd been talk of postponing the wedding, but Deborah and Eleanor had both been adamant that it should go ahead as planned. It had been the one thing they'd agreed on at the time.

'Top-up?' said Alice, lifting the teapot. Deborah's mention of their mother's pre-wedding visit was unanticipated. She hadn't intended to revive old grievances and was anxious that the misstep shouldn't prevent her from achieving her ends.

Deborah slid her cup and saucer across the table.

'We had good times there, didn't we?' Alice continued, tea gurgling from the pot's spout. 'Before Theo.'

'We did, though I always preferred London. That lovely house in Cadogan Square, Mr Allan bringing round the Daimler, the ballrooms and dresses and nightclubs. The country didn't hold enough excitement for me.'

'It was beautiful, though. The woods, the lake, all those picnics. The gardens.' Lightly did it. 'Of course, it should have been beautiful. Mother had a team of gardeners working round the clock.'

Deborah laughed. 'Those were the days. I'm hard-pressed finding someone to dust my mantelpiece now.'

'Old Mr Harris, wasn't it, the fellow in charge, and his son, the one who'd come back from the Somme with that dreadful brain injury.'

'Adam, poor soul.'

'Adam, yes, and there was another fellow, I'm sure there was. He came in on contract.' Alice could hear her own heartbeat thumping in her ears. The cafe noise seemed far away, as if she were speaking from within the glass vacuum tube on an old radio. She said, 'Benjamin something?'

Deborah frowned, straining to remember, and then shook her head. 'It doesn't ring any bells with me, I'm afraid – but then it was a long time ago, and there were so many who came and went. One can't be expected to remember them all.'

'Quite.' Alice smiled agreement and hid behind a sip of cooling tea. She hadn't realised she was holding her breath. Relief flowed, but with it came a strange deflation. For a split second she'd been fully prepared to hear Deborah say, 'Munro. His name was Benjamin Munro,' and the expectation had been thrilling. She fought a sudden temptation to push further, to force Deborah to remember him, as if in some way her sister's collusion would conjure him back to life, allow her to talk about him and therefore feel again the way she had back then. But it was a foolish urge, a madness, and she extinguished it. She had learned what she needed to:

Deborah had no memory of Ben, and Alice was safe. The wisest thing now was to move the conversation swiftly on to safer ground. She buttered a scone and said, 'What news of Linda?'

Alice only half listened as Deborah picked up the well-worn topic. The tedious story of The Errant Granddaughter mattered to Alice only insofar as she was planning to leave Loeanneth to Linda. She hadn't much choice in the matter. The house was entailed and she had no descendants of her own; those she might have had were little more than ghosts on the end of the bed on nights when she couldn't sleep, and to sell the house was unthinkable.

'Pippa's beside herself, of course,' Deborah was saying, 'that was her on my voicemail before – and one can hardly blame her. They call it a gap year, but Linda's been gone almost five.'

'Well, she's young, and exploring runs in the blood.'

'Yes, and we both know what happened to Great-Grand-father Horace.'

'I don't think there are Carib tribes in Australia. She's far more likely to lose herself to Sydney's beaches than cannibalism.'

'That's cold comfort for Pippa, I'm afraid.'

'Linda will find her way home eventually.' *When her allowance runs out*, Alice thought tartly, though she refrained from saying so. They'd never discussed the matter candidly, but Alice held grave reservations about Linda's character. She was quite sure Deborah felt the same way, but one didn't criticise one's sister's only granddaughter, not openly, it was bad manners. Besides, Deborah's difficulty conceiving had conferred the status of royalty onto her meagre issue. 'You'll see, she'll arrive back a new woman, a *better* woman, for the experience.'

'I hope you're right.'

As did Alice. The Lake House had been in the deShiel family for centuries and Alice had no intention of being the one to let it go.

It had been a shock when the house came to her in the aftermath of Eleanor's death. But then their mother's death itself had been a shock. It was 1946 and the war was over. After all that dying and destruction it had seemed scandalous that a person might step out onto the street and have her life extinguished by a bus en route from Kilburn to Kensington. Especially a person like Eleanor. It just wasn't the sort of death one expected for a woman like her.

The bus driver had suffered dreadfully. At the inquest he'd broken down and wept. He'd noticed Eleanor, he said, standing on the pavement, and he'd thought what a dignified lady she looked in her smart suit, carrying that leather briefcase. He'd wondered where she might be going. There was something about her expression, he said, as if she were lost in thought, but then a child at the back of his bus had begun screaming and he'd looked away from the road, only briefly, only for the merest second, you understand, and the next thing he knew, *thump*. That was the word he used. *Thump*. Alice could still hear him when she closed her eyes.

She hadn't wanted the house, Loeanneth, none of them had wanted it, but their mother's reasoning had seemed clear: Deborah was wealthy, Clemmie was dead, which left only Alice. Alice, however, knew Eleanor better than that; she understood that there was more to the legacy than met the eye. There were nights afterwards, when the darkness

closed in around her, when Alice was already feeling sorry
for herself, drinking too much at the bare table in the bleak
flat, her thoughts too loud in the peacetime quiet, when the
walls she'd built against the past began to tremble. It had
been back in her other life, just before she started writing,
before Diggory Brent gave her somewhere to funnel her fears
and regrets. Those nights, it would be clear to Alice that her
mother had been punishing her with the Loeanneth legacy.
That Eleanor had always blamed her for Theo's loss, even if
she'd never said it in as many words. And what an exquisite
punishment it was, how *right*, to be given possession of a
place she loved more than any other in the world but that
the past rendered out of bounds.

Thirteen

Alice caught the Tube home to Hampstead. An announcement advised of a person under a train at Goodge Street station so she took the Piccadilly line all the way to King's Cross. A pair of lovers travelled in the carriage with her, pressed together at the end amongst other people's suitcases. The girl was leaning against the boy, laughing a little as he whispered in her ear.

Alice met the eye of a pompous-looking man opposite. He raised his brows sniffily at the pair, but Alice refused to ally herself with him and looked away. She remembered love, all-encompassing, young-people love, even though it had been a long time since she'd felt it. There was beauty in love like that, just as certainly as there was danger. Love like that made the rest of the world disappear; it had the power to make even the most sensible person take leave of her senses.

Had Benjamin Munro asked Alice to die for him that summer she was quite certain she'd have done so. He hadn't, of course, he'd asked very little of her as it turned out. But then, he hadn't needed to ask; she'd gladly given him everything he wanted.

Alice had thought at the time she'd been so secretive. Silly child. She'd thought herself so clever and grown-up. But she'd been blind, love had blinded her to faults, both her own and his, just as William Blake had said it must. Love made people lawless, winged and unconfined; it made them careless. And they had been seen together, she and Ben. Deborah might not have known about them, but someone else had.

As the Tube rattled along, two long-ago voices came back to her as if from an old wireless, transmitting across the decades. It had been a winter's night in 1940, the height of the Blitz, and Clemmie had been in London briefly on un-expected leave, bunking in Alice's tiny flat. They'd been exchanging war stories over a bottle of gin. Clemmie's work with the Air Transport Auxiliary, Alice's tales of bomb-site recovery, and, as the hour got later, the bottle emptier and the sisters more sentimental, talk had turned to their father and the Great War, the horrors he must have seen and that they were only now beginning to grasp.

'He hid it well, didn't he?' Clemmie said.

'He wouldn't have wanted to burden us.'

'But he never said a *word*. Not one. I can't imagine living through all this, only to set it aside completely and abso-lutely when the war ends. I can see myself boring my grand-children to tears when I'm an old, old lady, talking their ears off with stories of the war and my part in it. But not Daddy. I never would've guessed he'd been through the trenches. The mud and the rats and the hell of watching his men die. Did he ever talk about it with you?'

Alice shook her head. 'I do remember him saying he was glad he'd had daughters, that no child of his would have to fight if another war came along.' She raised her glass to Clemmie's uniform and half smiled. 'I guess no one's right all the time.'

'Not even Daddy,' Clemmie agreed. 'And no matter what he said, he did want a son.'

'All men do, according to Grandmother deShiel.' Alice didn't add that the noxious old woman had made her pronouncement in October 1920, directly after Clemmie was born, chiding their mother that a third daughter was no way to welcome her husband home from the war.

'Anyway, he got one in the end,' Clemmie said. 'He got his son in the end.'

They'd sat in silence then, conversation having brought them to their childhood and the great taboo subject of their brother, each lost in her own gin-soaked memories of the past. The baby in the flat upstairs had begun to cry, a siren sounded in a distant part of London, and Alice stood, the room tilting as she gathered their empty glasses with one hand, carrying them between her fingers to the butler sink beneath the small, sooty window criss-crossed with tape. Her back was turned when Clemmie said, 'I saw that man on his way to France, the gardener who worked for a time at Loeanneth.'

The word crackled like a struck match in the chilly room. Alice balled her hands inside the sleeves of her knitted jumper. Steeling herself, she turned to face her sister and heard herself say, 'Which gardener?'

Clemmie was staring at the wooden tabletop, tracing its grain with her short fingernail. She didn't answer, knowing, of course, that there was no need, they both knew who she meant. 'Allie,' she said, the childhood nickname making Alice shiver, 'there's something I need to – that I've been meaning to . . . Something I saw, back when we were kids.'

Alice's heart thumped like the hammer on a clock. She

braced herself, one part of her wanting to close the conversation down, the other part, the drunk part, tired of running from the past, cavalier in this time of ever-present death and danger, almost inviting it. Frightening, the way alcohol took the restraints off confession.

'It was that summer, the last summer. We'd been to the air show a few months before and I was obsessed with planes. I used to run around the house, remember, pretending I was flying.'

Alice nodded, her throat was dry.

'I'd been down to the base, the one beyond Jack Martin's farm. I used to go there sometimes, just to watch the planes taking off and landing, imagining what it would be like to fly them myself one day. I was late coming home so I cut back through the woods, along the river. I wound up at the old boathouse.'

Alice's vision blurred and she blinked at a painting on the wall, something left by the flat's previous occupant, a ship in a stormy sea. That ship was moving now. Alice watched, mildly surprised, as it listed from side to side.

'I wouldn't have stopped, I was hungry and in a hurry to get home, but I heard a voice inside, a man's voice.'

Alice closed her eyes. For years she'd dreaded this moment, envisaged different scenarios, rehearsed explanations and excuses in her mind; now it was upon her she couldn't think of anything to say.

'I knew it wasn't Daddy or Mr Llewellyn and I was curious. I went to the window. I couldn't help it. I climbed up on the upturned boat and I saw, Alice, I didn't mean to but I did. That man, the gardener—'

'Look out!' Alice interrupted, leaping to grab the gin

bottle from the table, knocking it over in the process. Glass smashed and Clemmie jumped from her seat. She brushed at her clothes, startled by the sudden clatter, the cold liquor.

'I'm so sorry,' Alice said, 'your elbow – the bottle was about to drop. I tried to catch it.' She hurried to the sink and brought back a cloth, dripping water everywhere.

'Alice, stop it.'

'God, you're soaking wet. Let me fetch you another shirt.'

Clemmie protested but Alice insisted, and by the time clothes had been changed and the spill cleaned up, the mood for disclosure was gone. Next morning, Clemmie was gone, too. The space on the floor where she'd rolled out her kit was empty and all trace of her removed.

Alice had felt a swell of relief so great it rendered her light-headed. Even the note on the table couldn't put a dent in her spirits: *Had to go, early flight scheduled. See you when I'm back. Need to talk. Important. C.*

She'd scrunched that piece of notepaper into a tight ball and thanked God for the reprieve.

It turned out God could be cruel. Two days later, Clemmie was shot down over the ocean, four miles from the English coast. Her plane washed up but her body was never found. *The pilot is presumed to have ejected*, the report read, *immediately before the plane was hit*. Just one more loss in a world that had decided life was cheap. Alice was not self-absorbed enough to believe that other people's fates were lived out in service to her own life's lessons; she abhorred the expression 'everything happens for a reason'. Certainly there were consequences to everything that happened, but that was an entirely different prospect. So, she chose to see it as an instance of simple coincidence, that the death of one sibling had spared her implication in the death of another.

Alice still saw her sister when she least expected it. On summer's days, when she glanced towards the pulsing sun and her vision starred; a black speck shooting through the sky, turning a graceful arc, falling silently into the sea; that little girl who'd run circles in the fields, arms outstretched; the second of Alice's siblings to disappear. *Oh that I had wings like a dove! for then would I fly away, and be at rest.*

The train slid into King's Cross and the lovers hopped off, heading towards the exit. Alice fought an urge to follow them; just to remain, for a brief time, on the periphery of their heady infatuation.

She didn't, of course. She switched to the Northern line and travelled to Hampstead where finally she took the lift to the surface. She hadn't time for wistfulness or nostalgia; she had to get back, to see Peter and set repairs in motion. It was a lovely afternoon up top. The day's heat had slid away, the sun had lost its dazzle, and Alice walked the familiar path home.

Peter took up a yellow highlighter and drew it neatly over the lines. It was the end of a long day, and he allowed himself a moment of silent celebration. Alice's publisher wanted the website up in a month's time and he'd been tasked with providing the text – a job made rather more difficult than it might have been by the ardent refusal of the site's subject to involve herself in its preparation.

It wasn't anything so simple or clichéd as an octogenarian's refusal to admit the newfangled; indeed, Alice made it a point of pride to keep up-to-date with technology. The internet had made a huge difference to policing practices during Diggory's lifetime and Alice was stringent about maintaining realism in her books. Where she took umbrage was with the 'insidious infringement' of the public sphere into the private. Marketing was all well and good, she said, but when the author became more important than the books the world had surely tipped off-kilter. Only with the fiftieth anniversary upcoming, and a personal plea from the head of the publishing company, had she been induced to accede, and only on one condition: 'I don't want to know about it, Peter. Just make it happen, will you?'

Peter had promised that he would and proceeded gingerly, careful to avoid all mention of words like 'online' and 'platform' in her hearing. The author bio had been easy enough – they already had a standard document he kept updated for press releases – and Peter was rather proud of the special page he'd put together from the perspective of Diggory Brent himself, but he was working now on the Frequently Asked Questions section and things were progressing slowly. The problem was, the job necessarily relied on Alice's responses. Without her cooperation he was stuck hunting through the archives for articles from which he might pluck answers.

He had focused on the subject of writing and process, partly because he knew it would please Alice and partly because it made life easier. Alice didn't grant a lot of interviews these days, and those she did were conducted under the strict condition that she would talk only about her work. She guarded her privacy with a fervour Peter worried sometimes (quietly, to himself and never where she might intuit his concern) was verging on the neurotic.

He had, however, included a few personal questions out of deference to Alice's publicist, who'd sent through a 'short list' of thirty suggestions, and in order to find answers he'd needed to go back decades. Alice's own archives were less than ordered. There'd been some interesting and varied filing systems implemented over the years, and the task was more complicated than it might have been.

But here, finally, success. In an interview with the *Yorkshire Post* dated August 1956, he'd found a quote from Alice that, with a little massaging, could be made to fit one of the problematic personal questions:

Q: What kind of child were you? Were you a writer even then?

Peter looked back over the lines he'd just highlighted.

A: I was always a scribbler, the sort of child told off for writing on walls, or carving my name into furniture. I was fortunate to be given great encouragement by a family friend, a published writer who never seemed to tire of indulging a child in her flights of fancy. One of the greatest gifts I ever received was my first journal. My father gave it to me. How I treasured that book! I carried it with me everywhere and developed a predilection for notebooks I've never lost. My father gave me a new one every year. I wrote an entire mystery novel, my first, in the notebook I received for my fifteenth birthday.

It would do perfectly. Humming to himself, Peter scrolled down the document on his computer screen, hunting for the blank space awaiting an answer. Warm afternoon light spilled across the keyboard. A bus sighed to a stop on the road outside, a woman with laughter in her voice called for someone to 'Hurry up!', and down on the High Street a busker played Led Zeppelin on an electric guitar.

Peter was already mentally packing his bags, envisaging the long bus ride home with Pip and Abel Magwitch for company, when another question in the document caught his attention. Or, more properly, the answer he'd typed below it.

Q: In the Blink of an Eye *was your first published Diggory Brent novel, but was it the first manuscript you ever completed?*

A: It was. I'm one of those rare, lucky authors who never had to contend with a rejection notice.

Peter stopped humming. He glanced again at the high-lighted lines.

The two answers didn't exactly contradict each other. There was a difference between completing a manuscript and writing a novel in a teenage journal, yet something tugged at Peter's memory.

He scrabbled back through the pile of photocopies on the desk, seeking the pages from which he'd taken the second Q&A. He found it in a 1996 interview with the *Paris Review* and read on.

INTERVIEWER: In the Blink of an Eye *was the first manuscript you completed, but surely not the first you'd started?*

EDEVANE: In fact it was.

INTERVIEWER: You'd never set pen to paper to write fiction before beginning In the Blink of an Eye?

EDEVANE: Never. It hadn't crossed my mind to write a story, let alone a mystery, until after the war. The character of Diggory Brent came to me in a dream one night and the next morning I started writing. He's an archetype, of course, though any series writer who tells you their character doesn't share his or her preoccupations and interests is lying.

Peter heard the clock on the mantelpiece ticking. He stood up, stretched, finished his glass of water, then went to the window. It didn't matter how he tried to twist it, the two interviews were in direct contradiction.

He went back to stand behind the desk. His cursor was blinking by the word 'lying'.

Alice was not a liar. Indeed, she was scrupulously honest; honest to the point of causing offence in many cases.

The discrepancy was a mistake then. Forty years had passed between the first and second answers being given, in which time she'd forgotten. Alice was eighty-six years old. There were parts of Peter's childhood he couldn't remember with any certainty and he was only thirty.

Still, he wasn't about to put anything on the web that risked Alice being called out. It wasn't easy to get away with untruths or disparities anymore. Everything was instantly verifiable. Discrepancies were caught like insects in the web. It was no longer possible to be forgotten.

Peter reached down to tap the keyboard idly with one finger. Not a big deal, just an irritation. He couldn't exactly ask Alice directly which interview was accurate. He'd promised to make the website happen without bothering her and he valued his life too much to risk insinuating she'd told a fib.

His eyes drifted again to the screen.

It hadn't crossed my mind to write a story, let alone a mystery, until after the war . . . How I treasured that book! I carried it with me everywhere and developed a predilection for notebooks I've never lost . . . I wrote an entire mystery novel, my first, in the notebook I received for my fifteenth birthday.

Footfalls scuffed on the steps outside, and Peter looked at the clock. The front door opened and he heard Alice in the hall.

'Peter?'

'In the library,' he called, hitting the shutdown button so his page reduced to a single electronic speck. 'I was just finishing up. Cup of tea before I go?'

'Yes, please.' Alice appeared at the door. 'I've a few matters I'd like to discuss with you.' She looked tired, more fragile than he was accustomed to seeing her. She seemed to be wearing the day's warmth in the creases of her clothes, her skin, her manner. 'Any messages?' she said, sitting down to remove her shoes.

'Jane called about the new novel, Cynthia wants to talk about publicity, and there was a call from Deborah.'

'Deborah?' Alice looked up sharply.

'Only half an hour ago.'

'But I just saw her. Is she all right? Did she leave a message?'

'Yes.' Peter shifted interview files aside to find his note. 'It's here somewhere. I wrote it down so I wouldn't forget.' He found the piece of paper and frowned at his own scrawl. Deborah was always formal on the phone, but today she'd been unusually circumspect, insisting that he repeat her message to Alice verbatim, that it was important. 'She said to tell you that she *did* remember him, and that his name was Benjamin Munro.'

Fourteen

Cornwall, 23 June 1933

On his last morning at Loeanneth, Theo Edevane woke with the birds. He was only eleven months old and far too young to understand about time, let alone to be able to tell it, but if he had and he could, he'd have known that the hands on the big nursery clock had just gone to six minutes past five. Theo only knew that he liked the way the morning light caught the silver arrowheads of the hands and made them shine.

With his thumb stuck in his mouth, and Puppy warm beneath his arm, he rolled contentedly onto his side and gazed through the half-light to where his nanny was asleep on the single bed within the nook. Her spectacles were not on her nose, and without their metal arms to hold things together, her face had collapsed against the pillow, a series of lines and creases and soft saggy pockets.

Theo wondered where his other nanny was, Nanny Rose. He missed her (though the details of what it was he missed were already fading). This new one was older and stiffer with a smell that made his nose tickle. She kept a damp handkerchief tucked inside her black cotton sleeve and a bottle of castor oil on the window ledge. She often said 'there's no such word as "can't"' and 'self-praise is no recommendation', and liked to sit him in the big black perambulator and wheel him up and down the bumpy driveway. Theo didn't like sitting in the baby carriage, not now that he could walk; he'd tried to tell her so, but he hadn't many words and Nanny Bruen had only said, 'Quiet, Master Theodore. We did not ask Mr Rude along.'

Theo was listening to the birds outside his window, watching the dawn creep along his ceiling, when the sound of the nursery door opening made him roll onto his tummy and peer eagerly through the cot rails.

There, peeking back at him in the gap between the door and its jamb, was his big sister, the one with the long brown braids and freckles all over her cheeks, and Theo felt excitement and love explode inside him. He scrambled to his feet and grinned, slapping his hands on the edge of his cot so the brass knobs on the corners rang.

Theo had three big sisters and he loved them all, but this one was his favourite. The others smiled at him and cooed and told him he was a sweet baby, but they couldn't be counted on in quite the same way. Deborah put him down if he got too excited and clutched at her hair or clothes, and Alice could be laughing one minute, playing a tremendous game of peek-a-boo, when suddenly she'd get a funny look in her eyes, as if she could no longer see him, and with no explanation she'd be on her feet, way up high in the distance where the grown-ups lived, stabbing at her notebook with a pen instead.

This one, though, Clemmie, never tired of tickling him and pulling funny faces and blowing big, wet raspberries on his belly. She carried him places, her warm, skinny arms wrapped tightly around his middle; and when she finally plonked him down, she didn't stop him, as the others did, just as he'd found something really interesting to explore. She never used words like *dirty* and *dangerous* and *no!*, and when she came for him first thing in the morning, like she had today, she always took him through the kitchen where there were warm loaves of fresh bread cooling on the racks, and pots of lumpy strawberry jam in the larder.

Theo snatched up Puppy in anticipation and lifted his arms high, wriggling his body as if he might somehow free himself from his cot if he just tried hard enough. He waved his hands, stretched his fingers out wide in joy, and his big sister smiled so that her eyes lit up and her freckles danced, and just as he'd *known* she would, she reached into the cot and dragged him over the edge.

As she carried him joltingly towards the door, and Nanny Bruen snuffled a snore into her pillow, exhilaration made a star of Theo's body.

'Come on, Chubby Wubby,' his sister said, smudging kisses on the top of his head, 'let's go and look at the planes.'

They started down the stairs together and Theo beamed at the red carpet runner and thought of warm bread with butter *and* jam spread on it, and ducks by the stream and the treasures he would find in the mud, and his sister's arms out wide as she pretended they were flying; and, as they crossed the hall, he clucked laughter round his warm, wet thumb just for the joy of being happy and loved and here and now.

Eleanor heard the squeak on the stairs, but her sleeping mind took it for fodder, stirring it into a piquant dream in which she was the ringmaster in charge of a large, chaotic circus. Tigers who wouldn't be tamed, trapeze artists whose feet kept slipping, a monkey who couldn't be found. When she woke finally to the reality of her bedroom, the noise was already a distant memory, lost in the dark cavernous void with all the other night-time detritus that was shed in the crossover.

Light, solidity, morning at last. After months of planning, Midsummer had arrived, but Eleanor did not leap with alacrity from bed. The night had been interminable and her head felt like a wet sponge. She'd woken in the dark and lain for hours, her mind full and the room hot. Each sheep she'd counted had turned into a job on the list of things to be done today, and not until dawn had she finally fallen back into tumultuous sleep.

She rubbed her eyes and stretched, and then collected her father's old watch from the bedside table, squinting at its loyal, round face. Not even seven and it was stinking hot already! Eleanor collapsed back against her pillows. If this were any other day, she'd have put on her bathing suit and gone down to the stream for a dip before breakfast, before the others woke up and she had to be Mother. She'd always loved to swim, the silken water against her skin, the clarity of light on the rippling surface, the way sound thickened when her ears dipped beneath the surface. As a child, she'd had a favourite spot, particularly deep, down near the boat-house where verbena grew wild on the steep banks and the air was sweet and rotten. The water was wonderfully cold there, as she disappeared beneath the surface, twirling her body lower and lower till she was nestled among the slippery reeds. The days had been much longer then.

Eleanor reached out, brushing an arm against the sheet beside her. Anthony wasn't there. He must've risen early and was probably upstairs, avoiding the turmoil he knew from experience the day would bring. Until recently, she'd have worried to discover him gone already, tied herself in knots until she found him, alone; but no longer. She'd fixed things, and that particular fear could be laid to rest.

A mower started up outside and Eleanor let go of a sigh she hadn't realised she was holding. A mower meant the weather was fine, and thank God for that; it was one less thing to worry about. Rain would have been a disaster. There'd been thunder in the night, that's what had first woken her, and she'd rushed to the window and pulled aside the curtains, dreading the wet world she knew she'd see outside. But the storm had been far away, sheet lightning and not the jagged sort that hurled down rain; the garden had been dry and moonlit, eerie in its stillness.

In her relief, Eleanor had stood for a time in the darkened room, watching the faint undulations on the lake, silver-rimmed clouds being drawn across the pewter sky, nursing the uncanny sense of being the only person on earth awake. The feeling was not unfamiliar, it made her think of those nights when her children were babies and she'd fed them herself, much to her own mother's distaste, curled up in the armchair by the nursery window. Little animal squeaks of satisfaction, tiny velvet hands on the moon of her swollen breast, the vast, still quietness of the world beyond.

Eleanor had been fed as a baby in the same room, though under vastly different conditions. Her mother had not held with such 'vampiric' tendencies in infants, instructing Nanny Bruen – younger then, but no less ancient in attitude – to prepare sterilised cow's milk for 'the little stranger', in one of the teated glass bottles that had been ordered specially from Harrods. To this day, Eleanor couldn't smell rubber without experiencing a peaky wave of nausea and isolation. Nanny Bruen, naturally, had approved wholeheartedly of the regime and the bottles had been produced with military precision at intervals dictated by the cold-faced nursery clock, regardless of the rumblings of Eleanor's small stomach. It was just as well, the two women had agreed, that the child should begin her education in matters of 'order and punctuality'. How else was she to become a proper subordinate, taking her place gladly at the bottom of the family pile? Those were the bland, blancmange days before Eleanor's father came and rescued her from her Victorian childhood. He'd stepped in when talk turned to the hiring of a governess, declaring there to be no need, he would teach his daughter himself. He was one of the cleverest people she'd ever met – not formally educated, like Anthony or Mr Llewellyn, but a great gentleman scholar with a mind that remembered everything it read and heard, that cogitated constantly, fitting pieces of knowledge together, questing for more.

She propped herself against the pillows, strapping on the beloved watch, and a memory came of sitting on his lap before the fire in the library while he read aloud from his William Morris and A. J. Wyatt translation of *Beowulf*. She'd been young, too young to comprehend fully the meaning of the old English words, and she'd been drowsy. Her head had been resting against his chest and she'd listened to the burr of his voice from the inside out, a warm, echo-y hum that was everywhere all at once. She'd been mesmerised by the flicker of orange flames reflected in the glass of his watch and in that moment the object had become an emblem for the feeling of absolute safety and contentment that had enveloped her. There, with him, in the eye of the storm, the centre of the spinning universe.

Perhaps fathers and their daughters were always tied? Anthony was certainly a hero to their girls. He had been since his return from the war. At first they'd been awed, two little faces peering curiously from behind the door of his study, wide-eyed and whispering, but in no time at all they were smitten. Little wonder. He'd camped with them in the meadows, shown them how to weave boats from grass, listened patiently to all their tears and tales. A houseguest had once turned to Eleanor over mint juleps on the lawn, as Anthony played leapfrog with Deborah and Alice, as tiny tottering Clementine took her turn and he suddenly became a horse, galloping round the garden while all three girls dissolved with laughter; the houseguest had asked, mischief disguised as sympathy, whether it bothered her that her husband was so clearly the favourite. Eleanor had answered that of course it didn't.

It had almost been true. After the privations of the war, four long years during which the two of them had been forced to live apart, to grow up and take on new responsibilities, having him back where he belonged and seeing the unadulterated love and wonder on his face as he watched the children they shared was a panacea. It was like having her very own time machine, travelling back to an age of innocence.

Eleanor took up the photograph she kept beside the bed, the two of them in the kitchen garden in 1913, Anthony in his straw hat, brand-new then. He was staring directly at the photographer, his smile lopsided as if he'd just made a joke; she was looking at him with adoration, a scarf tying up her hair; they were both holding shovels. It was the day they'd dug out the strawberry patch and made a complete mess of it. Howard Mann had been behind the camera. He'd arrived in his Silver Ghost one day, anxious 'to see that the two of you hadn't fallen off the edge of the earth', and had ended up staying all week. They'd laughed and teased and argued fiercely about politics, people and poetry, just as they had in the Cambridge years, and when finally he returned to London, it was with reluctance and promises to come back soon, and a car boot filled with leftovers from their first harvest. Looking at the photograph now, remembering the two of them back then, Eleanor felt the gulf of time keenly. She felt humbled by those happy young people. So sure, so whole, so untouched by life . . .

  She clicked her tongue, impatient with herself. It was lack of sleep making her nostalgic, the tumult of the past few months, the weight of the day ahead. Carefully, she put the frame back on the table. The sun was gaining strength now, a dazzling constellation of pinpricks had appeared in the brocade curtains. Eleanor knew it was time to get up and yet a part of her resisted, clinging to the irrational notion that by staying in bed she might somehow stop the countdown from starting. Keep the wave from crashing. *There's no way to hold back the tide.* Her father's voice. The two of them watching the sea down by Miller's Point, waves collapsing on the rocks at the base of the cliff before relenting and being dragged back out again. *It's as inevitable as day following night.* It was the morning he'd told her he was ill and made her promise she would remember who she was when he was gone, *remember to remain good and brave and true.* The old, much-loved line from *Eleanor's Magic Doorway.*

Eleanor blotted out the memory and focused. The first guests would arrive at eight o'clock that night, which meant she needed to be robed and ready, with a stiff drink under her belt, by half past seven. Oh, but there was still so much to do! The girls would have to be pressed into service. To Alice she would give the simple (some would say pleasurable, though not, she knew, Alice) task of filling the guestroom vases with flowers. Deborah would do a superior job, but she'd been in a foul mood lately, petulant and opinionated, filled with the child's naive faith that she was going to do everything better than her parents, and Eleanor wasn't in the mood for an argument. As for Clemmie, poor child, it was enough that she stay out from underfoot. Dear Clemmie, already the most unusual of Eleanor's children, and now stuck in that awkward foal-like phase, toothy and long-limbed, refusing to leave her childhood behind.

The door opened abruptly and Daisy arrived with the silver breakfast tray held proudly aloft. 'Morning, ma'am,' she said with grating cheerfulness. 'Big day's here at last!'

The maid set down the tray, babbling breathlessly about the menu and the guests and the parlous state of things in the kitchen. 'Last I saw, Cook was chasing Hettie round the table with a guinea fowl in one hand and a rolling pin in the other!' Then she moved to draw back the curtains, allowing light, remarkable full light, to flood through the glass and sweep away any lingering trace of night.

And while Daisy began an unsolicited narration of the preparations taking place on the lawn below, Eleanor poured tea from the small silver pot and wondered how on earth she was going to manage all that the day required.

*

The curtains in the bedroom window lurched open and from where she sat on the garden seat, Constance could see that twit of a housemaid, Daisy, flapping her wings as she crowed and cawed by the glass, doubtless driving Eleanor to the brink of ear-stabbing distraction. It was no less than she deserved. Fancy lying in so late when there was a party to host! But then Eleanor had always been a most mercurial child.

Constance had had her own breakfast an hour ago. She always rose at the crack of dawn; it was the habit of a lifetime. Constance was not above vice – indeed she'd always felt it was a woman's duty to keep herself interesting – but punctuality was a virtue, she'd been taught as a child, without which one disrupted the lives of others. Such rudeness was not to be countenanced.

The garden was already a hive of activity. Constance had her stationery set with her and a list of letters to write, but it was almost impossible not to give in to diversion. A number of burly men were erecting elaborate firework-launchers on the oval lawn and vans had started arriving with deliveries for the kitchen. Nearby, a pair of inelegant local boys with decorative wreaths were busy trampling the flowerbeds as they looked for somewhere to set down their ladder. One of them, a liverish-looking fellow with a rash of fresh pimples on his chin, had made the mistake of approaching Constance when they first arrived, looking for 'the boss', but Constance had soon got rid of him with a blank stare and some prattle about the weather. Senility was a useful costume. It was true her thoughts wandered these days, but not as much as she let them all believe. She could still set her mind to accomplishing tremendous things if she were sufficiently inspired.

Yes, it was going to be a good day. Though she never would have admitted it aloud, and certainly not to Eleanor, Constance relished Midsummer. The Edevanes did not entertain often, but the tradition of Midsummer was one that Eleanor hadn't been able to let go, and thank God for that. The celebration at Loeanneth was the highlight of Constance's year, the only thing that made up for the fact she had to live here in this godforsaken place where the smell of the sea, its horrible crashing sound when the breeze blew a certain way, was enough to make her blood run cold. Constance despised the sound. It reminded her of that terrible night all those years ago; she'd thought herself rid of it when they'd left the house more than twenty years before, but life could be cruel like that.

Anyway. The purpose and excitement of the party preparations reminded her of happier times past: the anticipation she'd felt as a young woman, dressing in her silk and jewels, spritzing her cologne and pinning up her hair; the moment of arrival, making her grand entrance, casting her gaze across the crowd, catching the eye of a worthy conquest; and then, the excitement of the chase, the warmth of the bright dance floor, the hushed flight along dark corridors to claim her prize ... Sometimes, lately, the past was so vivid, so *real*, she almost believed herself to be that young woman again.

Movement broke her reverie and Constance felt her smile drop away. The front door had opened and now Daffyd Llewellyn emerged, stumbling over the threshold as he adjusted his hat and hoisted his easel onto his hip. She sat very still, hidden in the shadows. The last thing she wanted was to be drawn into conversation with him. He was moving more slowly than usual, almost as if he were in some sort of discomfort. Constance had noticed it the other afternoon, too, when they were all out on the lawn and Eleanor made the announcement about the award he was soon to receive. Heartburn, apparently – not that it was any of her care or concern; Constance had no time for the silly, weak man. The way he'd lurked about the house and garden when she was mistress, with his eccentric clothing and his sad eyes, his ridiculous fairy tales – every time she'd turned around he'd been there. And as for that breakdown of his! Constance sniffed with contempt. The man had neither pride nor shame. What had he to feel despondent about? *She* was the one who ought to have felt aggrieved. He'd taken her child from her, spouted his rubbish about magic lands and redemption, and then presumed to intrude upon her hospitality. She'd ordered Henri to send him away, but Henri, pliant and meek in every other respect, had refused.

And now it was Eleanor's turn to cosset and indulge the man. She'd adored him as a girl, and he her, and the pair still shared a singular friendship. Constance had seen them in a cosy tête-à-tête a couple of weeks ago, sitting on the garden seat near the roses. Eleanor had been telling him something, her face a study in anguish, and he nodding, and then he'd touched her cheek with his fingertips and Constance had realised Eleanor was crying. She'd known then what the conversation was about.

A warm breeze blew lightly and petals scattered like confetti. Constance saw many things these days. She'd have preferred to keep her youth and beauty, but it did no good to rail against the inevitable and it turned out there were benefits to ageing. When she lost her ability to turn heads, she gained the capacity to sit very still, to breathe very quietly, to pass unnoticed. And so, she saw things. She saw Deborah giving her mother a hard time since she'd become engaged; Alice sneaking away to meet in secret that gardener with the dark hair and the gypsy eyes; that business between Anthony and the pretty young nanny.

It was a pity Eleanor wasn't as watchful as Constance. She might have figured things out sooner. Constance had wondered how long it would take for the penny to drop. Of course, she could have told her daughter what she'd seen, but people were inclined to shoot the messenger, and evidently Eleanor had got there in the end, for the young nanny was gone now. She'd been sent packing with very little warning and no fanfare. And good riddance. The covert smiles, the snatched conversations when they thought no one could see. Constance had seen, though. She'd even observed the young woman handing over a gift one afternoon, a book. Constance's eyes weren't what they'd used to be and she hadn't been able to make out the title, not then, but she'd taken it upon herself to creep into Anthony's study later and there she'd seen it, among the butterflies and magnifiers, the same green cover. A book of poems by John Keats.

It wasn't the infidelity to which she took exception – Constance saw no reason men and women shouldn't take their pleasure where they found it – but discretion was key. It behoved people of their kind to make the right choices, so that news wasn't leaked outside the circle, where it could be twisted into gossip. And therein lay the rub. A person in one's employ was most certainly *not* within the circle, and to entangle oneself in such a way was not only foolish but unkind. It gave the servants ideas above their station and no good could come from that.

Comfort had a habit of breeding transgression, and Rose Waters had become far too comfortable, particularly in her handling of baby Theo. The nanny had maintained none of the professional barriers one might expect, kissing the child and crooning softly into his ear, cuddling him close as she carried him about the garden instead of sitting him as was proper in his perambulator. It was the sort of gushy treatment one might have tolerated from a doting family member, but *not* from the hired help. And the liberties taken had not ended there. Rose Waters had repeatedly overstepped her bounds, culminating recently in a moment of madness when she'd dared remonstrate with Constance for venturing inside the nursery 'during rest time'. Constance was the boy's grandmother, for goodness' sake, and had only wanted to sit by the cot and watch the little lad, his compact chest rising and falling with rude good health.

Thank God Nanny Bruen had returned. Constance was cheered by the very thought. It had been good to see her old stalwart again recently, brought back into the fold and placed in charge of Theo. Constance took a special interest in her little grandson, and the restoration of proper standards was sorely overdue. She made a mental note to have a word with Nanny Bruen later. She'd seen something quite unacceptable not thirty minutes before. Clementine, that unfortunate freckled child with the horsey teeth, had appeared at the side of the house with the baby riding high on her back! Constance had felt a rage rise within her. She'd called out, intending to remonstrate, but the girl had ignored her.

Now Constance glanced back down the garden to where she'd last seen the girl, disappearing around the lake. The mower clattered away on the lawns behind her and she took up her stationery set, using it as a fan. Mechanical noises always made the heat seem worse and it was going to be *dreadfully* hot today. People did strange things in hot weather, unexpected things. It was not unheard of that a person might go a little mad when the temperature sweltered. Constance had never enjoyed Shakespeare – for the most part he was an utter bore – but he had one thing right: Midsummer was a strange and unpredictable time.

There was no sign of Clementine and the baby. Theo's laughter still pealed in her memory and Constance felt her heart soften. He really was the most delightful child: a bonny nature, a smile that collapsed into dimples, those plump, sturdy legs. She wondered, sometimes, what the other little boy would have been like, the first one, had he been given half a chance.

She would sit with Theo this afternoon, Constance decided, and watch him sleep. It was one of her favourite things to do these days, and with Rose Waters gone, Eleanor busy and Nanny Bruen mindful of her proper place, there would be no one to stop her this time.

Clemmie took the narrow path of beaten grass along the stream. There were other, quicker ways to get there, but Theo liked to splash in the shallow water at the crossing and Clemmie liked to make him happy. Besides, it was Midsummer's Eve and the house would be in uproar all day. The longer they were out and away, the better. It occurred to her, with dispassion and not self-pity, that they probably wouldn't even be missed.

'Just as well we've got each other, little Wub,' she said.

'Gah!' came Theo's gurgled reply.

A surge of emotion that felt as much like loss as love came suddenly upon her and she tightened her grip on his legs, so round and squishy. He might have replaced her as the baby in the family, but Clemmie couldn't now imagine the world without her brother in it.

The rising sun was behind them and their long, jumbled shadow stretched ahead, her elongated body with his little legs stuck out at midway. His head was peeking over her shoulder as he clung to her back and every so often he extended a small, excited fist to waggle a plump finger at something they were passing. It had taken a bit of practice, but he was good now at holding tightly round her neck. She could even stretch her arms out wide when the mood struck her, gliding them through the air, listing this way and that as she made elaborate aerobatic manoeuvres.

She stopped when they reached the rock crossing, tossed aside the picnic bag she'd brought with her (party cakes stolen from the kitchen), and let Theo slide down the back of her legs into the large mound of dry grass clippings on the bank. He landed with a delighted giggle and clambered to his feet. 'Wah,' he said importantly, pointing at the stream. 'Wah.'

While Theo tottered through clover to the muddy edge, squatting on his bottom among the reeds, Clemmie hunted for the perfect skimming stone. It had to be small and flat and smooth, but beyond that, it had to sit just so in her

fingertips. She took one up and judged its weight, the round-
ness of its edges, before discarding it again as too uneven.

This process she repeated once, twice, three times, before
finding one that, though not perfect, looked as if it might do
the trick. She put it in her pocket and started searching for
the next.

Alice was the best at finding stones. She was one of those
people who always won at games because she had a love for
detail and a stubborn nature that refused ever to give up.
They used to spend hours down here selecting and then tossing their prized skimmers. They'd cartwheeled, and made
swings with the long, sinewy boat ropes, and built elaborate
cubby houses in the gorse. They'd fought and tickled and
laughed, administered sticking plasters to one another's
knees, and fallen asleep, tired and sweaty, beneath the May
bushes as the afternoon sun bleached colour from the
garden. But Alice was different now, this summer, and Clemmie had been abandoned.

She picked up a light-coloured stone with funny speckles
and rubbed it clean with her wet thumb. It was ever since
they'd come down from London. They were all used to the
way Alice became lost behind her notebooks, in the make-
believe worlds of her stories, but this was different. She was
moody, swinging from over-the-top glee to sullen exasperation. She'd taken to making weak excuses to be alone in her
bedroom – *I need to lie down . . . I'm busy writing . . . I have
a headache . . .* – and then sneaking away so that when
Clemmie went to find her she wasn't there.

Clemmie glanced back to where Theo was digging with a
stick in the dirt by the stream. He hooted happily as a grass-
hopper leapt from one reed to another and she smiled

wistfully. Theo was a glorious little fellow, but she missed Alice and would have done anything to have her back, for things to be as they had been before. She missed both her sisters. The two of them had gone on without her, becoming grown-ups without so much as a backward glance. Alice with that mooning expression, and Deborah engaged to be married. Clemmie felt it as a betrayal. She was never going to be like them, never going to grow up. Grown-ups were mystifying. Clementine despaired at the weary tedium of their instructions (*not now*, *slow down*, *stop it at once*), the dull conversations, the mysterious headaches, the excuses they made for absenting themselves from any activity that might prove fun; and she resented the infinite small betrayals, the realm of insinuation and nuance in which they moved, of saying one thing and meaning another. Clemmie lived in a rather more black-and-white world. For a pilot, there was much to be said for binary choices: yes or no, up or down, right or wrong.

'No!' she hissed, a self-reproach. Her mood had already cast a shadow over the sunlit morning and now the very thing she'd been trying not to think of was back in her mind. The thing she'd seen. Bodies, naked, twisted and moving—

No. Clemmie screwed her eyes shut and shook it away.

She knew why the awful pictures were back. It had been a day like this one when she saw them; she'd been down to the base, watching the planes, and was on her way home.

Clemmie stabbed at the ground with her foot. If only she'd gone home earlier, anything to have stopped her from cutting back through the woods right then and past the boathouse. The awful sight of them, the fright and confusion as she tried to make sense of what they were doing.

'Poor love,' Deborah had said when Clemmie confided the horrible scene, unable to keep it to herself any longer. 'You've had a terrible shock.' She'd taken Clemmie's hands and said she wasn't to worry about it anymore. She was absolutely right to have told, but now she must put it out of her mind. 'I'll take care of things, I promise.' Clemmie had thought that sounded a bit like promising to put a shattered eggshell back together, but Deborah had smiled, and her face was so serenely beautiful, her voice so certain, that Clemmie's cares had momentarily flown away. 'I'll speak to her myself,' Deborah had vowed. 'You'll see – everything will be all right.'

Clemmie jiggled the stones in her pocket and bit absently at her thumbnail. She still wondered whether she should have gone to Mother or told Daddy what she'd seen. When she'd asked Deborah, though, her sister had said not. She'd told her to forget all about it, that she mustn't tell anyone, not another soul. 'It would only upset them, Clem, and we don't want that, do we?'

She seized a pinkish oval-shaped stone, lined it up between her thumb and index finger. Clemmie had considered going straight to Alice after she saw them, and perhaps if they'd been closer she would have, but with the way things were, the new distance that had appeared so suddenly between them . . . No, she'd done the right thing. Deborah was the sort of person who knew what to do in every situation. She would take care of it.

'Mi-mi?'

Theo was watching her solemnly, his baby face intent on hers, and Clemmie realised she was frowning. She rustled up a smile and, after a second's consideration, he mirrored the happy expression, his little face crinkled and bonny, his equilibrium restored. Clemmie felt a wave of melancholy, gladness and dread combined. What faith he had in her! What faith he had, that one little smile was all it took to transform his mood entirely. She made her face serious again and the joy left his eyes. She had complete power over him and for Clemmie, powerless in so many other ways, the realisation was heady. She felt his vulnerability keenly. How easy it would be for a bad person to misuse that sort of trust!

Clemmie was distracted then by the noise of the mowing machine. Rather, its cessation. The burr of the mower was so much a part of summer mornings that she hadn't noticed it until the rattling stopped and other sounds – the stream, the early birds, her brother's baby chatter – were suddenly louder.

A cloud fell across her face. She knew who it was behind the mower and the last thing she wanted was to see *him*, that man. Not now, not ever again. She wished, wished, wished he'd go away, far from Loeanneth. Then maybe she'd be able to forget what she'd seen in the boathouse and everything would go back to how it had been before.

Clemmie hoisted Theo onto her hip. 'Come on, Wubba-dub-dub,' she said, dusting off his muddy hands. 'Climb aboard, time for take-off.'

He was an amenable child; she'd heard Mother say as much to Nanny Bruen when she replaced Nanny Rose a fortnight before (*amenable and very good-natured*, the pleased, surprised tone implying that the preceding child, Clemmie, had been neither). He didn't protest, leaving his explorations behind and nestling into position on her back, Puppy tucked safely in the crook of his elbow. Keeping her balance, Clemmie stepped across the stones to the other side of the stream and set off towards the airbase beyond Jack Martin's farm. She went at a clip, arms hooked under Theo's knees, and she didn't look back.

Ben jumped down from the mower and crouched on the grass by its motor. The chain was where it should be, there was nothing stuck in the blades, the ground he was trying to mow was flat. There ended his knowledge of things mechanical. He supposed there was nothing for it but to give the machine a few minutes to rethink its position.

He sat back and fumbled in his shirt pocket for matches. Morning sun warmed the back of his neck and promised a sweltering day. He could hear sparrows clearing the trills from their throats and an early train leaving the station, and could smell the sweet tea roses and fresh-cut grass.

A biplane flew overhead and Ben watched until it turned into the merest speck and disappeared. His gaze fell and he saw that the sun had hit the side of the house. It reached along the leadlight windows up top – the bedrooms, he knew – and he felt the same pull of longing he always did. He cursed himself for a fool and looked away, drawing on his cigarette. His feelings were irrelevant; worse than that, they were a liability. He'd already crossed too many lines. He was ashamed of himself.

He was going to miss this garden when he went. His contract had only ever been temporary – he'd known that when he started, he just hadn't known how soon it would end and how much he'd want to stay. Mr Harris had offered to extend his employment but Ben had told him he had other things to attend to. 'Family business,' he'd said, and the older man had nodded and patted Ben on the shoulder as Adam pottered about in the shed behind them, thirty-three years old but wide-eyed as a puppy. Ben didn't offer any more details, he certainly didn't mention Flo and her problems; he didn't have to. Mr Harris understood the responsibilities of family better than most. Like all who'd celebrated the safe return of a loved one from the Great War, he knew that those boys might've come back but they never really came home.

Ben ducked beneath the arbour and paused by the fish-pond when a memory crept upon him like a shadow. This was the spot where Alice had first read to him from her manuscript. He could still hear her voice, as if it had some-how been captured by the leaves around them and was being played back now, just for him, like a gramophone recording.

'I've had a brilliant idea,' he heard her say, so young and innocent, so full of joy. 'I've been working on it all morning and I don't like to boast, but I'm quite sure it's going to be my best yet.'

'Is it?' Ben had said with a smile. He'd been teasing, but Alice had been far too excited to notice. She'd leapt on with telling him about her idea, the plot, the characters, the twist, and the intensity of her focus – her passion – changed her face completely, bringing an animated beauty to her features. He hadn't noticed she was beautiful until she spoke to him of her stories. Her cheeks flushed and her eyes shone with intelligence. And she was *very* clever. It took a certain kind of clever to figure out a puzzle – to look ahead and see through all the possible scenarios, to be so strategic. Ben didn't have that kind of brain.

In the beginning he'd simply enjoyed her enthusiasm, the

indulgence of being told a story while he worked, the chance to bat ideas back and forth, which was so much like play. She made him feel young, he supposed; her youthful pre-occupation with her work, with the very moment they were in, was intoxicating. It made his adult worries disappear.

He'd known her parents wouldn't approve of them meeting like that, but he hadn't thought it would do any harm. And it hadn't at first. He'd never imagined at the start – neither of them could have guessed – where it would lead. But he was older than Alice; he should have known; he should have been more careful. The human heart, life, cir-cumstances – they were tricky things to govern; by the time he realised what was happening, it was too late.

His cigarette was finished and he knew he should be get-ting on. Mr Harris had given him a list of things to be done in preparation for the party, there was still a bonfire to stack, and he'd have to send someone back to sweet-talk the mower.

Ben glanced around to check there was no one lurking and then took out her letter. He'd done this so many times before, the fold marks were worn soft and the parts of the words that had once been there had disappeared. Ben remembered them, though, like whispers. She certainly knew how to write; she had a beautiful turn of phrase. He read each line slowly, carefully, and paragraphs that had once made him joyous now made him heavy with regret.

He would miss this place. He would miss her.

A bird flew low overhead, sounding a reprimand, and Ben folded the letter and put it back inside his pocket. There were things to be done and it did no good to focus on the past. 'She's going to be a huge fire tonight,' Mr Harris had said, nodding at the stack of wood they'd chopped during the week, a half-smile forming. 'They'll be able to see it from Caradon Hill. You know, there's an old saying round here that the bigger the Midsummer fire, the better a man's luck in the year to come.'

Ben had heard the saying before. Alice had already told him.

Fifteen

Cornwall, 2003

Clive Robinson was a thin, spry man of almost ninety years. He had a high, lined forehead and thick white hair, a large nose and a broad smile. He still had all his teeth. His gaze was clear and keen, the sort that suggested a quick mind, and he was watching Sadie through enormous glasses with brown Bakelite frames that she'd immediately suspected he had been wearing since the 1970s.

'The heat of that summer,' he said, shaking his head, 'it was the sort that gets right under your skin, makes it near impossible to sleep. Dry, too, weeks without a drop so that the grass was beginning to fade. Not at the Lake House, mind. They had people, gardeners, to make sure that didn't happen. It was all done up when we got there, lanterns, streamers, floral wreaths. I'd never seen anything like it, ordinary lad like me, a place like that. It was so beautiful. They sent out cakes for us at teatime. Can you imagine that? Day after their little boy went missing, and they sent out fairy cakes. Prettiest things I'd ever seen, all iced specially for the party the night before.'

Sadie had made contact with the retired policeman as soon as she'd received his letter. He'd printed his phone number at the bottom and she'd gone straight inside to ring him, the ramifications of her discovery on the 1664 floorplan still pulsing beneath her skin. 'I've been waiting for you,' he'd said when she told him who she was, and the fact wasn't lost on Sadie that it was precisely what the old man in *Eleanor's Magic Doorway* had said when Eleanor arrived to right his wrong. The way he said it, Sadie hadn't been sure at first whether he meant for the twenty-four hours since he'd written or the seventy years since the case was stamped unsolved. 'I knew someone would come eventually, that I wasn't the only one who still thought about them.'

They'd talked briefly over the phone, each sounding the other out, swapping police credentials (Sadie neglecting to mention she was in Cornwall on enforced leave), and then they'd broached the case. Despite its pressing newness, Sadie had restrained herself from blurting out her tunnel theory, saying only that she was finding information hard to come by, that she'd been limited so far to Pickering's account, to which Clive had given a snort of amused derision.

'He's a little short on solid information,' Sadie agreed.

'That's not all the poor man was short on,' said Clive with a laugh. 'Not to speak ill of the dead, but I'm afraid Arnold Pickering wasn't standing in line when the Almighty handed out brains.'

He'd asked if she wanted to come and see him, and Sadie had suggested the following day. 'Make it morning,' he'd said. 'My daughter Bess is coming at midday to take me to an appointment.' He'd paused before adding, sotto voce, 'She doesn't approve of my ongoing interest in the case. She calls it obsessive.'

Sadie had smiled into the phone receiver. She knew the feeling.

'She'd rather I took up bridge, or stamp collecting.'

'Secret's safe with me. I'll see you at nine.'

And so, here she was, on a bright Saturday morning, sitting in Clive Robinson's kitchen in Polperro with a pot of tea and a plate of digestive biscuits and sliced fruitcake between them. There was an embroidered cloth spread over the built-in table, iron creases suggesting it had been laid out freshly. Sadie had been unexpectedly touched when she noticed a small tag on its hem and realised it was the wrong side up.

If Clive had seemed genuinely pleased to see her, the enormous black cat he lived with was clearly incensed by the incursion. 'Don't take it personally,' Clive had said when Sadie arrived, ruffling the hissing animal beneath the chin. 'She's cross with me for going abroad. Quite possessive, my Mollie.' The animal was watching proceedings now from the space between two pots of herbs on the sunny window ledge, purring sourly as her tail flickered a warning.

Sadie took a biscuit and surveyed the remaining questions in the list she'd made for Clive. She'd resolved to test the waters before deciding whether or not she could trust the old policeman with her theory; there was also the small matter of verifying his competence as a source. Although she'd been thrilled to line up the interview, Sadie had been dubious as to how much a man pushing ninety would remember of a case he'd worked on seventy years before. But Clive had quickly assuaged her doubts and several pages of her writing pad were now filled with scribbled notes.

'I've never been able to forget it,' he'd said as he poured their tea through a strainer. 'Might not think it to look at me but I've got a good memory. The Edevane case in particular has stuck with me. Couldn't have got rid of it if I'd tried.' He'd lifted narrow shoulders that sloped away beneath his well-pressed collared shirt. He was of the generation that put stock in such matters of personal grooming. 'It was my first, you see.' He considered her through his thick lenses. 'Well, you're with the police, you know what I mean.'

Sadie had said that she did. No amount of training prepared a person for the storm and stress of their first real case. Hers had been a domestic-violence call. The woman had looked like she'd gone ten rounds in the ring, her face was black and blue, her lip split open, but she'd refused to press charges. 'Walked into the door,' she told them, not even bothering to think up an original lie. Sadie, fresh out of training and nursing her own demons, had wanted to arrest the boyfriend anyway. The injustice had burned. She couldn't believe they had no choice; that without the victim's cooperation there was nothing to do but issue a warning and walk away. Donald had told her to get used to it, that there was no limit to what a frightened spouse would do to protect their abuser, that the system made it hard for them to leave. The smell of that apartment was still as fresh as if it happened yesterday.

'It was my first taste of grief,' Clive Robinson had continued. 'I'd been sheltered as a lad, happy family, nice-enough house to live in, brothers and sisters and a granny up the road. Hadn't even been to a funeral when I started with the police. Went to my fair share afterwards, though, I can tell you.' He frowned at something beyond her shoulder, remembering. 'That house, those people – their helplessness, the desperate looks on their faces – even the air inside the rooms seemed to know that something had been lost.' He swivelled his teacup on its saucer, small adjustments as he chose his words. 'It was my first time.'

Sadie had offered a slight smile of understanding. Nothing like the police force for bringing the horrors of life up close and personal. The only people who had it worse were paramedics. 'So you started with the theory that Theo Edevane had wandered?'

A brief nod. 'We just presumed that's what had happened. Nobody thought of kidnappings in those days. There'd been the Lindbergh case in America the year before but that made news because it was so rare. We were sure we'd find the lad within hours, that being so young he couldn't have got far. We searched until nightfall, combed the meadows and the woods on the edge of the estate, but we couldn't find a trace. Not a clue. Next day, we brought in divers to check the lake, and when nothing turned up, that's when we started looking at who might have wanted to take him.'

Which led Sadie to her second series of questions, scribbled down the night before. Ordinarily, she fought against questions of 'why', particularly when she was just getting started on an investigation. 'Motive's for fiction writers,' Donald was fond of grumbling. 'Fiction writers and TV detectives.' Typically blunt, but he had a point. Police officers needed evidence; they had to satisfy questions of *how* the crime was committed and *who* had the chance to commit it. *Why* was a distraction, and oftentimes misleading.

In this case, however, with evidence particularly scant and seventy years having elapsed since the crime's commission, Sadie figured exceptions had to be made. Plus, the new map changed things. That mysterious alcove in the wall cavity, the possibility of another tunnel connecting the house to the outside world, a tunnel that had long ago disappeared from most maps and memories. If it were so, then one of the most puzzling aspects of the case, the *how*, might be solved. And with it, hopefully, the *who*, for the group of people who knew of the tunnel's existence must have been small and exclusive. A line from *A Dish Served Cold* had been going round and round in Sadie's head since she'd made the appointment with Clive: *Diggory always started with the family. It was a mistake to presume that grief and guilt were mutually exclusive.* The line had preceded Diggory Brent's first visit to the dead man's ex-wife and daughter. Sadie said, 'You interviewed the parents?'

'First thing we did. There was no evidence to incriminate either, and both had alibis. The boy's mother, in particular, had been very visible as hostess of the party. She spent most of the night at the boathouse, where they had gondola rides set up for the guests. Everything they told us checked out. No real surprise there; why would a parent kidnap their own child?'

A valid point, but Sadie wasn't prepared to let them off the hook so easily, even if she had developed a certain feeling of kinship towards Eleanor Edevane. 'The Pickering book suggested a period of about three hours between the end of the party and the discovery that the boy was missing. What were the whereabouts of the parents then?'

'They both retired to bed at the same time. Neither left the bedroom until eight a.m., when the maid came to tell them the lad wasn't in his cot.'

'Anything to suggest either was lying?'

'Nothing.'

'That they might have acted together?'

'To spirit the boy away, you mean? After they'd said goodnight to their three hundred guests?'

It sounded absurd now he put it like that, but Sadie was nothing if not thorough. She nodded.

'We couldn't find anyone who didn't say how well-loved the boy was. More than that, how *wanted*. The Edevanes had waited a long time for their son. They had three daughters already, the youngest was twelve in June 1933, and the boy was prized. All those wealthy families wanted boys back then, someone to pass the name and fortune on to. Not anymore. My granddaughter tells me all her friends want girls – better behaved, more fun to dress, easier all round.' He raised his neat white brows incredulously. 'Having had daughters myself, I can assure you that's not the case.'

Sadie gave a slight smile as Clive helped himself to a biscuit. 'I'll have to take your word for it,' she said, focusing with assiduous care on the list of family members he'd given her when she first arrived. 'You said the boy's grandmother lived with the family?'

A slight frown crossed his otherwise kind face. 'Constance deShiel. Insufferable woman. One of those snooty, overbred types who look as if they'd as soon eat you as answer your questions. Except when we asked about her daughter and son-in-law – she was rather more forthcoming then.'

'What did she say?'

'Little jibes of the "things aren't always as they seem" variety. She alluded more than once to infidelity, insinuating

there'd been some sort of affair, but pulled up short of offering specifics.'

'You pushed her on it?'

'Back then, someone in the gentry, especially a woman –
well, there were different rules of conduct, we couldn't press
her as we might have liked.'

'You looked into it, though?'

'Of course. As you'd know, family disharmony's a policeman's bread and butter; there're those who'll stop at nothing
to punish a spouse. The dad who turns up for a custody visit,
takes the kids and never brings them back; the mum who
feeds her kids a bunch of lies about their old man. The rights
of children are often lost in the battle between their parents.'

'But not in this case?'

'People went out of their way to tell us how devoted the
Edevanes were, what an inseparable couple.'

Sadie considered this. Marriages were mysterious things.
She'd never had one of her own, but it seemed to her that
each was its own beast, with secrets, lies and promises simmering beneath the surface. 'Why would Constance deShiel
have suggested otherwise if it wasn't true? Had she seen
something? Had her daughter confided in her, perhaps?'

'Mother and daughter weren't close; more than one
person told us that.'

'And yet they lived together?'

'Reluctantly, as I understand it. The old woman had lost
everything in a bad investment after her husband died and
relied on her daughter and son-in-law's charity, a situation
she resented.' He shrugged. 'Her insinuations might've been
a simple case of mischief-making.'

'When a child was missing?'

He waved a hand and his expression suggested nothing would have surprised him, that he'd seen people do all sorts of things in his time. 'It's possible, though there were other explanations. The old woman was suffering from the early stages of dementia in 1933. Her doctor advised us to take what she said with a grain of salt. In fact – ' they were alone but he leaned a little nearer, as if to share a confidence he didn't want overheard – 'Dr Gibbons suggested that Constance had been rather *in*constant in her own marriage, that it was possible her comments were actually confused memories rather than reliable reports. They say the past and the present become difficult to separate.'

'What do you think?'

He spread his hands. 'I think she was bitter but harmless. Old and lonely and she had a captive audience.'

'You think she was making herself seem important?'

'It was almost like she wanted us to ask her questions, to imagine her the architect of some great nefarious scheme. I dare say she'd have been well pleased if we'd arrested her. It would have given her all the attention she was seeking, and then some.' Clive picked a crumb from the tablecloth, setting it carefully on the edge of his plate. 'It's not easy, getting old, feeling one's relevance slip away. She'd been beautiful once, and important, mistress of the house. There was a portrait of her hanging over the fireplace in the library; formidable, she was. I still shudder to remember the way those painted eyes seemed to watch my every move.' He glanced at Sadie, his own gaze narrowing so that she glimpsed the hardened policeman he must once have been. 'All the same, a lead's a lead, Lord knows we hadn't many of them, and I watched the pair of them, Anthony and Eleanor, very closely after that.'

'And?'

'The loss of a child is like a grenade in most families, statistics on parents who split up in the wake of a tragedy bear that out, but they were lovely together. He was so careful with her, gentle and protective, making sure she rested, stopping her from tearing outside to join the search. He barely let her out of his sight.' His mouth tightened as he remembered. 'It really was a dreadful time. Poor woman, it has to be a mother's worst nightmare, but she handled herself with such grace. You know, for years after the family left she used to come back here.'

'To the village?'

'To the house. Just her on her own.'

This was new. Bertie's friend Louise had suggested that no one from the family had been near the place since Theo's disappearance. 'You saw her?'

'Police hear things, news would filter into town that there was someone back at the Lake House. I dropped in on her a few times, just to make sure she was all right, see if there was anything I could do to help. She was always polite, said it was kind of me but she was just enjoying a little respite from London.' He smiled sadly. 'I knew, though, she was hoping he'd come back.'

'It wasn't over for her.'

''Course it wasn't. Her baby was out there somewhere. She thanked me once or twice, said she appreciated the work we'd all put in, how hard we'd searched for her boy. Even made an exceptionally generous donation to the local station. Very dignified, she was. Very sad.' He frowned, lost in his memories. When he spoke again, a bitter, wistful note had crept into his voice. 'I used to hope I could still find the boy for her. Didn't sit well with me, that open file. Children don't just disappear, do they? They go somewhere. There's always a path, it's just a matter of knowing where to look.' He glanced at her. 'Ever had a case like that? Eats away at you.'

'Once or twice,' said Sadie, picturing Caitlyn Bailey in the hallway of that flat. Remembering the sensation of that little hand, warm and trusting in hers, the tickle of the child's messy hair when she fetched her storybook and laid her head on Sadie's shoulder.

'This was mine,' he said. 'Made all the worse because we had so little to work with.'

'You must have had theories, though?'

'There were leads, some of them stronger than others. Recent staff changes, a missing bottle of sleeping tablets we thought might have been used in the kidnapping, and a family friend who died in unusual circumstances, fellow by the name of Daffyd Llewellyn—'

'The writer—'

'That's him. Quite well known in his time.'

Sadie cursed herself for having left the library dissertation with its chapter on Llewellyn unopened. She remembered the introduction to *Eleanor's Magic Doorway* and its mention of a posthumous OBE awarded in 1934. She hadn't made the connection that his death had come so soon after Theo's disappearance. 'What happened?'

'A few days into the search we were down by the stream, a little way from the boathouse, and someone called out, 'A body!' But it wasn't the baby, it was an old man. Suicide, as it turned out. We thought it must've been guilt, that he'd had something to do with the boy's disappearance.'

'Are you sure he hadn't?'

'We looked into it, but there was no motive. He adored the boy, and everyone we interviewed confirmed him as Eleanor's closest friend. He wrote a book about her when she was a girl, did you know?'

Sadie nodded.

'She was completely devastated – collapsed when she was told. Awful.' He was shaking his head. 'One of the worst things I've seen.'

Sadie considered this. A child goes missing and a close family friend kills himself in the hours or days afterwards. 'The timing seems extraordinary.'

'Grant you that, but we spoke to the local doctor, who told us Llewellyn had been suffering anxiety in the weeks prior. We found a bottle of barbiturates in his pocket.'

'That's what he used?'

'The coroner confirmed an overdose. Llewellyn mixed the pills with champagne, lay down by the stream and never woke up. Extraordinary timing, as you say, given that the boy was taken at the same time, but nothing suspicious in it. Certainly nothing to link him to Theo Edevane's fate. Just a coincidence.'

Sadie smiled thinly. She didn't like coincidences. In her experience they were usually just links that hadn't yet been proved. And, now, her antennae were quivering. She had a feeling there was more to this Llewellyn fellow's death than met the eye. Clive had obviously dismissed the possibility a long time ago, but Sadie made a note to look into it later.

Llewellyn suicide – timing an accident or was he involved? Guilt?

In the meantime . . . she tapped her pen against the pad thoughtfully, circling the word *accident*. Because of course there was a third possibility in the case of Theo Edevane, perhaps most chilling of all: that the child had never left the house – at least, not alive. Sadie had seen cases where children had been injured or killed – accidentally or otherwise – and then the crime covered up. Those responsible invariably sought to make it look like a case of running away or kidnap because it focused attention away from the scene of the crime.

A series of *clicks* broke her train of thought and she noticed for the first time a large digital clock on the bench behind Clive. It was the sort with flip cards made from plastic and three had just turned at once to show the time as eleven o'clock. Sadie was suddenly aware that it was getting closer to midday, when Clive's daughter would arrive and bring their meeting to an end.

'What about the sisters?' she said, with renewed urgency. 'You spoke to them?'

'More than once.'

'Anything useful?'

'More of the same. The boy was loved, they'd seen nothing unusual, they promised to tell us if they thought of anything helpful. They all had alibis for the evening.'

'You're frowning.'

'Am I?' Clive blinked at her, light-blue eyes large behind his glasses. He ran a hand over the top of his white hair and then lifted a shoulder. 'I suppose I just always felt there was something the youngest one wasn't telling us. It was only a hunch, something to do with the awkward way she carried herself. She went red in the face when we were questioning her, crossed her arms and refused to look us in the eye. But she insisted she had no idea what could have happened to him, that nothing unusual had occurred in the household in the preceding weeks, and there wasn't a shred of real evidence to suggest she'd been involved.'

Sadie allowed herself to consider motive. Envy was the obvious one. A girl who'd been the baby of the family for almost twelve years until a little brother, a much-loved son, arrived to take her place. The party would have been the perfect time to do away with an obstacle, the noise and activity making it easy to slip beneath the radar.

Or else ... (and surely more likely than Clementine Edevane being a sociopathic little girl with murderous intent?) ... Sadie remembered Pickering's account of the girl's habit of taking Theo out with her in the mornings, her insistence that the door to the nursery had been closed when she went past, that she hadn't gone inside to fetch her little brother as she sometimes did. But what if she had, and something awful had happened to him, an accident, and she'd been too frightened, too ashamed, to tell anyone?

'There was a clean-up team in the grounds,' Clive said, anticipating her line of thinking. 'From the moment the last guest left, right through sunrise, contractors restoring the place to rights. No one saw anything.'

But what if, as Sadie suspected, there was another way to leave the house unseen? She wrote the word *Clementine* on her notepad and circled it. 'What was she like? Clementine Edevane.'

'A tomboy, you'd have to say, but fey with it. They were

all a bit different, the Edevanes. Charming, charismatic. I was rather taken with them. Awed. I was only seventeen, remember, and green as a bean. I'd never met people like them. It was the romance, I suppose – the big house, the garden, the way they spoke, the things they talked about, their fine manners and the sense of unspoken rules they followed. They were bewitching.' He looked at her. 'Would you like to see a photo?'

'You have one?'

The offer had been made openly, even eagerly, but now he hesitated. 'I'm not sure . . . well, it's a little awkward, you being a current member of the force . . .'

'Barely,' said Sadie, before she could help herself.

'Barely?'

She sighed in defeat. 'There was this case,' she began, and then, maybe it was the calm of that kitchen, its distance from London and her real world, the professional connection she felt with Clive, or the relief at finally being able to tell someone the secret she'd been keeping so diligently from Bertie, but Sadie found herself giving him a potted summary of the Bailey case, the way she'd refused to let it go, convinced herself and tried to persuade all and sundry that there was more to it than met the eye, that she was here in Cornwall not on holiday but on enforced leave.

Clive listened without interrupting, and when she finished, he didn't frown, or start a lecture, or ask her to leave. He said simply, 'I saw it in the paper. Terrible business.'

'I should never have spoken to that journalist.'

'You thought you were right.'

'I didn't give it enough thought, that's the problem.' Her voice curdled with self-disgust. 'I had a *feeling*.'

'Well, no shame in that. Sometimes "feelings" aren't as airy-fairy as they seem. Sometimes they're just the product of observations we haven't realised we've been making.'

He was being kind. Sadie had an instinctive antipathy towards kindness. Policing might have changed in the years since Clive retired, but Sadie was pretty sure breaking rank to go public on a hunch had never been considered acceptable practice. She managed a weak smile. 'You said there was a photo?'

He took the hint; didn't press further on the Bailey case. He seemed to consider for a moment before nodding. 'Back in a minute.'

He shuffled down the hallway and Sadie could hear him rummaging and cursing in a room at the back of the house. The cat was watching her, green eyes wide, tail pulsing in slow critical flecks. *Well, well, well*, that tail seemed to be saying.

'What do you want from me?' Sadie grumbled beneath her breath. 'I've already said it was my fault.'

She played idly with the tablecloth tag and tried not to dwell on Nancy Bailey. *Don't even think about making contact with the grandmother.* Tried to ignore the sensation of that warm little hand in hers. She glanced at the clock and wondered whether it was possible Clive was back there right now on the phone to the Met.

Another two numerals quivered and flipped, and finally, after what seemed a slow-motion age, Clive returned, looking, Sadie fancied, as nervous as she felt. There was an inexplicable animation to his expression and she decided that unless he was a sadist, and there'd been no indication of that so far, he was not returning from reporting her to

Ashford. She noticed that he wasn't carrying a photograph either; rather he had a thick folder under one arm. It was of a familiar type. 'I was waiting to see what I thought of you,' Clive said as he reached the table. 'Only, when I retired, I didn't think anyone would notice, let alone mind, so I took—'

'The file!' Sadie's eyes widened.

A short nod.

'You took the Edevane case file.'

'Borrowed. I'm going to put it back once the case is closed.'

'*You* . . . !' Admiration warmed her face as she considered the folder, now on the table between them, brimming with interview transcripts, illustrations, names, numbers, theories. 'You *devil*! You *wonderful* devil.'

He jutted his chin. 'Wasn't doing any good in archives, was it? There was no one there who'd miss it. Most of the others, their parents weren't even born when it happened.' His bottom lip trembled slightly. 'It's *my* case. *My* unfinished business.'

He handed her a large black-and-white photograph from the top of the file: a good-looking, well-heeled family whose hairstyles, dresses, suits and hats marked them as belonging to the 1930s. It had been taken outside during a picnic and they were lounging on a plaid blanket spread with plates and teacups; there was a stone wall behind them that Sadie recognised as belonging to the bottom garden near the stream. Eleanor and her husband Anthony were in the centre of the group. Sadie knew them from the newspaper photo, though they looked happy here, and therefore younger. An older woman, who must be Constance deShiel, was sitting in a

wicker chair to the left of her daughter, and three girls, teenagers or thereabouts, were gathered together on the other
side, legs outstretched, ankles crossed in the sun. Deborah,
the eldest and most conventionally beautiful, was sitting
closest to her father, a scarf tied over her hair; Alice was
next, her arresting gaze familiar from her author photo; and
on the end, a girl who was tall and rangy but obviously
younger than the others, who must be Clementine. Her
light-brown hair, wavy and side-parted, sat just above her
shoulders, but her face was difficult to make out. She wasn't
looking at the photographer, but rather was smiling at the
little boy sitting by his mother's feet. Baby Theo, an arm
outstretched towards his sister, a soft toy in his fist.

Despite herself, Sadie was moved by the photo. The tufty
grass, the spill of shadows on a long-ago summer's day, the
small white flecks of daisies in the picture's foreground. It
was a brief, single moment in the life of a happy family,
caught before everything changed. Clive had said the Edevanes were unlike anyone he'd met before, but it was the
ordinariness of these people, this scene, that struck Sadie
more. Anthony's jacket, tossed casually behind him, the piece
of half-eaten cake in Deborah's hand, the glossy retriever
sitting to attention, eyeing the prize.

She frowned and looked closer. 'Who's that?' There was
another woman in the photograph. Sadie had missed her at
first; she was lost in the dappled light beneath the stone wall.

Clive peered at the image. 'That's the boy's nanny. Rose
Waters was her name.'

'Nanny,' Sadie said thoughtfully. She knew a little about
nannies; she'd seen *Mary Poppins*. 'Didn't they used to sleep
in the nursery with children?'

'They did,' said Clive. 'Unfortunately she'd left the Lake House a couple of weeks before the party. It took us a while to find her. We traced her through a sister in Yorkshire in the end. Just in time, too: she was at a hotel in London, about to set sail to start another job.' He scratched his head. 'Canada, I think it was. We spoke to her, but she wasn't much help.'

'So there was no nanny at Loeanneth over Midsummer?'

'Oh, there was a replacement, all right. Hilda Bruen. A real old battleaxe, one of those ancient nannies, the sort who got her thrills from feeding cod-liver oil to children, making them cry and telling them it's for their own good. Younger than I am now, but to me as a lad she seemed like Methuselah. She'd worked at the Lake House when Eleanor was a girl and been pulled out of retirement after Rose Waters left.'

'She was there the night the boy went missing?'

'The very same room.'

This was rather big news. 'She must have seen or heard something?'

Clive was shaking his head. 'Sleeping like a baby. Seems she'd taken a draught of whisky to help shut out the party noise. Not an unusual occurrence, from what I could gather.'

'Bollocks!'

'Indeed.'

'There was no mention of her in Pickering's book.'

'No, well, there wouldn't be, would there? He was a fool of a man and no one gave him the time of day, so he was limited to what he could find in the papers.'

'I'm not sure I understand how something like this could be kept *out* of the papers – someone sleeping in the same room as the boy?'

'The family was insistent. Eleanor Edevane came to see my boss, seeking assurances that nothing would be said publicly about Hilda Bruen. The nanny had a long association with the family and they wouldn't permit her reputation to be tarnished. The Detective Inspector didn't like it – ' he shrugged – 'but as I said, times were different then. A family like the Edevanes, gentry, they were allowed a certain leeway that wouldn't be granted now.'

Sadie wondered how many other leads had been lost through such 'leeway'. She heaved a sigh and leaned back against her seat, swivelled her pen this way and that before tossing it lightly onto her writing pad. 'There's so little to go on.'

Clive smiled with sad apology. He gestured towards the bloated file. 'You know, in all that lot, out of hundreds of interviews, there was only one eyewitness who thought she might have spotted something useful.'

Sadie raised her brows in query.

'One of the party guests reported seeing the silhouette of a figure, a woman's figure, in the nursery window on the night of the party. Just after midnight, according to her. The fireworks were underway. Almost didn't tell us, she said. She'd been skulking around with a fellow who wasn't her husband.'

Sadie's brows went higher.

'Said she wouldn't have been able to live with herself if the boy wasn't found because she hadn't come forward.'

'Was she credible?'

'She swore to what she'd seen, but you could still smell the alcohol on her the next day.'

'Could it have been the old nanny she saw?'

Clive shook his head. 'Doubtful. She insisted the silhouette was slim and Hilda Bruen was decidedly stout.'

Sadie took up the picnic photograph again. There were a lot of women in the Edevane family and all of them were slim. Indeed, it struck her as she considered the image that Anthony Edevane was the only man among them – aside from baby Theo, of course. He was a handsome man; in his early forties here, but with dark-blond hair and a heavy, intelligent brow, and the sort of smile Sadie suspected was bestowed freely on those he loved.

Her gaze slid to the woman beneath the stone wall, obscured by shade but for one slender ankle that had sneaked into sunlight. 'Why did she leave? Rose Waters, I mean.'

'She was let go.'

'Fired?' Sadie glanced up sharply.

'A difference of opinion, according to Eleanor Edevane.'

'Which opinion?'

'Something to do with taking liberties. It was all rather vague.'

Sadie considered this. It sounded like an excuse to her; the sort of thing people said when they were trying to mask an unpleasant truth. She looked at Eleanor. At first glance, Sadie had presumed the photograph was of a happy, carefree family enjoying a warm summer's day. It occurred to her now that she'd fallen under the same spell Clive described. Letting the Edevane family's charm and wealth and attractiveness dazzle her. She peered closer. Was she imagining strain in the pretty features of Eleanor's face? Sadie gave a slow, thoughtful sigh. 'What about Rose Waters? Did she report the same?'

'She did. Very distressed she was, too. She described the dismissal as unexpected and unfair. Particularly upsetting because it had been her first nannying job. She'd been there ten years, ever since she was eighteen years old. Not much she could do about it, though; the means of making a complaint didn't exist back then. She was lucky to have been given a good reference.'

The timing, Rose Waters's sense of an injustice having been done to her, her familiarity with the family and their rhythms. Sadie had a funny feeling. 'She must have been a suspect.'

'Everyone was a suspect. Everyone and no one. That was half the problem: the field never got any narrower. Rose Waters became very agitated when we interviewed her, frantic when she heard what had happened. She was terribly worried about the boy. They'd been very close according to the other servants. More than one commented that she loved the boy like he was her own.'

Sadie's heart had started to beat faster.

Clive appeared to notice. 'I know how it sounds,' he said, 'but it happened a lot back then, after the first war. A whole generation was sunk beneath the mud in France and with them went the marriage hopes of millions of young women. Employment as a nanny by a family like the Edevanes was as close to having a child as most of them would ever come.'

'Must've been hard being sent away from a little boy she loved.'

Clive, anticipating the line of thinking, said calmly, 'No doubt, but loving someone else's child is very different from stealing them. There was nothing to link her to the crime.'

'Except an eyewitness who saw a woman in the boy's nursery.'

He nodded ambivalently, clearly of the opinion that, while anything was possible, he considered the theory unlikely. 'No one saw her on the estate, she wasn't at the party, and a fellow on the desk at the hotel in London said he'd served her breakfast on the twenty-fourth of June.'

Alibis could be flimsy things. There were any number of reasons why one person might be induced to vouch for another. As to Rose Waters not being seen at Loeanneth, if Sadie's tunnel hunch proved correct, it was irrelevant.

Sadie felt the divine zing of a credible lead opening. It was a sensation she didn't think she'd ever tire of. The nanny had loved the boy; she'd been dismissed suddenly, and in her view unfairly; an eyewitness had reported seeing a woman's silhouette in the nursery. Furthermore, Rose Waters had lived for a time within the house. It was not unthinkable that she'd learned, during her tenure, of the tunnel. From one of the daughters, perhaps? Clementine? Was that the secret Clive suspected the youngest Edevane daughter of keeping?

To take the boy was an extreme measure, granted, but wasn't all crime the execution of an extreme reaction? Sadie tapped her fingertips against the table rim. Rose Waters's dismissal was important, she just *knew* it.

'I'll tell you one thing. It was a great shame she wasn't at Loeanneth that night,' Clive said. 'More than one person we interviewed commented on how vigilant Rose Waters was when it came to the little lad. Even Eleanor Edevane said it never would have happened if Nanny Rose had still been there. Full of remorse, she was.'

'For firing the nanny?'

He nodded. 'Of course, parents usually find a way to blame themselves, don't they?' He took up the photo and inspected it, gently brushing away a piece of dust with the back of his fingers. 'You know, she stopped coming back to the house during the Second World War. I thought it was just the war, such a bloody mess that made of everything, but even when it was over Eleanor Edevane never came back. I wondered about her sometimes, whether she'd been hit by a bomb. Terrible thing to say, but the war was like that: we all got used to people dying. Sad to think of the house left all alone, but it made sense she stayed away. So much death and destruction, time just kept dragging on, six long, hard years of war. The world was a different place once it ended. More than eleven years since the lad went missing. Whatever vigil she was keeping here, I think she'd moved beyond it, finally let the little lad go.'

Sadie wondered if he was right, whether there was a point at which even the most determined sufferer of bereavement cut their losses. Whether half a decade of war and austerity, of mass destruction and waste, could blot out the memory of a comparatively small, personal grief, no matter how searing it had been. Perhaps a person could learn to live with a shadow child. Anything was possible – just look at Maggie Bailey. She'd walked away from her child. ('She did not, she *never* would've done a thing like that,' Nancy Bailey insisted. Sadie shook the voice away.)

'So,' said Clive with a sorry smile. 'There you have it. The Edevane case in a nutshell. Thousands of man-hours, the best of intentions, decades of personal obsession, and next to nothing to show for it. No more decent leads today than we had in the first days of the investigation.'

Sadie felt the suspension of her unspoken theory heavy between them. Now was the time to tell him. He'd trusted her with his file, the least she could do was return the favour. She said, 'I might have something new.'

Clive cocked his head as if she'd spoken in a foreign language and he was trying to decode her statement for meaning.

'A theory, I mean.'

'I heard you.' His eyes brightened and, at the same time, narrowed, as if he were guarding against his own eagerness. His voice when he spoke was gravelly. 'Go on then.'

Sadie started with the map Alastair had found for her, its age and obscurity, its unusual provenance, moving on to describe the floorplan with its small unnamed wall cavity and her theory that it might lead to a tunnel.

He nodded urgently as she finished and said, 'I knew there was at least one tunnel, we checked it in the days following, even though the trapdoor in the garden had been sealed, but I didn't know anything about a tunnel leading to that part of the house – nobody did. This map was old, you say?'

'Very. It had been tucked away with other bits and pieces in a waterlogged cellar somewhere and was only found during recent renovations. The whole lot was sent for restoration and wound up at the County Archives, which is how I came by it.'

Clive reached beneath his glasses to rub the bridge of his nose. Eyes closed, thinking. 'I wonder if it's possible . . .' he mumbled. 'But why wouldn't someone have mentioned it? Perhaps they didn't know?'

'*We* don't even know,' Sadie reminded him. 'Not for certain. I need to get inside the house to check. I've written to Alice Edevane—'

'Pah,' he said sharply, meeting her eyes. 'You'll as soon get blood from a stone as any help from her.'

'I've noticed. Why is that? Why isn't she as eager as we are to know what happened?'

'No idea. Perversity? Pig-headedness? She's a crime writer. Did you know that? Very famous.'

Sadie nodded distractedly. Was that why she hadn't heard back? Had her letters become lost amongst the hundreds of others a writer like A. C. Edevane must receive? Fan letters, requests for money, that sort of thing.

'Police officer called Brent,' Clive continued. 'I've read a few of them. Not bad. Found myself trying to read between the lines, see whether there was anything in there that'd help with the case. I saw her on TV a while back. She was just as I remembered her.'

'How do you mean?'

'High and mighty, enigmatic, sure of herself. She was sixteen when her brother went missing, only a year younger than I was, but a different species. Cool as a cucumber when we interviewed her.'

'Too cool?'

A nod. 'I wondered at the time whether it was an act. I couldn't believe a young girl could be so self-possessed. Sure enough, I saw another side of her later. My gift as a policeman back then was my meekness. Like a church mouse, I was, always slipping beneath notice. It made me very useful. My boss had sent me out to find him a new pen – his old one had run out of ink – and as I was returning to the entrance hall I saw her lurking on the stairs, creeping towards the door of the library where we were conducting the interviews, before changing her mind and sneaking back again into the shadows.'

'You think she was trying to work up the courage to knock on the door and tell you something?'

'Either that, or she was awfully anxious to hear what was being said in there.'

'Did you ask her?'

'She turned those cool blue eyes on me and told me to stop haranguing her, to get on with finding her brother. Her voice was full of authority, but her face – it paled to almost white.' He leaned closer. 'In my experience, people who know more than they should about a crime behave in one of two ways: they either make themselves invisible, or else they're drawn to the investigation like a moth to a flame.'

Sadie considered this. 'I need to get inside that house.'

'You do. *We* do.' He met her gaze. 'Don't think for a second I'm not coming with you.'

'I'll write to her again this afternoon.'

'Yes.' He seemed about to say more.

'What is it?'

Clive straightened both sides of his knitted vest, making a careful effort to avoid eye contact. 'Best, of course, to have the owner's permission . . .'

'Yes,' Sadie agreed.

'. . . but there *is* another option. Local man, paid to look in every so often, make sure the vandals and wildlife don't get too cosy.'

'He hasn't been doing much of a job.'

'Be that as it may, the man has a key.'

'Ah.'

'I could put you in touch if you like?'

Sadie took a deep, thoughtful breath. She liked all right. But she was going up to London in a few days and she couldn't afford to set a foot wrong if she wanted Donald on side . . . 'I'll give it one more try,' she said finally. 'See if I can get Alice Edevane's permission.'

'And if you can't . . .'

'Then I know where to find you.'

Sixteen

Bertie's place was empty when Sadie arrived home. There was a note on the table advising that her grandfather was out on festival business, and an unwrapped gift beside it, a framed cloth with words embroidered inexpertly in orange thread. *May your past be a pleasant memory, Your future filled with delight and mystery, Your now a glorious moment, That fills your life with deep contentment.* An attached card informed Sadie it was a Celtic blessing made 'with love' by Louise for Bertie. She wrinkled her nose and slapped a slice of cheese between two pieces of bread. The thought was nice enough, she supposed, but Sadie could just imagine what Ruth would have said about the message. Her grandmother had always hated that sort of shallow sentiment. As far as Sadie knew, Bertie had, too.

She took her sandwich upstairs and sat on the window seat in her room, notebook balanced against her knees. Clive had baulked at letting her take the Edevane file home but said she was welcome to sit at his table making notes. Naturally, Sadie leapt at the offer and had still been scribbling furiously when a knock came at the door and a stout woman with a surfeit of chins let herself in.

'Sadie – ' Clive's voice held a note of panic as it raced the intruder down the hall – 'this is my daughter, Bess. Bess, this is Sadie, my . . .'

'Bridge partner.' Sadie moved swiftly to reorder and conceal the file before meeting the other woman with an outstretched hand as she arrived in the kitchen. They exchanged brief, polite how-do-you-dos, during which Bess expressed approval that her father had finally found himself an acceptable hobby, and then Sadie made her excuses and left amid promises to catch up again over the weekend 'for another game'.

She planned to do just that. She'd only managed to scratch the surface of the file's contents. There were hundreds of different documents, and with time so limited she'd concentrated on building herself a timeline of the investigation.

Two days after Theo Edevane was declared missing, police had launched the biggest search in Cornwall's history. Hundreds of local people had turned up at daybreak each morning, eager to do their bit, along with a group of men who'd served with Anthony Edevane in his First World War battalion. The coastline was scoured, as were the fields and woods. Police knocked on every door of every house the boy and his abductor might have passed.

Posters displaying Theo's photo were distributed and displayed throughout the county, and in the days after Midsummer the boy's parents made an appeal through the newspapers. The disappearance became a national news item, capturing the popular imagination, and police were inundated with information, some of it given anonymously. Every lead was followed up, no matter how crazy or unlikely it seemed. On 26 June, police discovered the body of Daffyd Llewellyn, but, as Clive had said, despite initial suspicion no connection was ever found between the writer's suicide and the missing child.

The investigation continued throughout July and on the eighth of that month police were brought in from the Met to assist the local force. Sadie could just imagine how that was received. They were followed closely by the legendary former inspector, Keith Tyrell, who was employed as a private detective by a London newspaper. Tyrell left after a week, with nothing new to show for his time in Cornwall; the London police returned home soon after. As autumn stretched towards winter, the search was scaled down, police unable to continue with no results. Despite three months of rigorous investigation, they'd found no further clues and uncovered no other witnesses.

Over the years, police continued to receive occasional tip-offs, all of which were investigated, none of which led to anything concrete. A letter was received by a local newspaper in 1936, purporting to be from Theo's kidnapper, but it proved to be a hoax; in 1938, a psychic in Nottingham declared that the boy's body was buried beneath the concrete foundations of a shed on a local farm, however a search revealed nothing; and in 1939, police were called to a nursing home in Brighton to reinterview Constance deShiel, whose new nurse had become concerned by the old woman's incessant, tearful claims that a little boy, dear to her, had been killed by a family friend. The nurse, who'd grown up in Cornwall and was familiar with the case, connected the dots and telephoned the police.

'She gets very upset,' the nurse told investigating officers. 'Frets about the boy's loss, talks on and on about the sleeping pills that were used to keep him quiet.' Though initially

promising, particularly in light of a missing bottle of seda-
tives in the Edevane case, the lead ultimately came to
nothing. Constance deShiel was unable to provide police
with any new, verifiable information and descended under
questioning into a rambling narrative about her daughter
Eleanor and a stillborn baby. The old woman's long-time
doctor, interviewed upon his return from holiday, confirmed
she was suffering from the late stages of dementia and the
murder claim was only one of a number of topics to which
her muddled mind returned. She was just as likely, he said, to
tell police her other favoured story, a detailed account of a
royal visit she'd never actually made. Which left them precisely where they'd been in late June 1933. Sadie tossed her
notebook onto the far end of the window seat. Nowhere.

She went for a run that evening. It was warm and dry, but
the air hummed with the promise of rain. Sadie followed one
of the tracks through the woods, the rhythm of her footfalls
helping to drive out clamouring thoughts. She'd been studying the case notes like a woman possessed ('obsessed,' said
Donald), and her brain ached from the effort.

The sun was low in the sky when she reached the verge
bordering Loeanneth, and the long grass of the meadow was
deepening from green to mauve. The dogs were in the habit
of continuing on to the house and Ash whimpered uncertainly when Sadie stopped. Ramsay, typically aloof, stalked
back and forth some metres away. 'Not today, I'm afraid,
boys,' she said. 'It's too late. I don't fancy getting stuck in the
woods after dark.'

There was a large smooth stick nearby and she lobbed it
into the meadow for them, a consolation prize. They were

off like shots, leaping and tumbling. Sadie smiled, watching them wrestle for the stick, then her focus shifted to the distant thicket of yew trees beyond. Light was fading, the hidden crickets on the fringe of the woods had started their evening song, and hundreds of tiny starlings soared above the knotty, darkening copse. Beneath them, hidden within its walls of greenery, the house was hunkering down for another night. Sadie pictured it, the last of the sun's rays glinting off the leadlight, the cool navy spread of the lake out front, the lonely set of the roof.

Blades of grass tickled her legs and she tugged at them absently, unsheathing the stalks one by one. The action, surprisingly satisfying, brought with it the memory of an article in one of the Edevane girls' little newspapers: instructions on how to weave a grass boat. Sadie tried it now, taking two flat strands, folding one over the other to make a sort of braid. Her fingers were clumsy, though, and the schoolyard task too foreign. It had been a long time since Sadie had done anything fiddly or whimsical. She tossed the strands aside.

It struck her that one of the characters in the A. C. Edevane novel she was reading had mentioned a childhood summer spent weaving boats from long pieces of grass. No great coincidence, of course. It made sense that an author would raid her own life to furnish her characters with thoughts and memories. That's what Clive had meant about reading between the lines of Alice's novels, searching for clues that might shed light on the disappearance of Theo Edevane. He hadn't mentioned finding anything – indeed, he'd confessed to the habit with a wry, self-deprecating smile, as if inviting Sadie to laugh with him at just how desperate he'd become for credible information. Now, though,

Sadie wondered. Not about the A. C. Edevane books so much as whether it was possible Alice knew something important, something she'd kept secret all these years.

Sadie glimpsed another largish stick and picked it up, jabbing it restlessly against the ground. Did that explain why Alice hadn't replied to her letters? Was she guilty? Clive was right; the guilty could generally be divided into two groups: those who were constantly underfoot as they strove to 'help' officers with their enquiries, and those who avoided police like the plague. Was Alice one of the latter? Had she seen something that night, and was Clive right when he guessed she'd been returning to the Loeanneth library to report it to police? Perhaps it was Alice who'd told Rose Waters about the tunnel; perhaps she'd even seen the nanny herself that Midsummer's Eve?

Sadie drove the stick hard into the dirt. Even as she thought it, she knew it wasn't enough. Supposing Alice *had* told Rose about the tunnel – it wasn't a sufficient sin, surely, for her to lie, not when a baby was missing, not unless there was some other reason Alice owed Rose Waters her silence. Sadie shook her head, impatient with herself. She was over-reaching, trying too hard, and she knew it. This was exactly why she needed to keep running, to shut off whatever habit it was inside her that wouldn't stop assembling theories.

Ash had won the game of tug-o'-war and arrived back at Sadie's feet now, dropping the stick with a proud flourish. He panted imploringly, before nudging it with his nose. 'Oh, all right,' she said, tousling his ears. 'Once more, and then we have to go.' She hurled the stick, prompting the dogs to bark with pleasure as they raced through the grass.

Truth was, Sadie had gone a bit cold on her Rose Waters

theory since leaving Clive's. No matter which way she turned it, kidnapping a child seemed too extreme a reaction for an otherwise sane woman. And by all reports – the file had contained more than one – Rose Waters was sane. She was also described, variously, as 'efficient', 'attractive' and 'vivacious', with an impeccable service record. She'd had only one month off in the ten years since she'd started work with the Edevanes, and then only because she was called away on 'a family matter'.

Even if she had been unfairly dismissed, and even if she did desire revenge against her employers, the grievance suffered didn't seem strong enough to fit the crime. Plus, there'd have been enormous practical difficulties in executing the abduction. Could one woman possibly have acted alone? If not, who was her accessory – Daffyd Llewellyn, some other unknown person? – and how was he (or she) induced to assist with such a personal vendetta? No, she was clutching at straws, seeking to draw connections where there were none. Even the motive now seemed weak. There'd been no legitimate ransom request, which rather scotched suggestion, didn't it, that Rose had been seeking financial recompense?

Far-off thunder made the air contract and Sadie cast an eye to the horizon. The sun was setting, throwing light onto a heavy band of dark grey clouds out at sea. Rain was coming. She called for the dogs, eager to get going. Her shoelace had come undone and she leaned her foot against a nearby stone to retie it. Regardless of who took him and why, the question of what happened to Theo Edevane remained. Presuming he'd survived beyond Midsummer 1933, he must have gone somewhere. Children couldn't be stolen and then absorbed into a new situation without drawing attention. Someone *must* have noticed. There must have been suspicions, especially in a case that had received so much press coverage. The fact that nothing credible had come to police attention over the course of seventy years suggested that Theo had been very well hidden, and the best place to hide a child was in plain sight. By inventing a scenario so believable that no one thought to question it.

Sadie was tightening her other shoelace when something on the stone caught her eye. Time had eaten away at the letters and a fine speckling of lichen grew over them, but the word was still perfectly clear to Sadie, who'd been spotting versions of the same all fortnight. ALICE. Only this one was different from the others; there was more etched beneath it, lower on the stone. She knelt, pulling the grass away as the first fat splotches of rain began to fall. It was another name. Sadie smiled. The engraving read, ALICE + BEN. ALWAYS.

The cottage was dark and still empty when Sadie and the dogs returned, cold, drenched and hungry. Sadie found a dry towel for Ash and Ramsay and then heated up some leftover stew (lentils and love!). She ate hunched over her notes at the table as rain drummed steadily on the roof and the dogs snored with deep contentment at her feet. When she'd all but licked clean a second bowl, Sadie wrote her third letter to Alice Edevane, requesting permission to enter the house. She considered asking outright whether there was a concealed tunnel in the hallway near the nursery on the second floor, but thought better of it. Neither did she mention Rose Waters or the keen interest she had in discussing Clementine

Edevane and any information she may have harboured on the case. Sadie said only that she had a theory she was keen to follow up and she'd be much obliged if Alice would get in touch. She'd missed the Saturday collection, but took an umbrella and ducked out in the dark to post the letter regardless. With any luck it would reach Alice on Tuesday; in the meantime, Sadie would be glad to know it was already on its way.

She took the opportunity while she was in the village and had a single flickering bar of mobile reception to hunker down beneath the awning of the general store and check her phone for messages. There was still nothing from Donald and Sadie pondered the fact before choosing not to interpret his silence as reproach, rather as tacit agreement that she should resume work as she'd suggested, after making contact in London next week.

On a whim, before leaving, she put in a call to Clive to ask about the 1939 nursing-home interview with Constance deShiel. Something in the account she'd read was flashing dully on the switchboard of her mind, but she couldn't put her finger on what or why. Clive was pleased to hear from her but disappointed when she posed her question. 'Oh, that,' he said. 'There was nothing in it. She'd deteriorated terribly by then, poor thing. Awful way to go – spent her days ranting and raving about the past, mixing things up, getting herself upset. No, it's Alice Edevane who holds the key to solving this thing. She's the one we need to talk to.'

The lights of Seaview Cottage were on when Sadie rounded the bend in the narrow cliff road. Bertie was in the kitchen making a pot of tea and he took a second cup from the draining board when Sadie sat down at the table. 'Hello there, love,' he said. 'You've had a big day.'

'I could say the same thing about you.'

'Twelve boxes of toys packed and ready to be sold.'

'You must be hungry. You missed dinner.'

'I'm all right. I had a bite while I was out.'

With Louise, no doubt. Her grandfather didn't offer further details and Sadie didn't want to seem petty or begrudging so resisted prompting. She smiled – a little thinly – as he passed her a steaming cup and sat opposite.

She noticed the embroidered gift from Louise was hanging on a hook by the door. 'I haven't missed your birthday, have I?'

He followed her gaze and smiled. 'It was a just-because gift.'

'That's kind.'

'Louise is kind.'

'Nice enough message. A little simplistic, perhaps.'

'Sadie—'

'I know where Ruth would've put it. Remember that framed copy of "Desiderata" she kept on the back of the toilet door?' She laughed. It sounded hollow.

'Sadie—'

'She said if a person couldn't go placidly amid the noise and haste in the WC, then what hope was there?'

Bertie reached across the table and took her hand. 'Sadie. Lovely girl.'

Sadie bit her bottom lip. Unaccountably, infuriatingly, his words made a sob lodge halfway up her throat.

'You're like a daughter to me. I'm closer to you than I ever was to my own. Funny thing, that. My own child but I've nothing at all in common with your mother. Even as a little girl she was so worried about what other people might think, concerned that we weren't doing things "properly", that Ruth or I would embarrass her if we didn't dress or speak or think precisely like the other parents.' He smiled softly and brushed at the white stubbly beard he'd been sporting since he came to Cornwall. 'You and I, we're much more alike. I think of you as a daughter, and I know you look to me as a parent. But Sadie, love, I'm just a person.'

'You're different here, Granddad.' She hadn't known she was going to say it. She hadn't even known she felt it. She sounded like a child.

'I hope I am. I mean to be. I'm trying to move on.'

'You even got your licence.'

'I'm living in the country! I can hardly be relying on the Tube to get me from A to B.'

'But all that talk Louise goes on with, about magic happening and letting the universe decide, that wall-hanging. That's not you.'

'It used to be, when I was a boy. I'd forgotten—'

'It's certainly not Ruth.'

'Ruth's gone.'

'And it's up to us to remember her.'

His voice was unusually brittle. 'Your grandmother and I met when I was twelve years old. I can't remember a time *without* her. My grief, her loss – it would swallow me if I let it.' He drained his teacup. 'The wall-hanging was a gift.' He smiled again, but there was sadness behind it and Sadie felt chagrin at knowing she was its cause. She wanted to say sorry, but then they hadn't really argued, and she felt criticised somehow, and prickly, and that made apology difficult.

She was still deciding what to say when he beat her to it. 'I'm missing my favourite colander. I might just pop upstairs and see if I can't find it.'

Sadie spent the rest of the evening sitting cross-legged on the floor of her room. She struggled through the first three pages of 'Fictional Escap(e)ades', before realising the chapter on Daffyd Llewellyn was an interpretation of his book rather than a biography of the man himself, and impenetrable into the bargain. She turned instead to the notes she'd taken at Clive's, flicking between them and the Edevane sisters' little newspapers. She'd been thinking about Clive's certainty that Alice held the key, and that had brought her to the engraving she'd found that afternoon in the stone. She had a vague feeling she'd come across the name 'Ben' somewhere over the past day, but couldn't for the life of her remember where.

Rain slid down the windowpanes, the sweet scent of pipe smoke seeped through the ceiling, and Sadie cast her gaze over the sprawl of pages, scribbled notes and books spread across the floor before her. Somewhere, within the mess, she just knew there were details itching to connect, she could *feel* it. Never mind that it looked like anarchy in paper form.

With a deep sigh, she extricated herself from her research and climbed into bed. She opened *A Dish Served Cold* and read for a while in an attempt to clear her mind. Turned out the restaurateur had indeed been murdered, and it was looking increasingly likely the man's ex-wife had done it. Twenty years they'd been divorced, decades in which the man had built his career and fortune, while his ex-wife devoted herself to the care of their disabled daughter. Her own career aspirations had been sacrificed along with her freedom, but she loved their daughter and the arrangement had seemed amiable enough.

The trigger, it transpired – Sadie turned the pages faster now – was the man's casual announcement that he was going away for a fortnight's holiday to South America. All her life, his ex-wife had nursed ambitions to visit Machu Picchu, but her daughter couldn't accompany her and wouldn't be left alone. That her ex-husband – a man who'd always found himself far too busy and important to help with their child's care – was now poised to live out her great dream was more than the woman could take. Decades of maternal grief, the isolation felt by all carers, the sublimation of a lifetime's worth of personal desires had snowballed, leading the otherwise mild-mannered woman to an inevitable conclusion that her ex-husband must be prevented from making the trip.

Surprised, satisfied and strangely invigorated, Sadie turned off the light and closed her eyes, listening to the storm and the choppy sea, the dogs dreaming and snorting on the end of her bed. A. C. Edevane had an interesting take on morality. Her detective had discovered the truth about the man's seemingly natural death but chosen not to disclose it to police. His duty as a private detective, Diggory Brent reasoned, had been to meet his brief by discovering where the money trail led. He had done that. No one had asked him to look into the manner of the restaurateur's death; it wasn't even considered suspicious. The man's ex-wife had shouldered an enormous burden for a long time and for very little recompense; if she were to be arrested, the daughter would be very much the worse off. Diggory decided he would say nothing and let justice take its course without him.

Sadie remembered Clive's description of a young Alice Edevane skulking around the library while police investigations were underway, his sense that she'd known more than she was letting on and his more recent hunch (somewhat desperate) that one of her books might reveal a clue. *A Dish Served Cold* might not mirror the events of Theo Edevane's disappearance, but it certainly suggested Alice had a nuanced outlook on matters of justice and its course. The novel had rather a lot to say about the complicated relationship between parents and children, too, describing the bond as both a burden and a privilege; an inextricable link, for better or for worse. Evidently Alice did not look kindly on those who shirked their responsibilities.

Sadie tried to sleep, but she wasn't a good sleeper at the best of times and thoughts of Rose Waters intruded. It was all the stuff about parenting and devotion and the commitment of carers, she supposed. The love the nanny had shown towards Theo, 'like he was her own'; her spotless employment record and the sudden, 'unfair' dismissal that had left her devastated; the eyewitness who'd sworn she saw a slim woman's figure moving in the nursery after midnight . . .

With a huff, Sadie rolled over and tried to clear her mind. An image came to her unbidden of the Edevane family picnic. The husband and wife at the centre, the loved little boy in the foreground, that slender ankle and leg in the shadows. She heard Clive's voice telling her how wanted the little boy had been, how long the Edevanes had waited for him, and she thought about the 1939 interview with Constance deShiel, in which the old woman was said to have 'rambled on about Eleanor and a stillborn child'. Perhaps it hadn't been a figment of her addled imagination after all. Maybe

Eleanor had been pregnant between Clementine and Theo. *'It was no secret they'd wanted a son,'* one of the interviews in Clive's file had read. *'It was such a blessing when they had him. So unexpected.'*

Sadie opened her eyes in the dark. Something else was flagging her attention.

She turned on the light and leaned over the side of the bed, riffling through the papers on the floor for the page she was after. It was one of the little newspapers written and produced by the Edevane sisters on the old printing press. She was sure she remembered reading something about Nanny Rose.

There it was.

She took the old pages up into bed with her. An article by Alice, detailing Clementine Edevane's punishment for having referred to Nanny Rose as fat. Sadie checked the date, did a quick mental calculation, and then jumped out of bed to get her notebook. She scrabbled through the pages until she came to her notes outlining Rose Waters's employment record – in particular, her absence of a month in July 1932 when she was called away on 'a family matter'. The dates matched.

Sadie looked through the window – the moonlit cliffs, the turbulent inky sea, lightning on the horizon – trying to straighten her thoughts. Clive had said, *Why would a parent kidnap their own child?* He'd been talking about Anthony and Eleanor Edevane and the question had been rhetorical, a joke, because of course parents didn't need to kidnap their own children. They already had them.

But what about in cases where they didn't?

Sadie's face was pulsing warm. A new scenario was

forming. She could think of a reason why a parent might kidnap their own child.

Details folded into place, as if they belonged together, as if they'd been *waiting* for someone. A maid in trouble . . . A little boy in need of a home . . . A mistress who couldn't have her own child . . .

It had been a solution that suited everybody. Until suddenly it didn't.

Seventeen

London, 2003

The message was curt, even by Alice's standards. She had gone out, she would be back later. Peter pondered the piece of paper – he couldn't bring himself to call it a note – and wondered what it meant. Alice's behaviour lately had been odd. She'd been prickly, even more so than usual, and very distracted. Peter suspected things weren't going well with the new book, beyond the typical authorial angst he'd come to expect, and that Alice's creative problems were a symptom rather than the cause of her troubles.

He had a feeling he knew the cause. Her face when he'd relayed Deborah's phone message on Friday had drained of colour, and her reaction, the slight quiver in her voice, had reminded him of earlier in the week when the letter from the detective had arrived, asking about the old unsolved police case. The two things were connected, Peter was sure of it. Furthermore, he was convinced they related to the real-life crime in Alice's family's past. He knew now about the little boy, about Theo. Alice had tried to conceal her shock when the letter arrived, but Peter had noticed the way her hands started to shake, how she'd hidden them beneath the table where he couldn't see. The reaction, combined with her vehement denial of the letter's contents, had piqued his interest sufficiently that when he was sitting at his home computer that night, he found himself typing *Edevane* and *missing child* into the internet search engine. That's how he knew Alice's baby brother had disappeared in 1933 and never been found.

What he didn't know was why on earth she'd lie about it, and why the whole affair had her so rattled. He'd arrived for work one morning and found her passed out in an armchair in the library. His heart had thumped and for a split second he'd feared the worst. He'd been on the verge of administering uncertain CPR when she emitted a spluttery snore and he realised she was sleeping. Alice Edevane did not take naps. Peter would have been less surprised had he opened the door and found her belly-dancing in coin-rimmed silken robes. She'd woken with a jolt and he'd slipped back into the hall so they could both pretend he hadn't seen. He'd made a noisy show of removing his shoes and given the coat rack an extra shake for good measure, before returning to find her reading over a draft chapter, red pen in hand. And now this. An unexpected break from routine. Only Alice Edevane did not break routine, not once in the three years he'd been working for her.

The unexpected turn of events was perplexing, but it did at least give him an opportunity to finish the website FAQ page. Alice's publishers had been in contact again, patience straining as the publication date drew nearer, and Peter had promised he'd have the final content to them by the end of the week. He would, too. All that remained was to ascertain whether or not Alice had written a manuscript before *In the Blink of an Eye*. The *Yorkshire Post* article from 1956 that he wanted to crib his answer from quoted Alice as saying she'd written an entire mystery novel, her first, in the note-book she'd received for her fifteenth birthday, and Peter figured it would be simple enough to confirm. Alice was pathological about her notebooks; she never went anywhere without the current one and she kept all of them, without exception, on a set of shelves in her writing room. All he had to do was check.

He started up the stairs, caught himself whistling self-consciously and stopped. There was no need for an outward show of innocence. Only guilty people did that and there was nothing untoward in what he was doing. Entry to Alice's office was not forbidden; at least, nothing had ever been said to that effect. Peter didn't ordinarily go in there, but that was merely a matter of circumstance. The opportunity rarely arose. They always held their meetings in the library, and Peter worked at the large kitchen table or, some-times, in the spare room that had long ago been given over to files.

It was a hot day and sun streamed through the narrow window at the top of the stairs. Warm air had risen up the stairwell, pooling on the landing with nowhere else to go, and Peter was glad to open the door to Alice's dim, cool writing room and slip inside.

As expected, on the shelf beneath all her international first editions he found the notebooks. The first was small and thin, clad in brown leather that had softened and faded with time. Peter opened the cover and saw, on the yellowing frontispiece, the careful, rounded penmanship of a conscien-tious child. *Alice Cecilia Edevane, age 8 years old*. He smiled. The handwritten line offered a glimpse of the Alice he knew – confident, formidable, set in her ways – as a diligent young

girl with her whole life ahead of her. He returned the notebook and counted lightly along the row. By his calculations,
the book he was looking for was the one she'd received in
1932 and used into the following year. He stopped and took
a rather larger volume from the shelf.

Peter knew at once something was amiss. The notebook
was far too light for its size, and too thin in his hand. Sure
enough, when he opened it, half the pages were gone, only a
thick fringe of rough stubs remaining where they'd been
torn. He confirmed that it was indeed the book from 1932–3,
and ran his finger thoughtfully down the tattered ends. In
and of itself it meant nothing. As Peter understood it, plenty
of teenage girls tore pages from their diaries. Only this
wasn't a diary per se, it was a notebook. And it wasn't a few
pages; more than half the book was missing. Enough for the
draft of a novel? That depended on the novel's length.

Peter skimmed through the early extant pages. The pecu-
liarity of the find had attached an air of unease to the task
and he felt suddenly like a thief. He reminded himself he was
merely doing his job. That this was what Alice paid him to
do. *I don't want to know about it*, she'd said when she told
him to get on with the website. *Just make it happen.* Simply
find the answer, he told himself, then put the book back and
be done with it.

The early pages looked promising. They appeared to be
filled with observations of her family (Peter smiled when he
recognised Alice's description of her grandmother – 'a skeleton in the ashes of a rich dress' – as a quote from *Great
Expectations*), and ideas for a novel about people called
Laura and Lord Hallington, who were involved in a terribly
complicated love affair. There were also frequent references

to a person called 'Mr Llewellyn', who Peter gathered was the published writer Alice had mentioned in her interview, her childhood mentor.

But then the plotting came to an abrupt halt, abandoned, it seemed, for a numerical list titled: *The Rules According to Mr Ronald Knox, Adapted from the Preface to* Best Detective Stories.

The list of rules, though old-fashioned and didactic by today's standards, seemed to usher in a new era of Alice's creative life, for afterwards there was no further mention of Laura and Lord Hallington (or Mr Llewellyn, for that matter), their childish interactions replaced by more general musings on life and love, earnest and touchingly idealistic in their naive tone of optimism.

Peter glanced quickly through Alice's teenage exhortations on the purpose of literature, her attempts to replicate the ecstatic descriptions of nature in the romantic poems she cited as favourites, her eager articulation of her aspirations for the future: *to desire fewer possessions and to possess greater love*. He was beginning to feel uncomfortably voyeuristic, ready almost to give up the search, when he came across something that made him start. The initials BM had begun to appear in Alice's jottings. *According to BM . . . , BM says . . . , I will ask BM . . .* Anyone else might not have remembered the name Deborah had asked him to pass on to Alice in her phone message, but Peter had gone to school with a boy called Benjamin and the two of them had worked a paper round for a shopkeeper called Mr Munro, so when Deborah said the name, the coincidence had cemented the name in Peter's mind. Benjamin Munro, the man whose mention had made Alice pale.

Around the same time references to 'BM' began to pepper the journal, Alice appeared to start plotting a new novel. *A mystery, this time, a proper detective story with an ingenious method that no one will ever guess!* Planning continued over the next few pages, arrows and scribbled questions and hastily sketched maps and diagrams – techniques that were familiar from her current notebooks – and then an entry dated April 1933: *I am going to start BBB first thing tomorrow. I already have the first and last lines in mind, and a clear idea of everything that needs to happen in between (thanks, in part, to BM). I know this is going to be the one I'll finish. It already feels different from everything I've written before.* Whether or not she started BBB, and whether or not she finished, Peter couldn't say. Beneath her mission statement, something had been scribbled out with such vehemence that a hole had been torn in the paper, and then there was nothing. The rest of the pages had been removed.

Why would Alice have expunged the draft of a novel? She who was meticulous, almost superstitious, about keeping everything that contributed to the creation of a book. 'A writer never destroys her work!' she'd told the BBC. 'Even if she loathes it. To do so would be akin to denying the existence of an awkward child.' Peter stood up and stretched, glancing through the window that overlooked the heath. It might mean nothing. They were missing pages in a teenage journal. Pages written seventy years before. But Peter couldn't shake the feeling of unease that had crept upon him. Alice's recent behaviour, the way she'd denied the old police case, her shock when he'd given her Deborah's message, when he'd spoken the name Benjamin Munro. Even the small inexplicable mystery as to why she'd started telling journalists she'd never written before her first published novel. Something was going on and Alice was worried.

Peter slipped the notebook back into place, taking extra care to do so quietly, as if that might somehow erase the fact that he'd ever taken it off the shelf and looked inside. He'd decided simply to omit the question about Alice's first completed work of fiction from the FAQ page. He wished he'd done that at the start instead of coming up here and opening Pandora's box.

Perhaps it was his haste to leave the attic and put the whole thing behind him that caused him to trip over the lamp. Perhaps it was simply his usual gift for clumsiness. Whatever the case, the lamp was tall and free-standing, and Peter sent the whole thing teetering sideways to land against Alice's desk. A glass, thankfully empty, was bowled over, and Peter was setting it back to rights when he saw the envelope addressed to Alice. This, in and of itself, was not unusual; they were in Alice's home, after all. However, the post was Peter's remit and this was a letter he had not seen. Which meant it had been intercepted from the morning's pile without his knowledge.

Peter hesitated, but only briefly. He was fond of Alice. They weren't exactly on a grandmother/grandson footing, but he cared for her, and in light of everything else that was going on he felt a responsibility to her. He opened the letter, just enough to see who it was from. *Sadie Sparrow.* It wasn't the sort of name a person with a predilection for words forgot and Peter remembered at once the letter that had arrived exactly a week before. The police detective investigating the old case of a missing child. The case from 1933, the same year BM made his appearance in Alice's journal and the disputed manuscript had been (presumably) torn out. Peter experienced the grim sense of pieces of a puzzle coming together, while remaining frustratingly in the dark as to what that puzzle's picture revealed. He tapped his fingers against his lips, considering, and then glanced again at the thin sheet of paper folded on the desk. This really was snooping. It most certainly wasn't part of his job description. Peter had a sense of himself perched on the edge of a cliff, deciding whether to jump or retreat. With a shake of his head, he sat down and began to read.

Alice decided to walk through the park. The fresh air, she told herself with more than a little constitutional irony, would do her good. She hopped off the Tube at Hyde Park Corner and rode the escalator to the surface. It was much warmer today than it had been earlier in the week. The air was still and the heat thick, that particular kind of city heat that seemed to magnify in the spaces between tarmac and building. The Tube lines, with their seething serpents hissing through the tunnels, belching out sweaty commuters at each station, were like something out of Dante. She started along Rotten Row, taking assiduous note of the rose gardens and the faint scent of lilac, as if she really were walking because she fancied being alone with nature, and not simply to put off a little longer the awful task she knew was ahead.

It was Deborah who'd forced today's meeting. Alice, after Peter gave her the phone message on Friday (the horrific chill of hearing her assistant speak Benjamin Munro's name!), had decided the best course of action was denial. There was no reason she and Deborah needed to see one another over the coming months. Eleanor's anniversary had been and gone, the next family gathering wasn't until Christmas, which left plenty of time for the whole thing to blow over. For Alice to make *sure* it blew over. But Deborah had been insistent, employing that particular brand of gentle force she'd always wielded as the eldest sister and further mastered during her decades as a politician's wife. 'There are things we simply must discuss.'

Whatever the extent of Deborah's knowledge about Theo, she'd evidently travelled a considerable distance down memory lane, arriving at a place that made Alice very nervous. How much, she wondered, did Deborah know? She remembered Ben, but did she know what Alice had done? She must. Why else would she insist they meet to talk about the past?

'Do you remember Nanny Rose?' Deborah had said before ringing off. 'Strange, wasn't it, how she left so suddenly.' Alice had felt the closing-in of walls she'd been holding back for a very long time. Extraordinary the way it was all happening at once. (Though in truth it was she, Alice, who'd triggered Deborah's interest, with her questions at the museum. If only she'd kept her mouth shut.) Just that morning, Alice had received a third letter from the detective, more brusque than the others and with a single worrying development. This Sparrow person was now seeking permission to go inside the house 'to test a theory'.

Alice stopped walking as a dragonfly hovered close. *Yellow-winged darter.* The name came to mind of its own accord. She watched as the insect flickered towards a nearby garden bed, a spectacular tangle of summer flowers, red, mauve and brilliant orange. Gardens really were a balm. A bee vacillated between blooms and Alice experienced a sudden flash of all-body memory. They came often lately. She could *feel* what it would be like to creep into that garden, her body lithe and ache-free, to snake beneath the cool foliage and lie on her back so that the sky broke into bright blue diamonds through the branches and her ears were filled with the choir of insect life.

She didn't, of course. She continued along the path, leaving the garden and the strange flash of memory behind her. It could only be the tunnel, she thought, this theory of Sadie Sparrow's. She must have learned somehow of the second tunnel. Alice waited to feel panic but instead was visited only by a dull sense of resignation. It had been inevitable, she'd always known that. One of the biggest pieces of luck in the whole event had been the failure (to this point) of anyone to mention the tunnel to the police. Because Alice hadn't been the only one who'd known about it in 1933. There were others. Her parents, her sisters, Grandmother deShiel and Nanny Rose, who'd had to be told the winter Clemmie managed to get herself stuck behind its tricksy latch.

Alice slowed down as she reached the part of Rotten Row where the path branched off to form a bridge across the Serpentine. Beyond the water was the great green stretch of the park. Alice could never look at it without thinking of the Second World War. There'd been sandbags then, and vegetables in rows, the whole expanse given over to productive purpose. It seemed a rather quaint idea now, a harking back to the medieval past, as if a starving, bomb-battered nation might somehow be fed with the pickings from His Majesty's royal vegetable patch. At the time it had seemed eminently sensible; more than that, it had seemed vital. Their boys were dying in foreign lands and bombs rained down on London at night and supply ships were being obliterated by U-boats before they could dock, but the people of Britain would not be starved out. They would win the war, one vegetable patch at a time.

At the Imperial War Museum some years ago, Alice had overheard a couple of schoolboys sniggering at a poster of Potato Pete boasting that he made a good soup. The boys were lagging behind their classmates and when the teacher chastised them, the taller one looked as if he might cry. Alice had felt a ripple of Schadenfreude. Why was it that so much of the paraphernalia left over from the war made it seem as if it had been polite or quaint or mannerly, when in fact it had been fierce and deathly? People had been different back then, more stoical. There was far less talk of one's emotions. People were taught from childhood not to cry when they were hurt, to be good losers, not to acknowledge fears. Even Nanny Rose, who was sweetness personified, would have frowned to see tears when she poured iodine onto scrapes and scratches. Children were expected to face their fate when it came for them. Very useful skills, as it turned out, during wartime; indeed, as they were in life.

The Edevane women had all pitched in when war broke out. Clemmie joined the ATA, moving planes between bases for the RAF; Alice drove a hearse-turned-ambulance through the bomb-broken streets; and Deborah corralled busy volunteers in the WVS. But it was Eleanor who surprised them all. Deborah and Alice had urged their parents to seek shelter in the country, but their mother had refused. 'We'll stay here and do our bit,' she'd said. 'We wouldn't think of skiving off, and you're not to suggest it. If it's good enough for the King and Queen, it's good enough for us. Isn't that right, darling?' She'd smiled at their father, who was already suffering with the pleurisy that would kill him, and he'd squeezed her hand in solidarity. And then she'd taken up arms with the Red Cross, bicycling around the East End offering medical assistance to mothers and children who'd been bombed out of their homes.

Sometimes Alice saw the city as a map in her mind, with pins dropped in all the places to which she could claim a connection. That map was covered, the pins piling up on top of one another. It was quite a thing to spend the majority of one's life in the same place. To acquire countless memories that layered in one's mind so that certain geographic locations gained an identity. Place was so important to Alice's experience of the world that she wondered sometimes how nomadic people gauged the passing of time. How did they mark and measure their progress if not against a constant that was so much bigger and more enduring than they were? Perhaps they didn't. Perhaps they were happier for the lack.

One of the things that had most intrigued her about Ben was his itinerant nature. There were countless people made homeless after the First World War, sad men whose presence in streets all over Britain, holding signs that asked for work or food or money, cast a pall over the decade. Alice and her sisters were told to give when they could and never to stare; they were taught to pity. Ben wasn't like those displaced soldiers, though. He was the first person Alice had met who lived that way by choice. Moving from job to job, no more possessions than what he could carry in his pack. 'I'm a wanderer,' he'd said with a smile and a shrug. 'My father used to say there was gypsy blood on my mother's side.' For Alice, whose grandmother had always had plenty to say about the gypsies and vagrants who passed through the woods near Loeanneth, the concept was anathema. She had grown up grounded in the sureness and solidity of her family's history. The legacy of her father's people, their story of hard work and enterprise, the building of the Edevane empire; and her mother's family, with its deep roots in the plot of land they still called home. Even Eleanor and Anthony's feted love story centred around his rescue and restoration of Loeanneth. Alice had always thought it a terribly noble story, gladly taking on her mother's passion for the Lake House. She'd never imagined there was any other way for a person to live.

But Ben was different and he made her see things differently. He had no desire to possess things or to accumulate wealth. It was enough, he said, that he was able to get himself from one place to the next. His parents had worked on archaeological digs in the Far East when he was a boy and he'd realised then that the possessions people coveted in the fleeting present were destined to disappear; if not to turn to dirt, then to lie buried beneath it, awaiting the curiosity of future generations. His father had unearthed many such items, he said, beautiful objects that would once have been fought over. 'And they all ended up lost or discarded, the people who'd owned them dead and gone. All that matters to me are people and experience. Connection – that's the thing. That flicker of electricity between people, the invisible tie.' Alice had blushed when he said that. She'd known exactly what he meant; she'd felt it too.

Only once had Alice heard him talk about his lack of money with unhappiness and regret. She remembered it because of the unpleasant emotion it aroused in her. He had grown up with a girl, he said, an English girl, a few years older, whose parents were working on the same dig as his. She'd taken him under her wing, being thirteen to his eight years old, and because they were two of a kind, together in a strange land, they'd bonded tightly. 'I was a little bit in love with her, of course,' he said with a laugh. 'I thought she was so pretty with her long plaits and hazel eyes.' When the girl – Florence was her name ('Flo', he called her, the intimacy of the nickname a barb to Alice) – left for England with her parents, the two of them continued to write, letters that became more lengthy and more personal as Ben grew up. Each remained a constant in the other's peripatetic life, and when he returned to Britain at the age of seventeen they reconnected. She was married by then, but insisted he stay with her whenever he passed through London; they remained the closest of friends. 'She's the most generous person,' he said. 'Fiercely loyal, very kind and always ready to laugh.' Recently, though, she and her husband had fallen on hard times. They had a business they'd struggled to start, putting all their savings together and working themselves to the bone, and now the landlord threatened to evict them. 'They've had other difficulties, too,' he said. 'Personal troubles. Such good people, Alice, with modest desires. This is the last thing they need.' He'd been sharpening the pruning shears when he said, 'I'd do anything to help them.' A new note of frustration entered his tone. 'But the only thing that will make a difference is money and I've no more of that than what's in my pocket.'

The plight of his friend made Ben bitter and Alice, helplessly in love by now, longed to fix things for him. At the same time, she was filled with blackest envy for this other woman (*Flo* – how she hated the casual brevity of that nickname) who'd played such a vital role in his life, whose unhappiness, hundreds of miles away in London, had the power to blight his mood, right here and now.

But time has a funny way of quieting even the most intense passions. Ben didn't mention his friend again and Alice, who was young, after all, and therefore self-centred, let Flo and her plight slip from memory. By the time she told him about the idea she'd had for *Bye Baby Bunting*, three or four months later, she'd quite forgotten about the time he told her he'd do anything – anything at all – to get the money necessary to help his childhood friend.

On the other side of the Serpentine, a child was running towards the water. Alice faltered and then stopped, watching as the little girl or boy, it was hard to tell, reached the water's edge and started tearing off small jagged pieces of bread, sprinkling them from a fist as a cluster of ducks gathered. A honking swan came quickly, seizing the remaining bounty in one fell swoop. Its beak was sharp and near and the child began to cry. A parent came, as parents do, and the child was easily mollified, but the incident put Alice in mind of the mallards at Loeanneth, so greedy and bold. She wondered if they were still there, and the wondering put a catch in her throat. That happened sometimes. After years of determined denial, a wave of brutal curiosity about the house, its lake and gardens that was almost breathtaking would come upon her.

When they were children at Loeanneth they'd spent the summer in and out of the water, their skin turning brown beneath the sun, their hair bleaching almost white. Despite her weak chest, Clemmie had been the most outdoorsy of them all, with her long, skinny foal's legs and windblown nature. She should have been born later. She should have been born now. There were so many opportunities these days for girls like Clemmie. Alice saw them everywhere, spirited, independent, forthright and focused. Mighty girls unbounded by society's expectations. They made her glad, those girls, with their nose rings and their short hair and their impatience with the world. Sometimes Alice felt she could almost glimpse her sister's spirit moving in them.

Clemmie had refused to speak to anyone in the months after Theo disappeared. Once the police had done their interviews, she'd shut her mouth, tight as a clam, and behaved as if her ears had switched off too. She'd always been eccentric, but it seemed to Alice, looking back, that during the late summer of 1933 she became downright wild. She hardly returned home, prowling around the airfields, slicing at the reeds by the stream with a sharpened stick, creeping inside the house only to sleep, and not even that most nights. Camping out in the woods or by the stream. God only knew what she ate. Birds' eggs, probably. Clemmie had always had a gift for raiding nests.

Mother was beside herself. As if the anguish over Theo wasn't enough, now she had to worry about Clementine, too, out there in the elements. Clemmie had come back eventually, though, smelling of dirt, her hair long and tangled, and none the worse for wear. The summer had ripened and rotted so that autumn when it fell was thick and sullen. With it, an interminable grief settled over Loeanneth, as if all hope that Theo would be found had died with the warmer season. When the police search was officially called off, the policemen full of apologies, the decision was made that the

Edevane family should return to London. Deborah's wedding was to be held there in November and it made sense that the family take a few weeks to settle in first. Even Mother, usually loath to leave the country, had seemed glad to escape the cold, stultifying sadness of the Lake House. The windows were sealed, the doors locked, the car loaded.

Back in London, Clemmie had been forced to wear shoes again. New dresses were bought to replace those she'd torn and outgrown and a place was found for her at a day school for girls that specialised in maths and science. She'd liked that. After a succession of old-fashioned governesses, none of whom had lasted long at Loeanneth, real school had been the sweetener, the reward for acquiescence. It had been a relief, in a way, to see her brought back from the brink, but Alice had quietly mourned the loss of her savage sister. Clemmie's reaction to grief had been so primitive, so raw, that even observing it had been a release of sorts. Her return to civilisation compounded the tragedy and made it permanent, for if Clemmie had given up hope, then there really was none left.

Alice had been walking faster than she'd meant to and an ache was tightening her chest. A stitch, she told herself, certainly not a heart attack. She reached a seat and sank onto it. She decided she would stay a moment and catch her breath. The breeze was light on her skin, and warm. In front of her was a bridle path and beyond it a playground where children were scaling colourful plastic equipment, chasing one another while their nannies, girls with ponytails, wearing jeans and T-shirts, chatted beneath a tree. Adjacent to the playground was a sand-covered enclosure where mounted officers from the Knightsbridge barracks were training. It struck Alice that this was very near the spot she'd sat with Clemmie that day in 1938. It was true what people said, that when one became old (and how sneakily that happened, how sly time was), memories of the long-ago past, repressed for decades, were suddenly bright and clear. A prim little girl had been taking riding lessons, round and round the sand in circles. Alice and Clemmie had been lounging on a picnic blanket discussing Clemmie's intention to begin flying lessons. It was before the war started, and life in London for the daughters of well-to-do families was much as it always had been, but there was talk everywhere if you knew where to listen. Alice had always known where to listen. So, it seemed, did Clemmie.

Seventeen by now, she had flatly refused to participate in the Season and only narrowly been stopped at the docks after selling a number of family heirlooms so she might travel to Spain and fight with the Republicans in the civil war. Alice, impressed by her sister's grit, had nonetheless been glad to see her dragged back home. This time, however, seeing Clemmie's doggedness, the fierce enthusiasm with which she brandished the newspaper advertisement for the flying school, Alice had promised to do whatever was necessary to help convince their parents to agree. The day was warm and they'd finished their lunch and a pleasant lull had settled over them, due in part to the recent accord they'd reached. Alice was leaning back on her elbows, eyes closed behind her sunglasses, when Clemmie said, apropos of nothing, 'He's still alive, you know.'

It turned out she hadn't given up hope, after all.

*

Now, Alice looked for the precise place they'd been sitting. It had been near a garden bed, she remembered, and between two enormous roots of a chestnut tree. There hadn't been a playground then and the nannies, in long dresses and cloth hats, had gathered by the Serpentine, holding the hands of their small charges, pushing the littlest in large black perambulators. By Christmas that year, the grass would be gone, making way for trenches built in preparation for future air raids; that day with Clemmie, though, the war with all its terror and death was still ahead of them. The world was in one piece and the sun still shone.

'He's still alive, you know.'

Five years had passed, but Alice knew at once whom Clemmie meant. It was the first time Alice had heard her sister speak of Theo since he disappeared and she felt the burden of confidante heavily. Adding weight to the responsibility was her certainty that Clemmie was wrong. Stalling, she said, 'How do you know?'

'I just do. It's a feeling.'

The girl on the horse was trotting now, and the horse shook its mane so that it glistened proudly.

Clemmie said, 'There was no ransom note.'

'So?'

'Well, don't you see? If there was no ransom note, whoever took him did so because they wanted him.'

Alice didn't reply. How was she to let her sister down gently while leaving no doubt? How was she to do so without confessing too much?

Clemmie's face, meanwhile, had become animated. She was talking quickly, as if she'd been waiting five years to speak and now that she'd started there must be no hesitation.

'I think it was a man,' she was saying, 'a father without a child, who was visiting Cornwall and happened to see our Theo and fell madly in love with him. That man had a wife, you see, a kind lady who dearly wanted children but had been unable to have them. I can picture them, Alice, the husband and his young wife. Well-off, but not stiff or pompous, in love with one another and the imagined children they intend to have. I can see them getting sadder as the years pass, and the woman fails to fall pregnant, and the realisation slowly dawns that they might never hear little footsteps in the hall or laughter from the nursery. A pall settles over the house, and all music and happiness and light leave their lives, until one day, Alice, one day when the man is away from London on business, or meeting an associate –' she waved a hand, 'it doesn't matter why – he comes near Loeanneth, and he sees Theo, and he knows this is the very child to bring joy back to his wife's soul.'

The trotting horse had whinnied right then and Alice saw Loeanneth in her mind, the surrounding fields of farmland, the neighbouring horses for whom they'd used to sneak Cook's apples. Clemmie's story was full of holes, of course, not least because nobody stumbled unwittingly on Loeanneth; it was also inspired, at least in part, by Deborah's troubles. ('Five years and still no baby,' the whispers skated off the walls at society gatherings.) A memory came of nightingales by the lake on the cusp of dawn and she shivered violently, despite the sun's strength on her skin. Clemmie didn't notice.

'You see, don't you, Alice? It wasn't the right thing to do, and it brought misery to our family, but it was understandable. Theo would have proven irresistible. Do you remember the way he used to wave his arms when he was happy, like he was trying to take off?' She smiled. 'And he was so *wanted*. He's growing up surrounded by love, Alice, happy. He was young when he went, he'll have forgotten us, forgotten that he was ever part of us, even if we could never forget him. I can live with my own grief when I think of him happy.'

There'd been nothing Alice could say to that. She was the writer in the family, but Clemmie had a gift for seeing the world through a different lens. If she were honest, Alice had always been in awe, even a little jealous, of her sister's imagination, as if her own claims to creativity, her stories, the product of so much effort and error, were rendered lesser beside Clemmie's innate originality. Clemmie's was a naivety of sorts that necessarily cast the other person in the role of realistic brute. Alice didn't want to play that part, and what point was there in arguing? Why destroy the enchanting fantasy her sister had created: a new life for Theo, a loving family? Wasn't it enough that she, Alice, knew the truth?

But Alice, greedy, had wanted to hear more of Clemmie's story. 'Where do they live?' she'd asked. 'How did Theo turn out?' As Clemmie spun her answers, Alice had closed her eyes and listened, envying her sister her innocence and certainty. It was such an alluring way to think, even if misguided. For Theo wasn't living a new life with a loving family in a beautiful home. Clemmie was right that there'd been no ransom note, but wrong about what it meant. Alice knew, though. The lack of ransom note meant that it had all gone terribly wrong and Theo was dead. She knew because it was exactly how she'd planned it.

Eighteen

The day she came up with it had started like any other. It was 1933, early spring but still cold, and she'd been sitting in the Loeanneth airing cupboard all morning with her feet against the hot-water tank, reading through the collection of newspaper clippings she kept beneath lock and key in the filigree metal box Grandfather Horace had brought back from India and she'd purloined from the attic. She'd found an article about the kidnapping of the Lindbergh boy in America and it had got her thinking about ransoms and notes and how a criminal might best baffle police. She'd realised recently (an awareness that coincided with her new obsession with Agatha Christie) that what her previous story attempts were missing was a puzzle, a complex, knotty twist of events designed to mislead and bewilder readers. Also, a crime. The key to the perfect novel, Alice had decided, was to revolve the story around a crime's solution, all the while tricking the reader by making it seem she was doing one thing when in fact she was merrily doing another. Pressing her woollen-socked toes into the tank's warm cladding, she scribbled and jotted, turning over ideas as to who and why and, most importantly, how.

She was still thinking along these lines after lunch when she rugged up in her mother's old sable coat and sought out Ben in the garden. It was blustery out, but he was by the fishpond where he'd been building the secret garden, the whole thing sheltered within a tall circular hedge. She sat down on the cold marble edge of the pond, digging the heels of her Wellington boots into the mossy surrounds, and experienced a jolt of pleasure when she saw the copy of *The Mysterious Affair at Styles* she'd lent him peeking from his kitbag.

Ben was on the other side of the garden clawing at weeds and hadn't heard her approach, so Alice sat for a moment. His forearms were exposed, perspiration beginning to bead and crumbs of dirt clinging to his damp skin. He flicked longer strands of dark hair from his eyes and finally she could stand it no longer. 'I've had a brilliant idea,' she said.

He turned quickly; she'd startled him. 'Alice!' Surprise gave way quickly to pleasure. 'An idea?'

'I've been working on it all morning and I don't like to boast, but I'm quite sure it's going to be my best yet.'

'Is it?'

'It is.' And then she said the words that later she'd have given anything to take back. 'A kidnapping, Ben. I'm going to write a book about a kidnapping.'

'A kidnapping,' he repeated, scratching his head. 'Of a child?'

She nodded eagerly.

'Why would someone want to take a child that wasn't theirs?'

'Because the parents are rich, of course!'

He looked at her perplexedly, as if not sure how one thing connected to the other.

'For money.' Alice rolled her eyes playfully. 'A ransom.' An edge of sophistication had sharpened her voice, making her sound, to her own ears, very much a woman of the world. As she continued outlining the plan for him, Alice couldn't help but admire the appealing element of danger her story lent to her, an impression that she knew an awful lot about the workings of the criminal mind. 'The kidnapper in my story will have fallen on hard times. I'm not sure how exactly, I haven't settled on the details. Perhaps he was cut out of a will and lost his inheritance, or else he's a scientist and he's made a tremendous discovery but his business partner, the father of the child, has stolen his idea and made loads of money from it and he's bitter and angry. It hardly matters why, only—'

'—he's a poor man.'

'Yes, and he's desperate. He *needs* the money for some reason, perhaps he's got himself into debt, or he wants to marry a young woman from a different sort of background.' Alice felt her cheeks warm, acutely aware she'd skirted very close to describing their own predicament. She went on hastily, picking up the threads of her plot. 'Whatever the case, he needs a lot of money quickly and figures this is the way to get it.'

'Not a very likeable chap,' said Ben, shaking clumps of dirt free from the roots of a large weed.

'The villain doesn't need to be likeable. He's not meant to be. He's the villain.'

'People aren't like that, though, are they, all bad or all good?'

'He's not a person, he's a character. They're different things.'

'Well,' Ben shrugged lightly, 'you're the writer.'

Alice wrinkled her nose. She'd been on quite a roll but

the interruption had made her lose her train of thought. She turned back to her notes, hoping to pick up her place.

'Only,' Ben drove the gardening fork into the dirt, 'it occurs to me now, it's one of the things I don't much like about these detective novels of yours.'

'What's that?'

'The broad brushstrokes, the lack of subtlety, the idea that morality is unambiguous. It's not the real world, is it? It's simplistic. Like something from a children's book, a fairy tale.'

Alice had felt his words like a knife. Even now, at the age of eighty-six, making her way past the football fields on Rotten Row, she flinched to recall them. He'd been right, of course, and well ahead of his time. These days *why* trumped *how* every time, but back then Alice had seen no merit in his suggestion that the fascinating subject of why ordinary people might be induced to commit a crime was worth addressing; she'd cared only for tricks and puzzles. A wave of anguish had hit her when he said it, as if it were *her* he was calling simplistic, and not the genre. The day was cold, but with the swell of embarrassment and hurt that enflamed her Alice was steaming. She ignored his critique, moving on crisply with her description of the story. 'The kidnapped child will have to die, of course.'

'Will she?'

'He. Better if it's a boy.'

'Is it?'

He'd been amused then, infuriatingly so. Alice refused to return his smile, her voice imperiously patient as she continued. She spoke as if she were explaining things to him that he really ought to know. More excruciating, she behaved as if she were educating him on a topic a man like him couldn't hope to understand. It was awful. She could hear herself play-acting the Little Rich Girl, a role she despised but was powerless to stop. 'Boys are more valuable, you see, in a familial sense. Heir to the lands and title and all that.'

'All right, a boy then.' His tone was as easy as ever. Even more infuriating! 'But why does the poor lad have to die?'

'Because a murder mystery needs a murder!'

'More of your rules?' He was teasing. He knew he'd hurt her and was trying to make amends. Well, she wasn't going to be so easily won over.

Coldly: 'They're not my rules. They're Mr Knox's, published in *Best Detective Stories*.'

'Ah, I see. Well then, that's different.' He took off his gloves, reaching for a paraffin-paper-wrapped sandwich. 'And what are some of Mr Knox's other rules?'

'The detective isn't allowed to be helped by an accident or unaccountable intuition.'

'Sounds fair.'

'No twins or doubles unless the reader has been earlier prepared.'

'Far too close to cheating.'

'And there should be no more than one secret room or passage. That one's important for my story.'

'Is it? Why?'

'I'll get to that in good time.' She continued reciting the rules, counting them off on her fingers. 'The criminal must be mentioned early in the story; the reader shouldn't be privy to his thoughts; and last but not least, the detective should have a stupid friend, a Watson, who is slightly, but no more than slightly, less intelligent than the average reader.'

Ben paused mid-bite and pointed casually between them. 'I'm getting the distinct impression I'm the Watson in this team.'

Alice felt her lips buckle and could resist no longer. He was so handsome, smiling at her like that, and the day was beginning to brighten, the sun peeking through the clouds. It was simply too hard to stay cross with him. She laughed, and as she did his expression changed.

Alice followed his gaze over her shoulder, through the break in the hedge. For one dreadful moment she was convinced she was going to see Nanny Rose behind her. Alice had been watching from the window the other day and had seen the two of them, Ben and the nanny, talking. Things had looked a little cosier than she'd have liked. But it wasn't Nanny Rose at all, just Mother, who'd emerged from the back door and was sitting now on the iron seat, one arm folded across the other, a faint ribbon of smoke rising from the cigarette between her fingers.

'Don't worry,' she said, rolling her eyes and ducking her head back out of view. 'She won't bother us – not today. We're not supposed to know she smokes.'

She was trying to sound offhand, but the carefree mood of the past half-hour had gone. Alice and Ben both knew how important it was that they keep their relationship secret, especially from Mother. Eleanor didn't approve of Alice liaising with Ben. There'd been a few general comments over the past few months about choosing one's company carefully, and then the other night a particularly awkward scene in which Mother had called her up to the library after supper. There'd been a strange tension in Eleanor's face, despite her pretence at ease, and Alice had intuited what was coming. Sure enough: 'It isn't seemly, Alice, for a girl like you to spend so much time talking with members of staff. I know you don't mean anything by it, but people will get the wrong idea. Your father certainly wouldn't approve. Imagine if he were to look out of his study window and see his daughter consorting with someone so unsuitable, a gardener, for goodness' sake.'

Alice didn't believe for a moment that Daddy would be so small-minded as to disapprove – he didn't care one whit for arbitrary class distinctions – but she didn't say so. She didn't dare. Mother could've had Ben fired in an instant if she decided he was too much trouble.

'Go on,' said Ben, with a wink. 'Get out of here. I ought to keep busy, and you've got a masterpiece to write.'

She was touched by his concern, the unspoken care in his voice. 'I'm not afraid of getting in trouble, you know.'

'I didn't think you were,' he said. 'Not for a moment.' He handed her the Agatha Christie novel. She shivered when their fingertips met. 'Let me know when you've worked out more of your story.' He shook his head with mock horror. 'Killing little boys. How very grisly.'

The No. 9 bus drove by as Alice waited to cross Kensington Road. It was one of the old Routemasters and had an advertisement for the Kirov corps de ballet's *Swan Lake* on its flank. Alice would have liked to see the production but was afraid she'd left it too late to organise tickets. She didn't go to the ballet unless she could sit close enough to hear the dancers' pointe shoes hitting the stage boards. Excellence was the result of hard work and Alice had no interest in pretending otherwise. She understood illusion was part of performance, that dancers strived for the appearance of ease; she knew, too, that for many in the audience the romance of effortless grace was the point; but it was not so for Alice. She was a great admirer of mental and physical rigour and considered a performance much improved by the sheen of sweat on the leading man's shoulders, the sigh of completion at the end of the ballerina's solo, the blunt thud of toes hitting wood as the dancer spun and smiled. It was just the same as spotting the scaffolding in other writers' books. Awareness of construction didn't diminish her pleasure, only added to it.

Alice was not of a romantic disposition. It was one of the ways in which she'd wilfully distinguished herself from Eleanor, a childhood resolve that had hardened into habit. To wit, her mother's favourite ballet story came from the summer she met their father. 'It was 1911, before the war, and the world was still filled with magic.' Eleanor had told it often over the years. 'I was staying with my aunt in Mayfair and had met your father earlier that week. He invited me to see the Ballets Russes perform and I said yes without thinking twice, without checking with my mother as it happens. You can imagine, Grandmother deShiel almost disowned me. Oh, but it was worth it. That night! How perfect it was, and how young we were. How impossibly young.' At that she always gave a small smile, acknowledgement that her children would of course never truly accept that their parents had been anything other than as they were now. 'Nijinsky in *Le Spectre de la Rose* was like nothing I'd seen before. He danced a fifteen-minute solo and it passed like a dream. He was wearing a silk tricot, palest nude, onto which were pinned dozens of silk Bakst petals, pink and red and purple. The most exotic creature, so *beautiful*, like a shiny, graceful insect on the verge of flight. He leapt as if it cost him no effort, lingering in the air far longer than was possible, and seemed not to touch the stage between times. I believed that night that a man might fly, that *anything* was possible.'

But no – Alice frowned. She was being unfair. Eleanor might have retained her childhood fluency in the fairy-tale language of fate and superstitions, but her romantic nature wasn't all love affairs and happily-ever-afters; it was a way of looking at the world, an entire moral system all of her own. She possessed an innate sense of justice, a complex system of checks and balances that determined the measure of something she called 'rightness'.

This instinct for moral balance had been in evidence during the last conversation they ever had. Eleanor had just returned home after seeing *An Inspector Calls* at the New Theatre and had telephoned Alice at once to declare the evening 'uplifting'. Alice, who'd seen the play already, had been silent for a moment before replying, 'The part where the innocent young girl is mistreated and driven to suicide, or the depiction of the despicable Birling family who couldn't care less about her suffering other than to save their own skins?'

Eleanor had ignored the irony, pressing on with her critique: 'The ending was so portentous, so *right*. Each member of the family was guilty in his or her own way, and one was left with an entirely satisfying sense that the truth would out.' She had also, rather predictably, admired the uncertainty of the Inspector Goole character. 'Oh, Alice,' she'd said disappointedly, when Alice suggested his appearance might feasibly have been explained more clearly. 'It's beside the point. He's an archetype, a symbol, justice personified. It doesn't matter how he knew about the poor girl, or just who, or what, he really was; all that matters is the restoration of proper order.'

Alice had grumbled something about characterisation and believability, but Eleanor, tired, had brought the conversation to a temporary close. 'I'll convince you yet. We'll revisit the topic in person tomorrow.' They never did, of course. Eleanor had been due to visit Alice at her flat in Shoreditch when she stepped out onto Marylebone Road in front of the driver who'd taken his eyes from the road. Alice sat in her dim kitchen all the while, a fresh pint of milk in the fridge and a salvaged cloth on the table, with no inkling that the world had been tipped off its axis while she waited.

That's where Ben had been wrong. Alice blinked away the sudden unexpected heat of loss. His preference for people over places was all well and good, but people had a nasty habit of changing. Or leaving. Or dying. Places were far more reliable. They prevailed. And, if damaged, could be rebuilt, even improved. People could not be trusted to stick around. 'Except family.' Alice heard Eleanor's voice in her head. 'That's why I had so many daughters. So you'd always have someone. I knew what it was to be alone.'

Walking down Exhibition Road towards the museums, Alice was anything but alone. There were people everywhere, most of them adolescents. Alice felt a surge of pity for them, stuck as they were within the white-hot glow of youth, when everything seemed so vital, so essential, so important. She wondered where they were going. To the Science Museum or the V&A, or perhaps even the Natural History Museum, where they would file past the insects that had fluttered their last in the sunshine of Loeanneth? 'I wish you wouldn't kill them,' Eleanor had said one day, the closest Alice had heard her come to criticising Daddy. 'It seems so cruel. Such beautiful creatures.' It was Alice, wearing the white assistant's gloves, who'd leapt to her father's defence, though in truth she hated those pins too. 'Nature *is* cruel. Isn't that right, Daddy? Every living thing has to die. And they're still beautiful. Now they'll stay that way.'

A group of girls rushed past, laughing, and turned to joke over their shoulders at a good-looking boy with black hair who shouted something indecipherable in return. Their youth and exuberance radiated off them in waves that Alice could almost see. Alice remembered what it was to be like them. To feel for the first time a passion that made everything hyper-real. Ben's pull, back then, had been inexorable; her attraction such that she'd have sooner stopped blinking than give him up. She'd ignored her mother's entreaties and continued to meet with him, she'd simply been more careful than before, more deceitful.

Over the next few weeks, as Ben listened and made occasional interjections, Alice refined her idea for how to stage the perfect kidnapping. One fine spring morning, when the air was clear after a night of rain and the trout were leaping in the stream, she set up her blanket beneath a willow. Ben was digging post holes for a new fence and Alice lay on her stomach, ankles folded, legs swinging as she frowned at her notebook. Suddenly, she said, 'It occurs to me that I'm going to need an accomplice. No one's going to believe the criminal acted alone.'

'No?'

She shook her head. 'Too hard. Too many loose ends to take care of. It isn't easy kidnapping a child, you know. It's certainly not a one-man job.'

'An accomplice then.'

'Someone who knows about children. Preferably someone who knows *this* particular child. A trusted adult, all the better to keep the little darling quiet as a mouse.'

He shot her a look. 'I didn't realise quite how devious you were.'

Alice took the compliment with a light shrug and sucked thoughtfully on a strand of hair. She watched as a blotted band of clouds drifted across the blue sky.

Ben had paused in his digging to roll a cigarette. 'Bit of a long shot though, isn't it?'

Alice looked up at him, shifting her head so his shoulder blocked the sun. 'Why is that?'

'Well, it's one thing for our criminal to plot a kidnapping. He's a criminal, he wants money. But what are the chances of him finding a second person, someone he trusts enough to reveal his dastardly plans to, who's also willing to get involved?'

'Simple. He has a criminal friend, someone he met in gaol.'

Ben sealed the tobacco paper. 'It's too weak.'

'A friend with whom he agrees to split the money?'

'It would have to be an awful lot of money. It's a huge risk.'

Alice pressed the end of her pen against her lips, tapping lightly as she pondered. She wondered aloud, 'Why would a person agree to such a thing? Why would someone help commit a serious crime? There has to be something in it for the woman as well.'

'Woman?'

Alice smiled slyly. 'People tend not to suspect women of crimes – not when they're to do with children, anyway. A woman will make the perfect accomplice.'

'Well then – ' he knelt by the edge of the blanket – 'they're in love. People do all sorts of things they shouldn't for love.'

Alice's heart thumped against the hard earth as if it might burst free from her ribcage. His words were full of hidden meaning. Suggestions, a promise. Lately he'd been saying a lot more things like that, steering the conversation onto subjects like love and life and sacrifice. She tried to keep the quiver out of her voice. 'Love. Yes.' Her mind was filled with the things she'd willingly do for love. She could feel the skin on her neck beginning to flush; she was sure Ben would notice. She forced herself to think of her story, to concentrate only on its plot. 'At least, he *thinks* that they're in love.'

'They're not?'

'Sadly for him, no. She has her own reason for getting involved.'

'She's a white-slaver?'

'She wants revenge.'

'Revenge?'

'Against the boy's family.'

'Why?'

Alice hadn't thought that far ahead. She waved her hand

impatiently. 'What's important is that she plans to double-cross her lover. She agrees to help him, they come up with a scheme, steal the child from his nursery, and then they take him to another place. They write the ransom note but they never send it.'

'Why not?'

'Because . . . because . . .' The swell of a plot break-through warmed her from within. She sat up quickly. 'Because you're right. The woman doesn't want half the money. She wants the child.'

'She does?'

'She doesn't want to send him back; she wants to keep him. She's come to love him.'

'That was quick.'

'He's a lovely child, or else she already loved him, she's related to him in some way. It doesn't matter why, only that she does. Perhaps it's been her plan all along, to keep him for herself.'

'Our criminal isn't going to like that.'

'No, he certainly isn't. He *needs* that money, it was *his* plan in the first place, and he's gone to a lot of trouble and expense already to carry out the kidnapping.'

'So?'

'So, they argue. The woman tries to take the child, the man threatens her, they struggle.' A smile of realisation spread across her face and she sighed with delighted satisfaction. 'The child dies!'

'In the struggle?'

'Why not?'

'It just seems rather grim.'

'Then in his sleep . . . it hardly matters why. Perhaps he's already unwell and he's sleeping very deeply. Or else – ' she sat bolt upright – 'they've drugged him. They meant to make the kidnapping go more smoothly, but they miscalculated. The sleeping pills are for adults and the dose is too strong. They foil their own plan. The ransom note is never sent, and neither one of them gets a single penny *or* the child. Oh, Ben . . .' She reached out impulsively to squeeze his hand. 'It's *perfect*.'

Crossing at the lights near South Kensington Tube station, Alice spotted the green-painted flower stall on the nearby traffic island. In the tub at the front of the display were bunches of roses and one arrangement in particular caught her eye, an assortment of colours that brought to mind her mother's description of the costume in *Le Spectre de la Rose*. On a whim, she decided to take a bunch for Deborah, who would be waiting now, glancing at the clock in her morning room, the elegant black mantel clock that had been a wedding gift, and wondering when Alice would arrive. She wouldn't be idly waiting, mind, that was not Deborah's way. She would be using the time wisely, dealing with correspondence or polishing silver heirlooms, taking care of one of the many tasks with which genteel ladies of a certain age and class filled their time.

A small dark-haired man in a florist's apron appeared and Alice gestured at the roses. 'Are they fragrant?'

'Very.'

'Natural?' She leaned and sniffed.

'As the rain that falls.'

Alice was dubious. She couldn't abide the spritzing of flowers with scented oils, but made the purchase anyway.

The day of reckoning was upon her and she felt strangely reckless. She waited as the florist wrapped the stems in butcher's paper and tied the bundle with brown string, and then continued towards Chelsea, eyeing the blooms as she walked. Deborah would be pleased with them and Alice was glad. Her satisfaction was only slightly soured by the creeping concern that Deborah might suppose the gift an attempt to soften her up.

It was a strange thing to be on the way to confess a terrible secret to someone who knew her almost as well as she knew herself. Alice had never told anybody else. In the immediate aftermath of Theo's kidnapping she'd come very close to telling the police everything she knew. 'It was Ben,' she practised over and over in her mind, going so far as to tiptoe down the stairs and lurk by the library door. 'Ben Munro took Theo. I told him about the tunnel, it was my idea, but I never meant for this to happen.' She imagined their uncertain glances and heard herself saying, 'I *saw* him that night, on the edge of the woods. I left the party and went for a walk. It was dark, but the fireworks had started and I saw him near the tunnel trapdoor. I know it was him.'

Each time, though, she stopped herself, her instinct for self-preservation too strong. She'd been weak and frightened and so she'd fallen back on faith. There would be a ransom note, she reasoned; her parents had money, they would pay the sum it asked and Theo would be returned. Ben would have the amount he needed to help his friends and no one would ever know the part Alice had played.

The days dragged by and she kept one eye on the investigation and the other on the post. She heard one of the housemaids tell police about a missing bottle of sleeping pills but she thought as little of it then as they did. It wasn't until day three, when news came of Mr Llewellyn's suicide and her mother's grief threatened to overwhelm her, that Alice realised things were much worse than she'd thought. She overheard Dr Gibbons warning Mother that the sleeping pills he'd prescribed were very strong – 'Too many and you won't wake up' – and her mind had gone back to that afternoon with Ben, the way she'd laboured the importance of having help on the inside, made the case for using sleeping tablets to drug the child, raised the spectre of what would happen if the boy was given too many.

All of a sudden she realised what the lack of ransom note meant. But by then it was too late to raise the alarm. Where once her confession might have led police to Theo, now there was no point. And she would have had to explain why she'd waited three days to say anything. They would know she was responsible, not just for Theo's disappearance but for his death. They would never forgive her. How could they? And so she'd said nothing. She'd kept her secret for seventy years and told no one. Until now.

If she had to tell anyone, Alice was glad that it was Deborah. They were close, the pair of them, a closeness that did not express itself in a need to spend copious amounts of time in one another's company, but was something else entirely, something intrinsic. They had formed from the same soup. They were both still here. And as Deborah never tired of reminding her, she had been there the day Alice was born. 'You weren't at all what I'd expected. Red and indignant – and naked! What a surprise that was. I watched you squirming your raw little neck and screwing up your face the way babies do. Mother didn't know I'd crept inside the room and was quite astonished when I walked up to the bed, held out my arms, and demanded that she give me my baby. It took us a few tense moments to sort out our differences. She'd told me so many times during the pregnancy that a new baby was coming, that I was to be the big sister and it was my job to take care of you for as long as we both should live. I'm afraid I took her quite at her word. I was rather shocked and terribly disappointed when she laughed and told me you weren't, after all, mine to keep!'

Good, kind, responsible Deborah. What was she going to say when she learned what Alice had done? Alice had spent much of the past week trying to guess. Her own guilt she'd come to terms with long ago. She had acted neither malignantly nor deliberately. She was culpable because the whole thing had been her idea, but there was no need to make a grand confession to the police; not now; it was too late for anything to be done, and her offence was not of the kind they prosecuted. Murder, she wrote? Besides, she had already been punished. She continued to be. Eleanor had been right. The world had its own way of keeping the scales in balance. Guilty characters might escape prosecution, but they never escaped justice.

For all her attempts to differentiate herself from Eleanor, it was when she realised that her mother had been right about justice that Alice's writing had taken a leap for the better. She'd left behind her slavish adherence to the rationalism of Golden Age detective stories and Diggory Brent had stepped into her life, taking the place of the priggish, self-satisfied cypher sleuths she'd been working with to that point. She told people – journalists, readers – he'd come to her in a dream, which was almost true. She'd found him at the bottom of a whisky bottle in the dying months of the war. She'd been thinking of Clemmie, the conversation they never got to have about what Clemmie had glimpsed through the boathouse window. It still made Alice grimace to think that her younger sister had been there that afternoon when she finally offered herself to Ben. She'd been so pleased with herself when she knocked lightly on his door, manuscript in hand. Agatha Christie was the only other mystery novelist she knew of who'd dared to kill a child, and Alice couldn't wait for Ben to read her book and see how clever she was, the way she'd woven their plot into her story. Her sixteen-year-old voice came floating back to her now across the decades, the day she'd come up with the idea: 'A tunnel, Ben, there's a secret tunnel.'

'Underground, you mean, beneath the earth?'

'I know what you're going to say, so you needn't bother saying it. You're going to say that it's unrealistic, simplistic, pantomime-like. And it's not!' She'd smiled then like the cat that had got the cream, and she'd told him all about their own hidden tunnel. The concealed entrance near the nursery on the second floor of the house, the latch with the old-fashioned mechanism that had to be jiggled just so to open, the final ladder hewn into the hard stone wall that led to the woods and the way to freedom. Everything he needed to know to sneak a child out of Loeanneth.

Alice had reached Chelsea already. Shoppers with bags from boutiques along the King's Road brushed past in both directions, and down the road she could glimpse the stairs that led up to Deborah's house. The number 56 was painted in glossy black on the white column out front and a pair of pots with red geraniums stood either side of the bottom step. She steeled herself and headed towards them.

A leafy communal garden filled the middle of the square, its black iron gate locked against outsiders, and Alice hesitated beneath a thick sweep of ivy. It was quieter here, the bustle of the main road softened by the tall Victorian buildings that stood on all four sides of the square. Swallows twittered to one another in the branches above, the sound more enchanting and otherworldly for its contrast with the general urban hum. Through the dimpled glass of Deborah's morning-room window Alice could just make out the shape of a tall, lean figure. Alice Edevane was not a person who made a habit of breaking engagements, certainly not when the other party was there waiting for her, but oh, how a part of her longed to keep on walking. Her heart gave a flutter at this glimpse of escape. She could simply pretend that she'd forgotten, laugh when Deborah rang to check on her, blame it on old age. She was old, after all. Not *older* or *ageing* or any of those other words people used because they thought they were softer and more palatable. Alice was old and old people were accorded certain privileges. But, no, she knew it was a fancy. The reprieve would only be brief. It was time.

She knocked on the door and was caught off guard when it opened almost immediately. More surprising was the fact that it was Deborah herself who opened it. She was beautifully dressed as always, in a draping silk dress that tied about her narrow waist. Her hair was scooped into an elegant silver chignon.

The sisters nodded at one another but neither said a word. With a slight smile, Deborah stood aside, indicating with her hand that Alice should come in.

The house was spotless and gleaming, bountiful floral arrangements exquisite on every surface. Alice remembered now. Fresh flower deliveries arrived every third day from a shop in Sloane Square, the order was long-standing. She looked at the bunch of roses in her hands. They seemed paltry suddenly, a folly. She held them out nevertheless. 'Here. For you.'

'Oh, Alice, thank you, they're lovely.'

'It's nothing. Silly. They reminded me of Mother, that's all, Nijinsky—'

'The Bakst costume.' Deborah smiled, lifting the flowers to her nose, as much, it seemed to Alice, to steal a moment as to sample their fragrance. Of course, she was dreading the meeting as much as Alice was. Kind-hearted Deborah would take no joy from the conversation to come.

Alice followed her sister into the morning room where Maria, more personal assistant than housekeeper, was unloading tea things onto the coffee table. She straightened, empty tray under her arm, and asked whether there was anything else they needed.

'A vase, if you wouldn't mind, Maria. Alice brought these. Aren't they beautiful?'

'Lovely colours,' Maria agreed. 'Would you like them here, in the morning room?'

'My bedroom, I think.'

Maria swept the flowers from Deborah's hand and left in a streak of brisk efficiency. Alice fought the urge to call her back, to ask after her mother or her many siblings, to keep the housekeeper there just a little longer. But she didn't, and the room's air particles settled to fill the space Maria had left behind.

The sisters met each other's gaze and without a word sat down opposite one another on the linen settees. Alice noticed then a book on the table between them, a leather bookmark holding a place near the end. Recognition was instant and visceral. Their father had carried the edition of Keats's poems with him always, a favourite from which he drew comfort over the years, clasping it to him even on his deathbed. The sight of it now made her cheeks warm, as if her parents were with them in the room, waiting to hear what she had done.

'Tea?'

'Please.'

The clean, crisp gurgle of tea being poured from the pot was excruciating. Alice felt that all her senses were sharpened. She was aware of a fly teetering on the side of the tray, of Maria moving about upstairs, of the faint lingering scent of lemon furniture polish. The room was very warm and she slipped a fingertip beneath her collar to lift it from her neck. The weight of her impending confession pressed. 'Deborah, I need to—'

'No.'

'Pardon?'

'Please.' Deborah set down the teapot and pressed her fingertips together firmly. She clasped her hands and pushed them into her lap. The gesture was one of anguish. Her face was pale and drawn, and suddenly Alice realised she'd got it all wrong. That she wasn't here to talk about Ben; that her sister was ill, dying even, and she, Alice, had been too self-absorbed to notice.

'Deborah?'

Her sister's mouth tightened. Her voice was little more than a whisper. 'Oh, Alice, it's such a burden.'

'What is it?'

'I should have said something years ago. I meant to, I did. There have been so many occasions over the years when I almost – and then, the other day at the museum, when you mentioned Loeanneth, the gardener. You surprised me, I wasn't ready.'

Not an illness, then. Of course not. Alice almost laughed at her own boundless instinct for self-preservation. Here she was, sitting in the confessional, still looking for an escape hatch. Outside, a taxi trundled up the street. Alice saw the flash of black through the gauze curtains. She wanted to be inside that taxi, going away, away, to anywhere but here.

'Theo,' said Deborah, and Alice closed her eyes, waiting for what she knew was coming. 'I know what happened to him.'

After all her agonising, after years of keeping the secret to herself, of living with the guilt, it was over. Alice felt surprisingly light. She hadn't even needed to say it herself, Deborah already knew. 'Deborah,' she started, 'I—'

'I know everything, Alice. I know what happened to Theo, and the fact of it is driving me mad. It was my fault, you see. Everything that happened was my fault.'

Nineteen

Oxford, 2003

It turned out Rose Waters had a great-niece living in Oxford. Margot Sinclair was headmistress of a fancy public school and 'a very busy person'. Her secretary had, however, managed to find Sadie a half-hour appointment at one o'clock sharp on Tuesday. She hadn't actually said the word 'sharp', but it had been implied.

The interview was a long shot – most people didn't maintain the closest of relationships with their great-aunt – but Sadie, eager as a hound and with not much else in the way of leads, was there by midday and focused on the questions she'd jotted down. Preparation was key. It was going to take a very delicate touch to draw out Margot Sinclair on the subject of her great-aunt's possible involvement in the kidnapping of her own illegitimate child; a boy born secretly and passed off as the son of her employers.

'You sure you're not turning out a novel?' Bertie had asked when she tried the theory out on him.

She rolled her eyes. It was breakfast time, the morning after they'd had their almost-argument, and both were trying extra hard to sound light and breezy.

'All right, all right. Remind me again why the Edevanes would have taken on the child?'

'Because they had trouble conceiving again after their third daughter and they wanted a son, desperately. A decade went by and although Eleanor finally fell pregnant in 1931, the baby was stillborn the following year – that's what Constance was trying to tell people, but no one listened. You can only imagine how awful it must've been, how unfair they must have thought it, particularly knowing that Rose Waters, their unmarried nanny, was also secretly pregnant, surely with a child she couldn't keep. It doesn't take that much of a leap to see what happened next. They'd have been falling over themselves to take the baby off her hands, don't you think?'

He scratched his whiskery chin, before conceding with a nod that it was possible. 'The craving for a baby is certainly a powerful thing. My mother used to joke that if I hadn't come along when I did she'd have started eyeing up babies in prams at the park.'

'Only Eleanor Edevane didn't have to steal a baby from a pram. A little boy in need of a good home fell right into her lap, so to speak. And everything worked out perfectly until Eleanor fired Rose, and Rose decided she wanted her baby back.'

'Pretty risky move, firing the child's natural mother.'

'Maybe it was becoming risky having her there. That's what I intend to find out.'

He sighed thoughtfully. 'I suppose it's not the craziest theory you've ever come up with.'

'Thanks, Granddad.'

'Now you just need to run it past someone who knew Rose Waters.'

*

Alastair was the one who'd found Margot Sinclair. The morning after she came up with the theory, Sadie had gone straight down to the library and been pacing back and forth on the pavement out front when he arrived to open up. 'Coffee?' she'd said, handing over a takeaway cup. He'd raised his snowy eyebrows but hadn't said a word, ushering her inside as she explained in a halting fashion what she was thinking. Evidently he caught the gist, because when she finished and drew breath he said, 'You need to find someone who knows what happened to Rose after she left Loeanneth.'

'Exactly.'

He'd spun into action pulling dusty folders off shelves, typing things into search engines on the computer, flipping through file cards, and then finally, 'Bingo!' Something about old employment records, the census, next of kin, and then he'd announced that Rose Waters's sister Edith had lived in the Lake District, and Edith had a granddaughter who could now be found in Oxford. Sadie's mate in Traffic had done the rest – she definitely owed him a bottle of something nice when she got back to London – leaving the school's address in a message on her phone. 'I hope this is all above board, Sparrow,' he'd said before signing off.

'Totally, Dave,' Sadie muttered, gathering her notes together and pushing them into her bag. 'Totally.' The dashboard clock read ten to one, so she locked her car and crossed between the pair of griffin-topped pillars, following a wide entrance path towards a building that wouldn't have looked out of place next to Buckingham Palace. It was lunch break and kids in boater hats and blazers were milling about in small groups on the vast stretch of manicured lawn. In

this world, this sunlit circle quite outside the one Sadie usually moved in, she felt suddenly underdressed in jeans and a
T-shirt. They gleamed, those kids, with their braces-clad
teeth and thick, glossy ponytails, their fearless laughter and
their shimmering futures.

She found the administration office and gave her name to
a demure young woman behind a dark wooden desk. 'Please
take a seat,' the woman said in a polite half-whisper.
'Dr Sinclair will be with you soon.'

The reception was quiet of voices but busy with the noise
of industry. The furious thrum of the receptionist's fingers on
the keyboard, the canter of the clock, an air-conditioner
humming importantly. Sadie realised she was biting her
thumbnail again and stopped. She told herself to calm down.

In the outside world, the *real* world, Sadie wore her lack
of formal education proudly. 'You and me, Sparrow,' Donald
had said on more than one occasion, flinging a look of withering disdain over his shoulder at the 'expert' they'd just got
shot of interviewing, 'we're streetwise. A hundred bits of
paper telling the world how clever you are doesn't equal
that.' It was a very agreeable worldview, equating education
with wealth and wealth with posh and posh with moral
bankruptcy. It made Sadie better at her job. She'd seen the
way people like Nancy Bailey flinched and withdrew when
Inspector Parr-Wilson started talking at them in his cut-glass
accent. It was only when she came to places like this that
Sadie felt the niggling of what might have been.

She straightened her collar as the clock's minute hand
leapt to vertical. One o'clock on the dot and the office door
opened. A statuesque woman in a cream suit appeared, sleek
brown hair grazing her shoulders as she tilted her head and

widened her sea-blue eyes at her visitor. 'DC Sparrow? I'm Margot Sinclair. Please, do come in.'

Sadie did as she was told, chiding herself for trotting. 'Thanks for seeing me, Mrs Sinclair.'

'Dr Sinclair. I'm not married,' said the headmistress, smiling briskly as she sat behind her desk. She indicated with a sweep of the hand that Sadie should do likewise on the other side.

'Dr Sinclair,' Sadie corrected herself. It wasn't the most auspicious of starts. 'I'm not sure how much your secretary told you?'

'Jenny told me you're interested in my maternal great-aunt, Rose Martin – Rose Waters, before she was married.' She had a way of glancing over her glasses and down her nose that suggested interest without suspicion. 'You're a police officer. Are you working on a case?'

'Yes,' said Sadie, before deciding Margot Sinclair was one for crossing 't's and dotting 'i's, and adding, 'Though not officially. It's a cold case.'

'Is it?' The other woman leaned back in her chair. 'How intriguing.'

'A missing child, back in the 1930s. His disappearance was never solved.'

'I take it my great-aunt is not a suspect?' Margot Sinclair seemed amused by the prospect.

Sadie smiled in return, hoping the gesture implied agreement. 'It was a long time ago, and I'm clutching at straws, really, but I was hoping to find out a little about her life before she married. I'm not sure whether you know, but she worked as a nanny when she was young.'

'On the contrary,' Margot Sinclair said, 'I know a great

deal about Rose's professional life. She was one of the subjects of my postdoctoral dissertation on women's education. She was a governess. She taught children of the aristocracy.'

'A governess? Not a nanny?'

'She started that way, when she was very young, but she went on to become a governess and later a teacher of some note. Rose was incredibly clever and self-motivated. It was no easy thing back then to acquire the necessary training to lift one's station in life.'

It wasn't so easy now, thought Sadie.

'I've a copy of my dissertation here.' Margot went swiftly to a wall of bookshelves and took down a leather-bound tome, pausing to wipe the dustless top. 'It doesn't get much of an airing these days, but I was passionate about the subject when I was studying. It sounds daft, perhaps, but Rose was, and continues to be, my inspiration. Throughout my career I've held her up as a shining example of what's possible with a bit of application.'

Returning to her seat, Margot began an enthusiastic description of her thesis argument, while Sadie's gaze lifted to take in the array of framed qualifications hung neatly on the wall behind the desk. A doctorate from Oxford in biology, a second degree in education, various other accomplishments and achievements. Sadie wondered what it would feel like to go through life with proof, gold-etched and ebony-framed, that you were worth something. Smart.

Sadie had been fifteen when at the urging of her headmaster she'd agreed to sit the scholarship exam for the fancy girls' school in the neighbouring town. She still remembered the letter arriving to tell them she'd been awarded a place for the sixth form, but the memory had taken on the surreal air of a dream. The trip to purchase her uniform, however, was burned into her psyche. Sadie and her mother had gone together, her mother dressed carefully in what she imagined the polo-set wore, tight with nerves as she walked beside Sadie, determined, as always, to perform perfectly. Everything was going well until they became lost between quadrangles. The assigned appointment was strictly one hour; the faithless clock on the stone tower was slicing further into it; and her mother had had one of the anxiety attacks they all agreed to call 'asthma'. Her mother was a perfectionist and a snob, and the grandeur of the place, the pent-up pressure to prove herself, the realisation that their tardiness was going to 'ruin everything', was too much. Sadie found a bench for them to sit on while her mother recovered, and then she flagged down a groundsman who gave her directions to the uniform shop. They arrived with twenty minutes left in the hour, which her mother spent in silent reproach while a woman ran a tape measure up Sadie's legs and spoke with reverent familiarity of 'the tweed coat' and 'our little velvet beret' and other things Sadie couldn't imagine wearing.

In the end she hadn't needed to. She met a boy over the summer, a good-looking boy with a car and a winning way, and by the time school started she was pregnant. She postponed her enrolment, planning to go back the following year, but by the time it was all over she was a different person.

Even if Sadie *had* been able to see herself right to start, when the new school year came round her parents wouldn't have her back – they'd told their friends she was finishing high school on exchange in America; how would it look if she came back a year early? – and the scholarship didn't include boarding fees. Ruth and Bertie had assured her they'd find some way to work things out, but Sadie knew they wouldn't be able to meet the costs without going into serious debt. It was too much to ask; she'd thanked them but told them no. They weren't pleased with her decision as they wanted the best for her, but Sadie promised herself, and them, that she was going to be a success on her own terms and she didn't need a fancy school for that. She finished her A levels at night school and joined the police. A surprise to her grandparents, but not an unpleasant one. They were just relieved by then that she wasn't going to wind up on the wrong side of the law. It had looked a little hairy for a while there, after the baby, when Sadie was in freefall.

'So there you have it,' said Margot Sinclair, passing her thesis across the desk to Sadie. 'I'm not sure it will answer all your questions, but it will certainly give you a better idea of who Rose was. Now, shall we get down to it? I'm afraid I've another appointment scheduled in fifteen minutes.'

Margot's manner was brisk but willing, which suited Sadie perfectly. She'd been wondering how the other woman would react to questions about Rose's personal life, just how carefully she'd have to tiptoe around the subject, but with the clock ticking and Margot Sinclair nodding her no-nonsense encouragement, Sadie decided just to jump. 'I believe your great-aunt had a baby when she was a young woman, Dr Sinclair. Before she was married. Back when she was working as a nanny for a family in Cornwall, the Edevanes.'

There was a moment's stunned silence as Margot Sinclair absorbed the statement. Sadie waited for her to exclaim or refute or deny it, but she seemed to be in a state of some shock, sitting very still as a small muscle in her jaw flexed. Sadie's matter-of-fact claim hung heavily in the air between them and it seemed, in retrospect, that a slightly gentler approach might have been in order. Sadie was trying to think of a way to smooth things over when the other woman drew a deep breath and then exhaled steadily. Something in her expression caught Sadie's attention. She was surprised, certainly, that was to be expected, but there was something else. Suddenly, Sadie realised: 'You already knew about the baby,' she said in wonder.

Margot Sinclair didn't answer, not at once. She got up from her desk and went with Swiss finishing-school deportment to check the office door was properly sealed. Satisfied, she turned and said quietly, 'It was always something of a family secret.'

Sadie tried not to let her excitement show. She'd been right! 'Do you know when Rose fell pregnant?'

'In late 1931.' Margot sat down again, folding her fingers into a neat plait. 'The baby was born in June 1932.'

Practically the same birthday as Theo Edevane. Sadie's voice was quivering a little as she said, 'And yet she resumed work at Loeanneth just a month or so later?'

'That's right.'

'What did she do with the baby?' Sadie waited for the answer she knew was coming.

Margot Sinclair removed her glasses, holding them in one hand as she looked down her nose at Sadie. 'DC Sparrow, I'm sure I don't need to tell you that times were different then. Young women who fell pregnant outside marriage did not have an easy time of it. Besides which, Rose had no means to look after a baby, not then.'

'She gave the baby up?'

'She had to.'

Sadie could barely contain her thrill. She was on the cusp of finding Theo Edevane after all this time. 'Do you know who she gave him to?'

'Of course I do. She had a sister up north who was willing to take the baby and raise it as her own. And it wasn't a boy, it was a girl. My mother, as it happens.'

'She—? What?'

Margot continued, 'That's why Rose was so upset when she was dismissed by the Edevane family. She felt she'd given up her own child, she'd poured all her love into their baby instead, only to be fired for something trivial.'

'But—' Sadie cleared her throat, still trying to catch up with her thoughts. 'But if Rose's baby went to live up north, who was Theo Edevane's mother?'

'Well, you're the detective, DC Sparrow, but I'd have rather thought his mother was Mrs Edevane?'

Sadie frowned. It made no sense. She'd been so certain. Eleanor's inability to conceive another child – a son – for so long, followed by a stillborn baby; Rose's secret pregnancy, the timing of which fitted so perfectly; Eleanor firing Rose; Rose taking back her son. Only she hadn't had a son, she'd had a daughter. Margot Sinclair's mother, raised from birth in the Lake District by Rose Waters's sister. And there was no proof anyway that Eleanor had lost the baby she was pregnant with, only the rambling testimony of Constance deShiel. The whole theory collapsed like a house of cards.

'Are you all right, DC Sparrow? You're very pale.'

Margot pressed a button on her desktop intercom. 'Jenny? Some water, please.'

The secretary brought in a round tray with a carafe and two glasses. Sadie sipped at hers, grateful for something to do while she collected her wits. Gradually, she felt her mojo returning and a host of new questions floated to the surface. Rose might not have been Theo's mother, but she was still fired suddenly and unexpectedly, suspiciously close to his abduction. Why? If it wasn't because Eleanor Edevane felt threatened by her maternal presence, what had Rose done to put her employer offside? There must have been a reason. People who were proficient at their jobs and well-loved by those they worked for were not usually let go. She asked Margot.

'I don't think she ever understood that. I know it hurt her a great deal. She told me she loved working at Loeanneth. When I was a child and she came to visit she used to tell me stories about that house on the lake, and I always felt a kinship, an envy, too, for the little girls who grew up there. The way Rose told it, I half believed there were fairies in that garden. She was fond of her employers, too; she spoke well of them, particularly Anthony Edevane.'

'Oh?' That was interesting. Sadie thought back to her meeting with Clive, his account of the interview with Constance deShiel in which she intimated there'd been some sort of infidelity going on that might be relevant to the child's disappearance. 'Do you think it's possible she became *too* close to her employer? To Anthony Edevane?'

'An affair, you mean?'

Margot Sinclair's frankness made Sadie wince at her own coy euphemism. She nodded.

'He's mentioned in her letters, I know she admired him. He was a very clever man, and she had sympathy for him, of course, but I never had the impression there was more to it than that. She does credit him at one point with the suggestion that she'd make an excellent teacher, encouraging her to pursue study in the future.'

'But no romance? Not even a hint?'

'Nothing of the sort. In fact, I think that after her pregnancy Rose was very cautious about getting involved romantically. She didn't marry until she was almost forty and there was no indication she was courted before then.'

Another dead end. Sadie sighed. She had lost the battle to keep desperation out of her voice. 'Is there anything else you can think of? Anything that might be relevant to Rose leaving the Edevanes' employment?'

'There is something. I don't know that it's relevant, exactly, but it is a bit odd.'

Sadie nodded encouragement.

'Rose never understood why she was fired, which made it all the more perplexing that the Edevanes gave her an excellent reference and a very generous parting gift.'

'What sort of gift?'

'Money. Enough to fund the travel and study that set her up for the rest of her career.'

Sadie took this in. But why fire someone and then reward them handsomely? All she could think of was that the money was a bribe, but there didn't seem to be a lot of point in bribing someone who had no idea what it was they weren't supposed to tell.

There was a knock and the receptionist poked her head

around the door to remind Margot Sinclair she was due at her meeting with the board of governors in five minutes.

'Well then,' the headmistress said, with an apologetic smile, 'I'm afraid I'm going to have to say goodbye. I don't know how much help I've been.'

Sadie wasn't entirely sure either, but she shook Margot Sinclair's hand and thanked her for her time. She was at the door when something occurred to her. She turned and said, 'One more thing, Dr Sinclair, if you don't mind?'

'Not at all.'

'You said before that Rose was sympathetic towards Anthony Edevane. Why sympathetic? What did you mean by that?'

'Only that her own father had been similarly afflicted, so she understood what he was suffering.'

'Afflicted?'

'My great-grandfather had a dreadful war. Well, I don't suppose there was any other sort. Gassed at Ypres, and then sent back into the trenches. He was never the same, Granny said. He suffered nightmares and dreadful dark patches; he used to keep them all awake with his ranting. Post-traumatic stress disorder we'd call it now. Back then it was just shell shock, wasn't it?'

'Shell shock,' Sadie repeated. 'Anthony Edevane?'

'That's right. Rose mentions it many times in her journal. She tried to help him, and in fact it was their interactions that inspired her later theories about the teaching of poetry, particularly the Romantics, to refugee adolescents.'

Shell shock. It was a surprise. Sadie replayed the conversation in her mind as she walked back to her car. Not a surprise that he'd suffered with the condition; after all, he'd fought in France for years. Rather, the fact she hadn't come across any other mention to date. Was it a secret? If so, why was Rose Waters privy to the truth? Perhaps, as Margot had said, it was as simple as the young nanny having been familiar with the signs, recognising symptoms that others overlooked. Sadie wondered whether it mattered or whether she was simply clutching at straws. She thought about ringing someone – Clive, Alastair, Bertie – to run it by them, to see whether they could shed light on the condition, but her phone when she pulled it out was dead. With the signal as bad as it had been at Bertie's, she'd fallen out of the habit of charging it.

A bell had rung and the students were filing back into class now. Sadie watched them through the car window. Charlotte Sutherland went to a school like this one. In the photograph she'd sent with her letter, she'd been wearing a fancy uniform with a crest on the blazer and a list of accomplishments embroidered beneath it. That list had been long. No doubt there was a tweed coat and a jaunty little beret for use in the colder months. Sadie remonstrated with herself for being churlish. She was glad to think of Charlotte in a place like this. What had it all been for if not to afford her daughter the sort of opportunity she could never have provided herself?

Sadie sweet-talked the car into starting and gave herself a stern injunction to forget about Charlotte, once and for all. The letter was gone, returned to sender, no one at this address. She was supposed to be feeling, and acting, as if it had never arrived. She turned her thoughts instead to finding her way out of Oxford, and once she was on the M40, heading east towards London, she replayed her meeting with

Margot Sinclair, extracting all the new information – the excellent reference given to Rose Waters, the large cash payment – twisting it this way and that, and wondering vaguely whether Anthony Edevane's shell shock changed things, and how.

Twenty

Afterwards, Eleanor treated herself to tea at Liberty. The appointment had ended sooner than she'd expected, leaving her with two hours to fill before the train was due to leave Paddington. She'd stood on the corner where Harley Street met Marylebone Road, grey clouds disintegrating into grey buildings, before deciding her spirits could do with cheering and waving down a taxi. And so here she was. She turned the dainty spoon in circles, stirring in her milk, and then tapped it against the cup's fine porcelain lip. She caught the eye of a well-dressed man at a nearby table but didn't return his polite, enquiring smile.

Stupid of her to have held out so much hope, but there you had it. There was no fool like an old fool. Anthony had been right: the doctor had nothing new to offer, just more of the same talk. Eleanor wondered sometimes whether hope, that awesome, awful habit, ever died; better still, whether it could be killed. Things would be so much easier if it could, if it were as simple as flicking a switch. But alas, it seemed hope's glimmer always hovered in the distance, no matter how long one journeyed towards it without success.

Eleanor set down her spoon. Even as she thought it, she knew that she was wrong. Anthony had lost his hope. Not on the fields of France, perhaps, but at some point in the decade that followed. And that was the rub, that was why she must keep trying. It had happened on her watch. She hadn't been paying close enough attention, for if she had she would surely have noticed and done whatever was needed to arrest it. She'd made a promise to him and to herself.

It was raining outside now and London was slate-coloured and smeary. The streets glistened with dark puddles and a tide of black umbrellas flowed above the human traffic beneath. People moved faster in the rain, their expressions set, their eyes focused, each intent on his or her goal. There was so much scurrying purpose out there that Eleanor was overcome with weariness. Here, in the warmth of the tea-room, she sat inert like a single piece of flotsam in a sea of determination that threatened to sink her. She had never been good at filling time. She ought to have brought a book with her from Cornwall. She ought to have brought her husband.

Anthony's refusal to accompany her had been predictable; it was his vehemence that caught her by surprise. 'Stop,' he'd said when she first broached the subject. 'Please. Just stop.'

But Eleanor hadn't. Ever since she'd read the article in *The Lancet* she'd been determined that she and Anthony must meet Dr Heimer. Apparently she hadn't been the only one. The appointment had taken weeks to make and she'd had to contain her excitement, her hope, as she waited for time to pass, knowing it was best not to burden Anthony too soon.

'Stop.' He hadn't raised his voice; it had been almost a whisper.

'This could be it, Anthony,' she'd pressed. 'This man, this Dr Heimer, has been working on the problem, studying other men with the same afflictions, and he's had success, it says here that he knows how to fix—'

'*Please*.' The word cut like a knife and the rest of her sentence fell away. He didn't look at her, his head remained bowed over the top of his microscope so that Eleanor didn't realise at first that his eyes were closed. 'Just stop.'

She went closer. She could smell the faint hint of his perspiration, mingling with the strange laboratory odour of the room. Her voice was soft but firm. 'I won't give up on you, Anthony, no matter how hard you try to push me away. Certainly not now when it seems as if we might have found someone who can help.'

He'd looked at her then with an expression she'd been unable to name. She had seen him aggrieved before, too many times to count, the nightmares that came even by day, the sweats that came at night, and the terrible shaking that couldn't be stilled, even by the full force of her own body wrapped around his; but this had been different. The stillness. The quiet. That expression on his face that made her flinch as if she'd been struck. 'No more doctors,' he'd said in a low steady tone that brooked no argument. 'No more.'

She'd left him in his study, hurried downstairs, her face hot and her thoughts scattered. Later, when she was alone, she'd conjured his face. She hadn't been able to help herself; that expression of his had accompanied her all afternoon as she shadow-walked through the day's tasks. Only in the dead of night, as he slept fitfully beside her and she lay wide awake listening to the night-birds on the lake, remembering the long-ago evening when they'd cycled together over stones made white by moonlight, did the word come to her. Revulsion, that's what she'd seen in his face. Those features she'd loved so long and so well had been arranged in an attitude of disgust and loathing usually reserved for one's worst enemies. Eleanor could have borne revulsion directed at her; it was knowing that his loathing was reserved for himself that made her want to weep and wail and curse.

By morning, though, he was amiable again. He'd even suggested a picnic down by the stream. Hope had been resurrected, and if he still refused to come with her to London, at least this time he did it with a smile on his face and a claim that there were things he should be getting on with in his study. So it was, she'd carried her hope with her. All the way from Looe station it had sat on the empty train seat beside her where her husband ought to have been.

Now, she tilted her teacup and watched the tepid dregs roll this way and that. She'd told the girls she was travelling to London to visit a dressmaker in Mayfair, and they'd believed her because that's the sort of person they thought she was. Mother. They didn't remember the early years of their lives, when Anthony was away at war and she'd been alone with them at Loeanneth. The time they'd spent combing the estate together, the stories she'd told them, the secret places she'd shown them. There were so many aspects of Eleanor her daughters didn't know. She took them out sometimes, those hidden traits, and turned them over, inspecting and admiring from all sides, as if they were precious seed pearls. And then she wrapped them up again safely and tucked them away. She would never reveal them again because then she'd have to explain why she'd changed.

Eleanor didn't discuss Anthony with others. To do so

would have been to break faith with the young man she'd fallen in love with that summer in London, twenty years ago now, and, more devastating perhaps, with her tightly held belief that one day this too would pass. When it did, when she found the way to return to him his levity of spirit and everything he'd lost, when he was well again, he would be glad that no one knew how low he'd sunk, no one but Eleanor. His dignity deserved that.

She certainly never let the girls know. Anthony loved their daughters. In spite of it all he was a good father and the girls adored him. They'd never known the young man and his exceptional ambitions; he was simply 'Daddy', and his eccentricities made him their own. The long walks through the woods, days at a time in which he disappeared, returning with his bag filled with samples of this fern leaf or that butterfly, treasures that the girls pored over and helped him to archive. They had not seen, as Eleanor had, the man with his old medical book on his lap, his eyes closed as he tried to remember the bones of the human hand, his own hand, once so elegant and capable and sure, shaking where it rested on the broad page. He'd sensed her presence and opened his eyes, a sad, tight smile appearing when he saw that it was her. 'I've become one of those men,' he said, 'one of those fellows who sit around trying to fill their empty hours with useless pursuits.'

'That's not true,' she'd said. 'You're working on your natural history book. You're having some time away from medicine, but you'll go back to it. You'll complete your clinical training and be better than ever.'

'When will you see that it's too late? Accept I'm not that man anymore? That he died in France? The things that happened, Eleanor, the terrible choices, the monstrous decisions . . .'

'Tell me about them. Tell me, please, and then I'll understand.'

But he never did, only looked at her and shook his head and turned back to his books.

A woman at the entrance caught Eleanor's attention. A handsome woman holding the hand of a small boy – three years old, Eleanor guessed – dressed very smartly for the occasion in a white sailor suit. He had a cherub's face, big blue eyes, round flushed cheeks, and cupid-bow lips parted in wonder as he peered around his mother's hand at the busy, brightly lit room.

Eleanor felt a familiar tug of longing. She still hoped for another baby. More than hoped, she yearned. Ached with her desire to hold a child in her arms again, to tickle and kiss and cuddle a small, plump body. She reminded herself, sometimes, of the queen in Mr Llewellyn's story, who'd lost her child and so craved another she was willing to deal with the devil to obtain one. Eleanor's wasn't an *entirely* selfish longing. There was a small part of her that wondered whether maybe another child, a little boy, was just what Anthony needed. He loved the girls, but didn't all men want a son who would grow in their own image? Her hand went absently to her flat, firm abdomen. There were still occasional tender moments between them, when he was able; it was possible she would fall pregnant again. But despite her willingness, her eagerness, it had not happened in ten years.

Wistfully, Eleanor forced herself to look away from the woman and child, sitting together now at a table, the little one careful to observe the manners he'd been taught, while his big round eyes gave him away, busily cataloguing the unfamiliar place. She turned back to the window. The dark grey clouds had lowered further over London and the city was gloomy. The lights were on inside the tearoom and as Eleanor took in the warm interior mirrored in the dark glass, ghosted commuters hurrying by beyond it, she met her own reflection by mistake.

It was always a shock to catch oneself unexpectedly in repose. The woman looking back at her was a model of discreet respectability. Her back was straight, her clothes were fashionable without being modish, her hair was neatly set beneath her hat. Her face was a pleasantly drawn mask that gave nothing away. The sort of face other people's gazes slid across. The woman in the glass was everything Eleanor had sworn she wouldn't become. Certainly not the sort of person Eleanor the Adventuress might have been expected to grow into. Eleanor thought of her sometimes, her childhood doppelgänger, that little girl with wild, wide eyes, hair that wouldn't be controlled and a fierce spirit of adventure. Eleanor liked to imagine she was still out there somewhere. That she hadn't been subsumed but, rather, had turned back into a pearl and rolled away. That she was waiting somewhere for the fairies to find her and the woods to bring her back to life.

The thought was upsetting and Eleanor did what she always did when dark thoughts threatened to undo her. She moved. A quick wave brought the waiter, she paid the account, gathered her handbag and the decoy dress she'd barely looked at before purchasing, and with a shake to open her umbrella, headed out into the rain.

*

The ticket office was teeming with people when she reached the station, the smell of wet clothing pervasive. Eleanor joined a queue of disgruntled travellers and made her way slowly to the front of the line. 'I have a fare booked in the name of Edevane,' she told the booking clerk on the other side of the counter.

The man began searching through his file box and as he muttered the names he was passing over Eleanor glanced behind her at the jostling crowd. 'I gather the train is full,' she said.

The man didn't look up. 'Previous train broke down. Been overrun all afternoon with folk trying to get themselves shifted onto the next one. Edevane, you say?'

'Yes.'

'Here we are then.' The man in the booth slid two tickets beneath the grille. 'Departing platform three.'

Eleanor turned to leave, looking as she did so at the pair of tickets in her gloved hand. She pushed back to the front of the counter. 'My husband won't be travelling with me,' she said when she had the clerk's attention. 'He was unexpectedly detained.' More excuses. She made them without thinking these days.

'No refunds,' the man said as he started serving the gentleman behind her.

'I don't want a refund, only to return this ticket.' Eleanor slid it back across the counter. 'I don't need it. The ticket might as well be used by someone else.'

She sat in the carriage, waiting for the train to leave the station. On the platform, men in suits strode busily this way and that, while porters pushed leaning towers of suitcases through the crowds and small groups of people performed the intimate rituals of farewell. It seemed to Eleanor as she watched them that some of the most vivid moments of her life had been enacted in stations like these. There'd been the day she first met Anthony, the lemonade in Baker Street Underground station, and then the morning in 1914 that she'd waved him off to war. He'd looked so dashing in his uniform, Howard there beside him, both men gleaming with youth.

When he told her that he planned to enlist, the two of them lying side by side on a blanket by the Loeanneth stream, a thousand reasons why he shouldn't had crossed her mind. 'But we're so happy,' she'd blurted.

'We'll be happy again, when I come home.'

'*If* you come home.'

It was petulant, the first thing that came to mind and the worst thing she could have said. Selfish, childish and true. She kicked herself afterwards. The four years ahead would teach her temperance, but at the time, fear, panic and her powerlessness to stem their flow made her fierce. 'It's a war, you know. It's not going to be a picnic.'

He reached to push aside a stubborn lock of hair that had fallen across her eyes. His fingertips on her temple made her shiver. 'I have medical training, Eleanor. I can be useful. Those men, my friends, are going to need people like me.'

'*I* need you. There are other doctors, men with clinical experience.'

He smiled softly. 'You must know there's nowhere else I'd rather be than here, with you, but who would I be if I didn't go? How could I live with myself if I didn't help? How would you look at me if I didn't do my bit? If a man cannot be useful to his country, he is better dead.'

She knew then that there was nothing she could say to change his mind and the knowledge burned. It tasted like ash in her mouth.

'Promise me you'll come back,' she said, throwing her arms around him and burying her face in his chest, holding on as if he were a rock in a raging sea.

'Of course I'll come back.' Not the merest shadow of doubt. 'Nothing will stop me. I won't let it.'

They walked together to the station the day he left and she sat with him in the carriage as other young soldiers in fresh new uniforms climbed aboard; he kissed her and she thought for a moment she wasn't going to be able to let him go, and then the whistle sounded and she was on the platform again, without him, and the train was moving away. The house, when she got back to it, was warm and still. The fire in the library was burning low in the grate, just as it had been when they left.

It was so quiet.

A photograph of the two of them stood on the desk below the window, and as she looked at his laughing face, Eleanor tried to convince herself that he was upstairs, or outside by the lake, and that he'd be back any minute, calling to her from the hall to come and join him. But his absence told everywhere, and Eleanor glimpsed, suddenly, how long the coming days, weeks, months were going to be, how unbearably long.

Thank God for her baby, for Deborah, who gave her somewhere to focus her attention. It was not so easy to wallow in the heat of electric fear when one was being watched by wide trusting eyes, a little person who wanted to smile and was reading her mother's expression, looking for the signal that it was all right to do so. But behind the cheerful expression Eleanor forced, beneath the nursery rhymes she sang and the stories she told, she hardly dared to breathe. Every knock on the door shot a prickling flare throughout her body. Every story from the village of another soldier's death was a wrench and, later, a secret reprieve because it wasn't Anthony. The relief at finding a letter and not a black-rimmed telegram was short-lived when she read the date at its top and realised he'd posted it days before and anything might have happened since.

The letters themselves gave nothing away, not at first. There were mentions of being shelled, of course, and of zeppelins being destroyed nearby, but his accounts made them sound like small inconveniences. When he had his first experience with German gas, it was 'under the most ideal circumstances', as they happened to have a fellow around showing them how 'effective the preventative measures were'. Eleanor knew he was obfuscating and it mollified and infuriated her in equal measure.

He had a weekend of leave in London and she met him, beside herself with nervous excitement, unable to settle to anything on the train, her book lying unopened on her lap the whole way. She'd dressed carefully but when she saw him she felt ashamed of her efforts, because it was Anthony, her heart's own love, and her anxiety, her focus on such trivialities as which frock suited her best, seemed somehow to mark a lack of faith in them, in what really mattered.

They both spoke at once when they met. 'Shall we—' 'I suppose—' and then, after an agonising hesitation in which it seemed for a moment as if everything they'd used to be had turned to dust, they both began to laugh, and they couldn't stop, and were still being set off by the least trigger while they sat in the refreshments lounge drinking tea. After that they were themselves again, Anthony-and-Eleanor, and she insisted that he tell her all about it. 'Everything,' she'd said, 'no softening things,' desperate to get beyond the polite, inadequate surface of his letters home.

And so he told her. About the mud, and the bones men broke trying to drag themselves through it, and the men whom it swallowed whole. He called the Somme a mincing machine and said that war itself was intolerable. He described the agony of failing 'his men'. They were dying, he said, one after the other after the other.

The letters home changed after that visit and she wasn't sure she was glad. It crossed her mind that she ought to have been more careful what she wished for. The censor removed the worst sections, but enough remained for her to know that things continued to be grim, that war asked men to do horrific things and that it did horrific things to them in return.

When Howard was killed, the tone of the letters changed again. There were no more references to 'his men', and Anthony never mentioned another friend by name. Most chilling of all, where his letters had always been filled with questions about home, hungry for the merest detail about Deborah and the new little baby, Alice – *I wish I were there, too. I ache to be so far away from all of you. Be strong, my love, and in the meantime, won't you send me a lock of my baby's hair?* – now they were little more than cool, statistical accounts of what was happening at the front. They might have been written by, and for, anyone. And so Eleanor had to wrestle at once with the twin griefs of Howard's death – the shock of the news, its impossible finality – and the subsequent loss of her husband, who was already so far away, behind a wall of impenetrable politeness.

On the day he returned for good, the twelfth of December 1918, Eleanor brought the two little ones to London to watch his train come in. There was an orchestra set up on the station, violins playing Christmas carols. 'How will we know it's Daddy?' Deborah had asked her. She was intensely curious about this person she knew only from the studio photograph in the frame beside her mummy's bed.

'We'll know,' Eleanor told her.

Smoke filled the station as the train arrived, and by the time it cleared, servicemen were climbing down onto the platform. When she finally saw him, in the split second before his eyes found hers, she felt the years keenly. Anxieties crowded like moths around a flame. Would they still know one another? Would it be as it was? Had too much come to pass?

'You're hurting my hand, Mummy,' Alice had said. Not even two, and already filled with an admirable talent for forthrightness.

'I'm sorry, Pumpkin. I'm sorry.'

And then he'd looked directly at her and briefly she'd seen something in his eyes, a shadow in the shape of Howard and all the others like him, and then it was gone, and he smiled, and he was Anthony, *her* Anthony, home again at last.

The whistle blew outside. The train was about to leave and not a moment too soon. Through the window, Eleanor watched the soot-blackened tracks. It had been so wonderful to have him home. The girls couldn't get enough of him. Loeanneth was brighter for him being there, things were clearer, as if someone had sharpened the focus on a camera. Life was to go on, just as he'd promised it would. More than four years had passed but the war was won and they would make up for lost time. And if sometimes his hands shook a bit, if he broke off mid-sentence and had to collect his thoughts before resuming, if occasionally he woke with a bad dream and refused ever to talk about Howard, well, they were understandable problems and would surely sort themselves out.

Or so she'd thought.

The first time it happened, they were outside in the garden. The girls had been chasing ducks and their nanny had shepherded them inside for supper. It was a glorious evening, the sun seeming to hesitate in the process of setting, as if it couldn't bear to end the day. It was teetering on the horizon, throwing ribbons of pink and mauve across the sky like life ropes, and the air was sweet with jasmine. They'd brought the white cane chairs down from the house, and Anthony, having spent the afternoon entertaining the girls, had finally opened the newspaper he'd brought with him, only to fall into a doze behind it.

Edwina, the new puppy, was leaping about at Eleanor's feet, pouncing on a ball the girls had found for her, and Eleanor was rolling it gently along the cooling lawn, laughing fondly as the puppy tripped over her ears to fetch it back. She was teasing the little dog, lifting the ball just out of reach for the pleasure of seeing her balance on her hind legs, cycle her little paws in the air, and then snap at it with her teeth. They were sharp teeth. The puppy had already managed to tear holes in most of Eleanor's stockings. Darling little menace, she had a sixth sense for rooting out the things she shouldn't have, but it was impossible to be cross with her. She only had to look up with those big brown eyes and cock her head just so and Eleanor melted. She'd wanted a dog when she was a girl, but her mother had declared them 'filthy beasts' and that was that.

Eleanor pulled back on the ball and Edwina, who loved nothing more than a bout of play wrestling, sank her teeth further into the rubber. Everything was perfect. Eleanor laughed, and Edwina growled excitedly at the ball before breaking into a rousing ruction with a duck, and the sun shimmered orange in the sky, and then suddenly Anthony was upon them with a mighty holler. In one swift movement, he'd grabbed the little dog and was holding her down, his hands around her neck. 'Be quiet,' he was hissing, 'be quiet.'

Edwina yelped and howled, the duck fled, and Eleanor, shocked, jumped to her feet.

'Anthony! No! Stop!'

She was so frightened; she had no idea what was happening.

'Anthony, please.'

It was as if he couldn't hear her, as if she weren't there at all. Only when she ran to his side, fell down beside him and seized his shoulders, did he glance her way. He shrugged off her grip and for a split second she thought he was going to pounce on her, too. His eyes were wide, and she glimpsed that shadow again, the one she'd seen briefly at the train station when they welcomed him home.

'Anthony,' she said again, 'please. Let go of her.'

He was breathing hard, his chest rising and falling, his

expression shifting from anger to fear to confusion. At some point he loosened his hold on Edwina for the little pup wriggled free, emitting a small yelp of self-pity as she tore off to the safety of Eleanor's chair to lick her wounds.

Neither of them moved. It seemed to Eleanor later they were frozen by a shared sense, an unspoken agreement, that by remaining still they might somehow stop the egg from cracking further. But then she realised he was shivering and on instinct Eleanor took him in her arms and held him tightly. He was freezing. 'There now,' she heard herself saying, 'there now,' over and over again, just as she might had one of the girls scraped a knee or woken with a bad dream.

Later, they sat together in the moonlit night, both of them silent and shocked by what had happened. 'I'm sorry,' he said. 'For a moment I thought . . . I could have sworn I saw . . .'

But he never did tell her what he'd imagined he saw. In the years since, Eleanor had read reports and spoken with doctors and learned enough to know that Anthony must have been reliving a wartime trauma when he attacked Edwina, but he never would speak about the things that moved in the shadows. And they came again, those ghosts. She would be speaking to him and then catch him staring into the distance, his jaw tightening, at first in fear, later in resolution. She gathered over time that it was something to do with Howard, about the way he'd died, but Anthony refused to talk about it so she couldn't be sure of the details.

She told herself it didn't matter, that he would get past it. Everyone had lost someone in the war, it would all be better with time. When his hands settled down he'd go back to his training; that would make a world of difference. He would be a doctor, just like he'd always planned – a surgeon; he had a calling.

But his hands didn't settle down, and things didn't get better with time. They got worse. Eleanor and Anthony merely got better, together, at hiding the truth. There were terrible nightmares, too, from which he'd wake howling or shaking, urging them to move quickly, to leave, to make the dog stop barking. He wasn't often violent, and it was never his fault when he was, Eleanor knew that. His great drive in life had always been to help and to heal; he would never knowingly harm another. Fear that he might, though, plagued him. 'If the girls,' he began, 'if it had been one of them . . .'

'Shhh.' Eleanor wouldn't let him speak the preposterous thought out loud. 'It won't happen.'

'It could.'

'It won't. I won't let it. I promise.'

'You can't promise that.'

'I can. I do.'

There'd been so much fear in his face, and his hands as they clutched hers were shaking. 'Promise me, if you ever have to make a choice, you'll save them from me. Save me from myself. I couldn't live with myself if—'

She pressed her fingers against his lips to stop him from saying the terrible words. She kissed him and then held him tightly as he shook against her body. Eleanor knew what he was asking of her, and she knew she'd do whatever she had to in order to keep her promise.

Twenty-one

London, 2003

Sadie's flat looked and smelled like the sort of place she was used to being sent out to on call. 'You can tell a lot about a person by the home they keep,' Donald had told her once, in a prim sort of way, quite out of character with his usual burly self and rather rich coming from a man whose wife did all his cleaning. She picked up the scattered layers of junk mail and bills from the mat and closed the door with her foot. The weather had come over grey, but when she switched on the light only one bulb of three complied.

Just over two weeks away and a layer of dust had already settled on every surface. The room's odour was sour and neglected, and Sadie's furniture, never lovely, had become sullen and reproachful in her absence, more tattered, too, than she remembered. Further adding to the air of ill-kempt, unloved, couldn't-give-a-damnness was the pot plant on her kitchen sink. 'Oh, my,' said Sadie, dropping her bag and tossing the mail onto the sofa as she approached the poor, sad carcass. 'What's become of you?' She'd picked it up from the local nursery-school Easter fete a couple of months before in a fit of domestic aspiration, a rebuke to the man she'd been sort of seeing whose parting shot had echoed down the stairwell as he left: 'You're so used to being alone you couldn't even care for a pot plant.' Sadie crunched the dry, curled leaves onto the stainless-steel sink. She'd shown him.

Noise outside, traffic and voices, made the room seem unnaturally quiet. Sadie found the remote and clicked on the television. Stephen Fry was on, being clever and funny about something, and Sadie lowered the volume to a hum and checked the fridge. It was a further disaster site. Almost empty except for a couple of whiskery carrots and a container of orange juice. She checked the use-by date on the juice and decided six days past was fine, they were always overly cautious with these things. She poured a glassful and went to her desk.

While the computer booted up, Sadie plugged in her phone to charge and then dug the Edevane file from her bag. She took a sip of piquant juice and sat wincingly through the anxious squeal of the dial-up modem connecting to the internet. All the way home she'd gone over the interview with Margot Sinclair in her mind. Sadie had been so convinced Rose Waters and Anthony Edevane were engaged in a love affair and that Theo was Rose's son, not Eleanor's, that she was having a hard time processing the new information. The pieces of puzzle had fitted together so well it took an enormous act of will to pull them apart and start again. Perhaps that was why she clung to her hunch that Anthony Edevane was important. When the search engine home page appeared she typed in *shell shock*.

A list of sites appeared on her screen and she skimmed through the options until she found an entry from a site called firstworldwar.com which seemed reputable. Sadie clicked and started reading the definition. *A term used to describe psychological trauma . . . intensity of artillery battles . . . neurotic cracks in otherwise mentally stable soldiers.* There was a black-and-white photograph of a uniformed man staring at the camera with a wistful half-smile, his body angled so that the right side of his face was concealed by shadow. The article continued: *Soldiers came to recognise the symptoms but recognition by military authority was slower to develop . . . panic attacks, mental and physical paralysis, fearful headaches, terrifying dreams . . . many continued to feel its effects for years afterwards . . . treatment was primitive at best, dangerous at worst . . .*

There was a link at the bottom of the page to a paper delivered by a Dr W. H. R. Rivers in which he outlined his theories based on observations of injured soldiers at Craiglockhart War Hospital between the years 1915 and 1917. Much of the article was spent explaining the process of repression, Dr Rivers suggesting that returned soldiers who spent most of the day trying to forget their fears and memories were far more likely to fall victim during the silence and isolation of night when sleep weakened their self-control and made them susceptible to the creep of ghastly thoughts.

It made sense. In Sadie's experience most things were more intense at night. That was certainly when her own dark thoughts escaped their bounds and turned into dreams to haunt her. She kept skimming. According to Dr Rivers, repression made the negative thoughts accumulate energy, resulting in vivid or even painful dream imagery and horrors that raced violently through the mind. Sadie jotted the line in her notebook, considered it and then circled the word *violently*. The doctor was referring to the passage of thoughts in the soldier's brain, but the word, especially in the context of Theo Edevane's mysterious fate, gave Sadie an uneasy feeling. She'd known all along there was a third grisly possibility, that the boy might not have wandered or been taken but had met instead with a violent end. When she'd talked with Clive she'd wondered whether Clementine Edevane could have been involved in her brother's death, accidentally or otherwise. But what if it had been Anthony? What if it had been Theo's father, all along?

Sadie flicked back through her notes to those she'd taken during her interview with Clive. Anthony and Eleanor had provided alibis for each other. Eleanor had been grief-stricken during interviews and needed sedation over the course of the week. Clive had noted that Anthony was particularly caring and attentive and that he'd been fiercely protective of his wife. *He was so careful with her*, Clive had said, *gentle and protective, making sure she rested, stopping her from tearing outside to join the search. He barely let her out of his sight.* Sadie stood up and stretched. When she wrote those things, she'd accepted Clive's observation as evidence of the Edevanes' strong bond, their love for one another, the natural actions of a couple experiencing the unimaginable; she certainly hadn't suspected anything untoward. But now, viewed through the lens of her developing theory (and that's all it was, she reminded herself, one hunch built upon another), the behaviour took on a more sinister tint. Was it possible that Eleanor knew what her husband had done and was covering for him? Would a mother do that? Would a wife? Had Anthony been placating her, standing guard so that she couldn't reveal to police what she knew?

Sadie glanced at the digital clock in the corner of her

screen. She'd decided on the drive back from Oxford that tonight was as good a night as any to catch up with Donald. She ought to be getting her head in the right space to convince him she was ready to come back to work, not chasing ghosts around the internet. She should switch off now and return to the website later. She should put her notebook away and shower. Nothing said 'ready to be professional' like observing the basics in personal grooming. But a scribbled note further down the page caught her eye – Clive's account of Eleanor's annual visits to Loeanneth – and she kept reading. Clive had said that Eleanor returned each year in the hope her son might somehow find his way home, but that had been supposition. Eleanor hadn't told Clive that was her expectation; it had been his reading of her actions. What if she hadn't been expecting Theo to return because she already knew that he was dead? What if her annual visit wasn't a vigil but a memorial, in the same way people made regular pilgrimages to the gravestones of those they'd lost?

Sadie drummed her pen on the notepad. She was presuming a lot. Nowhere in any of the interviews had anyone used the word 'violent' in relation to Anthony Edevane, and Dr Rivers wrote about dissociation, depression, confusion, a soldier's sense that his 'light' had gone out, but again made no mention of violent tendencies. She sat down and surfed through a few more webpages, scanning and clicking until she came across a quote from a war correspondent called Philip Gibbs, writing about the return of soldiers to their lives after war:

Something was wrong. They put on civilian clothes again and looked to their mothers and wives very much like the young men who had gone to business in the peaceful

*days before August 1914. But they had not come back the
same men. Something had altered in them. They were subject
to sudden moods and queer tempers, fits of profound depression alternating with a restless desire for pleasure. Many
were easily moved to passion where they lost control of
themselves, many were bitter in their speech, violent in
opinion, frightening.*

Sadie sucked in her lips and reread the passage. *Sudden
moods . . . queer tempers . . . lost control . . . violent in
opinion . . . frightening.* Conditions that could certainly lead
a person to make a terrible mistake, commit a heinous act
they would never be capable of when they were in their right
mind.

There followed an article about trench conditions on the
Western Front, descriptions of the horrific lack of sanitation,
the rats and the mud and the fungal decay of trench foot,
the lice that sucked off rotting flesh. Sadie was completely
absorbed by what she was reading and when the home
phone rang it jolted her back to the present so rapidly she
could almost see images of the mud and the slaughter fading
around her.

She took up the handset. 'Hello?'

It was Bertie, his warm, homely voice a welcome balm.
'Just calling to see that you made it back to London all right.
I couldn't get an answer on your mobile. You were going to
ring me when you got there.'

'Oh, Granddad, I'm sorry!' *I'm a hopeless excuse for a
granddaughter who doesn't deserve someone like you.* 'My
battery's flat. I stopped a few times along the way, and traffic
on the M40 was a nightmare. I've only just come in.' She
pictured him in the kitchen in Cornwall, the dogs asleep

beneath the table, and felt a physical pull of longing in her chest. 'How's the day? How are my lads?'

'Missing you. I went to put my shoes on and they gathered expectantly at my heels, ready for their run.'

'Well, you know what you have to do. They'll show you the way.'

He chortled. 'I can just imagine how much they'd enjoy a run with yours truly. More like a limping lope!'

Regret came in a sudden wave. 'Look, Granddad, about the other night—'

'Water under the bridge.'

'I was insensitive.'

'You miss Ruth.'

'I was snarky.'

'You snark because you care.'

'I like Louise, she seems kind.'

'She's been a good friend. I need friends. I'm not trying to replace your grandmother. Now tell me, how was your meeting with Rose's great-niece?'

'A dead end, sort of.'

'The baby wasn't the nanny's?'

'It would appear not.' Sadie gave him a potted summary of her conversation with Margot Sinclair, the disappointment that her theory appeared defunct, finishing with the unexpected news about Anthony Edevane's shell shock. 'I don't know that it's relevant, but I've been doing a bit of reading and it's hard to imagine a man going through all that without it impacting his life afterwards.' As she spoke she'd wandered over to the window and stood now looking down into the street where a woman was remonstrating with a child who refused to get into his buggy. 'Did any of our family go to the First World War, Granddad?'

'My mother's cousin fought on the Somme, but he lived up north so I never knew him, and my favourite uncle fought in the second war.'

'Was he different when he came back?'

'He didn't come back, he was killed in France. Terrible loss; my mother never got over it. Our next-door neighbour, though, Mr Rogers, came back from the First World War in a dreadful condition.'

'Dreadful how?'

'He'd been buried under the earth for eighteen hours after an explosion. Eighteen hours! Can you imagine? He was out in the middle of no-man's-land and his mates couldn't get to him for all the shelling. When they finally managed to dig him out he was in a catatonic state of shock. He was shipped back home and treated at one of those hospitals they set up in country houses, but he was never the same according to my parents.'

'What was he like?'

'His face was fixed in a permanent expression of horror. He used to have nightmares where he couldn't breathe, and he'd wake up gasping for air. Other nights we'd be woken by a God-awful wailing that travelled right through the walls into our house. Poor man. The neighbourhood children were all frightened of him; they used to take dares to see who was brave enough to walk up to his door and knock before running away and hiding.'

'But not you.'

'No, well, my mother would have tanned my hide if she'd even suspected I was capable of that sort of childish cruelty.

Besides, it was personal with Mr Rogers. Ma had taken him under her wing. She cooked an extra plate of supper every night, brought in his washing, made sure his house was kept clean. She was like that, the kindest of hearts, never as happy as when she was helping someone less fortunate.'

'I wish I'd known her.'

'I wish you had, too.'

'She sounds a lot like Ruth.' Sadie remembered how willingly Ruth had welcomed her into their home when she had nowhere else to go.

'Funny you should say that. After Ma died and we took over the shop, Ruth took over with Mr Rogers, too. She was adamant that we couldn't just leave him in the lurch.'

'I can just hear her saying that.'

Bertie laughed and then sighed, and Sadie knew he'd be climbing the stairs to the attic when they finished their phone call, digging through his boxes for some small reminder of Ruth. He didn't mention her again, though, changing the subject to more immediate, tangible and solvable concerns. 'You all right for dinner?'

Sadie felt a swell of emotion. That was love right there, wasn't it? Someone in your life who cared that your next meal was coming to you. She opened the fridge and wrinkled her nose. 'Just dandy,' she said, pushing the door shut. 'I'm heading out to meet a friend.'

The Fox and Hounds did a roaring trade on Tuesday nights, due in no small part to its position across the road from a backpackers' hostel and its institution of a four-hour happy hour. There were other pubs closer to the Met, places that were teeming with police officers, but Donald reckoned he saw enough of the guys from work at work and it was worth the extra walk to have a break from talking shop. Sadie had taken him on faith for a long time, until she realised he always let her tag along, and they always talked shop, usually at his instigation. Truth was, the Fox and Hounds had the cheapest pints this side of the Thames and Donald was a cheapskate. A lovable cheapskate, but a cheapskate nonetheless. Tuesday was also the night all four of his daughters came home for dinner, and Donald had once told Sadie he needed all the fortification he could get if he didn't want to bust a cracking headache the minute he stepped across the threshold. 'The arguments, Sparrow, the bickering and the shifting loyalties. I can't make head nor tail of it. Women!' He shook his head. 'They're a mystery, aren't they?'

All of which was to say that Donald was a creature of habit and when Sadie set off for the Fox and Hounds, stomach growling, she knew she'd find him sitting on the bench below the framed picture of the frog who would a-wooing go. Sure enough, when she arrived, a telling fug of smoke sat thick above the booth. She paid for a couple of pints and then carried them gingerly across the room, ready to slide into the empty bench opposite him. Only it wasn't empty. Harry Sullivan was slouched in the corner, laughing uproariously at something Donald had just said. Sadie plonked her two beers on to the table and said, 'Sorry, Harry. Didn't realise you were here.'

Like all old cops, Donald had seen enough of the odd and the ugly to have lost the ability to look surprised. The closest he came was the slight suggestion of an eyebrow shift. 'Sparrow,' he said with a nod, as if she hadn't just spent two weeks in the wilderness at his insistence.

'Don.'

'Thought you were on holidays, Sparrow,' said Harry cheerfully. 'Tired of the sun and surf already?'

'Something like that, Sully.' She smiled at Donald, who drained the last of his current pint and wiped his moustache with the back of his hand before pushing the empty glass to the edge of the table.

'Cornwall, wasn't it?' Sully continued. 'I had an aunt who used to live in Truro, every summer me and the brother and sister would—'

'How about getting us another round, eh, Sull?' said Donald.

The younger detective eyed the fresh beers Sadie had brought with her, opened his mouth to point out to Don that he was already well served, before shutting it again. He wasn't the sharpest tool in the shed but realisation settled on his broad brow. He waved his empty glass in the general direction of the bar and said, 'Might just go and fetch myself a fresh one.'

'Righto then,' said Donald pleasantly.

Sadie stepped aside so Harry could leave the booth and then she took his place. The leather was warm, an unfortunate physical manifestation of her growing sense she'd been replaced. 'You and Sull have been partnering then?'

'We have.'

'Working on anything interesting?'

'B&E, pretty standard.'

Sadie itched for details but knew better than to press. She took up the menu and scanned it. 'I'm starving. You don't mind if I eat?'

'Not at all.'

The fashion for gentrification had bypassed the Fox and Hounds, and the menu displayed a basic list of four choices, all served with chips, just as it had since 1964. So proud was the management of its resistance to change, the fact was emblazoned in large print across the top of the menu card. Needless to say, Donald approved wholeheartedly. 'Bloody tapas,' he'd said to Sadie on more than one occasion when a case took them further afield. 'What's wrong with a good old-fashioned pie? When did people get so bloody fancy?'

The waitress came by and Sadie ordered fish and chips. 'Anything for you?'

Donald shook his head. 'Family dinner,' he said grimly.

The waitress left and Sadie took a sip of beer. 'Family well?'

'Very well.'

'And you're keeping busy?'

'Very busy. Listen, Sparrow—'

'I've been busy, too, working a cold case.' Even as she said it, Sadie kicked herself. She hadn't intended to mention the Edevane family. Digging around after a child who'd been missing seventy years, tracking down old maps and police files, conducting interviews with the descendants of those involved – it didn't exactly scream rest and recuperation, but seeing Sully sitting there in her place had pushed all her buttons. Dolt!

There was no taking it back now, though, and Sadie figured the best thing for it was to move on with a new subject, cover her mistake. But even as she thought it, she knew it was too late. Donald's ears had pricked up like an Alsatian who'd caught a whiff of rabbit. 'Cold case? Who for?'

'Oh, it's nothing really. An old officer in Cornwall who

was looking for a sounding board.' She took a swig of beer, bought herself some time before compounding the lie. 'A friend of my grandfather's. Couldn't really say no.' She started outlining the Edevane case before Donald could ask too much more about *how* it had come her way. Better he think her benignly helpful than weirdly obsessive. He listened, nodding occasionally as he shepherded tiny pieces of spilled tobacco across the table surface.

'I've got a feeling this shell shock is important,' Sadie said as the waitress deposited a plate of over-fried fish in front of her.

'You and your feelings, eh?'

Sadie cursed the poor choice of words but didn't bite. 'Know much about it?'

'Post-traumatic stress disorder? I know a little.'

She remembered then that Donald's nephew had served in the Gulf War. Her partner wasn't the most loquacious of people but there'd been enough veiled references for Sadie to gather that Jeremy hadn't had what might euphemistically be termed 'a good war'.

'Shit of a thing. Just when we think we've turned a corner, it hits him again. Terrible depression.' He shook his head as if the words to describe the depth of his nephew's suffering were not available. 'Not your usual sad-sack blues, something very different. Hopeless, despairing, terrible.'

'Anxiety?'

'That too. Heart palpitations, fear, nightmares that seem real.'

'What about violent urges?'

'You could say that. My sister-in-law found him with his old man's hunting rifle, pointing it at the door to his younger brother's room. He thought there were militants inside; he'd had a vision.'

'God, Don, I'm sorry.'

Donald's lips set thin. He allowed a quick nod. 'God-awful thing. Gentle kid, he was, real good heart, and I don't just say that because he's my brother's boy. I always knew when my girls were with Jeremy I could rest easy.' He swept the tobacco pieces off the table with one angry swipe. 'The things those boys had to do. The things they saw and that they can't forget. How does a person go back to normal after that? How do you tell a man to kill and then expect him to go back to normal?'

'I don't know.' Sadie shook her head.

Donald took up his beer and swigged savagely. When the glass was drained, he wiped the back of his hand across the bristles of his moustache. His eyes were bloodshot.

'Don—'

'What are you doing here, Sparrow?'

'I called, I left a message. You didn't get my message?'

'I was hoping you were joking. Friday the thirteenth and all that.'

'I wasn't. I'm ready to come back. If you could just trust me—'

'It's too late, Sparrow.' His voice had lowered, was almost a hiss. He leaned closer, glancing over his shoulder to where Sully was still propped against the bar, laughing with a blonde backpacker. 'Ashford's opened an inquiry into the Bailey case leak. I heard it from Parr-Wilson, who always knows before the rest of us. There's pressure from above, an example needs to be made, internal politics. You get the picture.'

was only forty-five, her ash-blonde hair hanging straight past her shoulders, her fringe long and blunt.

'Can I get you a cuppa, Nancy?'

'That'd be lovely.'

A quick scan of the kitchen revealed she was out of bags. 'How about a whisky?'

'That'd be even lovelier.'

Sadie was reminded how much she liked Nancy. In another life, they might've been friends. That was part of the problem. She took down two glasses and brought them and Johnnie Walker to the coffee table. She knew what she ought to do: refuse to enter into conversation about Maggie's 'disappearance', behave for all the world as if Nancy's daughter had just stepped out and there was every chance she'd returned home in the intervening fortnight, say something chatty like, 'Have you heard from Maggie yet?' But as she opened her mouth to do so, she closed it again. She'd been such a vehement proponent of the theory that Maggie had met with foul play, it would have seemed impossibly false. She resolved to let Nancy speak first. She poured whisky into the glasses and handed one over.

'So,' Nancy said, 'I went around to see the people moving into Maggie's flat. *Their* flat, now – the man she rented it from decided to sell, quick and quiet, as if my Maggie never existed.'

'You went to see the new owners?'

'I wanted to make sure they knew what had happened there. Just in case.'

She didn't explain further, but she didn't need to. Sadie knew what she meant. *Just in case Maggie comes back.* She could well imagine the conversation. In Sadie's experience most people did not enjoy the notoriety of purchasing and living in a place that had been part of a criminal investigation, though child abandonment was preferable to a murder scene she supposed. 'And?' she said. 'How was it?'

'They were nice. A young couple, newlyweds – their first home. They were still in the middle of unpacking but they invited me in for a cup of tea.'

'And you accepted?'

'Of course I did.'

Of course she did. Nancy's faith in Maggie was fierce, matched only by the lengths to which she'd go to prove that she'd been right, that her daughter hadn't abandoned her own child.

'I wanted to see inside, just one more time. She wasn't there, though, my Maggie. It was like a different place without her things.' Maggie's things were all in boxes, Sadie knew, piled on top of one another in Nancy's spare room, the one she'd had set up for Caitlyn. Nancy looked as if she were about to cry and Sadie wasn't sure what to say. She didn't even have a box of tissues to place meaningfully on the coffee table between them. 'I know there was no point,' Nancy continued. 'I know it was a stupid thing to do. They were nice, asked me questions about her, but I could tell by their faces they felt sorry for me, they thought I was mad. A crazy, sad old woman. I know it was stupid.'

It *was* stupid. A less forgiving couple and she might have ended up with the police arriving, a charge of harassment or even trespassing. But it was understandable too. Sadie thought about Loeanneth, still furnished seventy years after Theo's disappearance, and about Clive's account of Eleanor Edevane turning up year after year just to occupy the place where her son had last been seen. It was the same thing, only Nancy didn't have the luxury of maintaining a shrine to her missing daughter. All she had was a spare room loaded with boxes and cheap furniture.

'How's Caitlyn?' she asked, changing the subject.

That brought a smile to Nancy's face. 'She's well, little petal. Missing her mother. I don't see her as much as I'd like to.'

'I'm really sorry to hear that.' She was, too. Sadie had been struck when she interviewed Nancy the first time by the number of framed photographs of the little girl displayed in her flat. On top of the television set, hanging on the wall, standing amongst other photos on the bookshelf. Apparently they'd spent a lot of time together before Maggie upped and left. Nancy had taken regular care of Caitlyn when Maggie was working.

'I feel like I've lost them both.' Nancy fiddled with the edge of a cushion on Sadie's sofa.

'You haven't, though. It seems to me Caitlyn will need you more now than ever.'

'I don't know where I fit anymore. Whole new life Caty's got. They've decorated a room especially at Steve's place, filled it with toys, a new bed with a Dora the Explorer duvet cover. Dora's her favourite.'

'I remember,' said Sadie, picturing the little girl in the hallway, her pink Dora nightie. The memory came like a sharp pain in her chest, and she could see how much it hurt Nancy to think that her daughter had been replaced so easily in the little girl's affections. 'She's a kid. Kids like toys and TV characters, but they know what really matters.'

Nancy sighed and brushed back her fringe. 'You're a

good sort, Sadie. I don't know why I'm here. I shouldn't have come, I'll only get you in trouble.'

Sadie didn't mention that that horse had already bolted. Instead, she topped up their glasses.

'I suppose you're working on something else now?'

'No rest for the wicked.'

Sadie considered outlining the Edevane case, just to change the subject, but decided the parallels – a missing person never found – would be unhelpful. And Nancy wasn't really listening anyway, she was still thinking about Maggie. 'You know what doesn't make sense,' she said, setting down her glass and plaiting her fingers, 'is why Maggie would have left Caitlyn after she went through so much difficulty to have her in the first place.'

'To conceive her, you mean?' Sadie was mildly surprised. This was the first she'd heard of fertility issues.

'God, no, they only had to look at one another, those two. They had to move the wedding forward, if you know what I mean. No, I'm talking about *after* they divorced, custody. Maggie had to go to so much effort to prove she was a good mother; she had to get witness statements and put up with social services visiting and making their notes. Being so young the courts took some convincing, but she was determined not to let Caitlyn go. She said to me, "Mum, Caty's my daughter and she belongs with me."' Nancy looked at Sadie with an imploring, somehow triumphant expression. *Don't you see?* it seemed to say. 'Why would she go through all that only to walk out?'

Sadie hadn't the heart to tell Nancy that a court battle proved nothing. That there were very few separations where the parents *didn't* fight tooth and nail for custody, and that their determination frequently had less to do with a longing for parenthood than it did with one-upping their ex. She had seen otherwise mild, sane people fight viciously in the Family Court for guinea pigs and cutlery sets and the portrait Great-Aunt Mildred had painted of her terrier, Bilbo.

'Wasn't easy, neither. He's in a much better financial position than my Maggie, and remarried. She was worried the courts would decide that two adults, a mum and a dad, in the household were better than one. The judge got it right in the end, though. She saw what a good mum my Maggie was. And she *was* a good mum. I know what Steve told you, that business with her forgetting to collect Caitlyn from nursery, but that was a misunderstanding. She was only late because she'd started a new job, and as soon as she realised it was going to be tight, that's when I started helping. She was a terrific mum. When Caty turned two, all she wanted was a trip to the seaside and that's what we planned to do for her birthday. We'd promised and promised and talked about it for weeks, but the day before, she came over poorly. A high temperature, all floppy and sorry for herself. You know what Maggie did? She brought the seaside to Caty. Raided the storeroom at work for leftover supplies and spent the whole night making waves out of cellophane and cardboard, fish and seagulls and shells for Caty to collect. She put on a Punch and Judy show, just for Caty.'

Nancy's blue eyes gleamed with the memory. Sadie met the other woman's smile but her own was tempered with pity. She understood why Nancy had come tonight and it made her sad. There was no breakthrough in the case; she simply wanted to talk about Maggie, and rather than reach out to a friend or relative she'd chosen Sadie as her confidante. It wasn't uncommon during investigations for members of the victim's family to develop an abnormally tight bond with the police officer in charge. Sadie figured it made sense that someone whose life had been turned upside down by the shock and trauma of an unexpected crime would cling to the person who seemed to represent solutions and safety, who seemed to be in charge and able to fix things.

But Sadie was no longer in charge of finding Maggie, and she certainly wasn't able to fix things. Not for Nancy Bailey, not even for herself. Sadie glanced at the digital clock on the oven. She'd been hit suddenly by a wave of extreme tiredness. The day had been long and heavy and waking that morning in Cornwall seemed like something that had happened to someone else a very long time ago. She felt sorry for Nancy, but they were going over old ground which was in neither one of their best interests. She gathered their empty glasses into a cluster near the bottle of JW. 'Nancy, look, I'm sorry, I don't mean to be rude, but I'm very tired.'

The other woman nodded quickly. ''Course you are, sorry – I just get stuck, you know?'

'I know.'

'And there was a reason I came tonight.' She pulled something out of her pocket, a small leather-bound notebook. 'I've been going through Maggie's things again, just in case I found a new lead, and I saw in her diary she had a dinner date with a man called MT. It had been there the whole time but I didn't realise what it was. I remember now, he was a new fellow at work.' She was pointing at the initials with a fingernail bitten to the quick.

'You think this guy, this MT, might have been involved? That he had something to do with her disappearance?'

Nancy was looking at her like she'd lost her marbles. 'No, you duffer! I think he's proof that she didn't go anywhere, not by choice. Maggie never dated, not since she and Steve split up. She didn't think it was right to confuse Caty by parading one man after another across the threshold. But this one was different, this MT. She'd told me about him, you see, more than once. "Mum," she said, "he's so handsome and really kind and funny." She thought he might even be The One.'

'Nancy—'

'Don't you see? Why would she walk out right when everything was coming together for her?'

Sadie could think of any number of reasons, but reasons hardly mattered at this point. It was like Donald always said: thoughts about motive were a distraction. They stopped people from seeing what was right in front of them if they couldn't straight away explain it. All that mattered was that Maggie *had* walked out. They'd found unassailable proof. 'There was a note, Nancy.'

'Note.' Nancy waved her hand, frustrated. 'You know what I think of that note.'

Sadie did know what Nancy thought of the note. She thought very little of it indeed. Somewhat predictably, Nancy was convinced the note was a fake. This was despite having been told numerous times, by more than one handwriting analyst, with high degrees of certainty, that the message had been written by Maggie.

'It doesn't make sense,' Nancy said now. 'If you knew her, you'd agree.'

Sadie *didn't* know Maggie, but there were a number of things she did know. She knew there'd been a note, she knew

Caitlyn had been hungry and frightened when they found her, she knew the little girl was happy and safe now. Sadie looked at Nancy, sitting on the other side of the sofa, her face wretched with the effort of inventing endless possibilities for what might have happened to Maggie. It seemed the human brain had an unlimited creative ability when it desired something enough.

She thought again of Eleanor Edevane, whose child had also disappeared. Nowhere in Clive's notes had there been evidence that she'd made alternative suggestions as to where her son might be. In fact, Clive said she'd handled herself with grace, that she'd quietly let police get on with their work, that her husband had stopped her from tearing outside and helping with the search, that she'd decided against posting a reward but had donated money later to the police in gratitude for their efforts.

It suddenly seemed to Sadie very unnatural behaviour. Vastly different to Nancy Bailey's ferocious belief that the police were wrong, her tireless attempts to find new avenues of investigation. In fact, Eleanor Edevane's passivity could *almost* be read as further evidence she already knew the whereabouts of her child. Clive certainly hadn't thought so. He'd been convinced she was holding herself together with tremendous will and was brought unstuck only by the compounding tragedy of her friend Llewellyn's suicide.

But, then, investigating officers couldn't always be counted on to look beyond the personal relationship they'd forged with families, especially a young officer just starting out. Sadie sat very still, her mind suddenly active, ticking over the possibilities. Was the donation to police actually an apology of some sort, for wasting their time and resources in a search she knew would be fruitless? The search for a little boy who was already dead? Who had, perhaps, already been buried in the grounds of Loeanneth? In the woods, maybe, that gave the house its total privacy?

'I'm sorry. You're tired. I should go.'

Sadie blinked. Away with her thoughts, she'd almost forgotten her visitor.

Nancy gathered her bag by the straps, slinging it over her shoulder. She stood. 'It was good of you to see me.'

'Nancy – ' Sadie stopped. She wasn't sure what she wanted to say. *I'm sorry it didn't work out differently. I'm sorry I let you down.* She wasn't a hugger, and yet in that moment Sadie felt an overwhelming urge to embrace the other woman. And so she did.

Sadie sat for a time on the sofa after Nancy left. She was still tired, but her mind was too restless to sleep. She cursed herself for having returned 'Fictional Escap(e)ades' before leaving Cornwall; she could have used a good sedative right now. The other woman's sadness, her loneliness and the evident betrayal she felt in the face of her daughter's absconding had left a shadowy echo behind in the flat. It was a great pity she felt cut off from Caitlyn, but Sadie was glad for the little girl that she had another parent, a loving father with a second wife prepared to take on somebody else's child. There were some good people in the world, people like Bertie and Ruth.

When Sadie had found out she was pregnant that summer there'd been a dreadful series of rows with her parents. They'd been adamant that 'people mustn't know' and had demanded that she 'get it taken care of' as quickly and quietly as possible. Sadie had been bewildered and frightened, but she'd refused; things had escalated, her father had blustered and threatened, and then finally – she couldn't remember now whether it was he or she who'd given the ultimatum – Sadie had left home. That's when the social services had got involved, asking whether there was anyone else she could stay with while things cooled down, family or friends who might take her in. Sadie had initially told them no. It was only when they pressed that she remembered the grandparents she'd used to visit when she was younger. Vague memories came to her of the drive into London, the roast Sunday lunches, and the tiny walled garden. There'd been a falling-out, she remembered – her parents, like many of the blinkered and unyielding, were often falling out with people – and Sadie's mother had broken contact with her own mum and dad when Sadie was four years old.

Sadie had been nervous when she met Bertie and Ruth again after all those years. The circumstances of the reunion made her feel ashamed and therefore indignant. She'd stood with her back against the wall of the shop, shy disguised as surly, while Mr and Mrs Gardiner exchanged neighbourly pleasantries with the grandparents she could barely bring herself to look at. Ruth had chatted while Bertie stood quietly by, his wise brow furrowed, and Sadie focused on her shoes, her fingernails, the framed postcard by the cash register – anything other than the well-meaning adults who'd recently assumed control over her small world.

It was while she was standing there, looking at the postcard, a sepia photograph of a garden gate somewhere, that she'd felt the baby kick for the first time. *As if we shared the most amazing secret, that tiny hidden person and I*, Eleanor had written to Anthony on the ivy-rimmed paper, and that's exactly what it had felt like for Sadie, too. Just the two of them, against the world. That was when the whisper of the idea had first crept in, that perhaps she could keep her baby, that maybe everything would be all right so long as they were together. It made no practical sense: she was sixteen, she had no income or prospects, she knew nothing about raising a child – was still one herself – but the longing was so strong it knocked all sense out of her for a while. Hormones, or so the nurses told her.

With a sigh, she picked up the pile of mail from the end of the table and started sifting through, sorting bills from junk. She was almost finished when she reached an envelope that was neither. Her address was handwritten, the writing itself instantly recognisable, and for a split second Sadie thought it must be the same one she'd returned last week, that the postman had got it wrong and delivered it back to her rather than to the sender. Then she realised that of course it was a whole new letter, that Charlotte Sutherland had written again.

She poured herself a fortifying slug of whisky.

There was a part of Sadie that didn't want to open the envelope, but another part was itching to see what was written on the letter inside.

The curious part won. It usually did.

The first half of the message was very similar to the previous one, formal and polite, explaining who she was and telling a little about herself, her achievements and hobbies, her likes and dislikes, but when Sadie reached the last paragraph she noticed that the handwriting lost its composure, becoming jagged. A couple of lines in particular leapt out: *Please write back – I don't want anything from you, I just want to know who I am. I don't recognise myself, I look in the mirror and I don't know who I am anymore. Please.*

Sadie dropped the letter as if it burned. The words rang with truth. They might have been her own, fifteen years ago. She remembered vividly the pain of feeling she no longer knew herself. Of looking in the mirror at Bertie and Ruth's house, the tight swelling of her usually flat belly, the sensation of another life moving there. Worse, though, was afterwards, her skin bearing marks from the experience she'd been through. Expecting to be as she had been before, and realising, too late, that it was impossible ever to go back.

They were advised at the hospital not to name their babies. It was easier that way, apparently, and everyone was very concerned that things should be easy. Nobody wanted a scene. They had one every so often, the nurse had confided, no matter how careful they were. It was inevitable, she continued with quiet wisdom; regardless of how good a system they had in place, there were always some. There was one girl, dark-haired and Italian-looking, whose screams Sadie still heard sometimes. *I want my baby, give me my baby.* Running down the white-painted hallway, her gown gaping and her eyes wild.

Sadie hadn't shouted. She'd barely spoken. And when Bertie and Ruth came to collect her, when it was all over, she walked down that hallway with her old clothes on and her eyes on the door, as if nothing had happened and the whole episode could be left behind in that pale-green room with its crack in the wall, shaped like the River Nile.

During the course of her work Sadie had dealt with young mothers and she knew that agencies these days worked with the mums to arrange adoptions. They were allowed to see and name their baby after the birth, to spend time with them. In some cases, it was possible to receive updates on their child's progress, even to visit them.

But things had been different back then. There were more rules, different rules. As she lay in the bed, her arm still strapped to a monitor on the table beside her, nurses moving this way and that in the great bustle that follows a baby's birth, she'd held a strange, warm bundle in her arms, of skinny limbs and a rounded belly and cheeks that felt like velvet.

Ninety minutes.

Sadie had held her baby for ninety minutes before she was carried away, a small shaky hand startling over the top of the yellow-and-white-striped blanket in which she was wrapped. It was the same miraculous little hand Sadie had spent the past hour and a half stroking and cradling, that had closed tightly around her finger as if to claim her, and for a moment a void opened up in the room between them into which flowed all the things Sadie wanted to tell that baby girl, the things she wanted her to know, about life and love, the past and the future, but the nurses had a system and before Sadie could think, let alone speak, the small parcel was gone. The echo of her cry still made Sadie shiver sometimes. The warmth of that tiny new hand made her wake in an ice-cold sweat. Even now, here in her sitting room, she was cold, very cold. Sadie had only broken one of the hospital rules. She had given her daughter a name.

The pints with Donald, the whisky with Nancy, the fug of general maudlin thoughts had left her spent, and although it was only nine-thirty Sadie must have dozed, for the next thing she knew her mobile phone was ringing. She blinked in the dull light of her flat, trying to remember where she'd put the damn thing.

The charger. Sadie stumbled to answer it, shaking her mind clear. Her head was full of babies. Lost babies, adopted babies, abandoned babies. Maybe even a murdered baby.

She reached for her phone and saw a heap of missed calls on the screen, all from a number she didn't recognise. 'Hello?'

'DC Sadie Sparrow?'

'Speaking.'

'My name is Peter Obel. I work as an assistant for the novelist A. C. Edevane.'

Alice. Sadie felt a surge of adrenalin. Suddenly, she was very wide awake. 'Okay.'

'I'm sorry to call so late, but it's rather a delicate matter and I didn't want to leave a message.'

This was the bit where he threatened legal action if she didn't leave his employer alone.

'Ms Edevane received your letters regarding the disappearance of her brother, Theo, and asked me to call you.'

'Okay.'

'She'd like to set up a meeting to talk with you about the case. Does midday Friday suit?'

Twenty-three

Alice's first real memory of her father was of a day spent at the circus. It was a few weeks after she turned four, and the red-and-yellow tents had arrived like magic toadstools in a vacant field outside the village. 'How did they know it was my birthday?' she'd asked her mother, wide-eyed with delight as they passed the site. Excitement built over the next few days, posters appearing on walls and in shop windows, featuring clowns, lions and, Alice's favourite, a girl flying high above the ground on a glittering swing, red ribbons streaming behind her.

Little Clementine was suffering with a chest infection, so when the big day finally dawned, Mother stayed at home while they set off hand in hand across the fields. Alice skipped along beside her father, the skirt of her new dress bouncing pleasingly, trying to think of things to tell him, shy but filled with a sense of her own importance. It occurred to her now that Deborah must have been there, too, but Alice's mind had conveniently erased her sister from the memory. Upon arrival, they were hit with the smell of sawdust and manure, the sound of fairground music, children squealing and horses whinnying. A giant tent rose before them, its dark mouth wide and gaping, its pitched roof piercing the sky, and Alice stopped where she was to stare saucer-eyed at the jagged yellow flag hoisted up top, flapping in the breeze as tiny starlings sailed the wind currents above. 'It's whopping,' she said, pleased with the word, a new one she'd overheard Mrs Stevenson using in the kitchen and been longing to deploy ever since.

A line of people were jostling at the entrance, children and adults chattering excitedly as they filed beneath the big top and took their places on the raked bench seating. Static tension was in the air as they waited for the show to begin. The sun was hot and the stench of baking canvas mingled with the smell of anticipation, until finally a drum roll pummelled around the circle, silencing voices and bringing everybody to the edge of their seats. The ringmaster strutted and puffed, lions roared and elephants carried dancing ladies around the ring. Throughout it all Alice was transfixed, her attention leaving the action only occasionally and briefly to glance sideways at her father, to drink in his focused frown, the hollow of his cheek, his shaved jawline. He was still a novelty, the completing puzzle piece, the thing they'd been missing in the war years without even knowing it. The smell of shaving soap, the pair of enormous boots in the hall, the deep warmth of his whiskery laugh.

Afterwards he bought a bag of peanuts and they walked from cage to cage, reaching through the bars, unfurling their palms to receive a raspy licking. There was a man selling sweets from a cheery caravan and Alice pulled at her father's arm until he consented. With toffee apples in hand, filled with the warm and weary sense of pleasure spent, they headed for the exit, where they came across a man with wooden stumps for legs and a piece of metal covering half his face. Alice stared, thinking him another fairground attraction like the bearded lady or the dwarf clown with his top hat and sad painted face, but then her father surprised her by kneeling beside the man and speaking quietly with him. Time drew out and Alice became bored, kicking about in the dust and eating her apple down to its tacky stick.

They walked home along the cliffs, the sea crashing far below and daisies shifting in the fields, and their father explained that the man with the metal mask had been a soldier just like him; that not everyone had been lucky enough to return to a wonderful home like theirs, to a beautiful wife and children; that there were many who'd left a part of themselves in the mud of France. 'But not you,' Alice said boldly, proud of her father for returning unscathed, for retaining both sides of his handsome face. Whatever Anthony might have said in answer was lost when Alice, balancing along the tightrope of jagged rocks, slipped and fell, tearing a great gash in her knee. The pain was immediate and metallic and she cried hot spiteful tears of rage against the rock that had leapt into her way and tripped her. Her father mended her knee with his handkerchief, speaking gentle words that took her pain away, before scooping her onto his back and carrying her home.

'Your daddy knows how to fix things,' her mother told her later, when they'd arrived back with their sunburned faces and high spirits, been bathed, brushed and fed boiled eggs in the nursery. 'Before you were born, he went to a grand university where only the very brightest people in England can go. That's where he was learning how to make people better. That's where he was learning how to be a doctor.'

Alice frowned, considering this new information before shaking her head at her mother's mistake. 'My daddy isn't a doctor,' she said. 'He isn't at all like Dr Gibbons.' (Dr Gibbons had cold fingers and savoury breath.) 'My daddy's a magician.'

Eleanor smiled, and then she gathered Alice onto her lap and whispered, 'Did I ever tell you that your daddy saved my life?' and Alice settled in for the story that would become one of her favourites, her mother's retelling so vivid that Alice could smell the mix of exhaust fumes and manure, see the Marylebone street bustling with buses and motorcars and trams, feel her mother's fear as she glanced up and saw the LIPTON'S TEA advertisement bearing down on her.

'Alice?'

She blinked. It was Peter, her assistant. He was hovering. 'Won't be long now,' he said.

She glanced at her watch. 'Perhaps. Though very few people are punctual, Peter. You and I remain exceptions.' She was trying not to let her nerves sound in her voice but his kind smile told her she had failed.

'Is there anything you'd like me to do,' he said, 'when she's here? I could take notes, or make tea?'

Just be here, she wanted to say, *so there are two of us and only one of her. So I won't feel so unsteady.* 'Not that I can think of,' she said airily. 'If the detective's still here after fifteen minutes you may want to offer tea. It won't take me longer than that to establish whether or not she's a time-waster. In the meantime, you might as well get on with other things.'

He took her at her word and left for the kitchen, where he'd been working all morning on that blasted website. In his absence, the room was suddenly thick again with stubborn memories. Alice sighed. All families were a composite of stories and yet her own, it seemed, comprised more layers of tellings and retellings than most. There were so many of them, for one thing, and they all liked to talk and write and wonder. Living as they had at Loeanneth, a house rich with its own history, it was inevitable that they'd constructed their lives as a series of stories. But it seemed there'd been one very important chapter that was never told. A truth so important, so central, that her parents had made a life's work of keeping it secret. Alice had been wrong that day at the circus, when she'd pitied the man with the stumps and tin face as she skipped along beside her father and gloried in his wholeness. Her father had also lost part of himself in France.

'Mother told me just after VE day,' Deborah had said on Tuesday, as they sat together in her front room sipping tea, her inexplicable *mea culpa* still hanging in the air between them. 'We were in the midst of setting up for the celebration party and Daddy was resting upstairs. He was very near the end, and I caught her in a reflective mood, I suppose. I said something banal about it being wonderful that the war had finally ended, that all the young men could come home and get on with their lives, and she didn't answer. She was on a stepladder pinning a Union Jack in the window and her back was to me. I thought she mustn't have heard. It was only as I repeated myself that I saw her shoulders shaking and realised she was weeping. That's when she told me about Daddy, about how he'd suffered. How they'd both suffered after the first war.'

Alice, perched on the settee with a fine bone china teacup in her hand, was completely baffled. By the fact of her father's shell shock, but more than that, by Deborah's choice to disclose it now, on the day they'd met to talk about Theo. She said, 'There was never any indication he suffered with shock. They lived in London during the Blitz, for goodness' sake. I saw them many times and never once did he cower from the noise.'

'It wasn't like that,' Mother said. 'His memory wasn't as good as it had been, and his hands shook due to nerve gas exposure – he wasn't able to finish his training and work as a surgeon, which made him very depressed. But the real problem was something rather more specific, something that happened over there for which he couldn't forgive himself.'

'What was it?'

'She wouldn't say. I'm not entirely convinced she knew, and he refused to talk to doctors, but whatever it was he did or saw caused him nightmares all his life, and when he was in the grip of a terror he wasn't himself anymore.'

'I don't believe it. I never saw any sign.'

'They had an arrangement. Mother told me they were very careful to keep it hidden from us, from everyone. Daddy was determined that we shouldn't know. There'd been too much sacrifice, he said, for him to fail in his role as a father. I felt very sorry for her when she told me; I glimpsed how lonely she'd been. I'd always thought of them as self-sufficient, exclusive by choice, but it suddenly occurred to me that she'd withdrawn as a consequence of Daddy's condition. Caring for someone ill is difficult enough, but keeping their condition secret means cutting ties with friends and family, always maintaining oneself at a remove. She had no one to confide in all that time. I was one of the first people she'd told since 1919. More than twenty-five years!'

Alice had glanced at the ledge above Deborah's fireplace, where there stood a framed photograph of her parents on their wedding day, impossibly young and happy. The inviolability of Eleanor and Anthony's marriage had been a given in the Edevane family's mythology for as long as Alice could remember. To learn that the two of them had been keeping a secret all that time was to look at a touchstone and see it suddenly for a fake. Compounding the matter, and adding to Alice's indignation, was the fact that Deborah had known for near on sixty years while she, Alice, had been kept in the dark. It was not the way of things; *she* was the family sleuth, the one who knew things she shouldn't. Alice set her chin. 'Why the secrecy? Daddy was a war hero, there's no shame in that. We would have understood. We could have helped.'

'I quite agree, but evidently she'd made him a promise soon after he returned, and you know how she felt about those. There'd been some sort of incident, I gather, and afterwards she promised that no one would ever know. He never had to worry about frightening us, she simply wouldn't allow it. They came to recognise the signs of an impending spell, and she made sure to keep us from him until it passed.'

'Promise or not, surely we'd have *known*.'

'I was dubious too, but then I started to remember things. Hundreds of tiny, partial fears and thoughts and observations came back, and I realised that in some way I had already known. I'd always known.'

'Well, I certainly didn't know and I make a habit of preparedness.'

'I know you do. You're the original pre-emptive coper. But you were younger.'

'Only by a couple of years.'

'A vital couple. And you were off in your own world much of the time, whereas I watched the adults, eager to join them in the rarefied air up there.' Deborah smiled, but the gesture was devoid of cheer. 'I saw things, Alice.'

'What sorts of things?'

'Doors being quickly closed when I came near them, raised voices that were suddenly silenced, a look on Mother's face, a particular blend of concern and love when Daddy had gone off to the woods and she was waiting for him to return. All those hours he spent alone in his study and Mother's insistence that we mustn't trouble him, those interminable trips into town to collect parcels. On one occasion I sneaked up there and discovered the door locked.'

Alice waved a dismissive hand. 'He wanted privacy. If I had children, I'd lock my study door, too.'

'It was locked from the outside, Alice. And when I mentioned the fact to Mother, all those years later, when she finally told me about his shell shock, she said it had been at his insistence, that when he felt a turn coming on, especially when it felt like it was going to be a rage, there were no lengths to which he wouldn't go to spare us from harm.'

'Harm!' Alice scoffed. 'Our father never would have harmed us.' Not only was the suggestion ridiculous, Alice was at a loss as to why her sister was even raising it. They were supposed to be talking about Theo, about what happened to him. As far as Alice could see, her father's shell shock had nothing to do with Benjamin Munro and the kidnapping she'd scripted for him. She said again, 'He never would have harmed us.'

'Not intentionally, no,' said Deborah. 'And Mother was very clear that his rage was always directed at himself. But he wasn't always in control.'

Now, like a draught through the window, cold realisation came to Alice. They *were* talking about Theo. 'You think Daddy harmed Theo?'

'More than harmed.'

Alice felt her mouth open and a small soft puff of air escape. Things previously implied became clear. Deborah believed their father had killed Theo. *Daddy*. That he'd suffered some sort of shell-shock-induced traumatic rage. That he'd accidentally killed their baby brother.

But no, Alice *knew* that wasn't what had happened. It was Ben who'd taken Theo. He'd followed the plan she'd outlined in her manuscript, intending to send a ransom note, to blackmail her parents for the money he needed to help Flo, his friend in London who'd fallen on hard times. And although that might seem far-fetched, Alice wasn't relying on a hunch. She'd *seen* him in the woods of Loeanneth that night.

The alternative Deborah suggested was preposterous. Daddy was the gentlest man she knew, the kindest. He could never have done such a thing, not even in the grip of a terrible rage. The prospect was harrowing. It wasn't possible. 'I don't believe it,' she said. 'Not for a minute. If, for argument's sake, Daddy did as you say, then what happened to Theo? To his body, I mean.'

'I think he was buried at Loeanneth. Hidden, perhaps, until the police were gone, and then buried.' Despite the awful scenario she was describing, Deborah sounded preternaturally calm, as if she were somehow gathering strength from Alice's indignation.

'No,' Alice said. 'Violence aside, our father wasn't capable of that sort of deception. He and Mother loved one another. That was real. People remarked upon their closeness. No. Not only do I find it impossible to imagine Daddy capable of such a heinous act, I can't accept that he'd have kept that sort of secret from Mother. Burying Theo, for God's sake, while she was going out of her mind with worry as to his whereabouts.'

'That's not what I said.'

'Then—?'

'I've thought about it, Alice. I've thought about it until I fear it will drive me mad. Remember the way they were afterwards? Tremendously close at first, so that you never saw one without the other, but by the time we left Loeanneth and went back to London that strange distance had settled between them. Not so that anyone who didn't know them would notice, just a subtle shift. It was almost like they were play-acting, being very careful with each other. Still outwardly loving in their conversation and behaviour, but with a new stiffness, as if they were working very hard to do something that was once natural. And the way I saw her looking at him sometimes: concern, affection, but something else, too, something darker. I think she knew what he'd done and covered for him.'

'But why would she have done such a thing?'

'Because she loved him. And because she owed it to him.'

Alice racked her brain, struggling, again, to grasp the connection. It was an unfamiliar experience. She didn't like it. She felt cast back into the role of little sister for the first time in decades. 'Because of the way they met? Mother's idea that he saved her life on the day of the tigers, and that he'd then saved Loeanneth for her?'

'That, yes, but there was something else. It's what I've been trying to tell you, Alice. It's all to do with what Clemmie saw through the boathouse window.'

Heat was instant. Alice stood up, fanning herself.

'Alice?'

They were going to talk about Benjamin Munro after all. The memory came flooding back to Alice, the way she'd offered herself up to him that afternoon in the boathouse, only to be rejected, so kindly, so gently, that she'd wanted to crawl into a dark hole and lie there until she turned to soil and could no longer feel the agony and shame of having been so stupid, so unlovable, such a *child*. *You're a great kid, Alice,* he'd said. *I've never met anyone with a mind as clever as yours. You're going to grow up and go places and meet people and you won't even remember me.*

'Are you all right?' Deborah's face was full of concern.

'Yes. Yes, sorry, I just had a sudden . . .' *There's someone else, isn't there?* she'd spat at him, as all the great wronged romantic heroines must. She hadn't believed it for a minute, it had just been something to say, but then he didn't answer, and his face filled with sympathy, and she'd realised suddenly she was right. 'A sudden . . .'

'It's a lot to take in.'

'Yes.' Alice sat down again on Deborah's linen settee and an expression came to her, something she'd heard one woman say to another on the Tube and jotted down for use in a novel: *I told myself to put on my big-girl pants and get on with doing what had to be done.* Alice was tired of obfuscating. It was high time she put on her big-girl pants and confronted the past. 'You were talking about Clemmie,' she said. 'I gather she told you what she saw through the boathouse window.'

'Yes, and it's the reason I'll never be able to forgive myself,' Deborah said. 'I told Daddy, you see. I'm the one who tipped him into a rage that day.'

Alice frowned. 'I really can't see how the two things relate?'

'You know what Clemmie saw?'

'Of course I do.'

'Then you know how confusing it must have been for her. She came straight to see me and I told her I'd take care of it. Telling Daddy was the furthest thing from my mind at the time, but in the end I felt so sorry for him and so mad with *her*. I was naive and foolish. I should have kept my mouth shut.'

Alice was utterly confused. Him, her, mad with whom? Clemmie? How on earth had what happened between Alice and Ben in the boathouse enraged their father enough for Deborah to believe him capable of causing harm to Theo of all people! With an exasperated sigh, Alice held up her palms. 'Deborah, stop, please. It's been a very long day and my head is spinning.'

'Yes, of course, poor dear. Would you like another tea?'

'No, I would not like another tea. I'd like you to back-track a little, and tell me exactly what it was Clemmie saw.'

And so Deborah had told her, and when she'd finished Alice had wanted to get up and leave that lovely morning room, to be alone, to sit very quietly in a place where no one could bother her and she could concentrate. Call to memory every meeting she'd had with him, every conversation, every smile they'd exchanged. She needed to understand how she'd been so blind. Because it turned out she'd been wrong all this time. Clemmie hadn't seen Alice through the window, and Deborah knew nothing of Alice's crush on Ben Munro. She certainly hadn't suspected Alice of aiding him to kidnap Theo. She'd had her own personal reason for remembering the gardener's name after all this time.

Alice hadn't stayed much longer. She'd pleaded weariness and promised Deborah they would meet again soon, and then she'd left. On the Tube she'd sat motionless, a slew of emotions fighting for supremacy as she sifted through the new information.

She couldn't believe what a self-involved little fool she'd been. Such a desperate, longing child, so caught up in her own world she hadn't seen what was really going on. Clemmie had known, though, and she'd tried to tell Alice that dark night during the Blitz, but even then, almost ten years later when they were grown women and war had revealed to them the world's ills, Alice had been too stupid to listen. Too wrapped up in her own misguided view. Worried that Clemmie had seen her with Ben and could therefore link her to a kidnapper. But Clemmie hadn't seen Alice and Ben together. Alice had been wrong about that. Was it possible she'd been wrong about what happened to Theo, too?

Alice stayed on the Tube all afternoon, barely aware of the other passengers. She'd believed her own version of events for such a long time, but Deborah's revelation had brought small, niggling queries to the surface. She'd always taken the lack of ransom note to mean that something had gone wrong during the kidnapping. But now, seen from outside the swelter of her guilt, it seemed a long bow to draw, a presumption with scant evidence to back it up. It seemed an idea out of fiction, and bad fiction at that.

Her certainty that she'd glimpsed Ben in the woods that night – a sighting upon which she'd based her entire conviction – now seemed like the wishful thinking of an excitable young girl who'd wanted nothing more than to see him again. It had been dark, she'd been at some distance, there'd been three hundred strangers at Loeanneth for the Midsummer party. It could have been anyone. It might have been no one. The woods could be sly like that, casting shadows, playing tricks on a person. Would that she'd never gone there. A number of things might have turned out differently had she waited for Mr Llewellyn as she'd promised. Not least, her old friend might have lived. (Now there was a thought she tried ordinarily to keep at bay. Her failure to meet him as arranged, the 'important' thing he'd wanted to discuss with her, the poor old man lying down by the stream to die. Would she have been able to save him if she'd gone looking, instead of heading into the woods?)

The admission of doubts was like the lighting of a match. The whole idea now seemed an extraordinary folly: a gardener whose friend needs money kidnaps the child of his employer on the night of a huge party intending to extract a ransom. He uses a secret tunnel and a bottle of sleeping pills, executing the exact plan outlined to him by a sixteen-year-old girl with a bent for fiction . . . It was laughable. Ben wasn't a kidnapper. Alice had allowed her guilt to blind her. Teenage convictions had set like concrete, and no amount of adult reasoning had been able to shift them. But then she hadn't tried to shift them. She'd gone out of her way to avoid thinking about them at all.

Deborah's version of events, by comparison, though unpalatable, had a clarity to it that Alice's did not. There was a logic and simplicity underlying the sequence of events, an inevitability even. Theo had never left Loeanneth. That's why the police had found no trace of him out there in the world. He'd met his end at home, at the hands of someone he loved and trusted. Yet another casualty of the Great War and its enduring horrors.

The knowledge was an old death made new and there on the Tube, hiding behind her dark sunglasses, Alice had felt tears pricking her eyes. Tears for her baby brother, but also for her father, a good man guilty of the most heinous deed. Life in that moment had seemed impossibly cruel and cold, and she'd suddenly felt very tired. Alice didn't believe in God but she'd thanked Him all the same that Clemmie had died none the wiser. That she'd died believing her fairy-tale fiction about the childless couple and Theo's happy new life.

Embarrassment and remorse, horror and grief, and yet still another emotion had been playing at the edges of her experience when she finally made her way home that day, a lighter one whose tail she'd struggled to grasp. It wasn't until early evening, when she walked out of Hampstead station, that Alice realised it was relief. That all this time she'd blamed herself for telling Ben about the tunnel, but after seventy years, Deborah's revelation – the *possibility* it allowed that a different version of events occurred that night – had freed her in some way.

It wasn't relief that had made her decide to have Peter contact Sadie Sparrow, though: it was curiosity. Once upon a time, Alice would have laughed had somebody suggested she trust a stranger with the most intimate details of her family's history. Pride and a craving for privacy would have prevented it. But now Alice was old. Time was running out. And since hearing Deborah's story, lying awake at night as her mind went through every permutation, as one realisation led to another and the accepted facts of her life shifted like the gems in a kaleidoscope to form new pictures, Alice had to know the truth.

Years of plotting novels had trained her mind to sift through information and make of it a narrative, and it hadn't taken long to arrange the facts into linear form. But there were gaps, including the small matter of proof, and Alice wanted to fill them. She *needed* the full picture. She'd have carried out the necessary investigations herself, but there was a time and place to admit impediments, and at the age of eighty-six Alice had to concede certain physical limitations. At the risk of sounding too much like her mother, the arrival of a professional investigator, keen to get to the bottom of things right when Alice needed her, seemed somehow serendipitous. Besides, after the character research Alice had done since Tuesday, calling in favours from every contact she had within CID, Sadie Sparrow was no longer a stranger.

Alice took out her dossier and perused the notes, her glance lingering on the information she'd gathered about DC Sparrow's recent investigative work. By all accounts the woman was an excellent detective, described variously as passionate, dogged and downright pig-headed; it hadn't been easy to find anything even remotely grubby in her records. Even Derek Maitland had been reluctant to speak against her integrity and that really was saying something, but Alice could be very convincing. She'd followed the Bailey case in the press; Alice was always interested in a disappearing-person story. She'd seen the case declared closed, police confident that the little girl's mother had abandoned her, and she'd seen the subsequent article claiming a cover-up. She'd known someone in CID must have been talking, and now she knew who. It always paid to have a safeguard, and although Alice flinched at the very idea (the *sordidness* of blackmail, for really there was no dressing it up), with Derek Maitland's ace up her sleeve she felt sure she'd be able to trust Detective Sparrow to be discreet with the Edevane legacy.

She closed her file and glanced at the clock. The minute hand was almost at the twelve, which meant in a matter of seconds Sadie Sparrow would be late and Alice would be able to derive a petty but no less enjoyable sense of advantage. She would have the upper hand and all would be right with the world. She realised she was holding her breath and shook her head, amused at her own brief lapse into superstition. What a goose. Behaving as if the success of the meeting, the entire favourable resolution of her family's mystery, depended on her guest's tardy arrival. Alice composed herself, picked up the newspaper crossword she'd been trying to finish since breakfast, and watched impassively as the second hand ticked neatly towards the twelve. The minute hand prepared itself to leap, and when a knock came at the door, despite her best intentions, Alice's heart did the same.

Twenty-four

Sadie stood on the front steps, catching her breath. She'd run all the way from the bus stop, which wasn't easy in the dress shoes she'd extricated from the back of her cupboard at the last minute. They were dusty and musty and, as it turned out, the heel of one was hanging on by a single strip of glue. She bent down and swiped away a patch of scuff she'd missed earlier. Her feet looked like someone else's, someone she wasn't sure she liked, but A. C. Edevane was a snappy dresser, and Sadie had no intention of offending the old woman's sensibilities by presenting her usual sorry self on the doorstep. Neither had she had any intention of being late, no matter the trouble she'd had running in precarious heels. A. C. Edevane was pernickety about punctuality. She'd once refused to complete an interview with a tardy journalist, and had famously taken a BBC show host to task on air when he'd kept her waiting. Sadie knew this because she'd spent the better part of the last two and a half days in an electric swotting haze, watching old interviews and reading everything she could on A. C. Edevane. (It had been a surprisingly enjoyable task – there was something strangely compelling about Alice Edevane – made all the more agreeable for having distracted Sadie from the arrival of Charlotte Sutherland's second letter.) She also knew the author preferred shrubs to flowers and noted with a nod of satisfaction the pots of box on the windowsills of the house. So far so good. Sadie was pleased to feel a fresh wave of confidence wash over her as she straightened her sleeve cuffs. She was going to run this interview to script and she was not leaving without the information she needed.

Sadie lifted her hand to knock again, but before she could make contact with the door it swung open. It wasn't Alice Edevane standing on the other side, but a man of about thirty with long legs and a scrappy beard. He looked like an extra in a film about the Rolling Stones. Sadie felt a surprising and not entirely unwelcome frisson of attraction. 'Peter?' she guessed.

'DC Sparrow.' He smiled. 'Come on in, Alice is expecting you.'

The floorboards creaked as they walked and a clock somewhere was ticking time away. Peter led her to a sitting room off the hall, overly furnished, elegant, with a resoundingly masculine feel.

A woman Sadie recognised immediately from her publicity photos as Alice Edevane was sitting in a chair by the empty fireplace. As is often the case when one meets a very famous person in real life, Sadie experienced an overwhelming sense of familiarity. Not a wafty feeling of déjà vu, but an honest-to-goodness impression of already knowing the other woman. The way her trouser-clad legs were crossed and folded to one side, her casual grip on the newspaper, even the jut of her chin were somehow *known*. Though of course she wasn't known at all, not beyond the copious interviews Sadie had been bingeing on. A line came to her – *There is nothing so tiresome as a person who mistakes recognition for friendship* – and Sadie blushed, realising it was from the Diggory Brent she'd read the week before.

'Alice,' said Peter, 'DC Sparrow is here to see you.' He turned to Sadie and gestured kindly towards a green leather armchair with button studs. 'I'll leave you to it. I'm only in the kitchen if you need me.'

The clock on the mantelpiece grew immediately louder in his absence and Sadie felt a burning urge to say something. She bit her tongue, remembering a disdainful comment Alice had made in an interview about the inability of people these days to weather silence. Sadie was determined not to let the other woman catch even the merest whiff of trepidation; to do so, she suspected, would be calamitous.

Alice was watching her. Small, keen eyes that seemed unusually bright in an otherwise faded face. They were the sort of eyes, Sadie was suddenly sure, that could see inside a person's soul. After a few seconds that felt much longer, the old woman spoke. Her voice was that of a theatre actress, her elocution from another time. 'So,' she said. 'At last we meet, DC Sparrow.'

'Please, call me Sadie. I'm not working in an official capacity.'

'No, I should say you're not.'

Sadie pulled up short. It wasn't the words themselves – they were simple agreement – but the *way* Alice said them. Those eyes that *knew* things.

'I've made enquiries about you, Detective Sparrow. I'm sure you'd agree it was the prudent thing to do. You wrote requesting permission to enter my family home, to rifle through our archives, no doubt, and you expressed a special desire to discuss my brother's disappearance. I'm a very

private person, as you may have gathered, despite my occu-
pation; I wouldn't agree to talk about my family with just
anyone. I needed to know that I could trust you, and that
meant doing a little bit of research of my own to gain a
better picture of who you are.'

Sadie fought to hide dread beneath a calm smile, wondering what the hell that picture looked like.

Alice continued, 'I know about the Bailey case. In particular, I know about your off-the-record chat with the
journalist Derek Maitland.'

Sadie felt the blood drain from her head to her fingertips, where it proceeded to pulse as though it hadn't gone
far enough. *Alice knew she was the leak*. The words were
neon and for a moment their hot panicky glow prevented
any other thoughts from forming. Slowly, though, reason returned. Alice knew she was the leak and still she had invited
her here.

'I'm intrigued, DC Sparrow, as to what made you so
certain your missing woman, Maggie Bailey, met with foul
play when, from what I can tell, there was no evidence to
suggest such a scenario.'

Sadie had not expected to be talking about the Bailey
case today, but there was a reason the other woman had
brought it up. Alice could have reported Sadie to her superiors and refused to have anything else to do with her. Instead,
she'd invited her into her home. Sadie could only surmise
that Alice was trying to get beneath her skin. She knew this
play. Interview gamesmanship was one of Sadie's favourite
sports. She experienced a surge of collegial respect for the
old woman. 'It's not an easy thing to explain.'

Disappointment brought a sag to Alice's cheeks. The

answer was weak and dull and Sadie knew she had to do better. She continued quickly, 'To begin with, there was the way the flat looked, the small details that showed thought, if not money, had gone into the interior decoration: the piano that had been painted a bright sunny yellow, the wall devoted to pictures the little girl had drawn, her name printed proudly in the corner. I found it difficult to believe that a woman responsible for those showings of love would abandon her child. It didn't sit right with me and when we started talking to the people who knew her they agreed.'

'Which people?'

'Her mother, for one.'

Alice's eyebrows arched. 'But DC Sparrow, surely a mother is always going to support her child in a situation like this. Did you interview others who knew her? There was an ex-husband, wasn't there? Did he give you the same impression?'

'His character reference wasn't so glowing.'

'Wasn't it?'

'No, but surely an ex-husband is always going to be less than effusive in a situation like this.'

Alice allowed a fleeting smile, faintly amused, to cross her lips. She leaned back further into her chair and regarded Sadie over her steepled fingers. 'People can be unreliable, can't they? Even the most conscientious witness, eager to please and with nothing to gain, is liable to make mistakes, littering their testimony with small mis-recollections, assumptions and opinions rather than facts.'

Sadie's mind went to Clive's account of Alice as a reluctant interview subject in 1933. The way she'd lurked in the corridor outside the library, his sense that she was either hiding something or anxious to hear what the other interviewees said.

'We are all victims of our human experience,' Alice continued, 'apt to view the present through the lens of our own past.'

Sadie had the distinct impression they were no longer speaking generally. Alice had fixed her again with that birdlike stare. 'That's true,' she said.

'I'm curious, DC Sparrow; leaving aside witness statements for a moment, was there any actual evidence to support your feeling that something untoward had happened to the young mother?'

'No,' Sadie conceded. 'In fact, there was a letter, signed by Maggie, supporting the theory that she'd walked out.'

'I remember from the newspaper reports. You found the letter a week after you found the child.'

'Yes, by which time we'd gone a fair way down the path of investigating other possibilities. It had fallen somehow and become lodged down the side of the fridge.'

'But even after it was found, you didn't accept that Maggie Bailey had simply left.'

'I had difficulty letting go of my theory.'

'So much so that you went outside the Met and spoke to the press.'

Sadie met Alice's gaze. Denial was not an option; Alice wasn't a fool. Besides, Sadie didn't want to deny it. The old woman had the information necessary to ruin her career and the fact was unexpectedly liberating. In the time since she'd taken leave, there'd been very few people Sadie could talk to honestly about the Bailey case. Donald refused to hear a word, Sadie had needed to maintain some professional standing with Clive, and she hadn't wanted to disappoint Bertie with the truth. But now, suddenly, she could speak freely. There was nothing to lose: Alice already knew the worst. 'I saw no other way to keep Maggie's fate in the public eye. The Met had moved on – there's not a lot of sympathy for officers intent on spending taxpayers' money on cases without a shred of real evidence – but I couldn't stand to think something *had* happened to her and no one was prepared to keep looking.'

'You'll lose your job if they find out it was you.'

'I know.'

'Do you enjoy your job?'

'Wholeheartedly.'

'Yet you still did it.'

'I had to.'

'Are you a reckless person, DC Sparrow?'

Sadie considered the question. 'I hope not. I certainly didn't approach Derek Maitland hastily. And I'd like to think I was being responsible to Maggie, rather than irresponsible to my job.' She exhaled decisively. 'No, I'm not a reckless person. I'm conscientious. Maybe with a dash of headstrong.'

As she was offering up her own psychological profile, Peter had arrived back in the room. Sadie glanced at him expectantly, wondering whether she'd somehow triggered a hidden removal button so that he was here to see her to the door. He didn't say anything, but looked queryingly at Alice. She nodded once, efficiently, and said, 'I think we'd like some tea, thank you, Peter.'

He seemed inordinately pleased. 'Oh, brilliant news. I'm so glad.' He flashed Sadie the warmest of smiles as he went, leaving her touched, though unsure what she'd done to deserve it. Yes, she was definitely attracted to him. Strange, because he wasn't at all her type. He intrigued her, with his long, shaggy hair and old-fashioned manners. He couldn't be much older than she was, and he was charming in a bookish sort of way. How had he ended up here, working as a modern-day Lurch?

'He's a doctor, literature not medicine,' said Alice Edevane, reading her mind. 'And quite the best assistant I've ever had.'

Sadie realised she'd been staring and glanced away, her gaze falling to her knee, where she flicked avidly at an invisible piece of lint.

'Have you read any of my books, DC Sparrow?'

Sadie gave her trousers a final brush. 'One.'

'Then you've met Diggory Brent.'

'I have.'

'You might not realise that he became a private investigator after being kicked off the force for something very similar to your own recent misdemeanour.'

'I did not realise that.'

'No, well, once upon a time authors were expected to provide a little background summary in the beginning of each new book when one wrote a series, but the publishers stopped insisting and after so many books I was pleased to let the habit go. There are limited ways to say the same thing over and over again and I'm afraid it had become a rather tedious task.'

'I can imagine.'

'Diggory was not a natural fit in CID. A very driven man, but one who'd suffered dreadful privations in his personal life. He lost his wife and young child, you see, losses that gave him a tenacity that was not always appreciated by his peers, to say nothing of his superiors. Losing a child does tend to create a gnawing absence in a person, I've observed.'

Not for the first time, Sadie had the uncanny sense the other woman knew more about her past than she had any reason to know. She smiled noncommittally as Alice Edevane continued.

'Diggory was far better suited to an investigative life outside the strictures of the law. Not that he's an unlawful man, quite the contrary; he's a man of honour, extremely conscientious. Conscientious with a – how did you put it? – a dash of headstrong.'

Peter returned with a tea tray, setting it down on the desk behind Sadie. 'How would you like it?' he asked, and gracefully served up the white-and-one she requested.

'Thank you, Peter.' Alice accepted her own from him, black, sugarless. She took a sip, hesitating briefly as she swallowed, and then set down her cup and saucer, swivelling the handle just so. 'Now,' she said, her tone suggesting another change of gear, 'let's get down to business, shall we? In your letter you mentioned a theory. You wanted to get inside the Lake House to investigate it. I take it you've discovered the second tunnel at Loeanneth?'

And, like that, they'd left Maggie Bailey and Diggory Brent behind and Alice was leading the interview about her brother's disappearance. Sadie was glad to be back on topic, bemused as to how they'd got there, but eager to push ahead. 'Yes,' she said, sitting taller, 'but my thoughts have changed since I wrote to you. I wondered if I could ask instead about your father.'

Alice barely blinked, almost as if she'd known what was coming. 'You could ask, DC Sparrow, but I'm old and my time is precious. It would be more agreeable to me, and surely more useful to you, if you'd simply cut to the chase and tell me your theory. What do *you* think happened to Theo?'

In ten years working at the Met, Sadie was quite sure she'd never interviewed a subject like Alice Edevane. She tried not to appear flummoxed. 'I believe your brother died that night at Loeanneth.'

'As do I.' Alice seemed almost pleased, as if she were conducting an examination and Sadie had given the right answer. 'I didn't for a long time, I thought that he'd been kidnapped, but recently I've come to see that I was wrong.'

Sadie steeled herself to continue. 'Your father suffered from shell shock after the war.'

Once more, Alice was unflappable. 'He did, although, again, I only learned that recently. It was a secret kept very well by my parents. My sister Deborah told me, and she herself only learned about it in 1945.' Alice's long fingers were stroking the velvet piping on the armrest of her chair. 'So, DC Sparrow,' she said, 'we've established that my father suffered from shell shock, we've agreed that my brother most likely died at Loeanneth. How do you imagine these two things relate?'

Here it was. Sadie held Alice's gaze. 'I believe your brother was killed, Ms Edevane, accidentally, by your father.'

'Yes,' said Alice. 'I've recently come to believe the same thing.'

'I think he's buried at Loeanneth.'

'It is the scenario that makes most sense.'

Sadie breathed a sigh of relief. It was her experience that people did not usually appreciate the suggestion that their nearest and dearest was capable of committing a major crime. She'd imagined herself having to convince Alice, to gently cajole and explain and take great care not to trample her feelings. This frank agreement was far preferable. 'The only problem,' she said, 'is that I don't know how to prove it.'

'That, DC Sparrow, is where I might be able to help you.'

Sadie experienced a flutter of tentative excitement. 'How?'

'After such a time lapse, I doubt there'll be much in the way of physical "clues" remaining, but there are other sources we might turn to. My family are of the type to write things down. I don't know if you're a writer?'

Sadie shook her head.

'No? Well, never mind, it's not your secrets we're hoping to uncover. My father kept a journal that he wrote religiously, and my mother, though not a diary-keeper, was a great one for letters. She was one of those children who left little notes for the fairies, terribly charming, and then our father went away to war just after they were married and the habit of letter-writing stuck.'

Sadie remembered the ivy-rimmed love letter she'd found in the boathouse, Eleanor's note to Anthony, written while he was away at war and she was pregnant with Alice. She considered mentioning it now, but her interest, seen through the eyes of their daughter, seemed somehow voyeuristic. Besides, Alice had already moved on.

'There's a study in the attic at Loeanneth, where the family's records dating back generations are kept, and where

wondering whether she'd said too much. The prim little typist in the corner, relaying everything to her machine as Eleanor spoke, had been unsettling enough at the time, but to recall her now was nauseating. Eleanor knew it was important to be honest with the doctors, to tell them exactly what Anthony said and did, yet as she'd framed her descriptions in her mind, as she'd heard the words she spoke, she'd felt the sick weight of having betrayed the husband she'd sworn to protect.

He was so much more than the symptoms that plagued him. She'd wanted to communicate to the doctor how kind he was with the girls, how good-humoured and handsome and eager he'd been when she met him, how unfair it was that the war should be allowed to hollow out a man's core, to rend the tapestry of his life, leaving only the tattered threads of his earlier dreams with which to patch it. But no matter the words she chose, she couldn't make the doctor see how much she loved her husband, couldn't convey that she wanted only to save Anthony as he'd saved her. She'd wanted the doctor to absolve her from her failure, but instead he'd sat solidly behind his grey suit and wire-rimmed spectacles, pen pressed to his lips as he nodded and sighed and jotted occasionally in the margin of his lined pad. Her words beaded as they reached him, sliding off his oiled hair like water from a duck's back, and all the while, in the staid, clinical quiet of the room, the tippity-tap of that machine constantly reproached her.

Eleanor didn't realise she was crying until the man sitting opposite leaned to pass her his handkerchief. She looked up, surprised, and noticed they were now alone in the train carriage, except for an elderly woman sitting on the edge of the bench, closest to the door. Eleanor had been too wrapped up in her thoughts to notice the train making stops along the way.

She took the handkerchief and dabbed beneath her eyes. She was embarrassed – more than that, infuriated – to be this person, a weeping woman eliciting kindness from a stranger. It seemed an intimacy, this acceptance of a young man's handkerchief, and she was painfully aware of the old lady by the door, pretending interest in her knitting while stealing glances over its top. 'No,' he said when she tried to give the handkerchief back, 'you keep it.' He didn't ask after her troubles and Eleanor didn't volunteer them, he simply smiled politely and went about his business.

His business, she noticed, was the manipulation of a small piece of paper, his fingers working quickly but neatly, performing multiple tucks and folds, making triangles and rectangles, turning the paper over and doing the same again. She realised she was staring and glanced away, but she didn't stop watching, observing instead in the reflection of the train window. He made a final adjustment and then held the paper in one hand, inspecting it from all angles. Eleanor felt unexpectedly pleased. It was a bird, a swan-like figure with pointed wings and a long neck.

The train lumbered on, dragging itself west, and darkness fell outside the window as absolute as a theatre black after a show. Eleanor must have slept deep and long, for the next thing she knew the train had reached the end of the line. The stationmaster was blowing his whistle, ordering disembarkation, and passengers were brushing past the carriage window.

She tried to get her bags down from the racks and when she couldn't reach he helped her. It was that simple. The shopping bag had become stuck on a jagged piece of metal, it was awkward, and she was still disoriented from sleep, weary after a day that had begun before dawn.

'Thank you,' she said. 'And for before. I'm afraid I've ruined your handkerchief.'

'Don't mention it,' he said with a smile that brought a shallow dimple to his cheek. 'It's yours. As is this.'

Their hands brushed as she took the bag from him and Eleanor met his eyes briefly. He'd felt it too, she could tell by the way he straightened, the brief, bewildered expression on his face. It was electric, a spark of cosmic recognition, as if in that moment time's weave had opened and they'd glimpsed an alternative existence in which they were some-thing more than strangers on a train.

Eleanor forced her thoughts to order. She could see Martin, her driver, on the well-lit platform through the window. He was studying the other passengers, looking for her, ready to take her home.

'Well,' she said, in the same efficient tone she might have used to excuse a new housemaid, 'thank you again for your help.' And with a short nod she left the young man in the carriage, lifted her chin, and walked away.

If she hadn't seen him again their meeting would surely have been forgotten. A chance encounter on a train, a handsome stranger who'd shown her a small kindness. A trivial moment consigned to the recesses of a memory already brimming with others.

But Eleanor did see him again, some months later on an overcast day in August. The morning was unusually warm, the air thick, and Anthony had woken to one of his bad heads. Eleanor had heard him tossing and turning in the pre-dawn, battling the terrible visions that came upon him in the night, and she'd known to expect the worst. She'd also known from experience that the best defence was offence. She'd sent him upstairs immediately after breakfast, pre-vailed upon him to take two of Dr Gibbons's sleeping tablets, and given firm instructions to the staff that he was busy with an important project and not to be disturbed. Finally, as it was Nanny Rose's day off, she'd gathered the girls and told them to find their shoes; they were going to spend the morning in town.

'Oh no! Why?' That was Alice, always the first and the loudest with complaint. Her reaction could not have been more horrified had Eleanor suggested they spend a week down the mines.

'Because I have parcels to collect from the post office and I'd appreciate some arms to carry them.'

'Really, Mother, more parcels? You must have bought one of everything in London by now.' Grumble, grumble.

'That's quite enough, Alice. One day, God willing, you'll find yourself in charge of a household and then it will be your decision whether or not to purchase the necessary items to keep it running.'

The look on Alice's face screamed, *Never!* and Eleanor was startled to recognise her own younger self in the stub-born set of her fourteen-year-old daughter's features. The awareness riled her and she drew herself to full height. Her voice was more brittle than she'd intended. 'I won't tell you again, Alice. We're going into town, Martin has already been sent to fetch the car, so go at once and find your shoes.'

Alice set her mouth in a haughty line and her eyes

glistened with disdain. 'Yes, Mother,' she said, enunciating the title as if she couldn't get it off her lips fast enough.

Mother. No one was particularly fond of her. Even Eleanor winced sometimes at the woman's incessant pedantry. She wasn't a bit of fun and could always be counted on to temper a boisterous occasion with a sermon on responsibility or safety. And yet, she was essential. Eleanor would have collapsed under the heartbreaking strain of Anthony's condition, but Mother was always equal to the task. She made sure the girls gave their father space when he needed it and was ever on guard to catch him before he slumped. Mother didn't worry that her children looked upon her as a harridan. Why would she? It was all in the interests of helping them to become their best selves.

Eleanor, in contrast, cared a great deal, lamenting the loss of those distant war years when the girls had curled up on her lap and listened to her stories, when she'd run with them across the estate, exploring and pointing out the magical places of her own childhood. But she'd long since stopped feeling sorry for herself. She'd witnessed other families where life had been made to revolve around the exigencies of an invalid and had come to the firm conclusion that the ancillary damage was simply too great. She didn't want the shadow of Anthony's disappointment and distress to spill across the lives of her growing daughters. If she could just absorb his troubles herself, then the girls would remain unaffected, and one day, when she found the right doctor, when she discovered a cure to restore him, no one would be any the wiser.

In the meantime, Eleanor committed herself to keeping Anthony's condition concealed, just as she'd promised him she would. It was in the service of this promise that she made sure always to place plenty of orders with the department stores in London. She didn't need half the things she bought, but that was beside the point. It was one of the simplest, most believable ways she'd concocted over the years to get the girls out from beneath his feet. Between visits to the beach, or field trips to the meadow, they were made to accompany her into town to collect parcels. For their part, they found it entirely credible (though manifestly irritating) that their mother was a compulsive shopper who wasn't content without the latest frippery from London. And so it was that morning.

'Deborah, Clementine, Alice! Come along! Martin is waiting.'

There was the usual kerfuffle as the girls tore about the house trying to find their elusive shoes. There would have to be a lecture later – young ladies, responsibility, a duty to themselves, that sort of thing. Mother was good at delivering lessons. But then she ought to be; she'd had the perfect example in Constance. Eleanor amazed herself how much the shrew she could sound, how cold and unamused. Their faces when she delivered her stern calls for improvement were studies in boredom and dislike. Worse, except for the merest, occasional flicker of hurt and confusion that crossed Deborah's face – as if she *almost* remembered a time when things had been different – they revealed an utter lack of surprise. This, for Eleanor, was the most terrifying aspect of all. Her daughters had no idea how much she envied them their freedom and cheered their lack of social graces; how like them she'd once been; what great friends they might have become if things were different.

Finally, her daughters arrived at the foot of the stairs, more dishevelled than Eleanor might have hoped, but with a shoe on each foot, which was at least something. Eleanor ushered them outside to where Martin had the car idling, and they all piled into the back. While the girls bickered about who was sitting near the window and whose dress was stuck beneath whose bottom, Eleanor glanced through the window and up to the attic where Anthony was now asleep. If she could just keep the girls out all morning, by afternoon, God willing, he'd be restored and they could salvage part of the day. Sometimes, their best family time came after mornings like these. It was a strange pattern of push and pull, in which the depth of his despair was later matched by the radiant relief of his recovery. They were jewels, those moments, rare but precious reminders of the man he used to be. The man he still was, she corrected herself, deep beneath it all.

The clouds had lifted by the time they reached town. Fishing boats were returning to the harbour and seagulls drifted and cawed above a still, slate sea. Martin slowed when he reached the High Street. 'Anywhere in particular you'd like me to set you down, ma'am?'

'This will be perfect, thank you, Martin.'

He pulled the car over and opened the door, letting them all out.

'Would you prefer me to wait while you do your shopping?'

'No, thank you.' Eleanor smoothed her skirt over her hips as a salty ocean breeze caressed the back of her neck. 'I'm sure you have other errands to run for Mrs Stevenson and we'll be a couple of hours yet.'

The driver agreed to return for them at twelve-thirty and the arrangement was met with predictable complaint: 'But two whole hours, Mother!' 'To collect a few parcels?' 'I'm going to *die* from boredom!'

'Boredom is the province of the witless,' she heard herself say. 'A state to be pitied.' And then, ignoring all further protestations, 'I thought we'd have some morning tea while we're here. You can tell me what you've been learning in your lessons.' Not a lot, was Eleanor's suspicion. Judging by the number of small newspapers in circulation, the tittering of housemaids when they ought to be busy doing other things, the girls were far more focused on the old printing press than they were on their schoolwork. Eleanor had been just the same, of course, but there was no need for her daughters to know that.

Cheered somewhat by the suggestion of cake, if not by talk of lessons, the girls followed Eleanor into the cafe on the promenade where the four of them shared a relatively cheerful time, the only hiccup when Clementine upset a jug of milk, and a bucket and mop had to be called for.

Alas, the geniality could only be stretched so far. The polite conversation and pot of tea had both dried up when Eleanor sneaked a glance at her father's wristwatch and saw there was still over an hour to fill. She settled the account and drew on plan B. She'd come prepared with invented reasons to visit the haberdashery, the milliner and the jeweller, and led the girls along the High Street. By the time she'd finished enquiring about repairs to a clasp on her gold link bracelet, however, they were beside themselves with boredom.

'Please, Mother,' said Alice. 'Couldn't we just go down to the sea while you finish up here?'

'Yes, please, Mother,' chimed Clementine, who'd almost broken three clocks in as many minutes.

'Let me take them, Mother,' said Deborah, who, at sixteen, was just beginning to glimpse her role as eldest daughter and adult-in-waiting. 'I'll keep an eye on things, make sure they behave properly, and have us all back to help you with the parcels before Martin returns.'

Eleanor watched as they went, releasing a long-held sigh. Really, she was as glad as they were. It was far easier to fill time when she didn't have to keep them entertained and in line. She thanked the jeweller, agreed with his suggested method of repair, and stepped outside the shop.

There was a wooden bench seat in the square and Eleanor was pleased to find it empty. She sat down and passed a quiet half-hour watching the comings and goings of the village. As a child, Eleanor had never realised how much enjoyment could be gained, as an adult, simply from sitting. The absence of demands and expectations, of queries and conversation, was a true, simple joy. It was with some regret that she noted there were only fifteen minutes remaining until Martin returned to collect them, and that it was time to brave the post office.

That is – Eleanor steeled herself – it was time to brave the postmistress. Marjorie Kempling was a gossip with a seemingly inexhaustible trove of material she was bursting to share. Presumably as a consequence of Eleanor's frequent visits to collect parcels, Miss Kempling had come to regard the pair of them as something akin to co-conspirators. It was a misguided assumption, and one which Eleanor did nothing to encourage. She had little desire to know the ins and outs of her neighbours' lives, but it seemed no amount of crisp silence could deter the other woman's enthusiasm. Indeed, it appeared the more space Eleanor allowed, the greater was Miss Kempling's commitment to fill it.

Eleanor hesitated briefly on the top step of the stone post-office building. There was a little bell positioned on the architrave on the other side of the door, and its effusive tinkle was a sound she'd come to dread. To Miss Kempling it was a clarion call; to Eleanor it signalled the beginning of the onslaught. She readied herself, determined simply to march in and politely but firmly extricate herself and her parcels with the minimum of fuss. And then, with more force, perhaps, than was necessary, she took hold of the door's handle and prepared to push. Right as she did so, the door slipped away from her and, to her immediate mortification, Eleanor fell straight into a man trying to exit the post office.

'I'm so sorry, forgive me,' she said, stepping back onto the landing.

'Not at all. It was my fault, I was hurrying. I had a sudden overwhelming need for fresh air and a moment's silence.'

Eleanor laughed, in spite of herself. She met his eyes and it took her a moment to remember where she knew him from. He had changed. His hair was longer, dark and curled, and his skin was a great deal browner than it had been. He looked quite unlike the neat young man she'd first encountered on the train home.

His smile caught. 'Have we met?'

'No,' she said quickly, remembering the journey, the

handkerchief, the thrill she'd felt when his fingers brushed hers, 'I don't believe we have.'

'In London, perhaps?'

'No. Never.'

A faint frown had settled on his brow, but he smiled as if he hadn't a care in the world. 'My mistake, then. Apologies. Good day.'

'Good day.'

Eleanor let her breath go. The incident had left her un-expectedly rattled and she waited a few seconds before proceeding inside. The bell tinkled merrily and she fought an urge to reach out and deliver it a stilling blow.

The postmistress's eyes lit up when she saw that it was Eleanor. 'Mrs Edevane, how lovely to have a visit. I've a number of parcels here for you. But my goodness, you look so peaky!'

'Good day, Miss Kempling. I'm afraid I've just run into a gentleman on the steps. Terribly careless of me. I'm a little shaken.'

'Oh my! But that will be Mr Munro. Here – sit down, my dear, let me fetch you a cool glass of water.'

Mr Munro. She might have guessed Marjorie Kempling would know who he was. Eleanor hated herself for being interested. She hated herself even more for the irrational flare of envy she'd felt at the postmistress's comfortable use of the man's name.

'But isn't he a dish!' Miss Kempling bustled back from behind the counter, a glass of water clutched in one paw. 'He could be in the films! Quite unlike the other young fellows we see around here. A jack-of-all-trades, from what I gather, he travels all over taking work where it's offered. He's been labouring for Mr Nicolson at the apple orchard over the summer.' She leaned close enough that Eleanor could smell the oily day cream on her skin. 'He's living in an old caravan on the river, just like a gypsy. You can tell by looking at him, can't you, that he's probably got some of the blood. That skin! Those eyes!'

Eleanor smiled thinly, disdaining the other woman's excitable manner, her taste for gossip, and yet unconscionably eager to hear more. Oh, but she was the worst kind of hypocrite!

'Not a gentleman, exactly,' the other woman was saying, 'but fine manners and a lovely way about him. I'm going to miss his visits.'

Miss them? 'Oh?'

'That's what he was in for just now, to let me know he won't be needing letter collection anymore. His contract with Mr Nicolson is expiring and he's moving on next week. He left no forwarding address, more's the pity. Quite the man of mystery. I said to him, "But what if post arrives and I've nowhere to send it on to?" and do you know what he replied?'

'I can't imagine.'

'He told me that all the people he cared to hear from would know where to write to him, and the rest he could do without.'

There was no forgetting him after that. Miss Kempling had given Eleanor just enough information to fuel her interest and she found herself thinking of him often over the next few weeks. Mr Munro. The name had insinuated itself into her mind and came to her at the oddest times. When she was visiting Anthony in his study, when she was watching the girls on the lawn, when she lay down to sleep and the night-birds started crying on the lake. He was like a song that got stuck in one's head and couldn't be escaped. She remembered the warmth of his voice, the way he'd looked at her as if the two of them were in on a private joke, how she'd felt when his hand brushed hers on the train, as if it were fate and the two of them were always destined to meet.

She knew such thoughts weren't safe and she knew that they were wrong. The illicit frisson accompanying them told her that. She was shocked by herself, and dismayed; Eleanor had never imagined she'd be capable of attraction to anyone but Anthony and it felt sullying in some way to find herself in this position. She assured herself that it was a temporary state of affairs, an aberration; that she would forget this other man soon enough; that in the meantime her thoughts were her own and no one else need ever know. The man himself had moved on weeks ago, and he'd left no forward-ing address. There was no real risk. Why shouldn't she take out a pleasant memory now and again, what harm was there in that? And so she continued to remember, sometimes even to invent. Mr Munro. That easy smile of his, the pull she'd felt when he looked at her, what might have happened had she said instead, 'Why, yes, I remember you. We've met before.'

But of course there is always a risk when the heart allows a breach, no matter how small or harmless it might seem. The next occasion on which Eleanor needed to take the girls away from Loeanneth was a glorious morning, the first after weeks of drizzling rain, and the last thing she felt like doing was lacing herself into one of her formal dresses to make the trip into town. And so, she decided, they would have a picnic instead.

Mrs Stevenson packed them a lunch and they set off down the path between the laurel hedges, circumnavigating the lake until they reached the stream that ran along the bottom of the garden. Edwina, never one to be willingly left behind, panted fervently beside them. She was a lovely dog, loyal and faithful to them all, but particularly fond of Eleanor. They'd bonded, the pair of them, over the incident with Anthony when Edwina was just a puppy. The dear old girl had arthritis in her joints now, but refused to let it stop her accompanying her mistress wherever she went.

The weather was exceptional, and perhaps because they'd been cooped up for days they walked further than they otherwise might have. Eleanor swore later to herself that she hadn't taken them to the edge of Mr Nicolson's orchard on purpose. Indeed, it was Clementine who'd led the way, running ahead, her arms outstretched, and Deborah who'd finally pointed to the flat, grassy spot beneath the willow on the water's edge and said, 'Oh, do let's sit there, it's perfect!' Eleanor knew where they were, of course, and endured a small flutter of embarrassment as the fantasies she'd harboured over the past month came rushing back to her. But before she could demur, suggest they move their picnic further upstream or across another meadow, the blanket was out and the two older girls lolling on it. Alice was frowning at her notebook, biting her lip as she willed her pen to keep up with her tumbling thoughts, and Eleanor had to accept, with a sigh, that there'd be no leaving now. And really, there was no good reason to go elsewhere. That man, Mr Munro – her cheeks flushed even as she thought his name – had moved on weeks before. It was only her guilty conscience that baulked at the idea of sitting in this particular field on this particular farm.

Eleanor unpacked the picnic basket and spread Mrs Stevenson's goodies across it. As the sun rose higher in the sky, the four of them ate ham sandwiches and Cox's Orange Pippins and far too much cake, washing it all down with fresh ginger beer. Edwina watched proceedings imploringly, snaffling up each small titbit as it came her way.

But really, the heat for October was uncanny! Eleanor undid the small pearl buttons at her wrist, rolling her sleeves back once, and then twice, so they sat in neat pleats. A somnolence had come over her after lunch, and she lay back on the blanket. Closing her eyes, she could hear the girls bickering lazily over the last slice of cake, but her attention drifted, sailing beyond them to pick out the *plink* of water as gleaming trout leapt in the stream, the thrum of hidden crickets on the rim of the woods, the warm rustling of leaves in the nearby orchard. Each sound was an exaggeration, as if a bewitching spell had been cast over this small patch of land, like something from a fairy tale, one of Mr Llewellyn's stories from her childhood. Eleanor sighed. The old man had been gone over a month now. He'd left, as he always did, when summer finished, seeking the warmer climes of Italy to soothe his restless legs and spirit. Eleanor missed him terribly. The winter months at Loeanneth were always the longer and colder for his absence, and she, personally, was stiffer without him, more contained. He was the only person who still looked at her and saw the slip of a girl with wild, tangled hair and a seemingly unquenchable spirit.

She fell asleep, aware, just, as she tipped over the cliff of consciousness, and dreamed she was a child. She was on her boat, its white sail full of breeze, and her father and Mr Llewellyn were waving from the shore. Her heart was full of happiness; she felt no uncertainty or fear. Light rippled off the water and the leaves glistened, but then, as she turned back to wave again, she realised she'd drifted further than she'd meant to, and the lake was no longer a shape she recognised, opening instead to spill away from the house and her family, and the current was strong, pulling her yet further from them, and the water was choppy, the boat rocking from side to side, and she had to hold on tightly so as not to fall—

She woke abruptly and realised she was being shaken. 'Mother! Wake up, Mother!'

'What is it?' It was no longer bright. Great, dark clouds were gathering in the west and the wind had picked up. Eleanor sat up quickly, glancing around to count her children. 'Clementine?'

'She's fine. It's Edwina we're worried about. She ran off after a rabbit half an hour ago and hasn't come back, and now it's going to rain.'

'Half an hour – but how long have I been sleeping?' Eleanor checked her watch. It was almost three. 'Which way did she go?'

Deborah pointed towards a distant copse and Eleanor stared, as if by scanning the trees with enough intent she might will Edwina into view.

The sky was mulberry. Eleanor could smell the coming storm, heat and moisture combined. It was going to rain, heavily and soon, but they couldn't just leave Edwina, not this far from home. She was old and partly blind, and with her joints as stiff as they were she wouldn't be able to get herself out of trouble.

'I'll go after her,' said Eleanor decisively, stacking the picnic items back into the basket. 'She won't have gone too far.'

'Shall we wait?'

Eleanor considered briefly before shaking her head. 'There's no point all of us getting wet. You take the others home. Make sure Clemmie stays out of the rain.'

After seeing off the girls with stern instructions not to dawdle, Eleanor started towards the copse. She called for Edwina, but the wind was strong and her words were whipped away. She walked quickly, stopping every so often to survey the horizon, to call and listen, but there came no bark of reply.

It was becoming very dark, very quickly, and with each minute that passed, Eleanor's anxiety grew. Edwina would be frightened, she knew. At home, when it rained, the old dog flew straight for her bed behind the curtain in the library, tail between her legs and paws over her eyes as she waited out the worst.

An enormous detonation of thunder filled the valley; the storm clouds were right above her now. The last patch of light sky had been absorbed by the tumultuous gloom, and without hesitation, Eleanor climbed through the kissing gate and started across the next field. A great swirl of wind encircled her and lightning tore open the sky. As the first fat drops began to fall, she cupped her hands and called again, 'Edwina!' but her voice was swept up into the storm and there came no reply.

Thunder rolled across the plain and Eleanor was drenched within minutes. The fabric of her dress slapped against her legs and she had to squint to see through the sheen of heavy rain. There was a tremendous crack as a shard of lightning hit nearby, and despite her fear for Edwina, Eleanor felt a surge of curious excitement. The storm, its danger, the driving rain, all combined to wash away the veneer of Mother. She was Eleanor again out here, Eleanor the Adventuress. Free.

She reached the top of a hill and there at the bottom, standing on the edge of the stream, was a small gypsy caravan, burgundy in colour, with faded yellow wheels. She knew whose it was and went towards it with a shiver of recognition. The caravan was empty now, faded curtains drawn across the windows. It was in a state of some disrepair, but beneath the peeling paint she made out a trace of the old floral design that must once have adorned it. She wondered vaguely where he was now. What it must be like to live one's life in such a way. Free to travel, to explore, to flee. She envied him for enjoying such liberty, and it expressed itself in that moment as a curious anger with him. Madness, because of course he owed her nothing. It was only the strength of her imaginings that fuelled her sense she'd been betrayed.

Eleanor had almost reached the stream and was debating whether to follow it towards Loeanneth or cross to the other side, when she glanced at the caravan and stopped in her tracks. A set of rudimentary wooden stairs led up to a landing and there, as dry as could be, was Edwina. Eleanor burst out laughing. 'Why, you clever old girl! Fancy you sitting up there, nice and dry, when I'm completely drenched.'

Relief was instant and immense. She raced up the stairs,

kneeling to cup the old retriever's dear face in her hands. 'You gave me such a scare,' she said. 'I thought you must've been stuck somewhere. Are you hurt?' She checked the dog's legs for injuries and then, with wonder, took in more of the precarious narrow landing. 'But how on earth did you get yourself up here?'

She didn't notice the caravan door opening. The first she knew he was there was his voice. 'I helped her,' he said. 'I heard her fretting beneath the caravan when the storm started and thought she'd be more comfortable up here.' His dark tangle of hair was wet and he was wearing only an undershirt with his trousers. 'I invited her in but she wanted to stay outside. I suspect she was watching for you.'

Eleanor could think of nothing to say. It was the shock of seeing him. He wasn't supposed to be here anymore. He was supposed to have moved on, to be working elsewhere. His post, those letters from the people he cared enough to know, was meant to be finding him somewhere new. And yet, it was more than that, too. A sensation similar to déjà vu but far more potent. An inexplicable impression, encouraged perhaps by the wild weather, the strangeness of the day, that he was here because she had conjured him. That there was an inevitability to this moment, this meeting here and now, that everything had always been leading to this. She didn't know what to do, what to say. She glanced over her shoulder. The weather was still foul. A tempest in the field. She felt herself in no-man's-land, neither fully here nor there, perched on a narrow bridge between two worlds. And then he spoke again and the bridge crumbled beneath her. 'I was just about to light the fire,' he said. 'Would you like to come inside and wait for the storm to pass?'

Twenty-six

London, 2003

Sometime after Sadie Sparrow had left, the keys to Loeanneth tucked safely in her bag, Alice went out into the back garden. It was coming on for dusk, and a melancholy stillness had fallen with the shade. She followed the overgrown brick path, noting odd jobs that would need to be undertaken in the coming weeks. There were a lot of them. Alice preferred a garden with personality, but there was a difference between character and chaos. The problem was, she didn't get out into the garden nearly often enough. She used to love being outdoors, back in the time of before.

A tangle of star jasmine spilled across the path and Alice knelt to pluck a sprig, holding it beneath her nose and breathing in the scent of captured sunshine. On a whim, she unlaced her shoes. A delicate iron chair stood in a nook beside the camellia, and she sat, slipping her feet free and peeling off her socks, wiggling her toes in the surprise of the balmy air. A late butterfly hovered at a nearby rose bush, and Alice thought, as always, of her father. All her life he'd been a devoted amateur scientist; never had she imagined he'd wished for anything other than that which he'd had. She'd known that once, in the long-ago past, he'd trained and aspired to practise medicine, but that, like all the dreams and desires belonging to one's parents, existed in a realm far less real than the bright, bold present in which she moved. Now, though, she glimpsed how much the war had stolen from him. Snatches of conversation came back to her, mumblings and curses about his unsteady hands, his difficulty focusing, the memory games he'd used to play so keenly, trying to keep his thoughts in order.

Alice shifted the soles of her feet against the warm bricks, aware of each pebble, each spent flower beneath them. Her skin was sensitive these days, not at all like the play-hardened feet of her childhood. During the long summers at Loeanneth they'd gone weeks without shoes, having to scurry to find them when Mother announced a trip into town. The mad dash around the house, crouching to check under beds, behind doors, beneath stairs, and then the final, triumphant discovery. The memory was so vivid Alice could almost touch it.

She sighed heavily. Giving Sadie Sparrow the keys to Loeanneth had awakened in her a long-repressed sadness. When her mother died and she inherited the house, Alice had tucked those keys away and promised herself she'd never go back. A small part of her, though, had known the promise to be temporary, had known that of course she must change her mind; Loeanneth was home, her beloved home.

But she hadn't changed her mind, and now it looked as if she never would. She had given the keys and the task of sorting through her family's secrets to somebody else, a young detective who was keen but detachedly so, her interest in the crime's solution purely academic. It seemed somehow an ending, an admission that she, Alice, would never go back herself.

'Fancy a G & T?'

It was Peter, a crystal jug in one hand, two glasses in the other. Ice cubes clinking like a prop from a Noël Coward play.

Alice smiled with more relief than either she intended or he expected. 'I can't imagine anything I'd fancy more.'

They sat together at the wrought-iron table and he poured them each a gin. Citric, astringent and icy cold, it was just what Alice needed. They made conversation about the garden and exchanged pleasant amiable chatter, which proved a welcome departure from her recent ruminations. If Peter noticed her bare feet and thought it an alarming break with protocol, he was too polite to say so. When he'd finished, he stood and tucked his chair back into place.

'I suppose it's time I headed for home,' he said. 'Unless there's anything else you'd like me to do?'

'Nothing I can think of now.'

He nodded but didn't leave, and it occurred to Alice that an expression of gratitude wouldn't go astray. 'Thank you for today, Peter. For organising the meeting with DC Sparrow, for keeping the wheels turning while she was here.'

'Of course, don't mention it.' He grabbed at an errant tendril of ivy and turned the leaf back and forth in his fingers. 'The meeting was fruitful, I hope?'

'I think it was.'

'Good,' he said. 'That's good news.' Still, he didn't leave.

'Peter?'

'Alice.'

'You're still here.'

He sighed determinedly. 'I'm just going to say it.'

'Please.'

'Now that the website's finished, I wonder if I might have some time off, if you might be able to spare me from my usual tasks for a while.'

Alice was taken aback. Peter had never asked for time off before and her instinct was to refuse the request. She didn't *want* to spare him. She was used to him. She liked having him around. 'I see.'

'There's something important – something I'd like very much to do.'

Alice looked at his face and was struck by a sudden flash of self-awareness. The poor boy had never asked for anything, he did everything she asked without complaint, he boiled her eggs precisely as she liked them, and here she was making things difficult for him. What a crosspatch she'd become. How had this happened to her? She, who had once been filled with boundless joy, who had looked at the world as a place of unlimited possibilities? Was this what had happened to Eleanor? Alice swallowed and said, 'How long do you think you'll need?'

He smiled, his relief an indictment. 'I imagine three or four days should do it, including the weekend.'

It was on the tip of her tongue to snap, *Should do what?* but Alice caught the words in time. She forced her face into the most pleasant smile she could manage. 'Four days it is. I'll see you back here Wednesday.'

'Actually . . .'

'Peter?'

'I was hoping you might come with me.'

Her eyes widened. 'On a holiday?'

Peter laughed. 'Not exactly. I think we should go to Cornwall, to Loeanneth. Not to get underfoot while DC

Sparrow is carrying out her investigation, just to be there.
You could oversee, and I could help with the diaries and
letters. Reading between the lines, textual analysis – that's
what I do.'

He was watching her keenly, waiting for a reaction. An
hour before she'd have said no, definitely not, but now the
words wouldn't come. While they'd been drinking their gin
and talking, there'd drifted on the afternoon breeze a familiar garden smell of sodden dirt and mushroom, and Alice
had experienced an unexpected jolt of memory and longing.
There was something at Loeanneth that she wanted, she
realised, an emblem of the girl she'd used to be, of the guilt
and shame she'd felt for all these years, and suddenly she
needed it more than anything she'd needed in a very long
time. She had a sense that if she were even to begin putting
things behind her, she would have to get it back.

And yet. To return to Loeanneth. She'd promised herself
she wouldn't . . .

She simply couldn't decide. That fact in and of itself was
disturbing: Alice Edevane did not suffer indecision. She
couldn't help but feel that things were starting to unravel,
that she was losing her grasp on the weave; moreover, that
relinquishing her grip might not be such a bad thing.

Peter was still standing there.

'I don't know,' Alice said at last. 'I just don't know.'

Alice stayed in the garden for another hour after Peter left.
She drank a second gin, and then a third, and listened as her
neighbours went about the reassuring business of their evening routines, as the traffic built and then began to thin on
the street beyond, as the last of the day's fraternising birds

sought shelter. It was one of those perfect summery evenings, when everything was at its zenith. One of nature's tipping points. The air was heady with fragrance, the sky was graded from pink to mauve to navy, and despite the things she'd learned in recent days, Alice was visited by a sense of enormous peace.

When she did finally venture inside, she saw that Peter had left her dinner on the stove. The table was laid with her favourite setting and a note with instructions on how long to heat the soup had been propped against the utensil holder by the cooker. Apparently Alice had given a very convincing impression of ineptitude. She wasn't hungry yet, and decided to read for a time instead. In the sitting room, though, she found herself holding the photograph of her family enjoying that long-ago picnic at Loeanneth. Just before everything broke. Though of course, she reminded herself, it had already been broken by then.

She studied her mother's face. Eleanor had been thirty-eight years old in 1933, ancient to the mind of a sixteen-year-old, but from where Alice sat now a mere child. She had been beautiful, her features striking, but Alice wondered how she'd missed the sadness in her mother's expression. Looking back with knowledge of the never-ending trial Eleanor had suffered as she looked after Daddy, kept his condition to herself, absorbed his disappointments as her own, Alice could see it clearly. In a way it made her mother even more attractive. There was a guardedness in her pose, a haunting aspect to her penetrating gaze, and a weight in her brow, of endurance or perhaps defiance. She was fragile and strong and bewitching. Little wonder Ben had fallen in love with her.

Alice set down the photograph. Clemmie had been distraught when she told Deborah what she'd seen. 'She was
twelve and a half,' Deborah said, 'but young for her age.
Loath to leave childhood behind her. And, of course, it was
Mother.' Alice could just picture her little sister climbing
onto the wooden porch of the boathouse, pressing her arm
up hard against the glass, leaning her forehead on the back
of her hand as she looked through the window. How confused she must have been to see Mother and Ben together
like that. And how devastated Daddy must have been when
he found out. Deborah, too. 'I thought I'd hate Mother forever after Clemmie told me,' she'd agreed, when Alice said as
much.

'But you didn't.'

'How could I after what happened to Theo? His loss
rather dwarfed her infidelity, wouldn't you say? I suppose I
felt she'd been punished enough and my sympathy out-
weighed my anger. Besides, she recommitted herself to
Daddy after it all happened. I figured if he could forgive her,
then I could, too.'

'What about Clemmie?'

Deborah shook her head. 'It was never easy to know
what Clemmie thought. We didn't discuss it again. I tried
once or twice but she looked at me as if I were speaking
gibberish. She was so devoted to her flying. It sometimes
seemed she managed to soar above the ordinary human
tangles that ensnared the rest of us.'

Had she, though? Suddenly the ongoing distance between
Clemmie and their mother was cast in a new light. Alice had
always presumed it simply an aspect of Clemmie's rebellious,

loner nature; she'd never guessed, not even for a moment, that something so specific, so traumatic, lay beneath.

And what about me? Alice managed not to say. Instead, rather more lightly than she felt, 'I have to wonder why you didn't tell me earlier? Not about the affair, I don't mean that, I mean all of it. Daddy, his shell shock, Theo.'

Deborah's lips quivered in their firm line. 'We all loved Daddy, but you, Alice – you idolised him. I didn't want to be the one to take that from you.' She tried to laugh but the sound was tinny. 'Goodness, that makes it sound as if my decision were noble and it wasn't. It wasn't that at all.' She sighed. 'I didn't tell you, Alice, because I knew you'd blame me for triggering Daddy's rage. I knew you'd blame me, I knew you'd be right and I just couldn't bear it.'

She'd wept then, guilt and grief combined, admitting that she'd wondered sometimes whether her own trouble conceiving had been punishment for what she'd done, but Alice had reassured her. For one thing, the cosmos did not work that way; for another, her reaction was entirely understandable. She'd felt a burning loyalty to Daddy and a fierce anger towards Mother. She couldn't have known the terrible events she'd set in train.

So many pieces of the puzzle, and everybody holding different fragments. The only person who'd known it all had been Eleanor, and she hadn't been talking. Sadie Sparrow had been mystified as to how Eleanor could possibly have forgiven her husband for what he did. The unspoken question had pulsed behind their conversation: *Didn't she love her baby?* But Mother had adored Theo. No one who knew her could have thought otherwise. She'd grieved for the rest of her life, returning to Loeanneth each year, yet she'd never taken it out on Daddy. 'Love keeps no record of wrongs,' Eleanor had told Deborah on the night before her wedding, and in her case it had been true. She'd had an additional reason for standing by her husband, too. DC Sparrow might have had difficulty comprehending, but Alice knew it was because her mother believed she was at fault. That everything that happened was a punishment for having made a promise to Daddy and then failed him.

Alice glanced again at the photograph. She wondered how long her mother's affair with Ben had lasted. Had it been a brief tryst, or had they come to love one another? When Deborah first told her, Alice had been embarrassed. Her thoughts had gone immediately to the boathouse on the afternoon Ben rejected her. She'd asked him whether there was someone else and the tenderness in his face had told her that there was. It hadn't, however, told her who.

She'd imagined the two of them laughing at her behind her back and felt incredibly stupid. But Alice no longer felt foolish. The potent emotions of days ago had faded to mere shadows of themselves. She'd been a child of fifteen when they met, precocious but naive, and she'd fallen in love with the first older man who showed an interest in her, mistaking his kindness for a love returned. It was a simple story and she forgave herself her youth. She knew, too, that her mother would never have laughed at her. On the contrary, she could see now why Eleanor had been so vexed, so insistent, when she tried to warn Alice against growing attached to someone so 'unsuitable'.

Neither was Alice jealous that Ben had chosen Eleanor instead of her. How could she envy her mother, who had suffered and lost so much? Who'd been so much younger then than Alice was now, who'd been dead herself almost six decades. It would be like envying one's own child, or the character in a book one read a long time ago. No, Alice wasn't jealous, she was sad. Not nostalgic; there was nothing general or inexplicable about her emotion. She was sad that her mother had borne it alone. It occurred to Alice now, as she stared at her mother's long-ago face, that perhaps that had been the attraction. Ben was a kind man, gentle, engaging, and free from the ties of responsibility that must have seemed at times to Eleanor an unendurable burden.

Alice's focus shifted to her father, sitting on the edge of the picnic blanket at the back of the group. There was a stone wall behind him and it struck Alice as she looked at the photograph that her father had always seemed as sure and stable to her as those ancient stone walls that crossed the fields of Loeanneth. Deborah had said Alice idolised him. She'd certainly loved him specially, and she'd wanted him to love her in return. But then they all had, they'd all competed for his affection.

Now, she took in every detail of his familiar face, trying to see beyond the beloved features to the secrets beneath. Alice knew a little about shell shock, the same things everybody knew, about tremors and bad dreams and damaged men who cowered when they heard loud noises. But Deborah had said it wasn't like that for Daddy. His ability to concentrate had suffered, and his hands had shaken sometimes, too much to resume his training as a surgeon; however it was something else that plagued him, one particular experience rather than a general weight of horrors. A battlefield ordeal that had, in turn, had devastating consequences for their peacetime family.

Alice's gaze fell then, as it must, to Theo. Sitting at Mother's feet, a beguiling smile lighting his face as he reached an arm towards Clemmie. His toy puppy dangled from his hand, and to the uninitiated it might have looked as if he were making a gift of it to his sister. But Theo never would have given Puppy away, not willingly. What had happened to the little toy? Puppy's whereabouts were of little consequence really in the grand scheme of things, but still Alice wondered. It was the novelist in her, she supposed, always seeking to square away the smallest details. Larger questions remained, too. From the most basic – How had it happened? When did Daddy realise what he'd done? How did Mother find out? – to the most pressing, as far as Alice was concerned: What on earth had happened to her father to make him react in such a way? Alice would have given anything to go back to talk to her mother and father, to ask them plainly, but all that remained was to hope that answers lay in the papers at Loeanneth.

She had entrusted Sadie Sparrow to find them, but it seemed clear to Alice now that she couldn't just sit idly by. She had made a promise to herself never to go back to Loeanneth, but suddenly it was the very thing she wanted more than anything else in the world. She stood abruptly, paced across the library, fanned her warm face. Go back to Loeanneth . . . Peter had said she only needed to call and say the word . . . Was she really going to allow herself to be held to a commitment made in the full heat of youth and uncertainty and fear?

Alice glanced at the phone and her hand quivered.

Twenty-seven

Cornwall, 1932

He led a blessed life. That's what made it so much worse. He had a wife whom he loved, three daughters whose innocence and goodness brought light into his life, and now there was going to be another baby. He lived in a beautiful house with a rambling garden, on the edge of a great, lush wood. Birds sang in his trees and squirrels built their stores and trout grew fat in his stream. It was so much more than he deserved. Millions of men had lost their chance of a normal life, had died in the mud and the madness; men who would have given everything for what he had. But while they were dead and forgotten, Anthony's blessings kept rolling in.

He rounded the lake and stopped when the boathouse came into view. It would always be a special place. Such simple days back then before the war, when the house was being restored and he and Eleanor had camped by the stream. He wasn't sure he'd ever been as happy since. Things had been so certain. He'd had purpose and ability and the confidence that came with being young and whole, untested. He thought he could honestly say he'd been a *good* man, then. Life had seemed like a straight road that lay ahead, just waiting for them to walk it.

When the war ended and he came home, Anthony had

spent a great deal of time down at the boathouse: sometimes he'd just sat and watched the stream, other times he'd read over old letters; there were days when he'd simply slept. He'd been so tired. Sometimes he thought he'd never wake; plenty of days he'd have been happy not to; but he did, time and again he did, and with Eleanor's help he set up his study in the attic of the house, and the boathouse passed to the girls. It had become a child's place for play and adventure, and now it served as accommodation for staff. The thought pleased him; Anthony pictured layers of time and usage, yesterday's ghosts making way for today's players. Buildings were so much bigger than one man's life and wasn't that a happy thing? It was what he liked most about the woods and fields of Loeanneth. Generations had walked them, worked them and been buried beneath them. There was much solace to be gained from the permanence of nature. Even the woods at Menin would be grown back now. Hard to imagine, but it must be so. Did flowers grow on Howard's grave?

He thought sometimes of the people they'd met in France. He tried not to, but they appeared in his mind's eye of their own accord, the villagers and farmers whose homes had sat in the midst of war. Were they still there, he wondered, M. Durand and Mme Fournier, the countless others who'd billeted them, happily or otherwise, along the way? When the armistice was signed and the guns were put away, did the people whose lives they'd disrupted, whose homes and farms they'd destroyed, begin the long, slow process of repair? He supposed they must have. Where else would they have gone?

Anthony skirted around the hedge and set off towards

the woods. Alice had wanted to come with him today, but Eleanor had told her no and invented a task to keep her busy instead. His wife had become expert over the years at reading his moods; there were times when it seemed she knew him better than he knew himself. Lately, though, things were slipping. Ever since Eleanor told him about the new baby, things had been getting worse. It worried him. She'd thought the news would make him happy, and in some ways it did; but more and more often, he found his thoughts drawn to that barn on Mme Fournier's farm. He heard phantom crying in the night, a child's cries, and every time the dog barked he had to stand very still and quiet and tell himself that everything was all right, that it was only in his head. As if that made things better.

A flock of birds cut swift across the sky and Anthony shivered. For a split second he was there on the ground behind the milking shed in France, his shoulder smarting from where Howard had punched him. He screwed his eyes tight shut and counted five breaths before opening them a crack and letting the light flood back in. He concentrated on seeing only the wide, open fields of Loeanneth, Alice's swing, the last gate that led from the meadows to the woods. Slowly, determinedly, he started walking towards it.

It was just as well he'd come alone today. Eleanor had been right. He was becoming unpredictable. He was worried about what he might do without realising it, what the girls might see or hear. And they mustn't know what he'd done, what he was; he couldn't bear for them to know that. Even worse, if they were ever to glimpse the thing he'd *almost* done, the monstrous line he'd nearly crossed.

The other night he'd been woken by a noise in the dark

of the bedroom he shared with Eleanor; he'd sat up in bed and realised there was something in the shadowy corner near the curtains. Some*one*. Anthony's heart had been racing. 'What is it?' he'd hissed. 'What do you want?'

The man had walked slowly towards him and when he stepped through a spill of moonlight, Anthony had seen that it was Howard.

'I'm going to be a father,' he was saying. 'I'm going to be a father, Anthony, just like you.'

Anthony had screwed his eyes shut and blocked his ears so that his hands shook against his temples. The next thing he knew Eleanor was awake and holding him and the bedside lamp was on and Howard was gone.

He would be back, though; he always came back. And now, with a new baby on the way, there was no chance Anthony could keep him at bay.

They'd been at war for two and a half years. Fighting had ground down at the front and they'd been rotating in a seemingly endless shuffle of frontline hostility followed by billeting back from the line. They knew the town of Warloy-Baillon and her people well, and had become as comfortable as was possible in their trench-warfare limbo. Word had passed down the line, though, that they were readying for a big push and Anthony was glad; the sooner they won this bloody thing, the sooner they could all go home.

He was just coming off his last day away from the trenches and was sitting at the oak farm table in the kitchen of their reluctant billet, M. Durand, enjoying a final cup of tea from porcelain instead of tin as he reread Eleanor's latest letter. She'd sent a photograph of Deborah and the new baby, Alice, a dear, fat little thing with a surprisingly fierce and determined air about her. After one last look he tucked the photo carefully in his jacket pocket.

The letter, written on the ivy-rimmed paper he'd given her, was exactly what he'd asked for: story after story of a life he was beginning to feel had only ever existed in fiction. Was there really a house called Loeanneth, a lake with ducks and an island in its centre, and a stream that tripped and swirled through the bottom gardens? Did two little English girls called Deborah and Alice spend their mornings in a kitchen garden planted by their parents, making themselves ill eating far too many strawberries? *They were both rather poorly afterwards,* Eleanor had written, *but what is one to do? They're a couple of little sneaks when it comes to their garden raids. Deborah keeps them in her pockets and feeds them to Alice when I'm not watching. I don't know whether to be proud or cross! And even when I do suspect, I haven't the heart to stop them. Is there anything better than to pick fresh strawberries from the vine? To gobble them up and feel oneself dissolve beneath their sweetness? Oh my, but the nursery, Anthony – those sticky little fingers – it smelled like warm jam for days afterwards!*

Anthony looked up to see Howard at the kitchen door. Caught in a private, weak moment, he folded the letter quickly and slipped it away with the photograph. 'Ready when you are,' he said, collecting his hat and straightening it into position.

Howard sat in the rustic chair on the other side of the table.

'You're not ready,' said Anthony.

'I'm not going.'

'Not going where?'

'Back to the front.'

Anthony frowned, perplexed. 'Are you joking? Are you ill?'

'Neither. I'm leaving, deserting, call it what you will. I'm going away with Sophie.'

Anthony was not often speechless but now words failed him. He had known Howard was sweet on M. Durand's housekeeper. The poor girl had lost her husband in the first weeks of the war. She was only eighteen and had a baby son, Louis, to care for, no relatives or friends left in the village. He hadn't realised how far things had progressed.

'We're in love,' Howard said. 'I know it sounds ridiculous at a time like this, but there you have it.'

The guns were never quiet here, always thumping in the background. They'd become used to the way the earth shook and cups and saucers rattled across the tabletop. They were good now at ignoring the fact that each rumble meant the death of more men.

Anthony stilled his teacup and watched as the surface of the remaining liquid quivered. 'Love,' he repeated. It was such an odd word to hear spoken when they were all much more used to talking about rats and mud and bloodied limbs.

'I'm not a fighting man, Anthony.'

'We're all fighting men now.'

'Not me. I've been lucky, but my luck's going to run out.'

'We need to finish what we started. If a man cannot be useful to his country, he is better dead.'

'That's rubbish. I don't know that I ever believed it. What

good am I to England? I'm of far more use to Sophie and
Louis than I am to England.'

He pointed vaguely towards the window, and Anthony
saw that Sophie and the baby were sitting on a garden seat
on the other side of the courtyard. She was cooing to the
boy – a lovely child, with big liquid brown eyes and a dimple
in each cheek – who was laughing and reaching up with his
little plump hand to stroke his mother's face.

Anthony lowered his voice. 'Look. I can arrange some
leave. You can go back to England for a few weeks. Get
yourself sorted out.'

Howard shook his head. 'I'm not going back.'

'You don't have a choice.'

'There's always a choice. I'm leaving tonight. We're
leaving.'

'You're coming back with me now – that's an order.'

'I want to be with her. I want a shot at a normal life. To
be a father. To be a husband.'

'You can be all those things, you *will*; but you have to do
it properly. You can't just walk away.'

'I wouldn't have told you, but you're more than a friend.
You're a brother.'

'I can't let you do this.'

'You have to.'

'We both know what happens to deserters.'

'They'd have to catch me first.'

'They will.'

Howard smiled sadly. 'Anthony, old friend, I'm dead
already out there. My soul is dead, and my body will soon
catch up.' He stood, pushing his chair in slowly, carefully. He
left the farmhouse kitchen, whistling a song that Anthony

hadn't heard in years, a dance song from their university days.

The whistle, that tune, the casual way in which his friend was signing his own death warrant . . . All the ghastly things they'd seen and done together, the relentlessness of the whole undertaking, everything Anthony had suppressed to make it this far – the wretched intensity with which he missed Eleanor and his girls, his baby Alice whom he'd never even met – now threatened to overwhelm him.

His thoughts blurred and he stood abruptly. He hurried out of the kitchen, across the grassed area, along the paths between the farm buildings. He caught up with Howard in the alleyway that ran behind the next-door neighbour's milking shed. His friend was at the far end and Anthony shouted, 'Hey! Stop there.'

Howard didn't stop; he called instead over his shoulder, 'You're not my commanding officer anymore.'

Anthony felt fear and helplessness and anger rise up inside him like a black wave that wouldn't be held at bay. He couldn't let this happen; he had to stop it somehow.

He began to run. He'd never been a violent man – he was training to be a doctor, a healer – but now his heart pounded and blood surged through his veins and every bit of rage and sorrow and frustration he'd felt over the past few years pulsed beneath his skin. He leapt when he got close to Howard and pulled him down onto the ground.

The two men rolled together, wrestling and scuffling, each trying to land a deciding punch on the other, neither quite managing it. Howard was the first to make contact, pushing himself back to gain sufficient distance before swinging a left hook. Anthony felt a blaze of liquid pain dart through his chest and shoulder.

Howard had been right, he wasn't a fighting man, and neither was Anthony, and the fracas was surprisingly exhausting. The two men let one another go, falling apart, backs flat on the ground, chests rising and falling as each struggled to catch his breath, the momentary madness over.

'Oh, God,' Howard said at last. 'I'm sorry. Are you hurt?'

Anthony shook his head. He stared up at the sky, more dazzling somehow for his lack of breath. 'Bloody hell, Howard.'

'I told you, I'm sorry.'

'You've got no food, no supplies . . . what are you thinking?'

'Sophie and I – we've got enough. We've got each other.'

Anthony closed his eyes and laid a hand across his chest. The sun made his cheeks burn pleasantly and turned the inside of his eyelids orange. 'You know I have to stop you.'

'You're going to have to shoot me to do it.'

Anthony blinked into the brightness. An arrowhead of birds flew black against the brilliant blue of the sky. He watched them and as he did his certainties seemed to crumble. This day, this sunshine, the birds, all of it was outside the sphere of war. It was as if a different reality was taking place just up there, if they could only get high enough to escape this place they called the world.

Howard was sitting now with his back against the brick wall, inspecting his bruised hand. Anthony went to sit beside him. His ribs hurt.

'You're determined to do this.'

'We are.'

'Then tell me the plan. You must have one. I can't believe you'd be stupid enough to take a woman and baby across the country otherwise.'

As Howard outlined his scheme Anthony listened. He tried not to think about the army and rules and what would happen if his friend were caught. He just listened and nodded and forced himself to believe that it might work.

'This aunt of Sophie's – she's in the south?'

'Almost at the Spanish border.'

'She'll take you in?'

'She's like a mother to Sophie.'

'And what about the journey, what about food?'

'I've been saving rations, and the package Eleanor sent, and Sophie has managed to get some bread and water.'

'From M. Durand's kitchen?'

Howard nodded. 'I plan to leave him money in exchange. I'm not a thief.'

'Where have you been storing these supplies?'

'There's a barn on the edge of Mme Fournier's farm. It's not used anymore. Shells have torn great holes in the roof and it leaks like a sieve.'

'A few rations, a cake, a loaf of bread – it won't be enough. You'll have to remain hidden for days and there's no telling what you'll find as you travel south.'

'We'll be all right.'

Anthony pictured the army kitchen store. The tins of bully beef and condensed milk, the flour and cheese and jam. 'You're going to need more,' he said. 'Wait until it's dark. Everybody will be busy preparing for the push tomorrow. I'll meet you in the barn.'

'No you won't. I don't want you involved.'

'I'm already involved. You're my brother.'

Anthony took a knapsack with him that night, filled with all he'd been able to take. He was careful to make sure he wasn't followed. As an officer he was accorded greater privileges than most, but he still couldn't afford to be caught in the wrong place with a bag full of stolen supplies.

He rattled the barn door when he arrived and then knocked once as they'd agreed. Howard opened it immediately; he must've been waiting on the other side. They embraced. Anthony couldn't remember them ever having done so before. Later, he would wonder whether each had felt a presentiment of what was to come. He handed over the pack.

Moonlight streamed silver through a hole in the roof and he could see Sophie sitting on a bale of hay in the corner, the baby strapped to her chest in a canvas sling. The child was sleeping, rosebud lips pursed, a look of intense concentration on his small face. Anthony envied the child his peace; even now he knew he'd never sleep like that again. He nodded a greeting and Sophie smiled shyly. Here, she was no longer M. Durand's housekeeper, but Anthony's best friend's love. It changed things.

Howard went to her and they spoke quietly. Sophie was listening intently, nodding quickly at times. At one point she rested a small fine hand upon his chest. Howard placed his own on top. Anthony felt like an intruder, but he couldn't look away. He was struck by the expression on his friend's face. He looked older, but not because he was tired. The mask of false humour he'd worn for as long as Anthony had known him, the protective smile that laughed at the world before the world could laugh at him, was gone.

The two lovers finished their tender conversation and Howard came quickly to say goodbye. Anthony realised this was it. All afternoon he'd wondered what to say when the time arrived, he'd run through a lifetime's worth of well wishes and regrets and seemingly random things he otherwise might never have the chance to say, but now it all evaporated. There was too much to express and too little time in which to do it.

'Look after yourself,' he said.

'You too.'

'And when it's all over . . .'

'Yes. When it's all over.'

Noise came from outside and they both froze.

A dog was barking in the distance.

'Howard,' Sophie called in a frightened whisper. '*Dépêche-toi! Allons-y.*'

'Yes.' Howard nodded, still looking at Anthony. 'We must go.'

He hurried to Sophie's side, tossed the army knapsack over his shoulder and picked up the other bag from near her feet.

The dog was still barking.

'Shut up,' Anthony said under his breath. 'Please, shut up.'

But the dog didn't shut up. It was growling and yapping and coming nearer, it was going to wake the baby, and now there were voices outside, too.

Anthony glanced around the room. There was a window cavity, but too high for them to get the baby out. An open door in the far wall led to a small anteroom. He gestured towards it.

They piled inside. It was darker without the moonlight, and they all held their breath, listening. Gradually their eyes adjusted. Anthony could see fear writ large on Sophie's face. Howard, his arm around her, was less easy to read.

The hinge of the barn door jolted and it swung open with a clatter.

The baby was awake now and had started to babble softly. There was nothing funny about the situation, but the child didn't know that. He was filled with the simple joy of being alive and it made him laugh.

Anthony held a finger to his lips, signalling urgently that they had to keep him quiet.

Sophie whispered in the baby's ear, but that only tickled and made him laugh with even greater spirit. *A game*, said his dark, dancing eyes, *What fun!*

Anthony felt his hackles rise. The footsteps were very close now, the murmur of voices loud and clear. Again, he pressed his finger hard against his lips, and Sophie jostled the baby, her whispers gaining a panicked edge.

But little Louis was tired of playing, and hungry perhaps, eager to climb down from his mother and confused as to why she wouldn't let him. His gurgles turned into a cry, and the cries grew louder, and in the blink of an eye Anthony was at Sophie's side, and his hands were on the child, and he was pulling the small bundle, trying to untangle it from Sophie's cloth sling, trying to get his hand to the child's mouth, to make the noise stop, to make it quiet so that they would all be safe.

But the dog was at the second door now, scratching the

wood, and Howard was behind Anthony, pulling him away, pushing him backwards with enormous force, and the baby was still crying, and the dog was barking, and Howard had his arm around Sophie, who was whimpering, too, and the door's handle rattled.

Anthony drew his gun and held his breath.

When the door opened the torch beams were blinding. Anthony blinked and held up his hand from instinct. His mind was a fog but he could just make out two burly men in the dark beyond. One, he realised, when the man began talking in rapid French, was M. Durand; the other wore British army uniform.

'What's all this?' said the officer.

Anthony could all but hear the cogs of the man's mind turning and it was no surprise when he said, 'Put down the sack and step away.'

Howard did as he'd been told.

Baby Louis was quiet now, Anthony noticed, and was reaching up to touch Sophie's pale cheeks. He continued to watch the child, fascinated by his innocence, its striking contrast with the horror of the situation they were in.

And into the silence flowed recognition of what he'd almost done, the depravity of his instinct in that awful moment before.

Anthony shook his head. But it was monstrous! It was impossible. Surely not he, Anthony, who had always been able to trust himself, his control and precision and care, his drive to help others.

Confused, he forced the thought away and concentrated again on baby Louis. It suddenly seemed to Anthony that in a world from which all the goodness had been sapped, they ought all to be watching this precious child, marvelling at his purity. *Stop talking,* he wanted to say. *Just look at the little one.*

He was losing his mind, of course. That was what happened in the moments before one faced death. For it was certain they were all going to die. To aid a deserter was akin to deserting himself. Strangely, it wasn't as bad as Anthony had imagined. At least it would be over soon.

He was tired, he realised, very tired, and now he could stop trying so hard to make it home. Eleanor would grieve for him, but when she'd adjusted, she'd be pleased, he knew, to learn he'd died trying to help Howard begin a new life. Anthony almost laughed. Begin a new life! At a time like this, when the world was turning to ruin.

There came a crashing sound and Anthony blinked. He was surprised to realise he was still in the French barn. The officer had opened the knapsack and shaken out the stolen army supplies. Tins of bully beef and maconochie and condensed milk lay all over the ground – Anthony had made sure to take enough that Howard and Sophie could hide for weeks if they had to.

The officer whistled lightly. 'Looks like someone was planning a bit of a holiday.'

'I'd have got away with it, too,' said Howard suddenly, 'if Edevane hadn't caught up with me.'

Anthony glanced at his friend, confused. Howard didn't meet his gaze. 'Bastard followed me. Tried to talk me out of it.'

Stop talking, Anthony thought, just stop talking. It's too late.

The officer looked at the gun in Anthony's hand. 'Is that

right?' He glanced between them. 'Were you trying to bring him in?'

But Anthony couldn't form sentences fast enough, each word was like a piece of confetti on a windy day and he couldn't put them together.

'I told him he'd have to shoot me here,' Howard said quickly.

'Edevane?'

Anthony heard the officer, but only as from a great distance. He wasn't in that godforsaken barn in France any longer; he was back at Loeanneth, in the kitchen garden, watching as his children played. He was tending the garden that he and Eleanor had planted together a lifetime ago, he could *smell* the sun-warmed strawberries, feel the sun on his face, hear his children singing. 'Come home to me,' Eleanor had said that day by the stream, and he'd promised that he would. He was going to get back to them if it was the last thing he did. He'd made a promise, but it was more than that, too. Anthony was going to make it home because he wanted to.

'I tried to stop him,' he heard himself say. 'I told him not to run.'

As they positioned Howard between them and marched back towards camp, as Sophie wailed in stuttering French, Anthony told himself he'd bought his friend more time. That this wasn't how it ended. That where there was life there was hope. He'd find a way to explain it all away, to save Howard, to make things go back to how they were. The front was miles away; there was plenty of time to think of a way out of this mess.

A half-mile outside camp, though, he still hadn't thought

of anything, and he realised he could no longer smell strawberries, only the stench of war rot, of mud and waste and the
acrid taste of gunpowder on his lips. He could hear a dog
barking somewhere, and – he was sure – a baby crying in
the distant night, and the thought came to him before he
could stop it, cool and dull and empty of emotion, that if
he'd only finished what he'd started back there, silenced that
baby, that dear little child who'd barely started to live,
who wouldn't have known what was happening, for whom
Anthony could have made it mercifully quick, then Howard
would have been spared. That it had been his only chance to
save his brother and he'd failed.

Twenty-eight

It didn't seem to Sadie there was much point sticking around in London after she'd spoken with Alice Edevane. The keys to Loeanneth were burning a hole in her pocket and by the time she arrived back at her flat she'd decided to leave immediately. She tipped a glassful of water over her desiccated plant, gathered her notes, and slung her bag, still conveniently packed from her last stint in Cornwall, over her shoulder. She locked the door behind her and without a backward glance took the stairs by twos.

The five-hour drive went surprisingly quickly. County after county passed in a greenish blur as Sadie wondered at the evidence Alice had promised she'd find tucked inside the repositories at Loeanneth. It was nearly nine-thirty and becoming dark when she turned off the A38 and headed for the coast. She slowed as she approached the leaning signpost that pointed the way towards the woods and the hidden entrance to Loeanneth; there was a great temptation to follow the forked road. Her impatience to get started was matched only by her eagerness to avoid the awkward task that lay ahead of explaining to Bertie why she was back so soon. She could just picture his querulous expression as he said, 'Another holiday?' But there was no electricity at the

Lake House, she hadn't brought a torch, and unless she planned to avoid the village and her grandfather altogether there would be music to face at some point. No, she decided, it was better to be done with the inquisition upfront.

With a sigh of reluctant determination, she continued along the coast road and into the village, where preparations were underway for the weekend Solstice Festival. Lengths of coloured lights were being strung along the streets, and in the village square piles of wood and canvas had been set down at regular intervals, waiting to be assembled into stalls. Sadie drove slowly along the narrow streets before beginning the climb to Bertie's cottage. She rounded the final bend and there it was, perched on its cliff-top, warm lights glowing in the kitchen and the starlit sky bright behind its pitched roof. The scene was like something from a family Christmas movie, minus the snow. Which made Sadie the interloping relative, she supposed, arrived from nowhere to scuttle the peace. She parked the car on the verge of the narrow street, collected her suitcase from the back seat, and made her way up the stairs.

The dogs were barking inside and the front door was open before she could knock. Bertie was wearing an apron, ladle in hand. 'Sadie!' he said with a broad smile. 'You've come down for the festival weekend. What a lovely surprise.'

Of course she had. Brilliant save.

Ramsay and Ash leapt from behind him, sniffing Sadie with unbridled joy. She couldn't help but laugh, kneeling down to give them both some love.

'Are you hungry?' Bertie fussed the dogs inside. 'I was about to have supper. Come on in and butter some bread while I dish up.'

*

Every flat surface in the kitchen was covered with jars of preserves and racks of cooling cakes, so they ate at the long wooden table in the courtyard. Bertie lit candles in the tall glass hurricane lanterns, and as the little flames flickered and the wax burned down, Sadie caught up on village news. As might have been expected, the countdown to the festival had been filled with intrigue and drama. 'But all's well that ends well,' said Bertie, running a crust of sourdough around his empty plate, 'and this time tomorrow night, it'll all be over.'

'Until next year,' said Sadie.

He rolled his eyes heavenwards.

'You don't fool me, you love it. Just look at your kitchen. You've cooked up an unholy storm.'

Bertie was aghast. 'Dear Lord, touch wood, don't tempt fate. You mustn't even say that word. The last thing we need tomorrow is rain!'

Sadie laughed. 'Superstitious as ever, I see.' She glanced across the garden and out to the moonlit sea, the clear starry sky. 'I think you're pretty safe.'

'Either way, we're going to have to get an early start tomorrow if we want to have everything set up in time. I'll be glad to have an extra pair of hands.'

'About that,' said Sadie, 'I'm afraid I haven't been completely honest about why I'm here.'

He raised a single eyebrow.

'I've had a breakthrough in the Edevane case.'

'Well, well, have you now.' He pushed aside his bowl. 'Tell me everything.'

Sadie explained about her meeting with Alice and the

theory they'd come to regarding Anthony Edevane. 'So you see, the shell shock was relevant after all.'

'My God,' said Bertie, shaking his head. 'What a terrible tragedy. That poor family.'

'From what I can gather, Theo's death was the beginning of the end. The family never came back to Loeanneth, the war started, and by the time it ended, or near enough, Eleanor, Anthony and their youngest daughter, Clemmie, were all dead.'

An owl soared unseen above them, its wings beating the warm air, and Bertie sighed. 'It's a strange thing, isn't it, uncovering the secrets of people who are no longer with us. It's not like one of your usual crimes, where the driving force is to arrest and punish the guilty. There's no one left in this case to punish.'

'No,' Sadie agreed, 'but the truth still matters. Think about the people left behind. They've suffered, too; they deserve to know what really happened. If you met Alice you'd see how much of a burden the not-knowing has been. I think she's led her whole life in the shadow of the terrible events of that night, but now she's given me the keys to the house and permission to search wherever I see fit. I'm determined not to leave without finding what we need to prove Anthony's part in Theo's death.'

'Well, I think it's tremendous what you're doing, helping her put the whole affair to rest. And what a coup! Solving a crime that's remained a mystery for seventy years. That must feel terrific.'

Sadie smiled. It *was* a coup. It *did* feel terrific.

'And jolly decent of the Met to give you more time off to tie up the loose ends.'

Her cheeks were instantly scarlet; Bertie, by comparison, was a picture of innocence, reaching down to stroke Ramsay's neck. Whether he was in earnest or his appearance of ease masked an unspoken question, Sadie wasn't sure. Either way she could've just lied, but in that moment she didn't have the spirit for it. Truthfully, she was tired of pretending, especially with Bertie, who was her whole family, the only person in the world with whom she could be completely herself. 'Actually, Granddad, I've had a spot of trouble at work.'

Bertie didn't skip a beat. 'Have you now, love? Want to tell me about it?'

And so Sadie found herself explaining about the Bailey case. Her strong feeling that Maggie had met with foul play, her refusal to follow the advice of her superior officers, and her ultimate decision to go outside the force and speak to Derek Maitland. 'It's the number-one rule: don't talk to journalists.'

'But you're an excellent detective. You must've felt you had a good reason to break the rules.'

His faith in her judgement was touching. 'I thought I did. I was convinced my instincts were right and it seemed like the only way to keep attention focused on the case.'

'So you acted in good faith, even if you went about it the wrong way. Surely that counts for something?'

'It doesn't work like that. I'd be in trouble enough if I'd been right, but I wasn't. I made a bad call, the case got under my skin, and now there's an inquiry.'

'Oh, love.' His smile was full of sympathy. 'For what it's worth, I'd back your instincts any day.'

'Thanks, Granddad.'

'What about Donald? Does he know? What does he say?'

'He was the one who suggested I take leave. A pre-emptive strike, so to speak. That way if they find out it was me, I can argue I'd already removed myself from action.'

'Will that help?'

'I've never known Ashford to err on the side of leniency. I'll be suspended at the very least. If he's had a bad day, stood down.'

Bertie shook his head. 'It doesn't seem right. Is there anything you can do?'

'The best plan I've been able to come up with, aside from lying low and avoiding Nancy Bailey, is to keep my fingers crossed.'

He held up a hand, his old fingers plaited. 'Then I'll add mine. And in the meantime, you've got the solution to the Lake House mystery to prove.'

'Exactly.' Sadie felt a spike of excitement as she anticipated the following day. She was silently congratulating herself on finally having told Bertie the truth, when he scratched his head and said, 'I wonder what it was about the Bailey case.'

'What's that?'

'Why do you think this particular case got under your skin?'

'Mothers and children,' she said with a shrug. 'They're always the difficult ones for me.'

'But you've had similar cases in the past. Why this one? Why now?'

Sadie was on the verge of saying she didn't know, passing it off as one of those inexplicable things, when the first letter from Charlotte Sutherland flashed into her mind. In that moment, an urgent swell of something awfully like grief rose up within her, and a wave she'd been holding at bay for fifteen years threatened to crash. 'There was a letter,' she said quickly. 'A few months ago. The baby, she's fifteen now, she wrote to me.'

Bertie's eyes widened behind his glasses. He said only, 'Esther?'

The name, spoken like that, was an arrow. The one rule Sadie had broken, naming her baby when she saw that little star-shaped hand appear above the yellow-and-white blanket.

'Esther wrote to you?'

Twice now, Sadie thought, but didn't say. 'A couple of weeks after I started working the Bailey case. I don't know how she got my address; I guess they keep records of names and give them out if people ask, and it isn't so hard to find a private address if you know where to look.'

'What did she say?'

'She told me a bit about herself. Her nice family, nice school, her list of lovely interests. And she said she wants to meet me.'

'Esther wants to meet you?'

'Her name's not Esther. It's Charlotte. Charlotte Sutherland.'

Bertie leaned back against his chair, a faint, dazed smile on his face. 'Her name is Charlotte, and you're going to meet her.'

'No.' Sadie shook her head. 'No, I'm not.'

'But Sadie, love.'

'I can't, Granddad. I've decided.'

'But—'

'I gave her away. What will she think of me?'

'You were little more than a child yourself.'

Sadie was still shaking her head, the action involuntary. She shivered, despite the balmy night. 'She'll think I abandoned her.'

'You agonised over what was best for her.'

'She won't see it that way. She'll hate me.'

'What if she doesn't?'

'Look at me – ' No spouse, few friends, even her houseplant was dying from neglect. She'd sacrificed everything in her life to her job, and even that was looking tenuous. She was bound to be a disappointment. 'I'm no kind of a parent.'

'I don't think she's looking for someone to tie her shoelaces. By the sounds of things she's done very well in that department. She only wants to know who her biological mother is.'

'You and I both know biology is no guarantee of fellow feeling. Sometimes the best thing that can happen to a person is to gain a new set of parents. Look at the way you and Ruth stepped in for me.'

Now Bertie shook his head, but not sadly. He was frustrated with her, Sadie could tell, but there wasn't anything she could do to change that. It wasn't his decision to make, it was hers and she'd made it. For better or for worse.

For better. She exhaled determinedly. 'Ruth used to say that if you did the right thing and you'd do it again, the only thing left to do was to move forward.'

Bertie's eyes turned moist behind his glasses. 'She was always wise.'

'And she was usually right. That's what I've done, Granddad, followed Ruth's advice. For fifteen years I've moved forward and I haven't looked back, and everything's been fine. All this trouble started because of the letter. It brought the past back into my life.'

'That's not what Ruth meant, Sadie, love. She wanted you to move forward without regrets, not to deny the past entirely.'

'I'm not denying it, I'm just not thinking about it. I made the choice I made and there's nothing to be gained by digging it all up again.'

'But isn't that what you're talking about doing for the Edevane family?'

'That's different.'

'Is it?'

'Yes.' And it was. She couldn't find the words to explain how, not then and there; she just knew it. She was irritated by Bertie's opposition but she didn't want to argue with him. She softened her voice and said, 'Listen, I have to duck inside and make a couple of phone calls before it gets too late. How about I put the kettle on and bring us up a fresh pot to share?'

Despite the soporific roll of the sea, Sadie couldn't sleep that night. She'd managed finally to put Charlotte Sutherland, Esther, out of mind, but her attention had shifted to the Edevanes and Loeanneth. She tossed and turned as visions of Midsummer 1933 filled her thoughts. Eleanor checking on baby Theo before returning to her guests, paddleboats and gondolas drifting up the stream towards the boathouse, the great bonfire raging on its island in the middle of the lake.

It was still dark when she gave up on sleep altogether

and slipped on her running gear. The dogs woke excitedly as she passed through the kitchen, hurrying to fall into step beside her as she set off. It was too dark to attempt a path through the woods, so she contented herself with the headland, going over all the things she needed to do when she got to Loeanneth. She was back at Bertie's and toasting her third round of bread when the first light of dawn began to tiptoe across the benchtop. Sadie left a note for Bertie under the kettle, loaded the car with her files, a torch and a Thermos of tea, and hushed the dogs to stay.

The horizon was golden as she drove east. The sea glimmered as if someone had sprinkled it with iron filings and Sadie wound down the window to enjoy the crisp, briny breeze on her face. It was going to be a warm, clear day for the festival and she was glad for Bertie. Glad, too, that she'd escaped before he woke, thereby dodging a rehash of their conversation from the previous night. It wasn't that she regretted telling him about the letter, only that she didn't want to discuss it further. He was disappointed, she knew, by her decision not to meet Charlotte Sutherland, convinced that she was wilfully misinterpreting Ruth's advice, but it was a situation he couldn't possibly understand. She would find the words to explain it to him, what it was to give up a child, how keenly she'd had to struggle to move beyond the fact that there was someone out there, her own flesh and blood, whom she could never know, but at the moment, with everything else going on, it was just too complicated.

Sadie reached the leaning signpost, its white paint peeling after years of bracing wind, and turned left. The road that led away from the coast was narrow, long clumps of grass encroaching on the faded tarmac, and it became thinner still as it snaked into the woods. Dawn hadn't breached the canopy yet, and Sadie had to switch on the car's headlights to make her way through the trees. She drove slowly, scouring the overgrown verge for the entrance to Loeanneth. According to Alice Edevane's instructions, the wrought-iron gates would be difficult to spot. They were tucked back from the road, she'd said, and the elaborate, woven design was such that even during the family's heyday, they'd been threatened with consumption by the ivy tendrils that reached out from the trees to climb and cling.

Sure enough, Sadie almost missed them. It was only as her headlights glanced off the edge of a tarnished post that she realised this was it. She reversed quickly, pulled off the road, leapt from the car and fiddled with the keys Alice had given her, looking for the one marked *Gate*. Her fingers were clumsy with excitement and it took a few attempts to slot the key into the latch. Finally, though, she managed. The gate was rusty and stiff, but Sadie had always been able to find unexpected physical strength when sufficiently motivated. She forced the pair of gates open, wide enough, just, to drive her car through.

She'd never approached the house from this direction, and was struck, when she finally emerged through the thick woods, by how emphatically hidden it was from the rest of the world, tucked within its own valley, the house and inner gardens concealed by a protective planting of elms. She followed the driveway across a stone bridge and parked her car beneath the boughs of an enormous tree in a gravelled area colonised by wily tussocks of grass. The sun was still rising as she hitched up the old gate and entered the garden.

'You're early,' she called, when she saw the old man sitting on the rim of the big planter.

Clive waved. 'I've been waiting for this for seventy years. I wasn't about to wait a minute longer than I had to.'

Sadie had called him the night before and brought him up to speed on her meeting with Alice. He'd listened, shocked when he learned their new theory that Theo Edevane had been killed by his father. 'I was sure the boy had been taken,' he'd said when Sadie had finished. 'All this time I held out hope that I could still find him.' There'd been a tremble in his voice, and Sadie could tell just how much he'd personally invested in the case. She knew the feeling. 'We still have a job to do,' she'd said. 'We owe it to the little boy to learn exactly what happened that night.' She'd told him then about the keys and Alice's invitation to search the house. 'I called her just before phoning you and mentioned your ongoing interest. I told her how invaluable you've been so far.'

Now they stood together beneath the portico as Sadie struggled with the front door. For one heartstopping instant it seemed as if the lock were stuck and the key wasn't going to turn, but then there came the welcome click of the mechanism giving way. Moments later, Sadie and Clive stepped across the threshold, into the entrance hall of the Lake House.

The room smelled musty, and the air was cooler than Sadie had expected. The front door was still wide open and when she glanced over her shoulder the waking world outside seemed brighter than it had before. She could see all the way along the overgrown path to where the surface of the lake was sparkling with the first rays of morning sun.

'It's like time stood still,' said Clive softly. 'The house hasn't changed since we were here all those years ago.' He craned to take in every angle and added, 'Except for the spiders. They're new.' He met her gaze. 'So now, where would you like to start?'

Sadie matched his slightly reverent tone. There was something about a house left sealed for so long that invited such theatre. 'Alice thought it most likely that we'd find what we're looking for in Anthony's study or Eleanor's writing bureau.'

'And what is it exactly that we're looking for?'

'Anything detailing Anthony's condition, particularly in the weeks leading up to Midsummer 1933. Letters, diaries – a signed confession would be ideal.'

Clive grinned as she continued, 'We'll get more done if we split up. How about you take the study, I'll take the desk, and we reconvene to compare notes in a couple of hours?'

Sadie was aware of Clive's silence as they climbed the staircase side by side, the way he glanced about him, his deep sigh as they paused on the first-floor landing. She could only imagine what it must be like for him to be back inside the house after so many decades. Seventy years in which the Edevane case had remained alive for him, in which he'd never given up hope of solving the crime. She wondered if he'd thought back over the initial investigation overnight, and whether pieces of the puzzle, previously innocuous, had slotted into place.

'I thought of nothing else,' he said when she asked him. 'I was on my way to bed when you rang, but there was no chance of sleeping afterwards. I kept thinking about the way he stuck close to her during the interviews. At the time I presumed it was so he could protect her, so she wouldn't fall apart in the aftermath of the boy's disappearance. But it occurs to me now there was something almost unnatural about their closeness. Almost as if he were standing guard, making sure she wouldn't, or couldn't, reveal what he had done.'

Sadie was about to answer when her phone rang in the pocket of her jeans. Clive signalled that he was going to head on up to Anthony's study and she nodded, pulling out her mobile. Her heart sank when she recognised Nancy Bailey's phone number on the screen. Sadie considered herself something of an expert at breaking up and had thought 'Goodbye and take care of yourself' was clear enough: a discreet, even gentle, way of letting the other woman down. Evidently it was going to require a more explicit approach. But not now. She muted the phone and shoved it back into her pocket. She would deal with Nancy Bailey another day.

Eleanor's bedroom was along the corridor, only two doors away, but Sadie didn't move. Her gaze was drawn instead to the faded red carpet runner, rotting in patches, which stretched up a further flight of stairs. There was something else she needed to do first. She climbed a floor higher and then followed the hallway to its end. It had become warmer as she rose and the air was stuffier. The walls were still hung with framed pictures commemorating generations of deShiel family members, and behind each partially opened door, the rooms were furnished, right down to the small decorative items on bedside tables: lamps, books, comb-and-mirror sets. It was eerie and she was overcome by a strong, though completely irrational, sense that she needed to walk without making a sound. The contrary part of her coughed, just to shatter the pervasive silence.

At the end of the hallway, the nursery door was closed. Sadie stopped when she reached it. She had envisaged this moment many times over the past fortnight, but now that she was actually standing on the threshold of Theo's nursery, the whole thing felt more real than she'd imagined it would. She didn't usually hold with rituals and superstitions, but Sadie made a point of picturing Theo Edevane, the wide-eyed, round-cheeked baby from the newspaper photos, reminding herself that the room she was about to enter was sacred.

She opened the door quietly and stepped inside. The room was stuffy, and although the once-white curtains were drawn they were grey now, and moth-eaten, and light spilled through them unhindered. It was smaller than she'd imagined. The quaint cast-iron cot in the middle was a stark reminder of how young and vulnerable Theo Edevane had been in 1933. It stood on a round woven rug, and beyond it, by the window, was an armchair covered in chintz that must once have been a bright and cheerful yellow but had faded and thinned to a sad, nondescript beige. Little wonder, after decades of dust and insects and summer sun stealing in. The shelf of vintage wooden toys, the rocking horse beneath the window, the ancient baby bath in the corner: all were familiar from the newspaper photographs, and Sadie experienced a slightly jarring sensation of distant recognition, as if it were a room she'd dreamed about, or one she remembered vaguely from her own childhood.

She went to inspect the cot. Its mattress was still made up with sheets, and a knitted blanket had been stretched smooth and tight at one end. It was dusty now, sad. Sadie ran her hand lightly over the iron rail and there came a faint jingling. One of the four brass knobs wobbled unevenly at the top of its post. This was where Theo Edevane had been put to bed on the night of the party. Nanny Bruen had been asleep on the single bed against the far wall, tucked beneath the slanting roof, and outside, on the lawn by the lake, hundreds of people had been ushering in Midsummer.

Sadie glanced at the smaller side window through which the single witness in the case claimed to have seen a slender woman. The party guest said that it was around midnight, but she must have been mistaken. Either she'd imagined the whole thing – and according to Clive she'd still been drunk the next morning – or else it had been a different window, a different room. It was possible she'd glimpsed Eleanor in the nursery, checking on Theo as was her habit, but if that were the case she'd been wrong about the time, for Eleanor had left the room at eleven o'clock, stopping on the stairs to give instructions to a housemaid. And witnesses had seen Eleanor by the boathouse where the gondolas were docked just before midnight.

A round clock with a stark white face loomed down from on high, its hands marking some long-ago quarter past three, and five Winnie the Pooh prints stepped along the wall. Those walls had seen everything, but the room wasn't talking. Sadie glanced at the doorway and a ghostly imprint of the night's events played out before her. At some point after midnight, Anthony Edevane had come through from the hall, crossing the room to stand above the cot, just as Sadie was doing now. What happened next? she wondered. Did he take the little boy from the nursery, or did it happen right here? Did Theo wake up? Did he recognise his father and smile or coo, or did he grasp somehow that there was something different about this visit, something terrible? Did he struggle or cry? And what happened afterwards? When did Eleanor learn what her husband had done?

Something on the floor beneath the cot caught Sadie's eye, a tiny, shiny something, lying on the rug in a patch of morning sunlight. She bent to retrieve it; a round silver button with a plump cupid on it. She was turning it over in her fingertips when something moved against her leg. She jumped, her heart racing, before she realised it was only her phone, vibrating in her pocket. Relief turned quickly to exasperation when she saw Nancy Bailey's number again. With a frown, Sadie hit 'cancel', turned off the vibrate function, and pocketed both the phone and the button. She glanced around the room but the spell was broken now. She could no longer picture Anthony creeping across the floor towards the cot, or hear the noise of the party outside. It was just a lonely old room and she was wasting time with lost buttons and morbid imaginings.

Eleanor Edevane's bedroom was dim and the air smelled stale, of sorrow and neglect. Thick velvet curtains were drawn against all four windows and the first thing Sadie did was drag them back, coughing as plumes of dust detached and dispersed. She opened the stiff sash windows as high as they would go, and paused for a second to admire the view down to the lake. The sun was bright now, and the ducks were busy. A faint twittering sound caught her attention and she glanced above her. Tucked beneath the shelter of the eaves she spotted the hint of a nest.

As a current of cool, clean air breezed through the open window, she felt a wave of motivation and determined to ride it. She noted the roll-top writing bureau against the far wall, exactly where Alice had said it would be. It was Eleanor who had started Sadie down this road; Eleanor with whom she'd originally felt a connection, sparked by the ivy-rimmed letter; and it was Eleanor who was going to help her prove what happened to baby Theo. Remembering Alice's instructions, Sadie felt beneath the desk chair, patting the tatty upholstery on the underside of the cushioned seat, running her fingertips along each wooden edge. Finally, where the right back leg joined the seat, her fingers met a pair of tiny keys hanging on a hook. Bingo.

Once unlocked, the bureau's wooden cover rolled back cleanly to reveal a neat desk with a leather jotter and pen-holder laid out on the writing surface. A series of journals lined the shelves at the back and a quick peek inside the first revealed them as the triplicate volumes Alice had said Eleanor used for correspondence. Her gaze ran greedily along the spines. There was nothing to suggest they were in chronological order, but a glance at the tidy, uncluttered desk suggested it was likely. The family had left Loeanneth at the end of 1933, which meant, presumably, that the last book covered the months leading up to Midsummer that year. Sadie slid it from the shelf and, sure enough, the first page was a letter dated January 1933, addressed in beautiful handwriting to someone called Dr Steinbach. She sat on the floor with her back propped against the side of the bed and started to read.

It was the first in what proved to be a series of letters to a series of doctors, each outlining Anthony's symptoms and asking for help in polite sentences that didn't quite manage to conceal her desperation. Eleanor's descriptions of his plight were poignant, the eager young man whose life's promise had been stripped from him by his service to his country, who'd tried over the course of years since his return to recover and regain his past abilities. Sadie was moved, but there was no time now to lament the horrors of war. There was only one horror she was interested in proving today, and to that end she had to stay focused on her search for references to Anthony's potential for violence, his condition leading up to 23 June.

If there was something guarded about the letters Eleanor wrote to the doctors in London, those to Daffyd Llewellyn – and there were lots of them – were far more personal in tone. They still addressed Anthony's medical condition – Sadie had forgotten that Llewellyn trained as a physician before throwing it all in to become a writer – but, freed from having to couch her descriptions in terms that upheld her husband's dignity and privacy in the eyes of a distant medical practitioner, Eleanor was able to describe his condition and her despair honestly: *I fear sometimes that he will never be free, that this search of mine has all been in vain . . . I would give up anything to make him well, but how can I help when he has lost the will to help himself?* There were some lines in particular that persuaded Sadie she was on the right path: *It happened again the other night. He woke with a howl, shouting again about the dog and the baby, insisting that they must get out now, and I had to hold him down with all my might to prevent him charging from the room. The poor love, when he gets like that, thrashing and shaking, he doesn't even realise that it's me . . . He's so remorseful in*

the morning. I find myself lying to him sometimes, pretend-
ing that I injured myself rushing about. I know your feelings
on such matters, and I agree, in principle, that honesty with
sensitivity is the best approach, but it would do him such
great harm to know the truth. He would never knowingly
hurt a fly. I couldn't bear to see him shamed so . . . Now you
must not worry! I would never have told you if I'd thought
it would cause you to suffer so dreadfully. I assure you I'm
all right. Physical wounds heal; damage to one's spirit is so
much worse . . . I made Anthony a promise and promises
must be kept. You're the one who taught me that . . .

As she read, it became clear to Sadie that Llewellyn was
also privy to Eleanor's affair with Benjamin Munro. *My*
friend, as you insist on quaintly (coyly!) calling him, is well
. . . Of course I am racked with guilt. It is very kind of you
to point out differences between my mother and me, but
beneath your generous words, I know our actions are not so
dissimilar . . . In my own defence, if I might be allowed to
make one, I love him, differently to Anthony of course, but I
know now it is possible for the human heart to love in two
places . . . And then, in the final letter: *You are quite right,*
Anthony must never know. Far more than a setback, it
would destroy him . . .

The last letter was dated April 1933 and the book contained no others. Sadie remembered that Daffyd Llewellyn's
habit was to live at Loeanneth through the summer months,
which explained why there'd been no further written correspondence between them. She glanced again at the line, *You*
are quite right, Anthony must never know . . . *it would*
destroy him. It wasn't exactly proof, but it was interesting.
Judging by Eleanor's response, Llewellyn had been very

worried about how Anthony might react if he learned of the affair. Sadie wondered whether his anxieties had even contributed to the depression that led him to suicide. She wasn't an expert, but it didn't seem impossible. It certainly helped to explain the timing, which still niggled in the back corner of her brain.

Sadie brightened. Alice had said her mother stored the letters she received in the drawers on either side of her desk. With any luck, those from Daffyd Llewellyn would be there. She could see exactly what he'd feared – and how much – written in his own words. Sadie unlocked both drawers. Hundreds of envelopes, raggedy where they'd been opened, had been bound into groups and tied with coloured ribbon. All were addressed to Mrs A. Edevane, some typed officially, others handwritten. Sadie riffled through, bundle by bundle, hunting for those from Daffyd Llewellyn.

She was still empty-handed when she came across a batch, unusual for the top envelope having neither an address nor a stamp on it. Perplexed, Sadie scanned through the rest. There were one or two that had arrived officially through the post, but the rest were as blank as the first. And then it dawned on her. The soft red ribbon, the faint powdery hint of perfume. They were love letters.

Not strictly what she'd set out to find, but Sadie was overcome with a frisson of curiosity. Besides, there was a chance Eleanor had shared with her lover the fears she harboured about Anthony's condition. She pulled at the red ribbon, so eager to open the bundle that she sent them scattering to the floor around her. She was cursing herself for having got them out of order when something caught her eye. Something that didn't belong in this bundle at all.

She recognised the stationery at once, the woven pattern of deep-green ivy tendrils snaking around the margins, the handwriting, the pen: it was a perfect match. This was the first half of the letter she'd found when she was exploring the boathouse, the letter Eleanor had written to Anthony when he was away at war. Sadie's heart was thumping even as she smoothed out the sheet of paper. Later, it would seem to her as if she'd experienced a presentiment of what she was about to discover, because as she started to read, a missing piece of the puzzle, a clue she hadn't even realised she was searching for, fell right into her lap.

'Sadie?'

She looked up with a start. It was Clive, standing in the doorway, a leather-bound notebook in his hand, an enlivened expression on his face.

'Ah, there you are,' he said.

'Here I am,' she parroted, her mind still racing with the implications of what she'd just uncovered.

'I think I've got it,' he said excitedly, walking as quickly as his old legs would allow him to sit on the edge of the bed near Sadie. 'In Anthony's journal from 1933. Alice was right, he was a prolific diarist. There's one for each year, filled mostly with observations of the natural world and memory exercises. I recognised them from my early days with the police, back when I was trying to teach myself to remember every detail from a crime scene. But there were diary entries, too, in the form of letters to a fellow called Howard. A friend, I gather, who'd been killed in the first war. That's where I found it. In June 1933, Anthony seems to enter a new dark patch. He tells his mate he'd felt himself declining over the past year, that something had changed, he just hadn't known what it was, and that the birth of his son hadn't made things better. In fact, when I looked over old entries, he mentioned a few times that the sound of the little fellow crying brought back memories of an experience he calls "the incident", something that happened during the war. In his last entry before Midsummer, he writes that his eldest daughter, Deborah, had come to see him, and that she'd told him something that changed everything, explaining his feeling of something amiss and "shattering the illusion" of his perfect life.'

'The affair,' Sadie said, thinking of Daffyd Llewellyn's concerns.

'It has to be.'

Anthony had learned of the affair just before Midsummer. It was enough, surely, to tip him over the edge. Daffyd Llewellyn had certainly been worried about that. Now, though, in light of what she'd just read, Sadie wondered if that was all he'd discovered.

'How about you?' Clive nodded at the envelopes still scattered over the carpet. 'Anything of interest?'

'You could say that.'

'Well?'

She filled him in quickly on the partial letter she'd found at the boathouse, the letter from Eleanor to Anthony, written when he was away at the war and she was alone at home, pregnant with Alice and wondering how she was going to manage without him.

'And?' Clive urged.

'I just found the other half, the first half. Here, amongst Eleanor's other correspondence.'

'Is that it?' He nodded at the leaf of paper in Sadie's hand. 'May I?'

She passed it to Clive, who skimmed the contents, his eyebrows lifting. 'Goodness.'

'Yes.'

'It's passionate.'

'Yes.'

'But it isn't addressed to Anthony at all. It says, *Dearest Ben.*'

'That's right,' Sadie said. 'And it's dated May 1932. Which means the unborn baby she's writing about isn't Alice. It's Theo.'

'But that means . . .'

'Exactly. Theo Edevane wasn't Anthony's son. He was Ben's.'

Twenty-nine

Eleanor hadn't meant to fall pregnant, not to Ben, but she didn't regret it for a second. She'd known almost as soon as it happened. Ten years had passed since she'd fallen with Clementine, but she hadn't forgotten. She'd felt immediate and immense love for the little person growing inside her. Anthony had sometimes shown her the view through his microscope, so she knew about cells and building blocks and the fabric of life. Her love for the baby was cellular. They were one and the same and she couldn't imagine life without the tiny being.

So intense, so personal was her love, that it was easy to forget the baby had a father, that she hadn't somehow brought him into being by strength of will alone – particularly when the promised child was so small, so safely tucked away. He remained her secret (she was sure the baby was a boy), and Eleanor was good at keeping secrets. She'd had a lot of practice. She'd kept Anthony's secret for years, and her own since meeting Ben.

Ben. In the beginning, Eleanor had told herself he was simply an addiction. Once, when she was a little girl, Eleanor's father had given her a kite, a special kite shipped all the way from China, and he'd taught her to fly it. Eleanor had loved that kite with a passion, the tremendous coloured tails, the strength of the quivering strings in her hands, the strange and wonderful writing on the kite's side that was more like an illustration than a language.

Together she and her father had scoured the fields of Loeanneth, looking for the best place to launch the kite, the finest winds to fly it. Eleanor became obsessed. She kept flight notes in a book, she drew copious diagrams and plans for design adjustments, and she found herself waking suddenly in the night, sitting up in bed going through the motions of letting out the anchor system, her hands winding the reel of a ghost kite as if she were still out in the field.

'You've developed an addiction,' Nanny Bruen had said with a look of stern distaste, before taking the kite from the nursery and hiding it. 'An addiction is a devil, and the devil goes away when he finds the door shut firm against him.'

Eleanor had developed an addiction to Ben, or so she told herself, but now she was an adult, in charge of her own destiny. There was no Nanny Bruen to burn the kite and shut the door and so she was free to walk right through.

'I was just about to light the fire,' he'd said, the day she came upon him in the caravan. 'Would you like to come inside and wait for the storm to pass?'

It was still pouring with rain and without the hunt for Edwina to fuel her, Eleanor realised how cold she was, how drenched. She could see beyond him into a small sitting room that seemed suddenly the height of comfort and warmth. Behind her, the rain was pounding and Edwina, solid at her feet, had clearly made up her mind to stay. Eleanor couldn't see that she had much choice in the matter. She thanked him, took a breath, and went inside.

The man followed, closing the door behind him, and immediately the noise of teeming rain reduced. He handed her a towel and then busied himself lighting a fire in a small cast-iron stove in the middle of the caravan. Eleanor took the opportunity as she patted her hair dry to look around.

The caravan was comfortable, but not plush. Just enough had been done to make it homely. On the windowsill, she noticed, were more of those delicate paper cranes she'd seen him folding on the train.

'Please, sit down,' he said. 'I'll have this lit in a moment. It's a little temperamental but we've been on good terms lately.'

Eleanor pushed aside a whisper of misgiving. She was aware that his bed, the place he slept, was visible behind the drawn curtain at the other end of the caravan. She averted her gaze, laid the towel across a cane chair and sat. Rain fell softly now and it occurred to her, not for the first time, that it was one of the best sounds she knew. To be inside, with the hope of soon being warm and dry, while rain fell outside, was a splendid, simple joy.

Flames leapt and the fire began to crackle and he stood up. He tossed a spent match into the fire and closed the grate. 'I do know you,' he said. 'The train, the full train from London to Cornwall some months ago. You were in my carriage.'

'As I remember it, you were in mine.'

He smiled and her heart gave a dangerous, unexpected flutter. 'I can't argue with that. I was lucky to get a ticket at all.' He dusted soot from his hands onto his trousers. 'I remembered you as soon as we parted at the post office. I went back, but you'd already left.'

He'd gone back. The fact was unnerving and Eleanor hid her disquiet beneath an inspection of the caravan. 'You're living here?' she said.

'For the time being. It belongs to the farmer who employs me.'

'I thought you'd finished working for Mr Nicolson.' She cursed herself. Now he would know she'd asked about him. He didn't react and she quickly changed the subject. 'There's no running water or electricity.'

'I don't need those things.'

'Where do you cook?'

He nodded at the fire.

'Where do you bathe?'

He inclined his head towards the stream.

Eleanor raised her eyebrows.

He laughed. 'I find it peaceful here.'

'Peaceful?'

'Haven't you ever wanted to drop out of the world?'

Eleanor thought of the rigours of being Mother, the hatred she felt when her own mother nodded approvingly, the constant watching that had made her bones stiffen and the cogs of her mind tighten as if elastic bands were holding them rigid. 'No,' she said, in that approximation of a light voice she'd perfected over the years, 'I can't say I have.'

'I suppose it's not for everybody,' he said with a shrug. 'Would you like a cup of tea while your things dry?'

Eleanor's glance followed his gesturing arm to a saucepan on the stovetop. 'Well,' she said. It was cold, after all, and her shoes were still wet. 'Perhaps just while I wait for the rain to stop.'

He brewed the tea and she asked about the saucepan and he laughed and told her he didn't have a kettle but it seemed to do the trick.

'You don't like kettles?'

'I like them well enough; I just don't own one.'

'Not even at home?'

'This is my home; at least it is for now.'

'But where do you go when you leave?'

'To the next place. I have itchy feet,' he explained. 'I don't stay anywhere for long.'

'I don't think I could bear not to have a home.'

'People are my home, the ones I love.'

Eleanor smiled, bittersweet. She could remember saying something very similar, many years, a lifetime, ago.

'You don't agree?'

'People change, don't they?' She hadn't meant to sound so tart. 'A house, though – a house with walls and a floor and a roof on top; with rooms full of special things; with memories in the shadows – well, it's dependable. Safe and real and . . .'

'Honest?' He handed her a cup of steaming tea and sat in the chair beside her.

'Yes,' Eleanor said. 'Yes, that's it exactly. Honest and good and true.' She smiled, embarrassed suddenly to have expressed such a vehement opinion. She felt exposed, and odd – what kind of person felt such things about a house? But he smiled, too, and she glimpsed that although he disagreed he understood.

It had been a long time since Eleanor had met someone

new, since she'd been able to relax enough to enquire and listen and respond. She let down her guard, and spoke with him, asking him questions about his life. He'd grown up in the Far East, his father an archaeologist and his mother an avid traveller; they'd encouraged him to make his own life and not to be bound by society's expectations of him. Sentiments Eleanor could almost remember feeling herself.

Time passed in a strange unnatural way, as if the atmosphere inside the caravan existed outside the ebbs and flows of the wider world. The fabric of reality had dissolved so it was just the two of them. Eleanor had observed over the years that even without a watch she was able to tell the time accurately to within five minutes, but here she lost track completely. It wasn't until she chanced to see a small clock standing on the windowsill that she realised two hours had passed.

'I have to go,' she gasped, handing him her empty teacup as she stood. Such carelessness was unprecedented. It was unthinkable. The girls, Anthony, Mother . . . what would they be saying?

He stood, too, but neither of them moved. That same strange current passed between them, the one she'd noticed on the train, and Eleanor felt a compulsion to stay, to hide, never to leave that room. She should have said, 'Goodbye,' but what she said instead was, 'I still have your handkerchief.'

'From the train?' He laughed. 'I told you: it's yours.'

'I can't. It was one thing before, I had no way of returning it to you, but now . . .'

'Now?'

'Well, now I know where you are.'

'Yes,' he said. 'You do.'

Eleanor felt a chill travel down her spine. He hadn't touched her but she realised that she wanted him to. She had a sense of herself at the edge of a precipice, and in that moment she wanted to fall. Later she would realise that she already had.

'You've certainly got a spring in your step,' her mother noted later that afternoon. 'It's a wonder what being caught out in the rain can do for one's spirits.'

And that night, when Eleanor climbed into bed beside Anthony, when she reached for him and he patted her hand before rolling away, she lay very still in the dark, tracing the lines on the ceiling, listening as her husband's breathing steadied and deepened, trying to remember when she'd become so isolated, and seeing in her mind's eye the young man from the train, the man whose first name, she realised only now, she still didn't know; who'd made her laugh and think and soften, and who was only a walk away.

At first it was simply about feeling alive after so many years. Eleanor hadn't noticed she was turning into stone. She knew she'd changed over the decade or so since Anthony had returned from the war, but she hadn't appreciated just how great a toll her determination to look after him, to protect and make him well, to keep the girls from being hurt, had taken. And there was Ben, so free and light and good-humoured. The affair offered escape and closeness and selfish pleasure, and it was easy enough to tell herself he was merely an addiction, a temporary balm.

But the symptoms of addiction – the obsessive thoughts, the disturbed sleep, the exquisite pleasure derived from the scribbling of someone else's name on a fresh sheet of paper, of seeing it written there, a thought made real – are remarkably similar to those of falling in love, and Eleanor didn't realise at once what was happening. Then again, she'd never imagined it was possible to love two people at once. She was shocked when she caught herself humming one day, an old ballet melody she hadn't thought of in an age, and realised that being with Ben made her feel just as she had when she first met Anthony, as if the world were suddenly, startlingly, brighter than it had been before.

She was in love with him.

The words in her head were astonishing and yet they rang with truth. She'd forgotten love could be like that, simple and easy and joyous. The love she felt for Anthony had deepened over the decades, and it had changed; life had thrown the pair of them challenges and love had adapted to meet them. Love had come to mean putting someone else first, sacrificing, keeping the patched-up ship from sinking in the storms. With Ben, though, love was a little rowboat in which one floated calm above it all.

When she fell pregnant, Eleanor knew at once whose baby it was. Even so, she made a point of counting back over the weeks, just to make sure. It would have been so much easier had the baby been Anthony's.

Eleanor never considered lying to Ben, and yet she didn't tell him at once. The human brain has a knack for tackling complex problems with denial and Eleanor simply focused on her joy: there was going to be a baby, she'd always dreamed of having another, a baby would make Anthony happy. More than that, another child would make him well. This idea had been part of her thinking for so long it didn't occur to Eleanor to question it.

The knotty issue of the baby's paternity she refused at first to acknowledge. Even as her belly began to harden and she felt the flutter of small movements, Eleanor nursed her secret to herself. At four months, though, having broken the wonderful news to Anthony and the girls, she knew that it was time to talk to Ben. She was starting to show.

As she considered how to tell him, Eleanor realised she was dreading it, but not because she feared Ben would make things difficult. Ever since the first day in the caravan, she'd been waiting for him to disappear, anticipating bleakly the day she'd turn up and he'd be gone. Each time she'd walked along the stream to meet him, she'd held her breath, preparing for the worst. She'd certainly never spoken the word 'love' out loud. The thought of losing him had been agony, but Eleanor continued to remind herself that he was a drifter, and that she'd known it from the start. It had been part of the attraction and the reason she'd allowed herself to become involved at all. His temporariness had seemed the very antithesis to the burden she carried. One day he would leave, she'd told herself, and it would be over. No ties; no regrets; no real harm done.

But she'd been fooling herself, and now Eleanor saw just how false and blustering her casual attitude had been. Faced with delivering the news that was bound to make him run, her bohemian lover, a man who didn't even have a kettle to his name, she realised how deeply she'd come to depend upon him: his comfort and humour, his kind and gentle ways. She loved him, and despite the practical solution his leaving would provide, she didn't want him to go.

Even as she thought it, though, Eleanor cursed herself for entertaining naive hopes. Of course things couldn't stay the same. She was going to have a baby. She was married to Anthony. He was her husband and she loved him, she always would. The only thing for it was to tell Ben he was going to be a father, and watch him pack his bags.

She hadn't counted on biology. She hadn't counted on love.

'A baby,' he'd said with wonderment when she told him. 'A baby.'

There was an unusual look on his face, a smile of joy and pleasure, but, more than that, of awe. Even before Theo was born, Ben had fallen in love with him.

'We've made a little person,' he said, he who had shied away from responsibility and commitment all his life. 'I never imagined it would be like this. I feel connected to the baby, and to you; the tie is unbreakable. Do you feel it too?'

What could she say? She *did* feel it too. The baby tied Eleanor to Ben in a way that was quite separate from the love she felt for Anthony, the future she envisaged for her family at Loeanneth.

Ben's excitement over the next few months, his optimism and refusal to countenance even the slightest suggestion that their baby's conception was anything other than perfect and desired, was contagious.

Ben was so convinced things would fall into place – 'They always do,' he'd said, 'I've lived my entire life letting things happen as they must' – that Eleanor started to believe him. Why couldn't things continue as they had, she and the baby at Loeanneth and Ben here? It had worked so far.

But Ben had different ideas, and in the summertime, as her due date drew near, he told her he was leaving the caravan. She'd thought at first he meant to move on from Cornwall, and the sudden change of heart burned, but then he pushed a strand of her hair behind her ear and said, 'I need to be closer. I've taken a new position I saw advertised in the local paper. Mr Harris said that I could start next week. There's a boathouse, apparently, where garden staff sometimes stay?'

Perhaps Eleanor's worry showed on her face, for he went on quickly, 'I won't make things difficult, I promise.' He placed both hands gently on her firm, round belly. 'But I have to be closer, Eleanor. I need to be with you both. You and the baby, you're my home.'

Ben started work at Loeanneth in the late summer of 1932. He walked up the driveway one afternoon, in the middle of a hot spell, looking for all the world as if he knew nothing of the estate except that a position on the garden staff had been advertised. Even then, Eleanor convinced herself that things would all work out. Ben had a secure position from which to watch his baby grow; she would be able to see him whenever it pleased her; and Anthony, dear Anthony, need never know the truth.

She was living in a fool's paradise, of course. Love, her excitement about the baby's impending arrival, the long stretch of summer – all had blinded her to reality, but it didn't take long for paradise to lose its sheen. Ben's proximity made the whole affair real. He had existed for Eleanor previously in a different realm, but now, here, he was transplanted into the life she shared with her family, and Eleanor's guilt, long suppressed, began to stir.

She'd been wrong to betray Anthony. Eleanor saw it so clearly now, she couldn't imagine what she'd been thinking. What had come over her? Anthony was her dear love. She saw his bright young face in her mind's eye – that morning so long ago when he'd rescued her from the path of the omnibus, their wedding day when he'd smiled and squeezed her hand and she'd glimpsed their future stretching ahead of them, the afternoon at the railway station when he'd gone off to war, so eager to be useful – and it made her want to curl up and die from shame.

Eleanor began to avoid the garden. It was a fitting punishment; the garden had always been her favourite part of Loeanneth, a place of comfort and solace, and she deserved to lose it. But there was another reason she stayed away. Her guilt had nurtured a neurotic fear that she would accidentally reveal herself, that there'd be an encounter with Ben and somehow she'd give up her secret. She couldn't risk it: the consequences for Anthony would be devastating. She turned away quickly from the window if she ever caught a glimpse of Ben striding across the grounds, and she began to lie awake at night, worrying about what would happen if he decided he wanted more of their baby than she was willing to give him.

But no matter how she berated herself, no matter how contrite she felt, Eleanor could never wholly regret the affair. How could she, when her actions had given her Theo? She'd loved the little boy specially from the moment she knew she

was carrying him, but after he was born she *cherished* him.
It wasn't that she loved him more than she'd loved her infant
daughters, rather that she was a different woman now to the
one she'd been back then. Life had changed her. She was
older, sadder, in greater need of comfort. She was able to
love this baby with a liberating selflessness. Best of all,
with Theo, when it was just the two of them, she could be
Eleanor. Mother was gone.

Never, not once, amongst all the scenarios she'd imagined
and worried about, had Eleanor considered the fact that
Anthony's condition might get worse, rather than better,
after Theo's birth. She'd come to believe so firmly over the
years that a new baby – a son! – was just what he needed to
get well, that there was room for no alternative in her mind.
But she'd been wrong. The trouble started almost immediately, when Theo was only a few weeks old.

Anthony adored him, cradling him gently, staring with
wonder into his small, perfect face, but his joy was often
tinged with melancholy, a bitter shame that his life should be
so perfect when others had suffered such privations. Worse
than that, sometimes when the baby cried, a look would
settle on his face, a blank expression, as if he were distracted
by other things, secret things, playing out inside his head.

It was those nights when the bad dreams came – the fearful shaking, the instructions to 'Stop the baby crying', to
'Keep him quiet', and Eleanor had to use all her strength
to prevent him charging down the hall to do it himself – that
she wondered what on earth she'd done.

And then on Clementine's twelfth birthday they gave her
the glider. It had been Anthony's idea, and a good one, but

Eleanor's hopes of avoiding the garden were shot. They'd already had their lunch when Clemmie unwrapped the gift and ran outside, so it was only the tea-and-cake course left before the formal part of the day was over. Eleanor told herself that no harm could come in so short a time, and issued weary instructions to the maid to bring the tray into the garden.

The weather was beautiful, one of those crisp, sunny autumn afternoons during which a daring person might still swim. Everybody had entered into the celebratory spirit of the day, larking about on the lawn, tossing the glider, laughing when it almost took a scalp; but Eleanor was tense. She was aware that Ben was working down by the lake, anxious that her family shouldn't see the two of them together, worried that Ben would notice Theo's basket and find a reason to make his way up to the lawn to join the party.

He wouldn't do that; he'd promised her he wouldn't. But fear makes a person think crazy things and she just wanted the day to be over, for them to have their cake and tea and return again to the safety of the house. Clementine, however, had other ideas. It felt, in fact, as if the whole family was involved in a conspiracy against her. No one wanted tea, they waved aside offers of cake, and she was stuck playing Mother, when all she wanted was to be alone.

And then Clemmie, who seemed to have a knack for choosing precisely the worst moments to exercise her natural recklessness, began climbing the great sycamore. Eleanor's heart was in her mouth, her nerves already jangling, she didn't think that she could bear it. She stood beneath the tree, focused intently on her youngest daughter as she scaled it, feet bare, skirts tucked, knees scraped, determined that if Clemmie were to fall, she, Eleanor, was going to catch her.

Which was how she missed it when it happened. Nanny Rose was the first to notice; she gasped and reached to clutch Eleanor's hand. 'Quick,' she whispered. 'The baby.'

The words were chilling. The world seemed to tilt on its axis as Eleanor glanced over her shoulder and saw Anthony heading towards Theo's basket. The little one was crying and she could see from Anthony's stiff and awkward stance that he wasn't himself.

Rose had already started up the lawn. She was one of the few people who knew about Anthony; Eleanor hadn't told her, she'd figured it out herself. Her father had suffered similarly, she'd said, on the night she came to tell Eleanor she'd be there to help if needed.

'Daffyd,' Eleanor said, 'take the girls to the boat.'

He must have heard the panic in her voice because it took only a split second for him to understand, and then, with his jolliest storyteller voice, gather Deborah and Clemmie to him and start for where the boat was moored in the stream.

Eleanor ran; she almost ran straight into Alice, who was hurrying to follow her sisters. Her heart was pounding and she could think only that she had to get to Anthony in time.

One look at his eyes when she reached him and she could see he wasn't there. He'd gone to wherever it was he went when the darkness came upon him. 'The baby,' he was saying, his voice frantic, 'make him stop, make him quiet.'

Eleanor held her husband tightly, steering him back towards the house, whispering to him that everything was all right. When she had the chance, she looked back at Nanny

Rose and saw that she was settling Theo. Rose caught her eye and Eleanor knew that she would keep the little one safe.

That night, when Anthony had fallen into a heavy, drug-induced sleep, Eleanor slipped out of the bedroom and walked, barefoot, along the hall. She went carefully down the stairs, avoiding the pull in Grandfather Horace's Baluch carpet, her shadow skulking along the floor behind her.

The flagstones of the garden path still held the day's heat at their core and Eleanor relished their solidity beneath the soft soles of her feet. Those soles had been tough once upon a time.

When she reached the edge of the lake, Eleanor stopped and lit one of the cigarettes that no one knew she smoked. She drew deeply on it.

She'd missed the garden. Friend of her childhood.

The lake lapped in the darkness, the night-birds rearranged their wings, a small creature – a fox, perhaps – darted away from her in sudden alarm.

Eleanor finished her cigarette and went quickly to the stream. She unbuttoned her dress and slipped it over her head so she was wearing only her slip.

It wasn't a cold night, though it was too cool really to swim. But Eleanor had a burning in her chest. She wanted to feel reborn. She wanted to feel alive and free and untethered. She wanted to lose herself, to forget everything and everyone she knew. *Haven't you ever wanted to drop out of the world?* Ben had asked her in the caravan. Yes, she had, she did, tonight more than ever.

She submerged herself and sank to the bottom, the reeds cool and slippery against her feet, the water thick with sediment on her hands. She imagined she was a piece of driftwood being buffeted back and forth by the current, no responsibilities, no worries.

She broke the moonlit surface and floated on her back, listening to the night sounds: a horse in a nearby paddock, the birds in the woods, the gurgling of the stream.

At some point she realised she was no longer alone, and somehow she knew that it was Ben. She swam to the bank and walked out of the water, then went to sit beside him on the fallen log. He took off his coat and wrapped it around her and without having to be told exactly what was wrong, he held her and stroked her hair and told her not to worry, that everything was going to be all right. And Eleanor let him say it, because she'd *missed* him, and the relief at being in his arms right here, right now, made her throat constrict.

But Eleanor knew the truth. She was just like the queen in *Eleanor's Magic Doorway*, who so desired a child she'd been willing to make a deal with the devil to get him. She'd opened the door and walked through it and loved where she should not, and now she must suffer the consequences. The world was a place of balance and natural justice; there was always a price to pay, and it was too late now to shut the door.

Thirty

Cornwall, 2003

'Well, I'll be damned.' Clive was staring at Sadie, his blue eyes wide behind his glasses as the implications of what they'd just discovered fell into place.

'I don't know why it didn't occur to me before,' she said.

'No reason it should. I was here in 1933 and met the entire family. No one even hinted at such a thing.'

'Do you think Anthony knew?'

Clive whistled softly through his teeth as he considered the possibility. 'It certainly lends a darker tinge to events if he did.'

Sadie had to agree. 'Was there anything in the journals?' she asked. 'Around the time Deborah paid her visit to his study?'

'If there was, it was too cryptic for me to grasp.'

'What about during the interviews in 1933? I know you said there was no hint that Anthony wasn't Theo's biological father, but was there anything else, anything at all? Some small detail that didn't seem important at the time but might matter now?'

Clive considered. At length he spoke doubtfully. 'There *was* something. I don't know that it means much, I feel a bit silly even mentioning it, but back when we first carried out our interviews, my boss recommended that the Edevanes talk to the media. He was of the opinion that enlisting the public's sympathy would mean a whole lot more eyes on the lookout for the missing lad. It was stifling that day, all of us in the library downstairs, a photographer, the journalist, Anthony and Eleanor Edevane sitting side by side on the sofa while outside police were searching the lake.' He shook his head. 'Terrible, it was. Just terrible. In fact, Eleanor suffered a bit of a collapse, and that's when Anthony called an abrupt end to the interview. I didn't blame him at all, but what he said stuck in my mind. "Have some pity," he said, "my wife is in shock, her child is gone."' Clive looked at Sadie, a new determination in his gaze. 'Not "our child", but "*her* child".'

'It might just be that he was empathising with her, describing *her* reaction in particular?'

Clive, with growing excitement, said, 'No, I don't think so. In fact, the more I think about it, the more suspicious it seems.'

Sadie felt a pull of resistance. As Clive became increasingly certain that Anthony had known he wasn't Theo's father, her urge grew to prove that he hadn't. There was no logic behind her obstinacy; she simply didn't want to believe it. To this point, she and Alice had been acting under the assumption that Anthony killed Theo accidentally, a terrible consequence of a shell-shock-induced rage. But if Theo, the long-awaited, much-adored son, wasn't his biological child, and if Anthony had somehow discovered the truth when he learned of his wife's infidelity, then a much grislier possibility opened up.

If Donald were here, Sadie knew, he'd accuse her of

letting the family get under her skin, and so, as Clive continued to list the many small observations he'd made of Anthony in 1933, twisting them now to fit his developing theory, she tried to keep an open mind. She owed it to Alice not to let her personal feelings cloud her judgement. But it was an ugly picture Clive painted. The thought Anthony would have had to put into selecting the perfect night to commit his crime, an annual party during which he knew his wife would be run off her feet performing her duties as hostess, with their staff too busy to notice anything unusual. The convenient removal of Rose Waters, whose vigilance, Eleanor had lamented in her police interview, would never have allowed any harm to befall her charge. The young nanny's replacement with old Hilda Bruen who could be counted on to furbish herself with a draught of whisky if party noise threatened her sleep. It was all so premeditated. And what about Eleanor, where did the theory leave her? 'Do you still think she knew?' Sadie asked.

'I think she must have. It's the only thing that explains her resistance to offering a reward. She knew it was a pointless exercise, that her son wasn't going to be found.'

'But why would she have helped to cover up the crime? Why didn't she say anything? She stayed married to Anthony Edevane, happily by all accounts!'

'Domestic situations are complicated. Maybe he made other threats, maybe he threatened Benjamin. That would certainly explain why Munro disappeared so completely off the scene. Maybe Eleanor felt that she was in some way to blame, that her infidelity had driven him to it in the first place.'

Sadie thought back to her conversation with Alice, the

description of Eleanor as possessing a strong and specific set of moral values. Presumably a woman with ethics like that would have felt tremendous guilt for having broken her marital vows. But could she possibly have accepted Theo's death as due punishment? No. It was one thing to forgive Anthony an accident – and even that was a stretch – but it was quite another to excuse the murder of her child. And no matter Sadie's determination to keep an open mind, she just couldn't marry the descriptions she'd read of Anthony Edevane, gentle father, beloved husband, brave ex-soldier, with this picture of a vengeful monster.

'So,' said Clive, 'what do you think?'

He was eagerly awaiting Sadie's agreement, but she couldn't give it. They were missing something. It could *almost* be made to make sense, but the missing piece of puzzle was crucial. 'I think we should go downstairs, crack open the Thermos, and have a cuppa. Let it all percolate for a while.'

Clive was deflated but he nodded. Sun was streaming into the room now and as Sadie gathered up the scattered envelopes he went to the open window. 'Well, I never,' he said. 'Is that who I think it is?'

Sadie joined him, scanning the familiar view, the tangled garden and the lake beyond. Two figures were making their slow way up the path. Sadie couldn't have been more surprised had she seen baby Theo himself toddling towards the house. 'It's Alice,' she said. 'Alice Edevane and her assistant, Peter.'

'Alice Edevane,' Clive repeated, with a soft whistle of disbelief. 'Come home at last.'

*

'I changed my mind,' was all Alice said by way of explanation when Sadie and Clive met her in the entrance hall and
she and Clive had been reacquainted. Peter, having delivered
his employer to the door, had been dispatched back to the
car to fetch something she referred to rather mysteriously
as 'the supplies', and Alice was standing on the dusty tiles
with a vaguely indignant air, looking for all the world like
a rakish country chatelaine who'd just popped out for a
morning stroll but was home now and none too pleased with
the efforts of her bumbling staff. She continued briskly, 'The
old place could certainly do with a polish. Shall we sit in the
library?'

'Let's,' Sadie agreed, offering Clive a slight, baffled shrug
as they followed Alice through a door on the other side
of the hall. It was the room Sadie had glimpsed through the
window the first day she'd stumbled upon Loeanneth,
the place where police had carried out their interviews in
1933, and where Clive said Anthony and Eleanor had met
the journalist and photographer the day after Theo was
reported missing.

Now Clive sat at one end of the sofa and Sadie the other.
It was all very dusty, but short of performing an emergency
spring clean, there didn't seem much to be done. Presumably
Alice was here for an update on their investigations and she
wasn't the sort of person to brook opposition or let a little
grime get in her way.

Sadie waited for Alice to sit in the armchair and begin
firing questions at them, but the old woman continued
pacing instead, from the door to the fireplace to the desk
beneath the window, pausing momentarily in each spot
before moving again. Her chin was held high, but Sadie, with

the detective's trained eye, could see through this performance. Though she was trying desperately to mask the fact,
Alice was nervy, unsettled. And little wonder. There could be
few experiences stranger than arriving at one's childhood
home, seventy years after having left it, only to find it still
furnished exactly as it had been. And that was before one
took into consideration the traumatic event that had sent the
Edevane family packing. Alice stopped near the desk and
lifted the sketch of the child's face.

'Is it him?' Sadie asked gently, remembering the otherworldly beauty of the illustration she'd glimpsed through the
window on the morning she discovered Loeanneth. 'Theo?'

Alice didn't look up and for a second Sadie thought she
hadn't heard. She was about to repeat herself when Alice
said, 'It was drawn by a friend of the family, a man by the
name of Daffyd Llewellyn. He sketched it the day Theo
died.' She glanced up at the window, her jaw tightening. The
encroaching brambles blocked most of the view but Alice
didn't seem to notice. 'I saw him carrying it back from the
stream. He used to stay with us over the summer, in the Mulberry Room upstairs. He'd head out early most mornings, an
easel over his shoulder, a sketch block under his arm. I'd
never known him to draw Theo until I saw this picture.'

'An interesting coincidence,' Sadie probed carefully. 'The
first time he drew your brother was the day Theo disappeared.'

Alice looked up sharply. 'A coincidence, perhaps, but I
wouldn't call it interesting. Mr Llewellyn had no part in
Theo's fate. I'm glad he drew the portrait, though; it brought
my mother great comfort over the weeks that followed.'

'Daffyd Llewellyn died very soon after Theo, didn't he?'

Sadie remembered her interview with Clive, the suspicions she'd had about the timings of the two events.

Clive nodded, as Alice said, 'Police found his body during the search. It was a most unfortunate . . .'

'Coincidence?' Sadie offered.

'Turn of events,' Alice said pointedly. She returned her attention to the sketch and her expression softened. 'Such a tragedy, such a dreadful waste. One always wonders, of course . . .' But whatever it was she wondered, she didn't say. 'We all cared a great deal for Mr Llewellyn, but he and Mother were extremely close. He didn't much enjoy the society of other adults and she was a notable exception. It was a double blow for her when he was found so soon after Theo disappeared. Ordinarily she'd have sought comfort in her friendship with him. He was like a father to her.'

'The sort of person she'd have told her secrets to?'

'I should imagine. She didn't have many other friends, not the sort in whom she might have confided.'

'Not her own mother?'

Alice had been gazing still at the sketch but she looked up now, her expression wryly amused. 'Constance?'

'She lived with you, didn't she?'

'Under sufferance.'

'Might your mother have confided in her?'

'Certainly not. My mother and grandmother never got on. I don't know the cause of the animosity, but it was old and it ran deep. In fact, after Theo died and we left Loeanneth, the last tenuous ties between them were broken. Grandmother didn't come with us to London. Her health wasn't good; she'd been confused in the months leading up to Midsummer and afterwards went quickly downhill. She was sent to a home in Brighton where she lived out her days. It was one of the only times I saw Mother show any real affection for her: she was very particular that only the best nursing home would do for Grandmother, that everything had to be perfect. Families are complicated, aren't they, Detective?'

More than you know, thought Sadie, exchanging a glance with Clive. He nodded.

'What is it?' Alice, as astute as ever, looked between them. 'Have you found something?'

Sadie still had the letter from Eleanor to Ben in her back pocket and she passed it now to Alice, who ran her gaze over its contents, a single brow lifting. 'Yes, well, we'd established already that my mother and Benjamin Munro were engaged in a love affair.'

Sadie explained then about the other page she'd found in the boathouse, in which Eleanor talked about her pregnancy. 'I presumed she was writing to your father when he was away at war. She mentioned how much she missed him, how difficult it would be to have the baby without him, but when I found this page upstairs I realised she'd been writing to Ben.' Sadie hesitated briefly. 'About Theo.'

Now, Alice sank slowly into the armchair and Sadie finally understood the expression about having the wind knocked out of one's sails. 'You think Theo was Ben's son,' she said.

'I do.' Short and sharp, but Sadie couldn't see that there was much else to say on the matter.

Realisation had drained Alice's face of colour and she was staring into the middle distance, her lips moving slightly as if she were adding numbers in her head. In London she had seemed formidable, but now Sadie glimpsed vulnerability. It wasn't that Alice appeared frail; rather, that having stepped out from behind her own legend, she'd revealed herself a human being with ordinary frailties. 'Yes,' she said eventually, a hint of wonder in her voice. 'Yes, it makes sense. It makes a lot of sense.'

Clive cleared his throat. 'It rather changes things, don't you think?'

Alice glanced at him. 'It doesn't change my brother's fate.'

'No, of course not, I meant—'

'You meant my father's motive. I know what you're suggesting and I can tell you there's no way my father would have harmed Theo on purpose.'

Sadie had felt the same way when Clive first floated the theory upstairs; but now, seeing Alice's vehement refusal even to consider the possibility, she wondered whether she, too, was letting a profound distaste for the idea cloud her judgement.

There came the tread of footsteps in the room outside and Peter appeared at the door, back from his mysterious task. 'Alice?' he said haltingly. 'Are you all right?' He turned to Sadie, his eyes wide with concern. 'Is everything all right?'

'I'm fine,' said Alice. 'Everything's fine.'

Peter was by her side now, asking whether she'd like a glass of water, some fresh air, some lunch, all of which she flapped away with her hand. 'Really, Peter, I'm quite well. It's just the surprise of being back here, the memories.' She handed the sketch to him. 'Look,' she said, 'my little brother. That's Theo.'

'Oh my, what a wonderful drawing. Did you . . . ?'

'Of course not.' She almost laughed. 'A family friend, Daffyd Llewellyn, drew it.'

'The writer,' said Peter, as pleased by the news as if he were learning the answer to a long-held question. 'Of course. Mr Llewellyn. That makes perfect sense.'

Mention of the writer reminded Sadie that the conversation had shifted course before she'd satisfied herself as to the timing of his suicide. It occurred to her now that he might have felt guilty, not because he harmed Theo, but because he'd failed to stop Anthony. 'Was your father close to Daffyd Llewellyn?' she asked.

'They got on very well,' said Alice. 'My father regarded him as a member of family, but beyond that they had a great professional respect for each other, both being medical men.'

They had more than that in common, Sadie remembered. Daffyd Llewellyn, like Anthony, had been unable to continue practising medicine after a nervous collapse. 'Do you have any idea what brought on Mr Llewellyn's breakdown?'

'I never got the chance to ask him. I've always regretted that – I meant to, he was behaving uncharacteristically before the Midsummer party, but I was focused on other things and left it too long.'

'There was no one else who might have known?'

'Mother, perhaps, but she certainly never said, and the only other person who knew him as a young man was Grandmother. Getting the truth from her would have been a feat; there was no love lost between them. Constance couldn't countenance weakness, and as far as she was concerned Mr Llewellyn was beneath contempt. Her pique when his OBE was announced was prodigious. The rest of us were immensely proud – I only wish he'd lived to accept it himself.'

'He was your mentor,' said Peter gently. 'Like Miss Talbot was for me.'

Alice lifted her chin, as if to stave off tears if they so much as dared to threaten. She nodded. 'Yes, for a time, until I decided I'd outgrown him. Such hubris! But then, the young are always so eager to shake off the old, aren't they?'

Peter smiled; sadly, it seemed to Sadie.

The memory must have triggered something in Alice for she sighed with determination and brought her hands together. 'But enough of all that,' she said, turning to Peter with renewed energy. 'Today is not for regrets, unless to overcome them. Have you got the supplies?'

He nodded. 'I've left them by the front door.'

'Splendid. Now do you think you might find—'

'The floorboard with the moose-head whorl? I'm on it.'

'Excellent.'

Sadie ignored talk of moose heads and took back Eleanor's letter when it was proffered. She couldn't imagine what it would feel like to read a letter like that, written by her own mother. A voice from the long-ago past, reaching into the present to complicate a truth she'd always held dear. It occurred to her that it was a very brave thing to do, to write one's feelings down on paper and give them to another person.

An image of Charlotte Sutherland came to mind. In all her panic at receiving Charlotte's letters, Sadie hadn't stopped for a moment to consider the act of courage involved in writing and sending them. There was something incredibly intimate about the transference of sentiment; and in Charlotte's case, to write not once, but twice, had been to risk rejection a second time. Sadie had all but tripped over herself in her rush to grant that rejection the first time – was Charlotte brave or foolhardy to come back for more? 'What I don't understand,' she said, as much to herself as to the others, 'is why anyone would keep a letter like this. It's one thing to write it in the heat of the moment, but to keep it forever after . . .' She shook her head. 'It's so personal, so *incriminating*.'

A smile appeared on Alice's face and she seemed more herself. 'That's a question you only ask because you're not a letter-writer yourself, DC Sparrow. If you were, you'd know that a writer never destroys her work. Even if she fears the power of its contents to implicate her.'

Sadie was wondering about that when there came a call from outside. 'Hello? Anybody there?'

It was Bertie's voice. 'My grandfather,' she said, surprised. 'Excuse me a minute.'

'I've brought lunch,' he said as she reached the front door, holding up a basket loaded with a huge Thermos and bread that smelled fresh from the oven. 'I tried to call, but your phone rang out.'

'Oh, bugger, sorry. I had it on silent.'

Bertie nodded understandingly. 'You wanted to focus.'

'Something like that.' Sadie took out her phone and checked the screen. There were six missed calls. Two from Bertie, the other four from Nancy.

'What is it? You're frowning.'

'Nothing. Never mind.' She smiled at him, suppressing a growing wave of concern. Nancy was single-minded when it came to her daughter's disappearance, but to make this many calls was unusual. 'Come inside and meet everyone.'

'Everyone?'

Sadie explained about the surprise arrivals, glad as she did that they were there. She had a feeling Bertie might otherwise have been angling swiftly to turn their lunch conversation to the subject of Charlotte Sutherland or the fallout from the Bailey case, two topics Sadie was eager to avoid.

'Well then, it's a good thing I always cook extra,' he said cheerfully as Sadie led him towards the library.

Alice was standing with her arms crossed, glancing at her watch and drumming her fingertips, and Clive looked relieved that Sadie had returned.

'This is my grandfather, Bertie,' she said. 'He's brought lunch.'

'How kind of you,' said Alice, as she came forward to shake his hand. 'I'm Alice Edevane.' All hint of nerviness had gone and she was suddenly mistress of the house, exuding the sort of effortless authority Sadie figured they must have taught in wealthy families back then. 'What's on the menu?'

'I've made soup,' said Bertie. 'And hard-boiled eggs.'

'My favourite.' Alice rewarded him with a short nod of surprised pleasure. 'However did you know?'

'All the best people prefer hard-boiled eggs.'

Remarkably, Alice smiled, a genuine show of appreciation that quite transformed her face.

'Granddad's been baking all week for the hospital stall down at the Solstice Festival,' Sadie volunteered, apropos of nothing really.

Alice was nodding approval when Peter returned, a small black pouch in hand.

'Ready when you are,' he said, and then, noticing Bertie, 'Oh, hello there.'

Introductions were briefly made, and there was a confused moment during which Alice and Peter debated whether to carry on directly with their planned task or stop first for a bite to eat, before deciding it would be rude to let Bertie's soup get cold.

'Splendid,' said Bertie. 'Perhaps you can show us the best place to eat. I wasn't sure how habitable the house would be so I brought a picnic rug.'

'Very sensible,' said Alice. 'This is a garden made for picnics. Rather overgrown at present, I'm afraid, but there are some lovely pockets down by the stream and not too far to walk.'

Alice left the room with Peter and Bertie, chatting busily about an enormous sycamore tree in the garden, a wooden glider, and the boathouse beyond. 'My sisters and I spent most of our time down there,' Alice was saying, her voice fading as they disappeared down the stone path. 'There's a tunnel in the house that leads all the way to the edge of the woods, right near the boathouse. We used to have the most tremendous games of hide-and-seek.'

The morning had taken a strange turn, and as silence fell, Sadie turned to Clive with a slight shrug of bewilderment. 'I guess we'll break for lunch?'

He nodded. 'Looks that way. I'll walk with you, but I won't be able to stay. My daughter and her family are taking me for an afternoon's antiqueing.' He looked less than thrilled by the planned outing and Sadie winced in commiseration. They walked to where the others were waiting, and it was only as they skirted the lake that Sadie realised they were heading in the opposite direction to where the car was parked. Furthermore, it occurred to her, she hadn't seen Clive's car when she arrived that morning. And in any case, the entrance gate had been locked. 'Clive,' she said, 'how did you get here today?'

'By boat,' he said. 'I keep a little dinghy moored with a friend's trawler in the village. It's the easiest way to get between here and there – quicker than driving.'

'A lovely journey, too, I'll bet. Such peaceful countryside.'

He smiled. 'Sometimes you can go the whole way without glimpsing another soul.'

Sadie's phone rang then, shattering the peace and quiet, and she pulled it out, grimacing when she glanced at the screen.

'Bad news?'

'It's Nancy Bailey. The case I was telling you about.'

'The little girl's grandmother,' he said. 'I remember. I wonder what she wants?'

'I don't know, but she's been calling all day.'

'Must be important for her to keep calling you on a Saturday.'

'Maybe. She's nothing if not dogged.'

'Will you ring her back?'

'I shouldn't really. There's an inquiry, and if the Super finds out I'm still in contact with her, it won't take long for him to put two and two together. Besides, we're busy here.'

Clive was nodding, but Sadie could tell he had reservations.

'You think I should call her?'

'It isn't for me to say, only sometimes when a case gets under your skin, it's because there's something that still needs your attention. Look at me, here, seventy years later.'

The phone rang again, Nancy Bailey's number showed on the screen, and Sadie glanced at Clive. He smiled encouragement and with a deep breath she picked up.

Thirty-one

Afterwards, Sadie found the others by the stream. The picnic blanket had been spread in the long grass beneath a willow tree, and a small dinghy called *Jenny* bobbed in the gentle current at the end of the boathouse jetty. Peter and Clive were in earnest conversation, and Alice, sitting neatly on an old chair salvaged from somewhere, was laughing at whatever Bertie had just said. Sadie sat on the edge of the blanket and absent-mindedly accepted a mug of soup. Her mind was racing, busily unpacking every piece of evidence she'd worked so hard over the past few weeks to shelve. There was a moment in the working of each case, a tipping point, when one particular clue provided a new lens through which everything else was suddenly rendered clearer, different, connected. What Nancy had just told her changed everything.

'Well?' said Clive. 'I couldn't leave until I knew what she said.'

Conversation had stopped and everyone was watching Sadie keenly. It occurred to her that all the people she'd confided in about the Bailey case and her ignominious attachment to it were assembled here on the picnic rug.

'Sadie, love?' Bertie urged gently. 'Clive said Nancy Bailey had been trying to get hold of you all day.'

The case was officially closed. She was already in about as much trouble as was possible. She feared she might just burst with the new information if she didn't let it out. Sadie took a deep breath and said, 'Nancy told me she'd had a call from the new owners of her daughter's flat.'

Bertie scratched his head. 'The new owners have her phone number?'

'It's a long story.'

'What did they say?'

'They rang to tell her that they'd spotted something written in pen on the Formica edge of the built-in kitchen table. The words read, "It was him." They wouldn't have thought much of it, she said, except that Nancy had recently been to see them and Maggie's disappearance was fresh in their minds.'

There was a moment of silence as everyone considered this.

'Who was he, and what did he do?' said Peter perplexedly.

Sadie realised Alice's assistant was the only one among them who wasn't familiar with the role she'd played in the Bailey case, her suspicion that there'd been foul play, and quickly brought him up to speed. When she'd finished he said, 'Then this "him", whoever he was, that's the man you're looking for.'

Sadie noted with vague appreciation that he'd assumed she was right in believing there was more to Maggie's disappearance than met the eye. 'I just need to figure out who he is.'

Alice hadn't spoken yet, but now she cleared her throat. 'If a woman in trouble says "It was him", it's because she thinks people will know who she meant. Did Maggie Bailey have many men in her life?'

Sadie shook her head. 'She didn't have many *people* in her life. Just her daughter Caitlyn and Nancy, her mum.'

'What about Caitlyn's father?'

'Well, yes . . .'

'Who now has custody of the little girl?'

'Yes.'

'He's remarried since separating from the child's mother, hasn't he?'

'Two years ago.'

'But they haven't any children of their own?'

'No.' Sadie thought of the time she'd seen Caitlyn at the police station, the way Steve's wife, Gemma, had done the little girl's hair in ribbons, how she was holding her hand and smiling down at her with a warmth that Sadie could feel even from where she stood. 'But his new wife seems very fond of Caitlyn.'

Alice was unmoved. 'What's the husband like?'

'Steve? Earnest, eager. I don't know him well. He was helpful with our enquiries.'

Clive frowned. 'How helpful?'

Sadie reflected on how Steve had led searches for Maggie, arrived at the police station of his own accord to offer information about her character and past, painting police a very clear picture of a flighty, irresponsible woman who liked a good time and was finding the pressure of caring for a child overwhelming. 'Very,' she said. 'In fact, I would describe him as exceptionally helpful.'

Clive made a soft noise of satisfaction, as if the answer corroborated some deep-held theory of his, and Sadie remembered, suddenly, his comment in relation to the Edevane case, about there being two ways in which the guilty usually behaved. Her skin prickled. There was the first type, he'd said, those who avoided police like the plague, and then there was the second type, the helpful ones, who sought out officers at every opportunity, putting themselves at the centre of the investigation as all the while they nursed their secret guilt.

'But there was a note,' Sadie said quickly, struggling to catch her tumbling thoughts as a terrible new picture began to form. 'A note from Maggie, in her own handwriting . . .' Her voice trailed off as she recollected the way Steve had lamented Maggie's carelessness, reproached her for forgetting he was going away that week. He'd said of the changed dates, 'I made her write it down,' before switching his words in the next sentence to, 'I wrote it down for her.' A small adjustment, but one Sadie had noticed at the time. She'd presumed it a simple slip of the tongue. He was upset and he'd mixed up his words. No big deal. Now, she wondered whether the slip had been rather more Freudian in nature. A gaffe that pointed to another instance in which he *had* forced Maggie to write down the lines he dictated.

'But *murder*?' She was thinking aloud. 'Steve?' He'd never been a suspect, not even before they found the note. He'd had an alibi, she remembered, the fishing trip to Lyme Regis. They'd verified the information he'd given them, but only because that was procedure. It had all checked out – the hotel, the time off work, the boat-hire company – and that had been the end of it. Now, though, far from absolving him, it suddenly seemed to Sadie that Steve's absence from London – a trip that took him to a distant part of the country, right when his ex-wife disappeared – presented a perfect opportunity. 'But *why*?' Against her own code of practice Sadie couldn't help but puzzle over motive. 'He and Maggie were married once. They'd loved each other. They'd had very little to do with one another since their divorce. Why on earth would he suddenly kill her?'

Alice Edevane's crisp voice cut through the tangle of Sadie's thoughts. 'One of my earliest Diggory Brent mysteries was based on a story my sister Clemmie told me. We were sitting together in Hyde Park before the Second World War and she told me about a man whose wife so longed for a child that he stole one for her. I never forgot that story. It seemed entirely plausible to me that a couple's desire for a child, and a husband's love for his wife, might lead him to take the most drastic of actions.'

Sadie pictured Gemma's kind, happy face, the way she'd been holding Caitlyn's hand as they left the police station, how naturally she'd swung the little girl onto her hip. Oh God, Sadie remembered feeling so pleased for Caitlyn when she saw them, relieved that despite the disappearance of her mother, the little girl had landed in a loving home with parents who would care for her.

Bertie's voice was gentle. 'What are you going to do, Sadie, love?'

Yes, a list of practical tasks. That would help. Far more useful than self-reproach. 'I need to re-verify Steve's alibi,' she said, 'figure out whether I can place him at Maggie's flat during the period he was supposed to be out of London. I'll need to talk to him again, but it won't be easy, not with the inquiry.'

'Could you call Donald? Get him to ask some questions in your stead?'

Sadie shook her head. 'I have to be absolutely certain

before I involve him.' She frowned as something else
occurred to her. 'I'm going to need to take another look at
Maggie's note, too, get forensics to examine it for evidence.'

'DNA?'

'That, and signs of duress. We've already had it analysed
by handwriting experts who compared it with other exam-
ples of Maggie's writing and said there were elements that
looked stilted; that it showed the hallmarks of being rushed.
It seemed neat enough to me, but they can see all sorts of
things that aren't visible to the rest of us. We presumed the
haste was due to the enormity of what she was about to do.
It made sense.'

The note had been written on an elegant piece of card
stock. Maggie had worked at WHSmith, and according to
Nancy had acquired a taste for nice stationery. The writing
had been neat as far as Sadie was concerned, but there'd been
a jagged scribble at the top of the card that had given her
pause. 'She was testing the pen,' Donald had said with a
shrug. 'I've done it hundreds of times myself.' So had Sadie,
and yet somehow it didn't fit. Why, Sadie had wondered,
would a person whose life gave the impression of a fastidious
nature, test a pen on the piece of expensive card she intended
to use for an important message?

'She wasn't in her right mind,' Donald had said when
Sadie raised it. 'She was about to walk out on her daughter,
she was under pressure, I doubt she was thinking about how
pretty the paper looked.' Sadie had bitten her tongue at the
time. The letter had been a shock, scuppering her theories
and making her seem a crazy fantasist. The last thing she
needed was to keep harping on about a bit of ink on a piece
of card. Nancy had agreed, though. 'Maggie *never* would

have done that,' she'd said. 'Maggie liked things neat and tidy, ever since she was small she needed things to be just so.'

Suddenly that scribble seemed rather important. What if it were proof that someone else had been there with Maggie? Someone who'd stood over her, perhaps even tested the pen before dictating the message she was to write?

Sadie managed to articulate these thoughts for the others, kneeling as she dug in her pocket for her phone. Thankfully, not remotely legally, she'd snapped a picture of the note before it was officially tagged and filed. Now, she searched through the photo library until she found it, handing over the phone so they could each take their turn.

She stood and began to pace. Could Steve have planned something so terrible, executed a plan so horrific? It was possible she was going mad, clutching at straws, but when she looked at the others, Sadie was reassured. An ex-cop, a crime writer and a PhD researcher. With their combined credentials, they were a crack investigation team, and they all seemed to think there was something in the new theory.

Bertie smiled, his kind, familiar face filled with something rather like pride. 'What are you going to do, Sadie, love?' he asked again. 'What happens next?'

Whether she was right or wrong, no matter what the consequences for her, if there was even the slightest chance that Steve had stood over Maggie as she wrote that note, if she'd anticipated that things were not going to end well and yet still summoned enough defiance to send a clue to investigators, then Sadie owed it to her to follow up. Or to make sure someone else did. 'I think I have to call it in,' she said.

Bertie nodded. 'I think you do, too.'

But not to Donald. There was a chance this new lead

would go nowhere. She couldn't risk getting him in trouble on her account again. She was going to have to go right to the top, even if it meant revealing herself as the leak. As Bertie and the others packed up the picnic, Sadie dialled the Met and asked to speak to Superintendent Ashford.

When the others went back to the village that afternoon, Sadie didn't go with them. Clive left in the *Jenny* straight after lunch, having extracted a firm promise from Sadie that she'd let him know as soon as she heard anything back from the Met, and Bertie, who was taking the first shift on the hospital stall, needed to report for duty by three o'clock, when the festival officially opened. He'd tried to entice Sadie with promises of fresh scones and clotted cream, but the thought of being surrounded by good cheer while every nerve in her body was wound tighter than a tick was nauseating.

Alice, however, gave Bertie one of her very rare smiles and said, 'I haven't had proper Cornish clotted cream in an age.' She frowned when Peter reminded her delicately about the mysterious task she'd been so intent on since they'd arrived, and then waved a hand declaring that it had waited this long, it could jolly well wait one more day. Besides, it would be better to check in at the hotel before the festival started and the village square became overcrowded. Alice had promised to sign books for their hotelier, a vital step in securing two rooms on festival weekend at such short notice.

So it was that Sadie stood alone, watching as the two cars disappeared down the driveway and were swallowed, one after the other, by the woods. The moment they were gone, she took out her phone. It was becoming a habit.

There'd been no missed calls – not a surprise given she'd turned the volume up as high as it would go – and she put it away with a sigh of deep disgruntlement.

Sadie hadn't been completely honest with the others when she'd told them the Met were grateful for the new lead. In truth, Ashford hadn't been remotely pleased with her call, and when he heard what she'd had to say he'd been incandescent with rage. Her ear still burned from the blasting she'd received. She couldn't swear that his spittle hadn't travelled down the phone line to scald her. She'd felt her own ire rising in response, but had fought to keep it contained. She'd let him say his piece, and then, as calmly as she could, she'd apologised for her misstep and told him she had new information. He hadn't wanted to hear it, and so, with the sinking stomach of someone gambling with the job she loved, Sadie reminded him she had Derek Maitland's number and it wouldn't look good if it turned out she was right, that a woman had been murdered, and the Met hadn't wanted to know about it.

He'd listened all right then, his breaths as hot as a dragon's, and when she finished, he'd said gruffly, 'I'll put someone on it,' and hung up in her ear. There'd been nothing more to do after that, other than to wait, and hope he felt inclined to give her the courtesy of a phone call to let her know what they'd uncovered.

And so, here she was. Sadie had to admit there were worse places to kill time. The house was different in the afternoon. With the changed angle of the sun, it was as if the whole place had breathed a sigh of settlement. The frenetic morning activity of the birds and the insects had ceased, the roof was stretching and cracking its warm joints with habitual ease, and the light that streamed through the windows was slow and satisfied.

Sadie poked about in Anthony's study for a while. His anatomy textbooks were still on the shelf above his desk, his name written neatly, hopefully, on the frontispiece, and in his bottom drawer she found his school prizes: first in Classics, Latin Hexameters and countless others. There was a photograph hidden in the dark back corner, a group of young men in scholars' gowns and caps, one of whom she recognised as a very young Anthony. The fellow standing next to him, laughing, was featured again in a framed studio portrait on the top of Anthony's desk, a soldier with wild black hair and an intelligent face. A sprig of rosemary had been placed beneath the glass, held in position by the firm setting of the frame, but Sadie could tell by its brittle brown colour it would crumble to dust and be blown away if released. There was a framed photograph of Eleanor on the desk, too, standing in front of a stone building. Sadie picked it up to have a closer look. The picture had been taken in Cambridge, she guessed, where they'd lived before Anthony surprised his wife with the rescue and return of Loeanneth.

Anthony's journals filled a whole shelf of the floor-to-ceiling bookcase against the far wall, and Sadie selected a few at random. She quickly became engrossed, reading until the dying light made her eyes strain. The entries gave no indication whatsoever that Anthony was harbouring murderous intentions. On the contrary, they were filled with his earnest attempts to 'fix' himself; his self-reproach for having let down his wife, his brother, his nation; and page after page of memory games, just like Clive had said, as he tried to force his fractured mind back together again. The guilt he felt for having survived when others had not was all-consuming; his letters to Howard, his lost friend, were heartbreaking. Simple, elegant descriptions of what it was to live, as he put it, *beyond one's usefulness*, to feel that one's life was an undeserved prize, stolen at the expense of others.

Expressions of the gratitude he felt towards Eleanor, and his deep shame in himself, were hard to read, but worse were the whispered descriptions of his terror that he would accidentally harm the people he loved most in the world. *You, dear friend, more than any other, know I'm capable of that.* (Why? Sadie frowned. Did it mean anything, or was Anthony simply saying that his friend knew him well?)

It was clear, too, that Anthony's inability to qualify as a surgeon plagued him. *It was the only thing in my mind*, he wrote, *after what happened in France. The only way I could make it right was to ensure my survival mattered, to get home to England, to work as a doctor, and help more people than I'd harmed.* But he hadn't, and Sadie felt desperately sorry for him. Her own brief taste of living without the work she loved had been punishing enough.

She turned around in the stiff wooden swivel chair to take in the rest of the dim room. It was a lonely space, sad and stale. She tried to imagine what it must have been like for Anthony, confined to such a place with only his demons and disappointments for company, frightened always that they'd overcome him. He was right to be fearful, too, for in the end that was just what happened.

Because of course Theo's death must have been an accident. Even if Ben Munro was Theo's father, and even if Anthony had learned of Eleanor's infidelity and been filled with a jealous rage, to kill his wife's child was about as heinous as a crime could be. People changed, life happened, but Sadie just wasn't able to believe it of him. Anthony's self-awareness, his anxiety that he might be capable of violence, the lengths to which he'd gone to prevent it, surely contradicted Clive's theory that he'd committed such a devastating crime on purpose. Theo's parentage was irrelevant. The timing – Theo's death and Anthony's discovery of his wife's affair – was a coincidence. Sadie frowned. Coincidence. That pesky word again.

She sighed and stretched. The long summery dusk had started to fall. Crickets had begun their evening chant in the hidden spaces of the sunburned garden and shadows within the house were lengthening. The day's warmth had pooled and was sitting now, still and thick, waiting for the cool of night to sweep it away. Sadie closed the journal and put it back into its place on the shelf. Shutting the door to Anthony's study quietly behind her, she crept downstairs to retrieve her torch. A quick shine of the light on her phone's screen – still nothing – and then she headed back up to Eleanor's writing bureau.

She had no idea, really, what she was looking for; she only knew that she was missing something and Eleanor's letters were the best place she could think of to look for it. She would start before Theo was born and read everything in the hope that along the way she'd find the vital piece of information, the lens through which all the rest would suddenly reveal itself as linked. Rather than read by correspondent, she went chronologically, starting with Eleanor's triplicate, and then finding and reading the relevant reply.

It was slow-going, but Sadie had time to fill, nowhere else to be, and a deep desire for distraction. She forced the Bailey case and Ashford out of her mind and let Eleanor's world come to life instead. It was clear that Eleanor's love for Anthony was the defining relationship of her life, a great love shadowed by the relentless horror and confusion of his awful condition. In letter after letter to doctor after doctor, she made continued pleas for help, her tone always cordial, her determination to find a cure undimmed.

But behind the polite entreaties, Eleanor was in agony, a fact made plain in her letters to Daffyd Llewellyn. For a long time he alone was entrusted with the topic of Anthony's diminishment and distress. The girls didn't know, and neither, it seemed – except in the case of a few notable, trusted exceptions – did the servants. Nor did Constance, with whom Eleanor, and Daffyd Llewellyn, too, apparently, shared a long-standing enmity.

Eleanor had made Anthony a promise, she wrote on more than one occasion, that she would keep his secret, and there was no question of breaking her word. For everyone else she had created a fantasy in which she and her husband were without a care: she busy with the running of the house; he occupied by his studies of the natural world and production of a Great Work. She wrote chatty missives to their few acquaintances about life at Loeanneth, filled with funny, sometimes poignant, observations of her daughters, *each more eccentric than the one who came before.*

Sadie admired Eleanor's stubborn insistence, even as she shook her head at the maddening impossibility of the task she'd set herself. Daffyd Llewellyn, too, had urged her to be honest with those around her, particularly, in early 1933, when her concerns took a worrying turn. She was anxious as always for Anthony, but now she feared, too, for her baby son, whose birth, she said, had triggered something terrible in her husband's mind.

A deep trauma had resurfaced, memories of a horrifying experience he'd had during the war when his best friend Howard had been lost. *It's as if it has all snowballed. He resents his good fortune, and regrets deeply his inability to work as a doctor, and somehow it has all become confused with his memories of the war, with one 'incident' in particular. In his sleep I hear him crying, calling out that they must go, that they must keep the dog and the baby quiet.*

And then, some weeks later: *As you know, Daffyd, I have been making my own quiet enquiries for some time. It had perplexed me when I could find no mention of Howard on the honour roll, so I dug a little deeper, and oh, Daffyd, it's awful. He was shot at dawn, the poor man, by our own army! I found a fellow who'd served in the same regiment as Howard and Anthony and he told me: Howard had been trying to desert and Anthony stopped him. My poor love must have thought he could keep it quiet, but evidently another officer got involved and things turned out as they did. The man I spoke with told me Anthony took it very hard and, knowing my husband as I do, I'm certain he will have blamed himself just as surely as if he'd been the one to pull the trigger.*

Knowing the reason behind Anthony's night terrors didn't explain why they should be increasing at that time, however, and didn't help Eleanor with the difficult task of soothing and steering him back to reality. He adored baby Theo, she wrote, and the fear that he might inadvertently harm him was causing him to despair and even, in his darkest moments, to talk about 'ending it all'. *I cannot let him,*

Eleanor wrote. *I cannot allow the hope and promise of that tremendous man to end in such a way. I must find how to fix things. The more I think about it, the more convinced I am that only by talking about what happened to Howard will he finally have a chance to escape the terrors that stalk him. I plan to ask him about 'the incident' myself, I must, but not until everything is settled here. Not until everyone is safe.*

Throughout it all, the one light in Eleanor's existence, her single place of respite, was her relationship with Ben. Evidently she'd told Daffyd Llewellyn about him, and in turn she'd confided in Ben about Anthony's state of mind. There was something about Ben's itinerant nature, Eleanor had written, his lack of roots, that made him the perfect person with whom to share her secret. *Not that we discuss it often, you mustn't think that. There is so much else to talk about. He has travelled so far and wide, his childhood is like a treasure trove of anecdotes about people and places and I am greedy for them all. A form of vicarious escape, if only for a while. But on occasion when I simply have to free myself of my burden, he is the only one, aside from you, dear Daffyd, in whom I can trust. Talking to him is like writing in the sand or shouting into the wind. His nature is so elemental that I know I can tell him anything and it will go no further.*

Sadie wondered how Ben had felt about Anthony's condition – in particular, the possible threat he posed to Eleanor and to baby Theo. *His* baby, after all. The letter Sadie had found in the boathouse made it clear that Ben had known the boy was his child. She fingered the pile of letters to Eleanor from Ben. To this point Sadie had avoided reading them. Poring over someone else's love letters had felt like crossing a line. Now, though, it seemed she had to take a peek.

She took more than a peek. She read them all. And when she reached the last letter the room was pitch-black and the house and garden so quiet she could hear the distant rolling of the sea. Sadie closed her eyes. Her brain was both weary and wired, a strange marriage of contradictory states, and everything she'd seen and read and heard and thought that day tumbled together. Alice telling Bertie about the tunnel entrance near the boathouse; Clive and his boat – 'the easiest way to get between here and there . . . you can go the whole way without glimpsing another soul'; Eleanor's promise to Anthony and her concerns for Theo; Ben's stories of his childhood.

She thought, too, of Maggie Bailey and the things a person would do to save their child from harm; of Caitlyn, and the way Gemma had smiled down at her; of Rose Waters, and the keen love a person could feel for a child who wasn't their own. She pitied Eleanor, who'd lost Theo, Ben and Daffyd Llewellyn within a week of each other. And she kept coming back to Alice's description of her mother: *She believed that a promise, once made, should be kept . . .*

It wasn't so much the discovery of a single clue, as the coming together of many small details. That moment when the sun shifts by a degree and a spider's web, previously concealed, begins to shine like fine-spun silver. Because suddenly Sadie could see how it all connected and she knew what had happened that night. Anthony hadn't killed Theo. Not on purpose, not by accident, not at all.

Thirty-two

Cornwall, 23 June 1933

Out in the middle of the lake, the bonfire burned. Orange flames leapt jagged against the night-starred sky, and birds cut black above. Constance loved Midsummer. It was one of the few traditions of her husband's family with which she held. She'd always appreciated an excuse for a party, and the fires and lanterns, the music and dancing, the shedding of inhibitions made it especially exciting. Constance had never cared a jot for all the superstitious talk the deShiels spouted about renewals and transitions, the warding off of evil spirits, but this year she wondered whether perhaps there might be something in it. Tonight Constance intended to undertake a momentous renewal of her own. After almost forty years, she had decided, at last, to let go of an ancient enmity.

Her hand went to her heart. The old ache was still there, lodged within her ribcage like a peach stone. After decades spent suppressing the memories, they came often these days. Strange the way she could forget what she'd eaten for dinner the night before, only to find herself right back in the frantic swirl of that room, that early morning as dawn was breaking outside and her body splintering inside. The gormless house-maid dithering with the flaccid cloth, Cook's sleeves pushed up to her raw elbows, coals spitting in the fireplace. There'd been men in the corridor, debating as to What Should Be Done, but Constance hadn't listened; their voices had been drowned out by the sound of the sea. The wind had blown ill that morning and as people started to move in the liminal dark around her, a confusion of rough hands and sharp voices, Constance had disappeared beneath the relentless heave and pound of the hateful waves. (How she despised that sound! Even now, it threatened to drive her mad.)

Afterwards, in the wasteland of weeks that followed, Henri had called in a number of doctors, London's finest, all of whom agreed it had been unavoidable – the cord had been wrapped tight as a noose around his little neck – and it would be best for everyone if the whole unfortunate incident were forgotten. But Constance hadn't forgotten and she'd known they were wrong. The 'incident' hadn't been unavoidable; her baby had been killed by incompetence. *His* incompetence. Of course the doctors had closed ranks around him – he was one of their own. Nature was not always kind, they'd advised, each more ingratiating than the one before, but she always knew best. There was nothing to stop them trying again.

Stiff upper lip.

Least said soonest mended.

Things would be different next time.

They were right about that. When Eleanor was born twelve months later and the midwife held her up for inspection – 'It's a girl!' – Constance had looked her over from top to toe, enough to see that she was wet and pink and squealing, before nodding shortly, rolling over, and sending for a hot cup of tea.

She'd waited for the feelings to come, the rush of maternal love and longing she'd felt the first time (oh! that plump waxen face, the long fine fingers, the sweet curled lips that would never utter a sound), but the days had passed, one rolling into the next, her breasts had swelled and ached and then settled, and before she knew it Dr Gibbons was back to declare her fit and usher her out of confinement.

By then, though, something between them had been silently and mutually resolved. The baby girl cried and shouted and refused to calm when Constance held her. Constance looked at the child's bawling face and could think of no name that suited it more than another. It was left to Henri to name and hold and pace, until the advertisement could be placed and Nanny Bruen arrived on the doorstep with her impeccable references and nursery standards. By the time Daffyd Llewellyn stepped in, with his stories and rhymes, Constance and Eleanor were as strangers. Over time she nurtured her rage against the man who had taken not one but two of her children from her.

But – Constance sighed – she was tired of being angry. She had held on to her molten hatred so long it had hardened into steel and she had grown stiff with it. As the band launched into another merry tune and people swirled about the lantern-lit dance floor within its ring of willows, she cut through the crowd to the tables where the hired waiters were pouring drinks.

'A glass of champagne, ma'am?'

'Thank you. And another, please, for my friend.'

She accepted the two brimming flutes and made her way to sit on the bench beneath the arbour. It wasn't going to be easy – her old antipathy was as familiar as her own reflection – but it was time to let it go and be freed at last from the anger and grief that had kept her prisoner.

As if on cue, Constance caught a glimpse of Daffyd Llewellyn on the edge of the crowd. He was heading directly towards the arbour, skirting around the revellers, almost as if he knew she was waiting for him. For Constance, the fact further cemented her certainty that she was doing the right thing. She was going to be polite, even kind; to enquire after his health – the heartburn she knew was giving him trouble – and congratulate him on his recent achievements and the upcoming honour.

A smile pulled nervously at the edge of her lips. 'Mr Llewellyn,' she called, standing to wave at him. Her voice was more high-pitched than usual.

He glanced around, his body stiffening in surprise when he saw her.

A flash of memory came and she saw him as a young man, the bright and dashing physician her husband had befriended. Constance steeled herself. 'I wondered if you might have a moment.' Her voice wavered, but she caught it. Determined, resolved, eager to be released. 'I was hoping we might talk.'

Constance was beckoning him with a glass of champagne from beneath the arbour, the very spot in which Daffyd was supposed to be meeting Alice in fifteen minutes. The girl had a sixth sense for Ben Munro's whereabouts and Eleanor had pleaded with him to keep her occupied tonight. 'Please, Daffyd,' she'd said. 'It would ruin everything if Alice were to turn up in the wrong place at the wrong time.'

He'd agreed, but only because Eleanor was the closest

he'd ever come to having a child of his own. He'd loved her since she was tiny. A poppet in a bundle, a permanent attachment to Henri, always in his arms, and then later, when she was older, riding on his shoulders or skipping along beside him. Would she have been so like her father if she hadn't spent so much time with him when she was small? It was impossible to say, but she was, and Daffyd loved her for it. 'Please,' she'd said, taking his hands in hers. 'I'm begging you. I can't do this without you.' And so, of course, he'd agreed.

In truth, he had grave misgivings about the whole idea. The worry he felt for Eleanor was driving him to distraction and distress. His heartburn had become chronic since she'd told him, and the old depression, the malaise that had once threatened to overwhelm him, was back. He'd seen firsthand what could happen to women who lost their children. It was the sort of plot invented by desperation that held together only in the long wee hours of night.

He'd pleaded with her to reconsider, during the many conversations they'd had in which she'd poured out her heart, but she had been adamant. He understood her loyalty to Anthony – he'd known them both when they were young and grieved as she did for the loss her husband had suffered – and he shared her fears for baby Theo. But to make such a sacrifice! There had to be another way. 'Show it to me,' she'd said, 'and I will take it.' But no matter how he twisted and turned the pieces of the puzzle, he could find no arrangement that pleased her. Not without making public Anthony's troubles, and that she refused to do.

'I made him a promise,' she said, 'and you of all people know that promises aren't for breaking. You're the one who taught me that.' Daffyd had remonstrated with her when she said that, gently at first, and then sternly, trying to make her see that the logic animating his made-up world of faerie, those luminous threads he wove together to make his stories, were not strong enough to support the complications of a human being's life. But she was not to be dissuaded. 'Sometimes to love from afar is as much as we can hope for,' she'd said, and in the end he'd consoled himself that nothing was forever. That she could always change her mind. That perhaps it was all for the best, a temporary safe haven for the little fellow.

So he'd done as she asked. Arranged to meet Alice here tonight, to keep her from stumbling where she shouldn't and scuppering their plans. Eleanor had been sure the girl's natural curiosity would be enough to ensure her compliance and he'd been readying himself all day, going over contingencies, anticipating problems; but he hadn't foreseen being intercepted by Constance. As a rule, Daffyd tried to think of Constance as little as possible. They'd never seen eye to eye, even before the terrible business of that night. Throughout her courtship with Henri, Daffyd had watched from the sidelines as she led his friend a merry dance. So cruel, so uncaring, and yet Henri had been smitten. He'd thought he could tame her, that when she agreed to marry him her days of playing the field were over.

Constance's grief after the baby's death had been real, though; Daffyd didn't doubt that. Her heart had been broken, she'd needed someone to blame, and her eye had turned on him. It didn't matter how many doctors explained about the cord, assured her that the outcome would have been the same no matter who was in attendance; she wouldn't believe them.

She'd never forgiven Daffyd for the part he'd played. But then, he'd never forgiven himself either. He'd never practised again. His passion for medicine had died that bleak morning. He was beset with images of the baby's face; the clammy heat of the room; the terrible keening that came from Constance as she clung to the stillborn child.

But now, here she was, holding out a champagne flute and asking to talk.

'Thank you,' he said, accepting the glass and taking a larger sip than he might have. It was cold and bubbling and he hadn't realised quite how parched he was, how nervous about the task that lay ahead. When he finally stopped drinking, Constance was watching him, a strange look on her face, surprised, no doubt, by his uncouth thirst.

And then it was gone. She smiled. 'I've always loved Midsummer. There's so much possibility in the air, don't you think?'

'Too many people for me, I'm afraid.'

'At the party, perhaps, but I was speaking more generally. The idea of renewal, a fresh start.'

There was something unsettling in her manner. She was as nervous as he was, Daffyd realised. He took another swig of champagne.

'Why, you of all people know the benefit of a fresh start, don't you, Daffyd? Such a transition you made. Such a surprising second chance.'

'I have been fortunate.'

'Henri was so proud of your literary endeavours, and Eleanor – well, she worships the ground you walk on.'

'I've always been inordinately fond of her, too.'

'Oh, yes, I know. You spoiled her dreadfully. All those

stories you told, writing her into your book.' She laughed lightly, before seeming to experience a sudden sobering of mood. 'I've become old, Daffyd. I find myself thinking often about the past. Opportunities missed, people lost.'

'It happens to us all.'

'I've been meaning to congratulate you on your recent honour, the royal order. There'll be a reception at the palace, I presume?'

'I believe so.'

'You'll meet the King. Did I ever tell you, I almost enjoyed the same privilege when I was a young woman? I fell ill, alas, and my sister Vera went in my stead. These things can't be helped, of course. Life is filled with twists and turns. Your success, for instance – a tremendous case of roses from the ashes.'

'Constance—'

'Daffyd.' She inhaled and drew herself to full height. 'I was hoping you might agree it was time to put the past behind us.'

'I—'

'One cannot hold on to ill feelings forever. There comes a time when one must decide to act rather than to react.'

'Constance, I—'

'No, let me finish, Daffyd, please. I've imagined this conversation so many times. I need to say it.' He nodded and she smiled brief appreciation, before lifting her glass. Her hand shook slightly, whether from emotion or advanced age, Daffyd didn't know. 'I'd like to propose a toast. To action. To remedy. And to renewal.'

He met her glass with his own and they drank, Daffyd almost gulping the last of his champagne. He was stalling; he felt overcome. It was all so unexpected and he wasn't quite sure what to say: a lifetime of guilt and grief welled up inside him and his eyes glazed. It was too much to bear on a night that was already heavy with distressing duties.

His tumult must have been evident, for Constance was scrutinising him, watching as closely as if she were seeing him for the first time. Perhaps because he was being observed, he felt himself sway unsteadily. He was hot suddenly. It was stuffy here, very warm. There were so many people fussing, and the music was too loud. He drained the last dregs of his champagne.

'Daffyd?' Constance said, frowning. 'You look peaky.'

His hand went to his forehead as if to steady himself. He blinked, trying to focus his vision, to stop seeing fuzzy haloes around everyone and everything.

'Shall I get you a glass of water? Do you need some fresh air?'

'Air,' he said, his throat very dry, his voice raspy. 'Please.'

There were people everywhere, faces, voices, all a blur, and he was glad to have her arm to steady him. Not in a million years would Daffyd have anticipated a scenario in which it would be Constance rendering him aid. And yet, without her, he feared, he might have fallen.

They passed through a group of laughing people and he thought he glimpsed Alice in the distance. He tried to say something, to explain to Constance that he couldn't go too far, that he had important business to take care of, but his tongue was lazy and wouldn't form the words. There was still time. Eleanor had said they weren't meeting until midnight. He would do as he promised; he just needed a bit of cool air first.

They followed the path beyond the hedge until the noise of the crowd seemed very far away. His heart was galloping. It was more than his usual heartburn or anxiety; he could hear his pulse coursing behind his ears. It was guilt, of course; memories of that terrible dawn so long ago; his failure to save the little lad. To think that Constance should be the one to make amends. Daffyd felt an overwhelming urge to weep.

His head was spinning. Voices, so many of them, cacophonous, distant, but one cut high above them all, close to his ear, in his ear. 'Just wait here. Rest a moment, I'll fetch you some water.'

He was ice cold suddenly. He glanced around him. The owner of the voice was gone. He was alone. Where was she? Where was who? Someone had been with him. Or had he imagined it? He was tired, so tired.

His head swirled with the sounds around him. Fish flicking their tails in the dark pools, mysterious dripping noises in the depths of the woods.

He glimpsed the boathouse. There were too many people there, laughing and squealing as they skylarked in the lamplit boats. He needed to be alone, to breathe, to regain his composure.

He would walk just a little further in the other direction. Along the stream. It had always been one of his favourite places. Such fine days they'd had, such long, sunny days, he and Henri, and, later, little Eleanor skipping along, delighting them with her perspicacity. Daffyd would never forget the look on Henri's face when he watched his daughter, the cast of absolute adoration. Daffyd had tried to sketch that expression many times but never managed to capture it on paper.

He stumbled and corrected himself. His legs felt very odd. Loose, as if all the ligaments had turned to rubber. He decided to sit down for a time. Just a short time. He fumbled in his pocket for one of his heartburn pills, popped it in his mouth and swallowed hard.

The earth was cool and damp beneath him, and he leaned his back against the strong, solid trunk of a tree. He closed his eyes. His pulse was like a river, flowing fast after rain, rhythmical. He felt himself, a boat caught by the current, swishing and turning and throbbing.

Daffyd could see Henri's face now. Such a gentlemanly face, a *good* face. Eleanor was right. Sometimes to love from afar was the most one could hope for. And it was better, surely, than never to have loved at all.

Oh, but it was hard.

The stream lapped at the banks and Daffyd Llewellyn's breathing slowed to match it. He had to see Alice; he'd promised Eleanor. He would go soon. Just a few more minutes here, the earth solid and cool beneath him, the tree faithful, the breeze light against his cheeks. And Henri's face in his memory, his old friend, calling him, motioning with his hand that Daffyd should follow soon . . .

Alice was glancing at her wristwatch when she almost ran into her grandmother. The old woman was walking very quickly, and seemed to be in a state of uncharacteristic excitement. 'Water,' she said when she saw Alice; her cheeks were red and her eyes bright. 'I need some water.'

Ordinarily, Alice would have found her grandmother's

unusual energy enough to spark her curiosity, but not that evening. Her whole world had collapsed and she was far too busy soaking in her own shame and distress to wonder at the peculiarities of others. It was only out of a deep sense of duty that she'd come to meet Mr Llewellyn tonight. Alice could hardly bear to think back to their conversation that morning; she'd been so keen to get rid of him, so excited to go and show her manuscript to Ben, so proud. What a mistake that had turned out to be.

Lord, but she could just about die of embarrassment! Alice sat on the chair beneath the arbour and pulled her knees to her chest, utterly miserable. She hadn't wanted to come to the party at all, preferring to lick her wounds in private, but Mother had insisted. 'You're not going to sit inside all night sulking,' she'd said. 'You're to put on your best dress and join the rest of your family outside. I don't know what's got into you, and why you have to choose tonight of all nights, but I won't stand for it, Alice. Too much planning has gone into the evening for you to spoil it with your mood.'

And so, here she was, under sufferance. She'd wanted to spend the whole night in her bedroom, hiding beneath the covers, trying to forget what a fool she'd been, what a stupid little fool. It was all Mr Llewellyn's fault. By the time she'd got rid of the old man that morning, she'd figured it would be cutting things too fine to show Ben the manuscript; Mr Harris and his son would be back any minute. And so, instead, she'd decided to take her pages straight to the boat-house later that afternoon. That way, Alice had reasoned, they could be together in private at last.

Her skin flamed as she remembered. The way she'd

skipped up the stairs to knock on the door, brimming with excitement, with confidence. The special care she'd taken with her clothing and hair. The spritz of Mother's cologne she'd sneaked beneath the buttons of her blouse and onto the insides of her wrists, just as she'd seen Deborah do.

'Alice,' he'd said when he saw her, smiling (confusedly, she could see that now; at the time she'd thought only that he was as nervous as she was. The mortification burned!). 'I wasn't expecting anyone.'

He opened the boathouse door and she stepped across the threshold, pleased at the waft of perfume that trailed her. It was cosy inside, with only room for a bed and a basic kitchen. Alice had never been inside a man's bedroom and had to work hard to stop herself from gawping like a silly child at the patchwork eiderdown draped casually at the end of the mattress.

There was a little rectangular-shaped gift on top, wrapped plainly but neatly, with a piece of twine tied around it, a card made from one of Ben's paper animals. 'Is that for me?' Alice said, remembering his promise that he had something to give her.

He followed her glance. 'It is. Nothing grand, mind you, just a small token of encouragement for your writing.'

Alice could have burst with pleasure. 'Speaking of which,' she said, before beginning an excited account of having finished the manuscript. 'Hot off the press.' She forced the copy she'd made specially into his hands. 'I wanted you to be the first to read it.'

He was thrilled for her, a broad smile bringing a dimple to his left cheek. 'Alice! That's tremendous. What an achievement! The first copy of many, you mark my words.' She felt so adult, basking in his praise.

He promised to read it and for a moment she held her breath, waiting for him to turn the cover and see the dedication, but instead he set it down on the table. There was an open bottle of lemonade nearby, and Alice was suddenly parched. 'I'd kill for a drink,' she said in a kittenish voice.

'No need to do that.' He poured her a glass. 'I'm more than happy to share.'

While his attention was elsewhere, she released the top button of her blouse. He handed her the glass and their fingers touched. An electric shiver shot right down her spine.

Without breaking his gaze, Alice took a sip. The lemonade was cold and sweet. She licked her lips delicately. This was it. Now or never. In one swift motion, she set down the glass, stepped towards him and took his face between her palms, leaning in to kiss him just the way she'd dreamed of doing.

For a second it had been so perfect! She breathed in his scent, leather and musk and just the faintest tang of perspiration, and his lips were warm and soft, and she swooned, because she'd *known* it would be just like this, all along she'd known . . .

And then, suddenly, the growing flame was snuffed. He pulled away, his eyes searching hers.

'What is it?' she said. 'Did I do it wrong?'

'Oh, Alice.' Realisation and concern competed on his face. 'Alice, I'm sorry. I've been so stupid. I had no idea.'

'What are you talking about?'

'I thought – I didn't think.' He smiled then, gently, sadly, and she saw that he felt pity for her and that's when she knew. It hit her in an instant. He didn't feel as she did. He never had.

He was still speaking, his expression earnest, his brow furrowed and his eyes kind, but the ringing of mortification in her ears was shrill and unrelenting. Occasionally the frequency slipped and she caught a fragment of platitude: 'You're a terrific girl . . . so very smart . . . a wonderful writer . . . a great future ahead of you . . . you'll meet someone else . . .'

She was parched and dizzy, she needed not to be here anymore, in this place where she had so disgraced herself, where the man she loved, the only man she'd *ever* love, was looking at her with pity and apology in his eyes, and talking to her in the tone of voice all adults used to placate confused children.

With all the dignity she could muster, Alice picked up her glass and finished the lemonade. She collected her manuscript with its nauseating dedication and started towards the door.

And that's when she noticed his suitcase. Later, she would reflect on the fact, and wonder whether there was something wrong with her that, even when her heart was breaking, a small part of her stood outside the emotional truth of the moment, taking notes. Later still, when she'd become better acquainted with Graham Greene, she would realise it was merely the splinter of ice that all writers held in their hearts.

The suitcase was open against the wall and it was full of neat piles of clothing. Ben's clothing. He was packing.

Without turning back to face him, she said, 'You're leaving.'

'I am.'

'Why?' Oh, horrid vanity, but she felt a resurgence of hope that he *did* love her after all and it was his love that was forcing him to leave. His respect for her youth and his duty to the family who employed him.

But no. Instead he said, 'It's time. Past time, in fact. My contract ended a fortnight ago. I only stayed on to help in the lead-up to Midsummer.'

'Where will you go?'

'I'm not sure yet.'

He was a gypsy, of course, a traveller. He'd never described himself in any other terms. And now he was leaving. Walking out of her life as casually as he'd walked into it. A sudden thought struck her. She turned. 'There's someone else, isn't there?'

Ben didn't answer, but he didn't need to. She could tell at once by the sorry look on his face that there was.

With a small dizzy nod, and without another glance at him, she left the boathouse. Head held high, gaze steady, one calm step after another. 'Alice, your gift,' he called after her, but she didn't go back.

Only when she'd rounded the bend in the path did she hug her manuscript to her chest and run as fast as her tear-blinded eyes allowed her, towards the house.

How had she got it so wrong? Sitting on the garden bench beneath the arbour, as Midsummer celebrations swirled around her, Alice still couldn't understand. Her mind spooled back across a year of interactions. He'd always been so pleased to see her, listening intently when she spoke about her writing, her family, even offering suggestions when she complained about Mother, the misunderstandings they'd been having, trying to mend the rift between them. Alice had never met anyone who cared so much, understood her like he did.

It was true, he'd never, not once, touched her, not properly, not the way she wanted him to, and she'd wondered at the things she'd heard Deborah saying about young men and their lecherous, leering attentions; but she'd simply supposed him too much of a gentleman. And that was the problem. She'd supposed too much. All along, she'd seen only what she wanted to see: her own desires reflected back at her.

With a heartsick sigh, Alice glanced about for Mr Llewellyn. She'd been waiting over fifteen minutes now and there was still no sign of him. She ought to leave. After dragging herself out to meet him, he hadn't even bothered to keep their appointment. He'd probably forgotten all about it, or had got caught up with more enjoyable company and was running late. It would serve him right to turn up and find that she wasn't here.

But where would she go? To the gondolas? No, they were far too close to the boathouse. She never wanted to set foot down there again. To the house? No, there were servants everywhere, all of them Mother's spies, only too happy to report that Alice had disobeyed instructions. The dance floor? Hardly! She couldn't think of anything she felt like less than kicking up her heels and whooping in the fashion of those other fools – and who, pray tell, would she dance with?

And there it was. The awful truth. She had nothing better to do and no one to do it with. Little wonder Ben didn't love her. She was utterly unlovable. It was ten minutes to midnight, the fireworks would begin soon and Alice was all alone. She was hopeless and friendless, and there didn't seem to be much point at all in going on.

She saw herself then, as if from above. A lone, tragic figure, dressed in her prettiest frock, hugging her knees; a girl whose entire family misunderstood her.

She looked, in fact, a bit like an immigrant girl, sitting on the wharf after a long sea journey. It was something about the curve of her shoulders, the bow of her head, her fine, straight neck. She was a steadfast sort of girl, dealing with great loss. Her family had all been killed (how? Horribly, tragically, the details didn't matter, not now), but with fierce determination she'd charged herself with avenging their deaths. Alice sat taller, as the kernel of an idea began to grow. She reached slowly into her pocket to stroke her notebook. Thinking, thinking . . .

The girl was alone in the world, utterly bereft, abandoned and forgotten by all those she might have presumed to trust, but she was going to prevail. Alice would make sure of it. She stood quickly as a spark of animation fired her from within. Her breaths had quickened and her head was swimming with shimmery threads of ideas that needed braiding together. She needed to think, to plot.

The woods! That's where she'd go. Away from the party, away from all these silly revelling people. She would concentrate on planning her next story. She didn't need Ben, or Mr Llewellyn, or any of them. She was Alice Edevane, and she was a storyteller.

The plan was to meet in the woods, five minutes after midnight. Eleanor only realised when she saw him waiting, right where he'd said he'd be, that she'd been holding her breath all night, expecting it to go wrong.

'Hello,' she said.

'Hello.'

Oddly formal. The only way they were going to get through the awful task ahead. They didn't embrace, rather brushed each other's forearms, elbows, wrists in an awkward approximation of the affection, the ease, to which they were both accustomed. Everything was different tonight.

'You had no trouble?' he said.

'I met a housemaid on the stairs earlier, but she was flustered, gathering champagne flutes for midnight. She thought nothing of it.'

'Probably a good thing. It puts you at the scene well ahead of time. It's less suspicious.'

Eleanor flinched at the blunt expressions. *At the scene. Less suspicious.* How had it come to this? A reeling sensation of panic and confusion swirled within her, threatening to fell her. The world beyond, the surrounding woods, the party in the distance, were all a blur. She felt entirely disconnected from it all. There was no lantern-lit boathouse, no guests laughing and flirting in their silks and satins, no lake or house or orchestra; there was only this, now, this thing they'd planned, that had seemed so reasonable at the time, so logical.

A peony shell whistled through the sky behind them, cycling higher until it burst, a cacophony of red sparks, falling back over the lake. It was a spur to action. The fireworks were scheduled to run for thirty minutes; Eleanor had instructed the pyrotechnician to mount a display that no one could resist, she'd given the servants permission to enjoy the show, Daffyd was keeping Alice occupied. 'We must get moving,' she said. 'There isn't much time. I'll be missed.'

Her eyes had adjusted to the dark of the woods and she could see him quite clearly now. His face was a picture of reluctance and regret, his dark eyes searching hers, looking, she knew, for a crack in her resolve. It would be very easy to show him one. To say, 'I think we've made a mistake,' or 'Let's give it a little more thought,' and retreat in different directions. But she hardened her heart and started towards the trapdoor that led down to the tunnel.

Maybe he won't follow, she thought, she hoped. And then she could go back alone, leave her sleeping baby where he was, return to the party as if she hadn't a care in the world. She could wake tomorrow, and when she next saw Ben they would shake their heads together in amused disbelief, astonishment at the madness that had engulfed them, the crazy thing they'd almost done, the enchantment they'd been under. 'A *folie à deux*,' they'd say, 'a lunacy shared by two.'

But even as she thought it, even as her spirit lifted and lightened, she knew it would solve nothing. Anthony was worse than ever. Theo was in danger. And now, in an unimaginable – a *devastating* – development, Deborah and Clemmie had found out about Eleanor and Ben. The very thought that her daughters knew she'd been unfaithful to their father made Eleanor want to shrink into a tiny speck of dust and float away. Which was weak, and lazy, and only served to heighten her self-loathing. No, this plan, this sickening, unthinkable plan, was the only way to stem disaster's flow. More than that, it was precisely what she deserved.

Eleanor started. Something had just moved in the woods,

she was sure of it. She'd glimpsed – or had she heard? – something in the dark. Was someone there? Had they been seen?

She scanned the trees beyond, hardly daring to breathe.

There was nothing.

She'd imagined it.

It was nothing more than a guilty conscience.

All the same, it was as well not to linger. 'Quickly,' she whispered, 'follow me down the ladder. Quickly.'

She reached the bottom and stepped aside to make room for him in the narrow, brick-walled tunnel. He'd closed the trapdoor behind him and it was blacker than night. Eleanor turned on the torch she'd hidden earlier and led him through the passage towards the house. It smelled of must and mould and a thousand childhood adventures. She longed suddenly to be a child again, with no more to worry about than how to fill the endless sunlit day. A sob burned her throat, threatening to burst free, and she shook her head angrily, cursing herself for such indulgence. She needed to be stronger than that. There would be far worse to come in the days ahead. Sometime tomorrow morning the discovery would be made, a search would be called, the police would become involved. There'd be interviews and an investigation, and Eleanor would have to play her ghastly part – and Ben would be gone.

Ben. She could hear his footfalls behind her, and the fleeting, stinging awareness came again that she was going to lose him, too. That in a matter of minutes he would turn and walk away and she would never see him again . . . No. Eleanor clenched her jaw and forced herself to focus only on her progress. One foot in front of the other, only stopping when she reached the set of stone steps that led up through the cavity in the wall of the house. She shone her torch's beam towards the door at the top and drew a deep breath. The air was thick inside the passage, still and earthy, and dust spores hung in the strip of light. Once they went through that door, there'd be no turning back. She was steeling herself to start climbing, when Ben grabbed her wrist. Surprised, she turned to face him.

'Eleanor, I—'

'No,' she said, her voice unexpectedly flat in the narrow bricked space. 'Ben, don't.'

'It kills me to say goodbye.'

'Then don't.'

She realised at once, from the brightening of his expression in the torchlight, that he'd misunderstood her. That he thought she was suggesting he need not leave. She hurried to add, 'Don't *say* it. Just do what has to be done.'

'There must be another way.'

'There isn't.' There wasn't. If there were, she'd have found it. Eleanor had thought and thought until she felt her brain would bleed from the effort. She'd enlisted Mr Llewellyn and even he had been unable to suggest an acceptable alternative. There was no way to do the right thing by everybody, to keep everybody happy. This was the closest she had come, this plan in which she would bear the brunt. Theo would be confused at first – God help her, he'd be distressed, too – but he was young and he'd forget. She believed Ben when he said he loved her, that he didn't want to be without her, but he was a gypsy and to travel was in his blood; eventually he would have moved on regardless. No, it was she who would suffer most, left behind to endure their loss, missing them both as the moon misses the sun, always wondering—

No. Don't think about it. With all the force of will she could muster, Eleanor pulled her hand from his and started up the stairs. She ought to be concentrating instead on whether she'd done everything she needed to in order to make the plan work. Whether the extra draught of whisky would ensure Nanny Bruen's continued slumber. Whether Mr Llewellyn was even now engaged with Alice, who'd been especially difficult all evening.

At the top, she peered through the hidden spyhole in the secret door. Her eyes were glazed and she blinked furiously to clear them. The hallway was empty. In the distance she could hear the booming fireworks. She glanced at her watch. Ten minutes left of the display. It was enough time. Just.

The handle was solid in her hand, very real. This was it. The moment she'd known was coming, but had refused to imagine, concentrating instead on the logistics, never allowing herself to picture how she would feel when she reached this threshold. 'Tell me again what kind of people they are,' she said softly.

His voice behind her was warm and sad and, worst of all, resigned. 'The very best,' he said. 'They're hardworking and loyal and fun; their house is the kind of place that always smells of good food, and no matter what else they might be short on, there's never any shortage of love.'

Where is it, she wanted to ask, *where are you taking him?* But she'd made Ben promise never to tell her. She couldn't trust herself. The whole thing would only work if she didn't know where to find him.

Ben's hand was on her shoulder. 'I love you, Eleanor.'

She closed her eyes, her forehead on the hard, cold wood of the door. He wanted her to say it back to him, she knew, but to do so would be fatal.

With a slight nod of acknowledgement, she lifted the tricky latch and crept out into the empty hallway. With the fireworks still sounding over the lake, red, blue, green light spilling through the windows and across the carpet, she readied herself to enter the nursery.

Theo woke suddenly. It was dark and his nanny was snoring heavily on the cot bed in the nook. A dull thump sounded, and a wash of green light spilled through the sheer curtains. There was other noise, too, happy noise, lots of people, far away, outside. But something else had woken him. He sucked his thumb, listening, concentrating, and then he smiled.

He knew before she reached his cot that it was Mummy. She picked him up and Theo nestled his head in beneath her chin. There was a spot where it fitted just right. She was cooing in his ear and his left hand wound its way up to stroke her face. He sighed contentedly. Theo loved his mummy more than anyone else in the world. His sisters were more fun, and his father could lift him higher, but there was something about the way his mummy smelled and the sound of her voice and the way her fingers stroked his face so gently.

There was another noise then, and Theo lifted his head. Someone else was in the room with them. His eyes were adjusting now to the dark and he could see a man behind his mother. The man came closer and smiled and Theo saw it was Ben from the garden. Theo liked Ben a lot. He made things out of paper, and told stories that ended in tickles.

His mummy was whispering softly in his ear, but Theo wasn't listening. He was busy playing peek-a-boo over her shoulder, trying to get Ben's attention. Mummy was holding him more tightly than usual and he wriggled to break free. She brushed a series of kisses on his cheek, but Theo pulled away. He was trying to make Ben smile. He didn't want to cuddle, he wanted to play. When Ben reached to stroke his cheek, a giggle burst out around Theo's thumb.

'Shhh,' whispered Mummy, 'shhh.' There was something different about her voice and Theo wasn't sure he liked it. He stared at her face but she wasn't looking at him anymore. She was pointing to something beneath the cot. Theo watched as Ben knelt down and then stood again, a bag over his shoulder. It wasn't a bag Theo recognised so he gave it no more thought.

Ben came closer then and lifted his hand to touch Mummy's cheek. She closed her eyes and leaned her head against his palm. 'I love you, too,' she said. Theo looked between their faces. They were both standing very still, neither saying a word, and he tried to guess what would happen next. When Mummy handed him to Ben, Theo was surprised but not unhappy.

'It's time,' she whispered, and Theo glanced at the big clock on the wall. He wasn't sure what time was, but he knew it came from there.

They left the nursery and Theo wondered where they were going. It was not normal to leave the nursery at night. He sucked his thumb and watched and waited to see. There was a door in the hallway, he'd never noticed it before, but now his mother held it open. Ben stopped and leaned close to Mummy, he was whispering in her ear but Theo couldn't hear the words. He made a whispering sound himself, *wisha, wisha, wisha,* and smiled with satisfaction. And then Ben carried him on and the door closed softly behind them.

It was dark. Ben turned on a torch and started walking downstairs. Theo looked around for Mummy. He couldn't see her. Maybe she was hiding? Was this a game? He watched hopefully over Ben's shoulder, waiting for her to jump out and smile and say, *Peek-a-boo!* But she didn't. Again and again, she didn't.

Theo's bottom lip trembled and he thought about crying, but Ben was talking to him, and his voice made Theo feel safe and warm. There was a rightness to it, the same way Theo's head fitted perfectly in the space beneath his mother's chin, the way his sister Clemmie's skin smelled just like his own. Theo yawned. He was tired. He lifted Puppy and tucked him on Ben's shoulder and then pressed his face against him. He slid his thumb into his mouth and closed his eyes and listened.

And Theo was content. He knew Ben's voice the way he knew his family, in that special way, knowledge that was as old as the world itself.

Thirty-three

It was pitch-black, except for the luminous white beams of their flashlights sweeping the ground a few metres ahead. Peter wasn't precisely sure why they were here, now, in the woods outside Loeanneth, rather than in the village enjoying the Solstice Festival. He'd rather fancied a bowl of fish stew followed by a cup of local mead, but Alice had been as stubborn as she was mysterious. 'Granted, it's not ideal to go while it's dark,' she'd said, 'but it needs to be done and I have to do it.' Which begged the question as to why they hadn't got in and done it earlier in the day like they'd planned. 'I wasn't about to undertake it with the detective and her grandfather around. It's private.'

The answer rang true, in part, Alice being one of the most private people Peter knew. He'd have wondered why she'd asked *him* along, except that the list of things she'd had him acquire for the excursion, 'the supplies' as she insisted on calling them, suggested clearly enough he'd been brought along for brawn. He'd managed to get everything she'd asked for. Not easy at such short notice, but Peter was good at his job and hadn't wanted to let her down.

The task was plainly very important to Alice, as evidenced by her late-night call to his home on Friday, when she'd announced that she'd thought about it and would be accompanying him to Cornwall after all. She'd sounded unusually excited, garrulous even, and it had crossed Peter's mind that she'd been liberal with the G & Ts after he left. 'I've no intention of taking over,' she'd said, before advising him she'd be ready and waiting for collection at five the next morning. 'Best to get a jump-start on the traffic, wouldn't you agree?' He'd said he did, and was about to hang up when she added, 'And Peter?'

'Yes, Alice?'

'Do you think you could lay your hands on a shovel and a pair of good-quality gardening gloves? There's something I'd very much like to do while we're there.'

All the way from London she'd sat beside him, a fixed expression on her face, a distracted air about her, uttering a determined 'not necessary' to every suggestion he made that they stop for air, food, water, or just to stretch their legs. She wasn't in the mood for chatting, which suited Peter. He'd simply turned up the volume of his audiobook and tuned in to the next instalment of *Great Expectations*. He'd been so busy over the past fortnight that he hadn't had time to finish the novel, but figured the long drive would be the perfect opportunity to do so. As they neared the village, he suggested they go straight to the hotel to check in, but Alice answered sharply. 'No. Unthinkable. We must go straight to Loeanneth.'

That's when she'd told him about the key she wanted him to fetch for her. 'There's a drying room upstairs,' she'd said, 'and in the floor beneath the rack there's a loose board. You'll know it because it has a whorl that looks uncannily like a moose's head. Inside the cavity you'll find a small leather pouch. There's a key inside the pouch. It's mine and I've been missing it for a very long time.'

'Got it,' he'd said. 'Loose floorboard, moose-head whorl, small leather pouch.'

Her determination had still been in evidence when they joined the others for the picnic at lunchtime. She'd had him cart the equipment with them, eager to head into the woods the moment they'd finished, but then Sadie Sparrow's grandfather, Bertie, had offered to show her around the festival and she'd accepted without a moment's hesitation. Peter would have been completely flummoxed, except that over the course of the morning he'd glimpsed something he thought might explain her change of heart. He couldn't be certain, but he had a feeling Alice had warmed to Bertie. She'd listened to him intently when he spoke, laughing at his jokes, and nodding keenly at his stories. It was decidedly un-Alice-like behaviour; she wasn't usually one for forming quick, close bonds, or any bonds at all, really.

Whatever the case, they'd gone back to the village, checked in to the hotel, and Alice had enjoyed a tour around the festival. Peter, meanwhile, had made his apologies and ducked out on his own. There'd been something playing on his mind all afternoon, a small personal niggle, and he'd wanted to stop by the library to check it out. But now, here they were, in the dark of night, following the same path they'd taken earlier, around the lake and down towards the boathouse. When they reached the stream, Alice didn't stop, urging him on instead towards the woods. Peter was wary, wondering whether it was reprehensible to bring an octogenarian into the woods at night, but Alice told him not to worry. 'I know these woods like the back of my hand,' she said. 'A person never forgets the landscape of their child-hood.'

Not for the first time, Alice thanked God Peter wasn't a talker. She didn't want to speak or explain or entertain. She wanted only to walk and to remember the last time she'd followed this path through the woods. A night-bird soared above them in the darkness and the sounds came back to her of that night, almost seventy years ago, when she'd crept out here to bury it: the horse whinnying, the lapping of the lake, the warblers in flight.

She stumbled and Peter caught her arm. 'Are you all right?' he said.

He was a good boy. He'd asked very few questions. Done everything she'd asked. 'Not much further,' she said.

They walked on in mutual silence, through the nettles, across the clearing where the tunnel trapdoor was hidden, and past the trout pond. Alice felt a strange elation to be back at Loeanneth, to be here in the woods tonight. It was just as she'd imagined as she sat in her library back in London the night before, listening to the clock tick on the mantelpiece, as her flame of longing for the place became a blaze of yearning and she put her call through to Peter. It wasn't that she felt young again, certainly not; rather that for the first time in seven decades she'd given herself permission to remember being that young girl. That frightened, love-struck, silly young girl.

At last they reached the spot that Alice had chosen back then, the place to which her guilt had been anchored all this time. 'We can stop now,' she said.

A smell came to her, of wood mouse and mushrooms,

and the wash of memory was so strong she had to steady herself against Peter's arm.

'I wonder whether you might do a bit of digging for me,' she said. 'Real digging, I mean, with dirt, as opposed to the other sort.'

Bless him, he didn't query her, merely took the shovel from the sack he was carrying, donned the pair of gardener's gloves, and started digging where she pointed.

Alice angled the torch to illuminate a circle for him to work within. She held her breath, remembering that night, the rain that had fallen, the muddy hem of her dress sticking to her boots. She'd never worn it again. She'd balled it up as soon as she got back to the house and burned it when she had the chance.

She'd made herself walk across the fields despite the rain. She could have used the tunnel. It wouldn't have been easy to go alone, not with the funny latch, yet she'd have managed. But she hadn't wanted to go anywhere that Ben had gone. She'd been so sure he was the one who took Theo, so caught up in her own theory. Petrified that someone else would put two and two together and discover the part she'd played.

'Alice,' said Peter, 'can you swing the light around a bit?'

'Sorry.' She'd let the torch's beam drift with her thoughts and corrected it.

There was a clunk as the shovel hit something solid.

He was down on all fours now, extracting the parcel from inside the hole. Unwrapping and removing what remained of the cloth bag she'd put it in.

'It's a box,' he said, looking up at her, his eyes wide with surprise. 'A metal box.'

'It is.'

He stood, sweeping dirt off the top with his gloved hands. 'Do you want me to open it?'

'No. We'll take it back to the car with us.'

'But—'

Her heart had begun to trip along when she saw it, but she managed to make her voice sound calm. 'There's no need to open it now. I know precisely what we'll find inside.'

Sadie pushed her way through the busy crowds at the Solstice Festival. The streets that met to form the village square were lined with stalls selling corn on the cob, and clothing, and handmade pork pies and pasties. Flames leapt from upturned barrels, and out on the harbour a floating pontoon was loaded with fireworks, waiting to be lit at midnight. Alice and Peter were staying at the hotel on the corner of the High Street, the white-rendered number with the hanging baskets of flowers along its wall and the snooty owner, but getting through the crowds was taking longer than Sadie had imagined. She just hoped they were there and not out amongst the revellers. She was desperate to tell them what she'd learned about Theo's death, for Alice to know that Anthony was in the clear.

Her phone was ringing; she could feel the vibration against her leg. She extricated it from her pocket, just as a kid with an enormous stick of candyfloss elbowed past her. Sadie looked at the screen and saw it was the Met. 'Hello?'

'Sparrow.'

'Donald?'

'Well, you've certainly managed to stir up a hornets' nest this time.'

Sadie stopped still. Her pulse had started to race. 'What happened? Have they talked to the husband, to Steve?'

'He's here now, in custody. Confessed to the whole thing.'

'What? Hang on, let me go somewhere quieter.' It was more easily said than done, but Sadie managed to find a nook along the stone harbour wall where she could tuck herself away from the crowds. 'Tell me exactly what happened.'

'Ashford brought in the new wife first. Got DI Heather to sit in and ask the questions, how things were going with Caitlyn, that sort of thing, all nice and friendly, and then they moved on to whether she had any other children, whether she wanted more. Turns out she can't have kids of her own.'

Sadie pressed her other hand against her ear. 'What's that?'

'She and the husband tried for a baby for over a year before seeing a doctor for tests.'

It was just as they'd hypothesised over lunch at Loeanneth, the same scenario Alice had described from her earlier Diggory Brent book, the story she'd said her sister had told her years before. 'So he went and got one for her?'

'That's about the sum of it. He said his wife had been devastated by the news of her infertility. She'd always wanted a baby, wanted a little girl more than anything in the world. The failure to fall pregnant was devastating, and all those fertility drugs messed her up even more. She was suicidal, he said, and he wanted to make her happy.'

'By finding her a daughter,' Sadie said. 'The perfect solution, but for the pesky fact that Caitlyn already had a mother.'

'He broke down under questioning. Told us what he'd done, where we'd find her body. Fishing holiday, my foot! We've got divers out there now. He was your typical first-timer, crying, saying he wasn't a bad person, he didn't want this to happen, he didn't mean for it to go so far.'

Sadie pressed her lips together grimly. 'He should have thought of that before he sat Maggie down and made her write that note, before he killed her.' She was seething. The way he'd picked at that polystyrene cup during his interview, the performance he'd given of the loving father, the put-upon ex-spouse, concerned and confused and willing to do what-ever was necessary to find the irresponsible runaway, when all the while he knew precisely where she was. What he'd done to her.

Maggie must have known what was coming. At some point in their final confrontation she must've figured it out. *It was him*, she'd scribbled desperately. *It was him*. The use of past tense had never been so chilling. Nor so brave. The one small mercy was that Caitlyn, to all appearances, hadn't seen what happened to her mum. 'Did he say what he did with his daughter while he was dealing with Maggie?'

'Put *Dora the Explorer* on. The little girl didn't budge.'

And knowing Caitlyn was still in the flat would've en-sured Maggie didn't make a scene, careful to shield her daughter from what she'd realised was about to happen. For the second time that evening, Sadie had cause to reflect on the lengths to which a parent would go to protect the child they loved.

Donald's voice turned sheepish. 'Look, Sparrow—'

'He left his daughter alone in that flat for a week.'

'Says he thought the grandmother was due to visit – that

the little girl would be found much sooner; he was about to call it in himself, he said—'

'Nancy Bailey will have to be told.'

'They've already sent a liaison officer.'

'She was right all along.'

'Yes.'

'Her daughter didn't walk out. Maggie never would've done that. Just like Nancy said.' She'd been murdered. And they'd almost let her ex-husband get away with it. Sadie felt relieved and vindicated, but sickened, too, and saddened, because it meant that Nancy's daughter wasn't ever coming home. 'What will happen to Caitlyn?'

'Child protection are looking after her now.'

'And afterwards?'

'I don't know.'

'Nancy adores the girl,' said Sadie. 'She used to care for her when Maggie was working. She's got a room set up for Caitlyn already. The child should be with family.'

'I'll make a note.'

'We need to do more than make a note, Donald. We owe it to the little girl. We failed her once. We have to make sure it doesn't happen again.'

Sadie wasn't about to let Caitlyn disappear inside the system. She was good at being a squeaky wheel, and more than happy to be as squeaky as she needed to be to make sure things turned out the way they should.

Just as she was making a silent resolution to call in every favour she was owed, to stop at nothing until Caitlyn and Nancy were reunited, she caught a glimpse through the crowd of two people she recognised.

'Look, Don, I've got to go.'

'All right, Sparrow, I get it, I should've listened and I'm—'

'Don't worry about it. I'll talk to you later. Just do me a favour.'

'Right.'

'Make sure that little girl and her grandmother are together.'

She ended the call and pocketed her phone, weaving through the crowd as quickly as she could towards the spot where she'd seen Alice and Peter. She paused a second when she got there, glancing this way and that, until she saw the tell-tale white hair.

'Alice!' She waved a hand above the crowd. 'Peter!'

They stopped and looked about, mystified, until Peter, a head taller than most other people, caught sight of Sadie and smiled. There was that spark again. No doubt about it.

'DC Sparrow,' said Alice, surprised, as Sadie reached them.

'I'm so glad I found you.' Sadie was breathless. 'It was Ben. It was him all along.'

She noticed then that Peter had a shovel in a sack over his shoulder and Alice was clutching something in her arms, a largish box of some sort. Now, the old woman seemed to hold it tighter. 'What on earth do you mean?' she said.

'Ben took Theo. Your father, Anthony – it wasn't him. He was innocent.'

'She's delirious,' said Alice to Peter. 'Help her, Peter, she's talking nonsense.'

Sadie shook her head. She was still reeling elatedly from the conversation with Donald, she needed to calm down, to start at the beginning, to make them see. 'Is there somewhere we can talk? Somewhere quiet?'

'There's the hotel,' said Alice, 'but I have serious doubts as to how quiet it will be.'

Sadie glanced up at the hotel. Alice was right; there'd be no escaping the noise there. She thought of Bertie's courtyard, high above the village, with its view to the sea. 'Come with me,' she said. 'I know the perfect place.'

Although Bertie was still down at the festival, he'd left the porch light on and the door unlocked. The dogs milled about the newcomers, sniffing curiously, before accepting they were friend not foe and following them into the kitchen.

'Would you like a cup of something?' Sadie offered, vaguely recalling there were certain duties concomitant with playing host.

'I suspect I'm going to need a glass of something,' said Alice. 'Something strong.'

Sadie found a bottle of sherry at the back of Bertie's pantry, gathered a clutch of glasses, and led the others outside to the courtyard. The fairy lights draped around the stone walls of the garden were already twinkling, and as Alice and Peter pulled up chairs at the table, Sadie lit the candles in the hurricane lamps. She poured them each a drink.

'So,' said Alice, clearly not in the mood for social niceties, 'what's all this about Benjamin Munro taking my brother? I thought we'd decided. My father, the shell shock . . .'

'Yes,' said Sadie, 'we had, and that certainly played its part, but Theo didn't die that night. Ben took him and he didn't act alone. He and your mother planned it.'

'Whatever are you talking about?' Alice's hand went to rest on the top of the metal box she'd brought with her. It was covered with dirt, and in the space of an instant Sadie connected the dirt with Peter's shovel before letting the oddity go and pressing on.

'We were right about the threat your father's shell shock presented, but wrong that he'd actually harmed Theo. Ben and your mother decided the baby needed to be protected, and the tunnel, the party, the fireworks display, all of it gave them the perfect opportunity to make him disappear. It's in their letters. At least, it is if you know what to look for. Your mother agonised, but she couldn't think of any other way to keep Theo safe. She couldn't leave your father, she loved him, and she'd made her promise not to go public with his suffering. As she saw it, there was no other choice.'

'And Ben was Theo's biological father,' said Peter, who'd been nodding along. 'The best possible person to whom she could entrust him.'

'The only person,' Sadie agreed.

'That's why she wouldn't offer a reward,' Alice said suddenly, connecting the dots with the speed and accuracy one might expect from a woman who'd been plotting mystery novels for half a century. 'It always troubled me. I couldn't understand why she was so adamant about it. At the time, she said the prospect of money brought desperate people, opportunists, out of the woodwork and muddied the water. Now it makes sense: she just didn't want people looking for Ben and Theo. She didn't want them found.'

'It also explains why she insisted there be no mention made in the press of Nanny Bruen's negligence,' said Sadie.

'And why she made sure Rose Waters and the local police were remunerated handsomely.'

'Did she?' said Alice. 'I didn't know that.'

'Rose was devastated by her dismissal, and little wonder – she was let go *because* she was so vigilant. There was no way the plan would've worked if Rose had been watching over Theo. When she was fired, your mother gave her a glowing reference, and a bonus that allowed her to study. It set her up for the rest of her life.'

'She was making restitution,' said Peter.

Sadie nodded. 'The "kidnapping" was a fiction of her own creation, so she made sure anyone who suffered as a consequence was compensated for loss of income and un-necessary trouble.'

'That sounds like Mother,' said Alice. 'Her sense of justice, of "rightness", was her guiding concern.'

'So what happened next?' said Peter. 'Ben took Theo through the tunnel and away from Loeanneth. Do you think he raised him?'

Alice frowned, rocking her sherry glass back and forth between her fingers. 'Ben fought during the Second World War. He was killed in the Normandy landings, poor man – so cruel, to die like that, right at the very end. He'd been fighting for a long time, too. My sister Clementine saw him in France in 1940.'

'Theo was still a boy during World War Two,' said Sadie, performing a quick mental calculation. 'Only seven when it started. If Ben enlisted at the beginning, he can't have been raising Theo as his son. Unless he married someone else?'

'Or Theo ended up somewhere else,' said Peter.

'Which leaves us no better off than when we started,' concluded Alice.

A despondency settled over the group, given vocal expression by Ash, who let out a long doggy sigh in his sleep. Sadie topped up their sherry glasses and they drank in silence. The distant burr of festival cheer, building towards midnight, drifted up from the village.

'What about the letters?' said Alice at last. 'Was there anything in them that might indicate where Ben and Theo went after leaving Loeanneth?'

'Not that I could see. In fact, your mother was very keen that Ben *shouldn't* tell her where they were going.'

'Perhaps he gave her a hint anyway?'

'I don't think so.'

'Something subtle. Something personal that you might have missed.'

Sadie's certainty was no match for Alice's obstinacy. 'It's worth a look,' she said. 'Let me get the file from inside. I brought a few of the letters home with me.'

Bertie was just coming in the front door when she reached the kitchen. 'Hello, Sadie, love,' he said, with a tired but happy smile. 'I managed to escape before the party really got going. Fancy some supper?'

Sadie explained that Alice and Peter were in the courtyard, talking over the Edevane case. 'We've had a breakthrough, but it's left us with a whole new list of questions.'

'Supper for four, then. Coming right up.'

'Aren't you tired of serving pear cake?'

'Never! What sacrilege.'

As she took the file from her backpack, Bertie hummed softly by the kettle. 'What about the other matter?' he said, dropping teabags into cups. 'Did you hear back from the Met?'

Sadie filled him in quickly about Donald's call.

'So,' he said with grim satisfaction. 'You were right. I told you your instincts were good.' He shook his head and his lips tightened in sympathy. 'That poor woman, that poor child. I trust you got your job back?'

'I'm not so sure about that. Ashford knows I was the leak. He's not going to want to condone my actions, regardless of how things turned out. I'll have to wait and see. In the meantime . . .' She held up the file and motioned over her shoulder towards the courtyard.

'Of course. I'll see you out there in a few minutes.'

Sadie rejoined the others just as Alice was saying to Peter, 'You know, I always thought I saw Ben in the woods that night.'

'Why didn't you say something to the police?' Sadie asked, sitting back down and sliding the file into the centre of the table.

Alice glanced to where a gusty breeze had set the string of fairy lights to rattling against the stones. 'I shouldn't have been there,' she said, shadows playing on her cheekbone. 'I was supposed to be meeting Mr Llewellyn at the party. I've always blamed myself for what happened to him; wondered whether it all might have ended differently had I stayed at the arbour a little longer. He'd come to me earlier in the day, you see, very keen that we should meet. Insistent that there was something he needed to discuss with me. I waited, but he never came.'

'That's another "coincidence" I don't like,' said Sadie, frowning. 'There's something not right about Mr Llewellyn's death. He was devoted to your mother, he knew what she was planning, how much was at stake for her – it doesn't sit right with me that he'd choose to end his own life then and there.'

'I quite agree,' said Alice. 'It makes no sense. But depression, like so many nervous conditions, is not a rational illness.'

'If only we knew more about his particular depression.' Sadie stood, pacing back and forth along the bricks. 'That initial breakdown, when he quit medicine and started writing books. In my experience, when someone makes a life-changing decision like that, there's something else behind it. If we knew what it was, maybe it would shed some light?'

Peter held up his hand. 'Actually, I think I might have the answer to that.'

Sadie spun around to face him; Alice peered over her glasses. 'Peter?'

'At Loeanneth today, when you were talking about Llewellyn's breakdown, wondering what had caused it, I vaguely remembered reading something about it in one of my undergraduate classes at university. I popped into the village library this afternoon and met a very helpful man—'

'Alastair,' Sadie offered.

'—precisely, who happened to have the perfect book just sitting there on his desk. It had come in on inter-library loan and was packaged, ready to return, when I spied it. It really was the most remarkable coinciden—'

'Don't say it.'

'—piece of luck. It had a chapter devoted to Llewellyn and *Eleanor's Magic Doorway*, a very interesting allegorical analysis relying on Kantian principles of symbolic—'

'Peter,' said Alice sternly.

'Yes, yes, sorry. The author argued that Llewellyn's story could be read as an allegory for the experiences of his own life, in particular the breakdown he'd suffered as a young doctor, when he was forced to attend an emergency situation at a friend's country house and he lost a patient.'

'A baby,' Sadie gasped. 'The patient was a newborn baby.'

'How do you know?' Alice said. 'Which baby? Whose baby?'

Peter met Sadie's gaze, processing for a moment, and then he grinned with realisation. 'You think it was Constance's baby.'

'Yes.' Sadie hurried to the table. 'Yes, yes, yes.' She thumbed quickly through the file, the candles in the hurricane lamps flickering beside her.

'That explains it,' said Peter, more to himself than to the others. 'The tension between them, the animosity she felt towards him. She really was a Miss Havisham.'

Confusion made Alice cross. 'Peter,' she said impatiently, 'what the dickens does Dickens have to do with anything?'

He turned to her, his eyes bright. 'When I was working on your website, you said not to bother you, just to do it, and I had to find an answer to a question so I looked in one of your journals, up in your office.'

'Yes, and?'

'And you made a comment about your grandmother: you described her as "a skeleton in the ashes of a rich dress", a quote from *Great Expectations*.'

'That sounds entirely likely. She was a dragon of a woman, and quite fond of dressing in the grand old frocks from her glory days – though not a wedding dress, I'm pleased to say. What in heaven's name does that have to do with a baby?'

'Here it is.' Sadie pulled out the page where she'd written her notes from the second interview that police had conducted with Constance at the care home. 'The nurse said that Constance kept talking about Eleanor and a baby boy who'd died. I thought Eleanor must have had a stillborn son before Theo, but it wasn't Eleanor at all.'

Alice drew quick breath. 'It was Grandmother's.'

Sadie nodded. 'And Daffyd Llewellyn was the doctor. It explains everything. His relationship with Constance; the cause of his depression; why he gave up medicine and sought solace in creating fairy tales for children . . .'

'It also explains the storyline of *Eleanor's Magic Doorway*,' said Peter, 'the old man crippled with regret and locked outside the kingdom, the cruel queen whose grief for her lost child casts an eternal winter, the girl Eleanor whose innocence is the only thing strong enough to heal the rupture . . .' He tapped his chin thoughtfully. 'The only thing it doesn't explain is why he became suicidal at the Midsummer party of 1933.'

'He didn't,' Alice said quietly, meeting Sadie's gaze. 'He didn't kill himself, did he?'

'No.' Sadie smiled, experiencing the delightful sense of pieces coming together. 'No, I don't think he did.'

It was Peter's turn to scratch his head. 'But we know he died from an overdose of barbiturates. There was evidence, a medical examination.'

'There was also a bottle of strong sleeping pills stolen from the house that night,' said Alice. 'For a long time I believed they'd been used to keep Theo quiet.'

'But they weren't,' said Sadie. 'It wouldn't have been difficult, just a few pills dissolved in a drink, and *voilà*. Because the loss of her baby had been eating her up for decades and she wanted—'

'—revenge,' Peter finished her sentence. 'Yes, I see what you're saying, but forty years had passed; why would she wait so long?'

Sadie pondered this. Ramsay had honoured her by coming to sit upon her feet and she reached down to scratch beneath his chin. 'You know,' she said thoughtfully, 'I just read a book that posed that question. A woman killed her ex-husband out of the blue after tolerating years of shoddy treatment. In the end it was the smallest thing. He decided to go on holiday to the very place she'd always dreamed of visiting and his announcement served as the perfect trigger.'

'*A Dish Served Cold*,' said Alice approvingly. 'One of my quieter mysteries, but a personal favourite nonetheless. What was Grandmother's trigger, though? As far as I can remember, Mr Llewellyn had made no exotic holiday arrangements.'

'But he had made a recent announcement,' said Peter suddenly. 'You mentioned it today. He was awarded an OBE, services to literature; you even said your grandmother took the news badly.'

'The royal honour,' said Sadie.

'The royal honour,' Alice repeated. 'Constance spent her life angling for an invitation to mingle with royalty. She'd been invited to the palace as a girl but was unable to attend. The number of times we heard about it as children! She never got over the disappointment.' Alice gave a smile of bleak satisfaction. 'It's the perfect trigger. I couldn't have plotted it better myself.'

They all sat quietly, listening to the crash of the ocean, the faraway festival noises, and enjoying the warm glow of solution. People could keep their drugs and alcohol, thought Sadie, there was nothing as thrilling as unravelling a puzzle, particularly one like this, so unexpected.

The reflective moment was brief. Alice – a woman after Sadie's own heart – straightened in her chair and pulled the file towards her. 'Right,' she said, 'as I remember it, we were looking for a hint as to where Ben took Theo.'

Peter raised his brow at Sadie in fond amusement, but they did as they were told, gathering around the table to rake through the file.

After a time, and having found nothing of use, Alice said, 'I wonder if there's a clue in Mother's behaviour, the way she returned each year to Loeanneth . . .' She frowned. 'But no, there's no reason to think Ben would have continued living in Cornwall, nor that he'd have brought Theo back to Loeanneth if he had.' She sighed, deflated. 'Far more likely it was simply a vigil of sorts, a way of feeling close to Theo. Poor Mother, one can only imagine what it would be like to know there was a child out there somewhere, one's own flesh and blood. The curiosity, the yearning, the need to know that he was loved and happy must have been harrowing.'

Bertie, who'd arrived in the courtyard carrying a tray loaded with pear cake and four cups of tea, shot Sadie a meaningful glance.

Sadie assiduously avoided it, pushing aside images of Charlotte Sutherland in her school blazer, of that tiny star-shaped hand appearing over the top of the hospital blanket. 'I suppose, having made the decision to give up the child, the only thing for it was to stay the course. It's the fair thing to do. Let the child get on with her life without the complication.'

'His life,' Peter corrected.

'His life,' echoed Sadie.

'How pragmatic you are, DC Sparrow.' Alice lifted a single eyebrow. 'Perhaps it's only the writer in me that presumes all parents who give up children must hold on to a small kernel of hope that one day, somehow, their paths will cross again.'

Sadie was still dodging Bertie's gaze. 'There might be cases where the parent feels the child will be disappointed in who they are. Angry and hurt that they were given up in the first place.'

'I expect so,' said Alice, taking up the newspaper article from Sadie's file, gazing at the portrait of Eleanor taken beneath the tree at Loeanneth, with three little girls in summer dresses gathered round her. 'But my mother always had the courage of her convictions. I've no doubt that having given him up for what she thought were the best possible reasons, she'd have been brave enough to weather the possibility that he resented her decision.'

'Oh my!'

They all looked up at Bertie, hovering behind the table with a plate of pear cake in one hand and a teacup in the other.

'Granddad?'

Peter was fastest, leaping up to take the cake and tea before they fell. He ushered Bertie into a seat.

'Granddad, are you all right?'

'Yes, I, it's just such a – well, no, it's not a coincidence at all, people often use that word incorrectly, don't they? They mean something is a remarkable concurrence of events but they forget, as I did, that there's a causal link. Not a coincidence at all, just a surprise, a huge surprise.'

He'd become flustered, he was babbling, and Sadie experienced a sudden rush of worry that the day had been too much for him, that he was on the verge of suffering a stroke. Love and fear combined to express as doggedness. 'Granddad?' she said sternly. 'What are you talking about?'

'This woman,' he said, tapping at the picture of Eleanor in Alice's newspaper article. 'I've met her before, when I was a boy working in my mum and dad's shop, during the war.'

'You met my mother?' said Alice, just as Sadie said, 'You met Eleanor Edevane?'

'Yes on both counts. A number of times. Though I didn't know her name. She used to come into the shop in Hackney when she was doing her volunteering.'

'Yes.' Alice was delighted. 'She worked in the East End during the war. She helped children who were bombed out of their homes.'

'I know.' Bertie was smiling widely now, too. 'She was very kind. One of our most reliable customers. She used to come in and buy a few odds and ends, things she certainly didn't need, and I'd make her a cup of tea.'

'Well, that *is* a coincidence,' said Peter.

'No,' said Bertie, 'that's what I'm trying to say.' He laughed. 'It's certainly a surprise to see her picture after all this time and realise she's connected to the business at the Lake House that's had my granddaughter so caught up, but it's not as random as you might think.'

'Granddad?'

'*She's* the reason I moved here, to Cornwall, she's the one who put the idea in my head in the first place. We used to have a picture hanging by the cash register, it was a postcard from my uncle, a photograph of a small wooden door set into a brick garden wall, covered in ivy and ferns, and she saw it once and told me about the gardens in Cornwall. I asked her, I think – I had a book set in Cornwall and the place had always seemed magical to me. She talked about the Gulf Stream and the exotic species that could be grown here. I never forgot it. She even mentioned Loeanneth, now I think about it, though not by name. She told me she was born and grew up on an estate that was famed for its great lake and gardens.'

'Incredible,' Peter said. 'And to think all these years later your granddaughter would discover her abandoned house and become obsessed with the case.'

'Not obsessed, exactly,' Sadie corrected. 'Interested.'

Bertie ignored the interruption, caught up in his memory of the long-ago conversations he'd shared with Eleanor Edevane about Loeanneth. 'She made it sound like a magical place, the salt and sea, smugglers' tunnels and fairy folk. She said there was even a miniature garden, a perfect, tranquil spot with a goldfish pond at its centre.'

'There was,' said Alice. 'Ben Munro built it.'

'Ben Munro?'

'One of the gardeners at Loeanneth.'

'Well now . . .' Bertie tilted his head. 'That *is* peculiar. That was my uncle's name, my favourite uncle who died in the Second World War.'

Alice frowned, as Peter said, 'Your uncle used to work at Loeanneth?'

'I'm not sure. It's possible, I suppose. He did all kinds of work. He wasn't the sort to stay put for long. He knew a lot about plants.'

Everyone looked at one another and Alice's frown deepened. 'It must be a different Benjamin Munro. The Ben we knew at Loeanneth couldn't have been anyone's uncle; he was an only child.'

'So was Uncle Ben. He wasn't my biological uncle. He was a good friend of my mother's. They grew up together and remained as thick as thieves. They both had archaeologist parents who travelled with their work. Ben and Mum met when their families were stationed in Japan.'

Everyone fell silent and the air around them seemed charged with static. The quiet was broken by an enormous crack and then the fizz of the first Midsummer firework being shot into the sky above the harbour.

'Where were you born, Bertie?' Alice's voice was light.

'Granddad was adopted as a baby,' said Sadie, remembering. He'd told her all about his mother and the troubles she'd had getting pregnant, how glad she was when he finally came along, how much he'd loved and been loved by her. It had been back when Sadie came to live with them, and had helped her to feel easier about her own decision to give up her baby. Only afterwards, the fact had faded from her memory. It had been such a confusing time, there'd been so many thoughts and feelings jostling for attention, and Bertie had spoken about his parents often over the years, with such love and warmth, that she'd simply forgotten that they weren't his biological family.

Bertie was still talking about his mother, Flo, and his Uncle Ben, unaware that Alice had stood very quietly and was making her way around the table to where he sat. She took his face between her shaking hands. Wordlessly, her eyes moved over his features, studying each one. A cry caught in her throat and Peter reached to steady her.

'Granddad,' Sadie said again, a note of awe in her voice.

'Bertie,' said Peter.

'Theo,' said Alice.

They were still sitting in the courtyard of Seaview Cottage when the stars began to fade and the promise of daylight cast a ribbon along the horizon. 'He used to write to me,' said Bertie, opening the wooden box he'd brought down from the attic. He took out a pile of letters. The earliest were dated 1934. 'Long before I could read, but my mum and dad used to read them to me. Sometimes they came with little gifts, or origami animals he'd folded to amuse me. Whenever he travelled for work, and when he went away to war, he'd write. I told you, he was my favourite uncle. I always felt close to him. A kinship, I guess you could say.'

'I know just what you mean,' said Alice again. It had become a mantra. 'I felt the same connection when we met this morning. A familiarity. As if I *recognised* you in some way.'

Bertie smiled at her and nodded, his eyes glazing afresh.

'What else is in the box, Granddad?' Sadie asked gently, sensing he could use the distraction.

'Oh, bits and bobs,' he said. 'Childhood mementoes.' He took out a bedraggled toy puppy dog, an old book, and a small romper suit. Sadie noticed it was missing a button and gasped. She reached into the pocket of her jeans and pulled out the round cupid she'd found at Loeanneth. A perfect match.

'Did your mother and father ever tell you about your biological parents?' Peter asked.

Bertie smiled. 'They used to tell me a story, about a tiger and a pearl. As a little fellow, I was more than happy to believe I'd been brought back from India in the form of an enchanted jewel; that I'd been born in the woods, weaned by fairies and then left on my parents' doorstep.' He took a necklace from the box, a tiger's-tooth pendant suspended on it, and ran his thumb over the dull ivory surface. 'Uncle Ben gave this to me, and as far as I was concerned, it was proof that the story was true. As I got older, I stopped asking. I would have liked to know who they were, of course, but my parents loved me – I couldn't have asked to grow up in a happier family – and so I made peace with the not knowing.' He glanced again at Alice, his eyes shining with a lifetime of emotion. 'What about you?' he said, nodding at the metal box that stood on the table in front of her, still covered in dirt. 'I showed you mine.'

She took the key from her purse and unlocked the filigree box, lifting the lid to reveal two identical piles of paper. *Bye Baby Bunting*, read the title on top, *by Alice Edevane*.

'They're manuscripts,' he said.

'Yes,' Alice agreed. 'The only existing copies of the first novel I ever finished.'

'What are they doing in the box?'

'A writer never destroys her work,' said Alice.

'But what were they doing in the ground?'

'Now that's a long story.'

'Maybe you'll tell me sometime?'

'Maybe I will.'

Bertie crossed his arms in mock castigation, and for a

split second Sadie glimpsed Alice in the gesture. 'At least tell us what it's about,' he said. 'Is it a mystery?'

Alice laughed. The first open, unguarded laugh Sadie had heard from her. A musical, youthful sound. 'Oh, Bertie,' she said. 'Theo. You wouldn't believe me if I told you.'

Thirty-four

London, 1941

She'd come as soon as she heard where the bombs had landed in the night. It had been two years since she'd received the letter, containing very little other than the news that he'd enlisted and an address in Hackney. To this point Eleanor had managed to stay away. Her war work took her close enough that when she saw children in the streets, watched them playing knuckles or running errands in their grey shorts and scuffed shoes, she could convince herself that one of them was him; but when she read about the bombings in the newspapers, when she reported for work that morning and was given the list of ravaged streets to visit, she'd turned on her heel and run.

Debris of stones and bricks and broken furniture littered the pockmarked road but Eleanor picked her way through quickly. A fireman nodded a greeting and she returned it politely. Her fingers were crossed – silly and childish, but helpful somehow – and her throat constricted a little more with each shell of a house she passed.

They hadn't counted on another war. When she made Ben promise never to get in touch, insisted that she mustn't know where Theo had been taken, she hadn't imagined a future like this one. She'd told herself it would be enough, it would *have* to be enough, to know he was with people Ben loved; that her child – her beautiful baby – would grow up happy and safe. But she hadn't counted on another war. It changed things.

Eleanor wasn't going to tell Anthony she'd come today. There was no point. She was only going to check the house hadn't been hit; she wasn't going to go inside. She certainly had no plans to see Theo. All the same, she felt the chill of the illicit. Eleanor didn't like keeping secrets, not anymore – their secrets, hers and Anthony's, had almost been their undoing.

She'd thought learning of the affair would destroy him, but it hadn't. He'd come to her calmly in the days afterwards and urged her to leave him. He'd realised by then that Theo wasn't his son and he said he wanted her to have another chance at happiness. He was tired of being a burden, inflicting damage on the people he loved most in the world.

But how could she have done that? Gone away with Ben and Theo, started again. She would never have left her girls and she couldn't take them away from Anthony. Besides, she loved her husband. She always had. She loved *both* of them, Anthony and Ben, and she cherished Theo; but life wasn't a fairy tale and there were instances when one couldn't have everything one wanted, not at the same time.

As for Anthony, learning of her affair with Ben seemed to lighten his load in some way. He said it made his life less perfect; that he had paid a price, gone some of the way towards restitution.

'Restitution for what?' she'd said, wondering if he was finally going to be honest with her.

'For everything. For surviving. For coming home to all of this.'

She'd known of course that there was more to it, that he was talking, however cryptically, about the great shadow that stalked him, and when Theo was safe, far away from Loeanneth, she'd finally asked him about Howard. He'd been angry at first, and more upset than she'd ever seen him, but eventually, with time and much coaxing, he'd confirmed the story she'd already uncovered. He told her everything, about Howard and Sophie, and baby Louis, too; the night in the barn when he'd almost helped his friend escape; the terrible line he'd nearly crossed. 'But you didn't,' Eleanor said at last, as he wept on her shoulder.

'I wanted to; I wished I had. I still wish it sometimes.'

'You wanted to save Howard. You loved him.'

'I should have saved him.'

'He wouldn't have wanted you to, not like that. He loved Sophie and baby Louis. He considered himself Louis's father, and a parent will always sacrifice themselves before their child.'

'But if there'd been another way.'

'There wasn't. I know you: you'd have found it if there were.'

Anthony had glanced at her then and she'd glimpsed the tiniest light of hope in his eyes that she was right.

She continued, 'If you'd done anything differently you'd have both been shot. Howard was right; he saw things clearly.'

'He sacrificed himself for me.'

'You tried to help him. You took a great risk to help him.'

'I failed.'

There'd been nothing she could say to that. She'd simply sat with him as he grieved for his lost friend. Finally, she'd squeezed his hand firmly and whispered, 'You didn't fail *me*. You made me a promise. You said you wouldn't let anything stop you coming home.'

There was only one other secret she still kept from him and that was the truth about what happened to Daffyd. Anthony had loved him and never would have borne knowing what Constance had done. But Eleanor had found the empty bottle of sleeping pills in her mother's room and she'd known. Her mother didn't bother to deny it. 'It was the only way,' she said. 'The only hope I had for renewal.'

Constance and Eleanor's relationship, never good, was untenable after that. There was no question of the old woman moving with them to London, but she couldn't be abandoned either. Not entirely. Eleanor searched all over before she finally found Seawall. It was expensive, but worth every penny. 'There's no better nursing home in England. Such a wonderful position,' the matron had said as she gave Eleanor a tour, 'immediately on the seafront. Not a room in the building from which one can't hear the ocean rolling in and out, in and out.'

'It's just right,' Eleanor had said, signing the admission forms. And it was. Just and right. The unrelenting sound of the ocean for the rest of her days had been precisely what Constance deserved.

Eleanor turned into the street, almost colliding with a stern-looking policeman on a bicycle. Her gaze ran along the houses until it reached the grocery store. Her breaths lightened when she saw the cheery sign out front: MORE OPEN THAN USUAL!

Relief was instant. It hadn't been hit.

Eleanor decided it was just as well while she was here to take a look at the shopfront. She continued walking until she stood close enough to peer through the taped front window. She took in the name of the shop painted proudly at the top of the glass, and the neat display of tins on the shelf inside. There were two levels to the brick house above, matching curtains in each window. This was a nice place. Comfortable. Eleanor could imagine the effort it took to keep the awning and the glass so clean during the air raids.

The bell tinkled softly when she pushed open the door. It was a small shop, but surprisingly well stocked given the shortages. Someone had gone to a lot of effort to make sure there were interesting items to offer war-weary customers. Ben had said his friend, Flo, was a force to be reckoned with – 'She never does anything by halves.' It had been one of the things, along with his assurance that his friend was kind and good and true, that had helped Eleanor warm to this woman she'd never met, to whom she was going to entrust so much of her heart.

The shop was very still. It smelled of fresh tea-leaves and powdered milk. There was no one behind the counter and Eleanor told herself it was a sign. She had seen what she'd come to see and now it was time to go.

But a door in the wall at the back of the shop was ajar and it struck her that it must lead into the house. The place where he slept at night and ate his meals, and laughed and cried and leapt and sang, the home in which he lived.

Her heart was beating quickly now. She wondered

whether she dared peek behind the door? Eleanor glanced over her shoulder and saw a woman with a black perambulator trundling along the street outside. There was no one else in the shop. All she had to do was slip through the opening. She drew a deep steadying breath and then startled when a noise came from behind her. She spun around in time to see a boy appear from behind the shop counter.

She knew him at once.

He'd been sitting on the floor the whole time and looked at her now with wide eyes. He had a mop of straight sandy hair that fell like an upturned pudding bowl and was wearing a white apron tied around his waist. It was too long for him and had been doubled over to fit.

He was about nine years old. No, not about, he *was* nine years old. Nine years and two months, to be precise. He was slight but not thin, and his cheeks were full. He smiled openly at Eleanor, like someone who knew the world to be a good place.

'Sorry to keep you waiting,' he said. 'We haven't much in the way of milk today, I'm afraid, but we've a few nice eggs just came in from a farm out Kent way.'

Eleanor was light-headed. 'Eggs,' she managed to say. 'Eggs would be lovely.'

'One or two?'

'Two, please.'

She took out her ration book and, as the boy turned to a basket on the shelf behind the counter and started wrapping the eggs in squares of old newspaper, she crept closer. She could feel her heart beating against her ribcage. If she just reached out her arm she'd be able to touch him.

She folded her hands together firmly on the counter and

noticed a book. It was scuffed and dog-eared and missing its dust jacket. It hadn't been there when she entered the shop. The boy must have brought it with him from his hiding spot on the floor. 'You like to read?'

The boy shot a guilty glance over his shoulder; his cheeks were instantly pink. 'My mum says I'm a natural.'

My mum. Eleanor winced. 'Does she?'

He nodded, frowning slightly and with great attention to detail as he finished twisting the ends of his second egg bonbon. He brought them both to the counter and then tucked the book onto a shelf beneath. He glanced at Eleanor, saying solemnly, 'I'm not actually supposed to read while I'm minding the shop.'

'I used to be like that when I was your age.'

'Did you grow out of it?'

'Not really.'

'I don't think I will either. I've already read that one four times.'

'Well then, you must know it almost by heart.'

He smiled proud agreement. 'It's about a girl who lives in a big old house in the country and discovers a secret door-way to another world.'

Eleanor steadied herself.

'The girl lives in a place called Cornwall. Have you heard of it?'

She nodded.

'Have you been there?'

'I have.'

'What's it like?'

'The air smells like the ocean, and everything is very

green. There are marvellous gardens filled with strange and wonderful plants you won't see anywhere else in England.'

'Yes,' he said, his eyes bright. 'Yes, that's just what I thought. My uncle told me so. He's been there too, you see. He said there really are houses like the one in my book, with lakes and ducks and secret tunnels.'

'I grew up in a place like that.'

'Wow. You're lucky. Uncle Ben – he's fighting in the war right now – he's the one who sent me this postcard.'

Eleanor looked where the boy was pointing. A sepia photograph of an overgrown garden gate had been taped to the side of the cash register. White cursive writing swirled across the bottom right corner, wishing the recipient *Magic Memories*.

'Do you believe in magic?' he asked earnestly.

'I think so.'

'Me too.'

They smiled at one another, a moment of perfect accord, and Eleanor felt herself on the threshold of something she hadn't foreseen and couldn't properly describe. Possibility seemed to infuse the air between them.

But then a swirl of noise and movement arrested their attention and a woman bustled in from the door at the back of the shop. She had dark curly hair and an animated face with full lips and bright eyes, the sort of indomitable spirit that filled a room and made Eleanor feel thin and flimsy.

'What are you doing there, love?' She ruffled the boy's hair and smiled at him with enormous love. She turned her attention to Eleanor. 'Has Bertie here looked after you?'

'He's been very helpful.'

'Not keeping you from getting on with things, I hope? My lad could talk the legs off an iron pot if I let him.'

Bertie grinned and Eleanor could see it was a running joke between them.

A pain seized her chest and she reached out to hold the counter. She was suddenly dizzy.

'You all right there? You look a bit green.'

'It's nothing.'

'You sure? Bertie – go put the kettle on, love.'

'No, really,' said Eleanor. 'I should be going. I've a lot of calls left to make. Thank you for the eggs, Bertie. I'm going to enjoy them. I haven't seen real ones in such a long time.'

'Hard-boiled,' he said, 'that's the only way to have eggs.'

'I couldn't agree more.' The bell above the door tinkled again as she opened it and Eleanor had a flash of memory, a day ten years before, when she'd pushed open the post-office door and run into Ben.

The boy called after her, 'I'll make you a cup of tea next time you come.'

And Eleanor smiled back at him. 'I'd like that very much,' she said. 'Very much indeed.'

Thirty-five

London, 2004

They met at the Natural History Museum, just as they always did on Eleanor's anniversary. They didn't hug, that wasn't their way, but they linked arms, each shoring the other up a little as they did the rounds. Neither spoke; instead they walked together quietly, lost in their own private memories of Anthony and Loeanneth and all the things they'd learned, too late to help him but soon enough to bring a measure of resolution to their own lives.

The others joined them afterwards for tea at the V&A. Even Bertie made the trip up from Cornwall. 'I wouldn't dream of missing it,' he'd said when Alice telephoned him with the invitation. 'Besides, I was already planning to come to London that week. There's a certain grand opening to attend after all . . .'

He was already holding a table when Deborah and Alice arrived, and waved them over. He stood, smiling, embracing them each in turn. Strange, Alice thought, as Deborah patted his cheeks and laughed, the way their abhorrence of physical greetings didn't extend to their little brother. It was as if, having missed so much time together, they felt a physical need to bridge the years. Or perhaps it was because they'd lost him when he was so very small that the love they felt demanded tactile expression, in the same way an adult cannot help but reach to hold a child. Whatever the case, they treasured him. It occurred to Alice how pleased Eleanor would be to know that they'd found each other again.

Sadie came next, a handful of papers in her arms. She walked as quickly as always, head down as she tried to shuffle the sheets back into order. 'Sorry,' she said, arriving at the table. 'Tube was delayed. I'm late. Story of my life at the moment trying to get things ready in time for the opening. Hope I haven't kept you waiting too long?'

'Not at all,' said Deborah, smiling fondly. 'We've only just arrived ourselves.'

'And here's Peter now,' said Bertie, nodding towards the entrance.

Sadie handed the manuscript to Alice. 'I've marked anything I could find, but there wasn't a lot. Just a few procedural things. Oh, Alice – ' she dropped her handbag and collapsed onto a spare seat – 'it's a good one. Very good. I couldn't turn the pages fast enough.'

Alice looked pleased but not entirely surprised. 'I'm happy to say that number fifty-one proved rather more obliging than number fifty.'

Peter arrived at the table, leaning to kiss Sadie on the cheek. She clutched his shirt and kissed him back. 'How did you go?' she said. 'Did you get it?'

'Right here.' He tapped his satchel.

'How did you manage that? They told me it would be at least another week.'

He smiled mysteriously. 'I have my ways.'

'I'll bet you do.'

'He does, and he's my assistant,' said Alice, 'so don't even think about stealing him.'

'I wouldn't dare.'

'Go on then,' said Bertie. 'Don't keep us all in suspense. Let's have a look at it.'

Peter took a flat rectangular parcel from his backpack and unwrapped the tissue paper. The metal gleamed silver when he held it up for them to see.

Alice put on her glasses and leaned closer to read the engraving. *S. Sparrow, Private Investigator. Please ring doorbell for assistance.* She folded her glasses again and tucked them in their case. 'Well,' she said, 'it's to the point and I like that. I don't hold with cute business names. As the Sparrow Flies, Bird's-Eye View . . .'

'The Early Bird Catches the Worm,' said Peter.

'Actually, I quite like that one,' said Bertie.

'Alas, I can't claim it,' said Peter. 'That was one of Charlotte's.'

'Is she coming?'

'Not today,' said Sadie. 'Too much homework. But she said she'd try to make it to the opening of the agency on Saturday night.'

'Well then,' said Bertie, with a smile of something like pride and satisfaction and deep contentment all wrapped into one. 'What do you all think? Shall we skip tea just this once and have some sparkling wine instead? It seems to me we have an awful lot to celebrate.'

Author's Note

People often ask where the ideas for books come from. The truth is that a novel is made up of thousands of little ideas, like pieces of a jigsaw puzzle, which join together to form a story. Three such disparate ideas formed the kernel of *The Lake House*: I'd long been toying with the idea of an abandoned house; I knew I wanted to write about a missing child (inspired, in part, by a very famous unsolved case in Australia); and I thought it would be fun to write a real, proper mystery. All of my books contain mysteries, but in *The Lake House* I included a detective character (off-duty, but still . . .), a grande dame mystery writer, and not one but two unsolved 'crimes'.

I was also eager to indulge my long-held love of Cornwall. I'm a very visual person, most inspired when I have interesting things to look at. Country or city, inside or out, natural or otherwise, I'm not particular: I love landscapes and laneways; the sky and the sea; chimney tops, hidden doorways and beautiful gardens. I also love music, art, theatre, and of course history, especially that lovely, shivery sense that the past still surrounds us. Most of all, I'm drawn to places that make me *feel* something. Cornwall – with its windy coastlines and spectacular wildflowers, its abundant gardens and gorgeous whitewashed houses, its enveloping atmosphere of history, mystery, myth and magic – is just such a place.

But while imagination and inspiration can take an author a long way, it's impossible to create a vivid and believable historical milieu without research. For me, this is one of the most engaging parts of being a writer. Indeed, I'm often at risk of becoming lost inside the research and never writing a word of fiction. The complete list of sources consulted for *The Lake House* is too long to include here, but some of the most useful and used were *The Perfect Summer: England 1911, Just Before the Storm* by Juliet Nicolson; *The Victorian House* by Judith Flanders; *Talking about Detective Fiction* by PD James; *The Reason Why: An Anthology of the Murderous Mind*, edited by Ruth Rendell; *For Love and Courage: The Letters of Lieutenant Colonel E. W. Hermon*, edited by Anne Nason; *A War of Nerves* by Ben Shephard; and *Testament of Youth* by Vera Brittain (from which I gleaned the grim headmaster's line, 'If a man cannot be useful to his country, he is better dead').

The website www.beaumontchildren.com provided information regarding the investigative process, and www.first worldwar.com contains a wealth of material on shell shock. It is also, incidentally, the very website that Sadie consults after her meeting with Margot Sinclair. I read many online accounts of young women's experiences with the adoption process. Most were anonymous and I am grateful to the authors for being brave enough to share their stories.

Unlike Alice Edevane, who fears that her editor Jane won't provide the kind of *real* criticism necessary to help strengthen her manuscript into a novel, I am fortunate to work with two wise and insightful editors who challenge me to make my books the best that they can be. Annette Barlow and Maria Rejt are precious gems and I appreciate them both.

My sister, Julia, was there from the very beginning, full of encouragement when the story was just a handful of odd puzzle pieces that seemed like they might fit together, and my mother Didee's unwavering love and compassion is an example, always, of the lengths to which a mother will go for her children. For being the best life-team a girl could hope for, I'd like to thank my husband, Davin, who is clever, funny and kind, and my three sons, Oliver, Louis and Henry, who have, between them, made me a more clear-sighted, multilayered, vulnerable, brave, (and, I hope, better) person and writer.

extracts reading groups
competitions books new
discounts extracts extracts
competitions new
books
events books
extracts
new reading groups
interviews
events extracts
discounts books
new books events
events new
www.panmacmillan.com
extracts events reading groups
competitions books extracts new